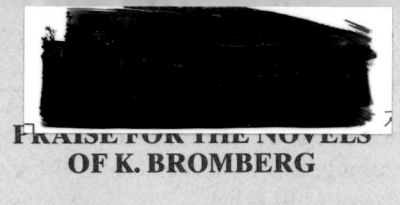

PRAISE FOR THE NOVELS
OF K. BROMBERG

"An irresistibly hot romance that stays with you long after you finish the book."
—# 1 *New York Times* bestselling author Jennifer L. Armentrout

"Captivating, emotional, and sizzling hot!"
—#1 *New York Times* bestselling author S. C. Stephens

"The more I read, the more I want. . . . Your emotions will be taken on one hell of an angst-filled, heartbreaking, gut-wrenching, mind-blowing, and wickedly sexy, beautiful journey."
—Book Crush

"There was a certain je ne sais quoi to the story that kept me reading till the very end."
—Smexy Books

"[A] highly emotional yet satisfying series, oh, and let me not leave out SEXY."
—Guilty Pleasures Book Reviews

"Well-written and with a great balance of dialogue and description."
—Love Between the Sheets

"An emotionally charged, adrenaline-filled, steamy, and passionate read. . . . K. Bromberg deliver[s]."
—TotallyBookedBlog

"This series is *everything* a true fan of romance would want or need."
—Sinfully Sexy Book Reviews

continued . . .

JAN 1 6

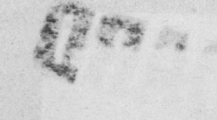

Also by K. Bromberg

Slow Burn
Sweet Ache

HARD
BEAT

A DRIVEN NOVEL

K. Bromberg

A SIGNET SELECT BOOK

SIGNET SELECT
Published by New American Library,
an imprint of Penguin Random House LLC
375 Hudson Street, New York, New York 10014

This book is an original publication of New American Library.

First Printing, November 2015

For more information about Penguin Random House, visit penguin.com.

ISBN 978-0-451-47681-4

Printed in the United States of America
10 9 8 7 6 5 4 3 2 1

Penguin
Random
House

Acknowledgments

The acknowledgments are the hardest part to write in every book. Thanking people never gets old but the fear that I will forget someone who should be thanked does. So this time around, I'll try to be short and sweet.

To my readers, thank you for continually taking a chance on me. Your unending support and unwavering faith has made all the difference in my success. I may write the books, but you are the ones who tell your friends about them. Not a day goes by that I take your support for granted. To the VP Pit Crew and the ladies who help run it, thank you for keeping my Driven world alive while I'm off writing.

To my author friends, thank you for making this wild ride a little more bearable. To be able to do what we love to do for a living and at the same time build a community that supports one another is a pretty incredible thing to be a part of.

To my friends and family, thank you for understanding that my computer is an extra appendage, that social media is a necessary evil, and that when I'm quiet, it's not you—it's those damn people in my head again.

To Amy and Kerry, thank you for believing in Beaux and Tanner's story when it was so very different from the other Driven books.

Kristy

Prologue

"Are you on a suicide mission, now?"

"What the hell are you talking about?" I shift in my seat to face Rafe, catching a glimpse of the world outside the windows of the Manhattan headquarters of Worldwide News. But what I really see in my mind's eye are the memories I wish I could wipe away.

Flashes of light against the stark black night. Piercing sirens drowning out my pleas for her to breathe. Her lifeless body, pale and clammy. Unresponsive.

Her eyes. Those blue eyes of hers, always so goddamn vibrant and mischievous, blank and fixed.

The smell of gunpowder mixed with the metallic scent of unexpected death lingering around us like a fog.

The ache. In my heart from what I knew to be true, and in my shoulders and arms from the force of the compressions on her chest as I tried to force life back into her.

Her lips. So cold. So blue.

The sound of my own voice pleading and begging for her to be strong. To stay with me.

Chaos. The feel of hands pulling me back because the medics needed space to do their job. The one I knew was useless.

The chill that settled in as they loaded her in the transport, and I shivered uncontrollably from the trauma. But I held on to the cold, wrapped it around me like a blanket, because it was so much easier to focus on that than the guilt already weaving itself around my psyche and soul.

I couldn't save her. I tried. But I failed.

"Tanner!" Rafe's voice pulls me from the nightmare on a constant repeat in my mind. It takes me a moment to pull myself from the painful recollections.

"Yeah. Sorry." I run my hand over my upper lip and wipe away the beads of sweat forming there. "I—"

"Got distracted? Like I said, you want a suicide mission."

"That's bullshit and you know it. It's always about the story. Always." I'm pissed at having to explain myself when usually the only question I get asked is if my bag is packed.

"I'm afraid you're going to become the story, given your mind-set." The sarcasm in his voice pisses me off further, and I know he's purposefully pushing my buttons. "You want the danger, the hard beat, somewhere where you can risk your safety as punishment for not being able to save Stella?" He squares his shoulders and braces his hands on his desk, staring down at me from the other side of it. A silent reprimand in a sense. I hold his glare because as right as he is, he's also so very wrong.

"Am I not your best reporter?" It's an arrogant question but one I know is damn well true. I glance out the window for a moment before scooting forward in my seat and bracing my hands on my knees. When I look back up to him, I make sure he sees the temerity in my eyes.

"That's not the issue. The—"

"Bullshit!" I shove my chair back as I stand up, letting the sound emphasize my point. "Shit's about to go down over there. You don't need some fresh-faced kid getting killed because he doesn't know the lay of the land. I can do the job better than any of them."

"You're gonna burn out, man. You've been going hard for years . . . and now with this, I mean it's only been two and a half months. . . ."

"And I'm going out of my fucking mind with boredom," I shout, throwing my hands up before I get hold of myself and rein it in. I have to show him I can do this. That I can go out in the field and be an asset instead of the loose cannon he thinks I am. And fuck yes, mentally I'm just that, but he doesn't need to know. "Put me in, coach. I'm begging you, Rafe. I need this, need to get the fuck out of Dodge and back to where I'm comfortable and feel at home. . . ." My begging is pathetic, but at this point I'm a desperate man.

"If home to you is a hotel full of journalists in bum-fuck Egypt, then I feel sorry for you, man. . . ." His voice fades off as his eyes search mine. His gaze holds compassion, understanding, and pity, and I hate fucking pity.

"It's not my home, but it's what I need right now. It'll help me process everything . . . make me focus on the job and not on her." Or her funeral and meeting her parents at the service instead of in Ibiza where we had all planned to vacation a week later.

"I get it, Tanner. All of it . . . shit." He steps away from the desk and shoves his hands in his pockets as he looks out the window, a sigh falling from his lips. He turns back around to face me. "Let me see what I can do. I don't even have a new . . ." His voice trails off, although both of us know what he's going to say next.

One of her cameras sits on my dresser at home where

the memory card is still loaded with pictures from the last night we spent together. I can't stand the thought of looking at them. I wish I could. Then maybe the horrible images in my mind would be erased.

"Rafe, it is what it is. You can say it because I need to get used to it. A new photographer."

I know he's upset too. The three of us started out in this business as fresh-faced kids thrown into the fire together. Now one of us is a suit, one of us needs to escape back into those flames to forget, and one of us is dead. "I still think you should stay stateside for a bit. Go spend time with your sister and her family for a while. Get some perspective."

"I've got all the perspective I need. Thanks." I'm being a sarcastic asshole, but if anyone can understand my need to get back into the field, it should be him. "Look, I'm not taking no for an answer. Do what you gotta do, man, but get me the fuck back there or I'll head over to CNN. I hear they're looking for someone."

I go in for the kill with that line since he knows the perks their executives have tried to entice me with in the past. And by the widening of his eyes and the set of his jaw, it seems to have worked.

"I'd have to get it cleared with the brass." He raises his eyes to the ceiling, referring to the executives upstairs. "They think that you . . . ." His voice fades off, the incomplete thought making my mind whirl.

"You're telling me that they blame Stella's death on me?" I walk to the opposite end of the room, needing to move to abate my anger, and shove a hand through my hair. It's shaggy and an inch too long, but fuck if I've cared enough to look after myself these last few months.

"I never said that." His exasperation over how to handle me is obvious in his voice.

"You don't have to. I live with it every goddamn day. . . .

Like I said, *the most trusted name in news*," I taunt, dropping CNN's slogan on him before I raise my eyebrows, making my intention clear as day. Then I walk toward the door, tossing, "Try me," over my shoulder as I step over the threshold.

After that I just have to hope my threat works.

Chapter 1

One month later

A hand slaps me firmly on the back. It's one of many in an impromptu celebration in the bar of the hotel to greet me.

"Welcome back, you crazy fucker!"

Burn out, my ass.

I turn to see Pauly's familiar face: broad grin, hair falling over his thick glasses, and belly leading the way. "Man, it's good to see you!" As I turn to shake his hand, I'm instantly pulled into his arms for a rough embrace.

He pulls back and cuffs the side of my cheek. "You okay?" It's the same look that everyone has been giving me, and it's driving me fucking insane. Pity mixed with sadness. But Pauly is allowed to look at me like that since he was there before all the shit hit the fan; he loved her like a sister too. And coming back here, I feared this moment—meeting him face-to-face—as if he'd judge me, think it was my fault . . . but all I feel right now is relief.

It feels so damn good to be back here, with people who get me, who understand why I'd return to work when so many others think I should have given it up to stay home for good. They don't get that once you're a nomad, you're always a nomad. Or that home isn't where your house is necessarily; it's where you feel comfortable. And yes, that comfort can alter over time—as your needs shift and wants change—but in the end, I feel more like myself right now than I have since Stella's death.

I pull my thoughts back to the here and now, to Pauly, the stale cigarette smoke that hangs in the air around me, and the pungent scent of spices coming in through the open windows of the bar.

"I'm better now that I'm back here." I motion to the barstool next to me for him to sit down.

"Thank God for that. Took Rafe long enough."

"Almost four months."

"Shit," he says in sympathy, knowing what a big deal that is to someone like me.

"Yeah. Tell me about it. The first two months were a mandatory leave of absence. Then once I threatened to go to CNN, he said he was speeding things up ... but then, fuck, they made me take another Centurian course." It's a course for foreign correspondents about what to do in a hostile environment and how to handle the multitude of things that can go wrong at any given time. "And then I was told they couldn't find a photographer who wanted to travel to this *paradise*. ... It was one damn thing after another."

"So in other words, he was dragging his feet so he could get you back here on his time frame."

"Exactly." I nod and tip my bottle up to my lips. "He thought I needed a break, said I was going to burn out." I motion to the bartender to bring us another couple of beers.

"We're all going to at some point. In the meantime ..." He taps the neck of his beer bottle against mine. "Might as well get our fix."

"Amen, brother. So, tell me what the hell has been happening while I've been gone." The need to change the subject is paramount for me right now. I know Stella is going to be everywhere here, but I need a way to make her not so present in my mind so that I can focus on doing my job.

At least it's a good theory.

"I'm hearing that some new players have moved into the game and that there's a high-official meet in the works, but we can talk shop later. Right now, we need to welcome you back properly." Pauly raises his voice to shout the last few words. In agreement, the crowd of people around us, mostly men, raise up a glass and call out a few *aye, ayes*.

The excitement around me feels palpable. It doesn't take much in this place to give people a reason to celebrate. We all live on that razor-thin edge of unpredictability, so we take the chances we get to party because who knows when we'll get another one? For all we know, tomorrow we could be on air-raid-siren lockdown in the hotel or out in the field in an embedded mission with a military unit.

When I turn back around, the bartender is busily filling the row of shot glasses on the bar top in front of me with Fireball whiskey. History tells me that this row is the first of many in tonight's welcome-back celebration. My inclination is to chug back the first shot and then slowly work my way out of the bar and to my room.

It's been a long ass few days. Between flights through multiple time zones and then a transport into the heart of the city, plus trying to reconnect with my sources to let them know I'm back in town, and grease their palms some, I'm exhausted, exhilarated, and feeling a little more like myself back in the thick of things, doing exactly what I love.

"C'mon, T-squared," Carson yells with a slap of his hand on the counter. Hearing the nickname referring to the initials of my first and last names is like a welcome mat laid before me, and right then I know there is no way in hell I'm skipping out on this party.

"I'm game if you're game!" I raise a glass up to him and wait for everyone close to us to grab a shot. The jostling of more people patting my shoulders accompanied by welcome-back comments causes the amber liquid to slosh over the sides of the shot glass.

"Shh. Shh. Shh," Pauly instructs our friends as he stands on the seat of his chair, holding up his own glass. "Tanner Thomas . . . We are so glad to see your ugly ass back in this shithole. I'm sure once you hand our asses to us time and again by getting the story first, we'll want you to leave, but for now we're glad you're here. Slainte!" As soon as he finishes the toast, the room around us erupts into cheers before we all toss back the whiskey.

I welcome the burn and before the sting even abates, my glass is already being refilled. When I look up from the pour, my eyes lock on a woman I hadn't noticed on the other side of the bar. The momentary connection affords me a glimpse of dark hair and vibrant eyes as she lifts her drink in a silent nod to me, but as soon as I register she's doing it on purpose, someone moves and blocks my view of her.

But I keep my eyes fixed in that direction, wanting another glance of the mysterious woman. She doesn't look familiar, but at the same time something more than curiosity pulls at me. It's been four long months—she could be anybody—but for a guy like me always in the know around here, it bothers me that I don't have a clue who she is.

"Ready, Tan?" Pauly's glass taps against mine, pulling me from my thoughts.

"Bottoms up, baby." God, it feels good to be back. Listening to the guys' war stories, getting up to speed on the shit that's happened at the grassroots level that no one back at home has any clue about.

The whiskey goes down a little smoother the second and third times while our crowd gets bigger from people coming in after fulfilling their assignments. And each wave of people joining us ushers in another round of shots.

Maybe it's the alcohol, maybe it's the familiar atmosphere, but soon I feel like I can breathe easier than I have in months. I think of Stella intermittently through the night, mostly how much she'd have loved this show of unity amongst all these people competing for the next big story, and for the first time in forever I can smile at her memory.

"So how long you here for this time?" Pauly asks.

"I don't know." I blow out a long breath and lean back in my chair, tracing the lines of condensation down the glass of water in front of me that's still full. Whiskey tastes so much better tonight. "This might be my last time. . . ." My own words surprise me. A confession from the combination of the nostalgia and my own mortality examined through the alcoholic buzz.

"Quit talking like that. This shit is in your blood. You can't live without it."

"True." I glance across the room while I nod my head slowly in agreement. "But dude, a dog only has so many lives."

"I guess that's why I prefer pussies. They've got nine of 'em."

"Christ, Pauly." I choke on the words. "I prefer to eat it rather than live it."

His arm goes around my shoulder as his laugh fills my ears. "I missed the fuck out of you, Thomas. Speaking of . . ." His hand grips me tighter before he lifts his chin to direct my line of sight. "The hottie at two o'clock has been eyeing you all night."

I shrug the comment away, even though a small part of me—one that I'm not too happy with right now— hopes that he's referring to the woman I'd glimpsed earlier. I'd told myself that she'd left. But secretly I want to be wrong. "I'm sure as hell hoping when you say 'hottie,' you're referring to a woman and not an IED."

"Cheers to that truth. Scary shit," he says, tapping the neck of his bottle against the rim of my empty glass, "and no, I'm referring to dark hair, great rack, killer body—"

"No, thanks." I cut him off, but my eyes dart to where I saw her sitting earlier, and immediately I chastise myself.

"You still seeing what's-her-name?" he asks with the same indifference as I felt toward her.

"Nah . . ." I let my voice drift off as my thoughts veer to our last fight when she accused me of cheating on her with Stella. "She took an assignment monitoring North Korea."

"She thought you and Stella were messing around?" he infers.

The thought brings a bittersweet smile to my face. Memories of Stella and me, young and in love, flash through my mind. It feels like forever ago. Probably because it was. Two young twenty-somethings on their first assignment with no one else to help occupy their time. Lust turned to sweet love and then the slow realization that we weren't any good as a couple. Then came an awkward phase when we had to get over the bitterness associated with lust gone wrong. The passage of time allowed us to realize we were really good at the best-friend thing which in turn made us a great team, reporter and photographer. Inseparable for almost ten years, except for the odd assignment that took us to other places of the world and despite the introduction of significant others.

"Yeah. I get it. I'd probably think the same thing, but ..." I shrug. "You've seen us together. Know how Stell and I were—"

"Mutt and Jeff," he mumbles as we both fall into a short silence thinking of her. "I liked what's-her-name."

"No, you didn't." I laugh loudly because his comment was the farthest thing from the truth. He nods his head in agreement—everyone knew they didn't get along. "But thanks. I think it had run its course before she changed assignments. You know what relationships are like with what we do."

"Man, do I know it. What am I on here? Wife number three? Four? You've got the right idea with the let's-have-fun versus the let's-get-hitched mentality ... but uh, she just looked over here again and fuck me, I'd make her wife number five for the night if she'd let me."

The deep belly chuckle he emits pulls a reluctant laugh out of me, and it takes everything I have not to glance in the woman's direction. Resistance is futile. Eventually I give in to curiosity and glance up, planning to avert my eyes before she looks our way again.

Intriguing eyes meet mine. Her dark hair is pulled back into a messy knot that should look unkempt but somehow makes her sexier. When our eyes connect, her lips fall open in surprise in an O shape before they correct themselves into a slow, soft smile. I nod my head at her and then casually look away, both hating and loving that pang in my gut that stirs to life.

Something about her—yet nothing I can put my finger on—tells me I should steer clear. So why the fuck do I glance back up to see if she's still looking? And why do I care?

"I'm sure you would," I finally answer Pauly, a little slow in my response.

"She's hot. I mean how often do we get someone that fine in this neck of the woods? Damn, dude, her eyes are back on you now. She's seriously checking you out." He snickers.

"Yeah, and she's probably some sheikh's wife. No, thanks . . . I'll keep the hand they'd cut off just for looking at her." I toss my napkin on the bar at the same time the barkeep slides another round in front of us.

"Better your hand than something else," Pauly deadpans.

"Got that right." I laugh.

"I might take the risk for her." I glance over and look him up and down. He can't be serious. "Okay. Maybe not."

"Maybe not." I scrub my hand over my clean-shaven face, knowing the smooth skin will soon be replaced by the scruff that just kind of happens when you live here. "She one of us?"

"She's been here about two weeks. Freelance, I think. Don't know much about her—heard she's a loose cannon of sorts. Always off on her own, taking unnecessary risks and getting into people's business. I've steered clear other than a nod in the lobby."

That's what I intend to do: steer clear of her. Too many newbies come in gung-ho, trying to get the next big story, and end up getting someone hurt. *Just like what happened to Stella.*

"Well, for what it matters, loose cannon or not, I think

you should go for it. She'll probably be gone sooner rather than later, which is always a good thing. . . . Prevents attachment, and shit, you never know when your next chance to taste those nine lives will be." He winks and I can't help but snort.

"Thanks but I've got enough to worry about with my new photog coming in tomorrow." I roll my eyes and bring the shot glass up to my partially numb lips as my mind veers back to the fact that it's been ten years since I've had to break in anybody new. I'm not looking forward to this.

"Well tough shit, man," he says, patting me on the back, "because she's making a move for you."

The resigned sigh falls from my mouth at the same time she slides into the chair next to me. Gone is the distinct smell of this crowded bar when the clean and flowery scent of her perfume surrounds me. I keep my head down, eyes focused on the scratches in the wood counter, acknowledging that I don't want the small zing I feel to flourish. At all.

But of course the longer we sit there, with me looking down and the full weight of her stare on me, I know I'm in a losing battle. I've got plenty of fight in me, just not for her right now. I need to head this off at the pass.

"Whoever you're looking for, I'm not him." I try not to sound too hostile, but my voice lacks any kind of warmth. I've been here, done this before. The newbies try to butter me up to get the scoop on everything in town—and coming off the heels of the mess with Stella, I'm not giving anything to anybody.

"I don't believe I'm looking for anything." Her voice sounds smooth as silk with a hint of a rasp. How did I know she was going to have a sexy voice?

"Good."

"Whiskey sour," she says to the bartender, and I have to admit the order kind of surprises me. "And put it on his tab."

I immediately look up to catch the smirk on her face and the taunting glimmer in her green eyes. Intrigue has me keeping my gaze on hers because I admire that she came back at me with her own line instead of scurrying away to lick her wounds. Can't say the freelancer doesn't have some chops.

"I don't believe I offered to buy you one." And the truth of the matter is I don't give a flying fuck about the drink. I would've bought it anyway out of plain manners, but something tells me I just walked right into her well-maneuvered game, and fuck me if I'm going to stay there.

"Well, I don't believe I asked you to be an asshole either, so the drink's on you." She raises her eyebrows as she brings the cocktail to her lips. And of course my eyes veer down to watch her run the tip of her tongue over the rim of her glass to the drop of liquid that falls there.

My mind drifts to the pleasure she could bring with her mouth and her tongue . . . purely out of male fascination.

"Then I guess you should steer clear of me and neither of us will have to worry about me being an asshole." I grunt out the words, unsure why I'm pushing her away so hard when she's done nothing wrong.

"So you're the one, huh?"

Her comment stops me with my drink midway to my mouth, and my thought process falters as I slowly look over to her, trying to figure out what she means. "The one?"

"Yep, the one that every reporter in this room hates and wants to be all at the same time."

I take in the glossy black hair pulled back so that little

pieces fall down to frame her face and soften her strong cheekbones as I mull over her comment. When our eyes meet, there's defiance laced with amusement in hers, and as much as I want to face her challenge head-on, I won't. Not here, not now—and definitely not with a room packed with other journalists who are watching my every move to see if I'm going to fall apart in some way or another.

I motion to the bottle of Fireball sitting across from me and look at the bartender as I slide my money across the counter. He picks up the bottle and sets it in front of me at the same time as I scoot my chair back. When I grab the neck of the bottle, I look back and give her a half-cocked smile. "Yep, I'm the one."

And without so much as another word, I head out of the bar. The guys give me shit as I walk past about being a pansy-ass until I hold up the whiskey bottle to show them I'm not really turning in early. Pauly catches my eye and nods, knowing where I'm headed and that I need the solitude I can find there.

The fucking problem, though, is even as I ascend the stairs up the dank stairwell, the only thing I can think about is her.

Chapter 2

The door is stuck.

A part of me likes that fact because it means that possibly no one has been up here, and another part of me appreciates the physicality it takes to get it open when I put my shoulder into it.

The metal door slams back and clanks against the concrete wall behind it. The sound cuts into the silence of the night as I stand there, momentarily cautious for some reason, even though in this place I've found more peace than anywhere else in the strife-torn country.

I was worried how I'd feel coming up here—wasn't sure I'd be able to face this the first night back—but standing here, I know it's for the best to face the memories head-on. To fight the ghost of her that's been haunting my dreams with reliving the memory of her in "our" place.

The noise from the city streets below is faint and comforting, but I don't notice much beyond the dust particles floating in the stream of light from the open door. I have to talk myself into stepping over the threshold. After making sure the door is secured so I don't get locked out,

I make my way across the rooftop to a little section on the far end. I walk around the stem walls erected in the shape of a plus sign that protects some air-conditioning units on three of the four sections to see if it's still here after almost five months.

When I turn the corner to see the tarp folded beside the covered mattress and the sign—a piece of paper taped to the wall bordering it that says WELCOME BACK, TANNER, I laugh aloud. At first the sound is one of amusement, and then it slowly fades off in relief when it hits me that the guys downstairs still drinking kept this up here for me. They preserved my little place of solitude in this crazy-ass world because they knew how much I needed it. And how much it meant to me.

Dropping to my knees on the mattress, I sit with my back against the wall so that the sign is beside my head. Once I've gotten comfortable, I look out at the lights of the city beyond that calls to me like a curse and a blessing. A necessity to make my blood hum with that adrenaline I thrive on and a damnation for the dreams it suppresses for so many others. Lights twinkle in the distance, beacons of life in a minefield of hopelessness and destitution.

When I bring the bottle of Fireball up to my lips, the burn feels good, reminds me that I'm still here, still alive. And that Stella isn't.

"Oh, Stell," I say into the night with a shake of my head. "This feels so weird sitting up here without you."

The bittersweet memory of the last time I sat here comes back with a vengeance, and it blazes ten times stronger than the sting of the whiskey.

"Do you ever wonder if you've missed that once-in-a-lifetime, Tan?" Stella looks over to me, the smear of dirt from the day riding with the embed like a badge of honor across her cheek. She has that look in her eye, the one that makes every guy in existence roll his eyes because it

means his woman is going to talk about shit he doesn't want to address. But first off, she's not my girl, and second, I kind of want to know what she's talking about.

"You're not going to get all sappy on me now, are you?" I pass the Styrofoam cup filled with Kahlua and coffee her way. She rolls her eyes and takes a sip, hissing when it scalds her tongue.

"Zip it, Thomas. You're stuck with me."

"Explain, then." I shake my head when she tries to pass back the coffee to me. It's been a rough day; I need something stronger than a keoke coffee, but I'll meet up with Pauly later for that. Right now I just need our routine, our wind down after a fucked-up day out beyond the city's walls of misconceived protection.

Stella's sigh pulls me from the images of blood-soaked camouflage and the sound of gunfire. I know she hates when I get all lawyer-ish on her, as she calls it, and so that's why I phrased my comment that way, needing to get us back to what has been our norm over the past decade.

"Never mind. You, Mr. I-fall-in-love-with-everyone, would not understand what I'm talking about," she says with a roll of her eyes, but I can tell something's bothering her.

"I don't fall in love with everyone. I prefer to call it infatuation." I try to lighten the mood by bringing up one of our long-standing conversations.

"Ah." She laughs aloud. "But it's such a short, slippery slope for you . . . one that lasts a whole two dates before you hit the barrel of love."

"Barrel of love?" I can't help but laugh at that, even though I don't appreciate the comment. "Fuck. Am I really that pathetic of a sap?"

Stella stares through the darkness before turning her face to the city beyond us. "No. You're not a sap. . . . You just have a good heart."

"That's what it's called nowadays? I guess I'd better work on changing that."

"No, it's endearing. This big alpha male with a soft heart. You'd never guess it was there beneath all of that testosterone." She falls quiet again, and I know whatever is bugging her is just beneath the surface, and yet here we are speaking about me. She reaches out and grabs my hand. "Don't ever change that, Tanner. Someday someone is going to appreciate that in you. Your quick love and big heart."

My mind immediately thinks to crack a joke about something else that I have that's big, but when I recognize the conflicted sorrow in her eyes, it dies on my lips. "What's going on with you, Stell? Talk to me."

"It's nothing."

Fuck. The most dreaded words in all of existence for a man to hear other than "I'm fine." "I'm not buying it. What did you mean about a once-in-a-lifetime?"

She refuses to look my way, so I poke her side until she starts talking. "I meant that one person that you're supposed to be with forever. The person that you're fated to love." She falls silent as she peers over the steam of the coffee cup to the city down below. "What if you've met that person already and screwed it up somehow? Or even worse, what if you met that one person but just at the wrong time in your life?"

I stare at her profile for a bit while I ponder what she's saying, taking in the slight upturn of her nose, and find comfort in the familiarity of her beside me. Is she right? It's not like I'm old, but I'm not getting any younger either. My life is transient at best and a mind fuck at its worst . . . but is there really such a thing as a once-in-a-lifetime? "There has to be more than one person in the universe you're fated to be with. That's just cruel if the powers that be only give you one shot, you know?"

"Yeah. I guess." She sounds less than convinced.

When I see the glimmer of tears welling in her eyes, I reach over and squeeze her hand. Who knows what's going on in that mind of hers? After all this time, if I can't figure it out, I know to stop trying. Her stubborn ass will tell me in her own time, when she wants to.

But when she doesn't squeeze my hand back, I scoot next to her and put my arm around her, pulling her in tight to my side. "Well, we both know that I'm not your once-in-a-lifetime," I tease with a laugh and press a soft kiss into the top of her head, but for some damn reason I question my own statement.

"We were a hot mess, weren't we?" She laughs softly as my mind flickers to the year we dated only to find out we were miserable as a couple. Explosive tempers leading to hot sex may be memorable but definitely not sustainable. How we broke it off but then were forced together because of our careers and in the end found out we could be incredible friends to each other.

"The Dynamic Duo." I reiterate Rafe's nickname for us, photographer and reporter, best friends and confidants. She looks up to me and holds my gaze through the night's darkness. "What?" I ask, trying to figure out what her expression is saying.

"I don't know. Sometimes I wonder if my being here, living this life we lead . . . if I've ruined my chances for it, that's all."

"Stell." I grab at straws to comfort her about a topic that makes me feel completely awkward. And even more disconcerting are the thoughts her damn question has stirred in my mind. She's my best friend. After a decade she knows all of my quirks, my pet peeves, everything. . . . What would happen if we tried a relationship now?

I bite back the laugh at the thought. Stella is like my sister, Rylee, to me. Well, all except that Stella and I had sex way back when we were actually dating.

But the thought lingers in the back of my mind, what if we are right for each other but met at the wrong time? *A backfire on the street down below has the both of us flinching, our instinctive training to duck at the sound of gunfire taking over.*

We laugh at how ridiculous we look and how only here, only with us, would this be normal. "Look," I tell her, "if in ten years we are still nomads, still single, then we'll revisit this conversation."

"What about it?" *she asks, her eyebrows narrowing as she tries to figure out what I'm saying.*

"If we are each other's once-in-a-lifetime."

Her sharp inhale makes me realize what I just said, the stupid inferences she could make from it. But at the same time, when she laughs, I hear her nervousness, and the look in her eyes is so real, so vulnerable, that when I glance down to her lips, I'm forced to swallow over the lump in my throat.

It has to be the moment, a simple slice of time when two friends who have lived a lifetime together as a result of their volatile careers fall into that trap of need mixed with comfort and a splash of loneliness. The minute I lean forward and brush my lips to hers, I hate myself for it, and yet at the same time, the immediate recoil I thought would happen on my part doesn't happen. It's just a whisper of a kiss, but my lack of reaction scares the fuck out of me.

I rest my forehead against hers. "Sorry," *I murmur, my hands threading through her hair.*

"Well, that wasn't exactly the birthday present I was planning for you tomorrow, but . . ." *Her voice fades into a laugh.*

"I told you I don't want anything," *I say to squash that argument again, but then feel the need to repeat it.* "I'm sorry."

"Don't be. After ten years, that's the only time we've

*ever crossed that line." The heat of her breath hits my lips
and tempts me when I'm never tempted by her.*

*"I guess we have ten more years to see if it happens
again." I can hear the smile on my lips in my tone, and
even though we both are in agreement that what just happened shouldn't have, we sit in the darkness for a minute —
foreheads touching, lips so close — almost as if the both of
us knew what was going to happen the next night.*

*How this moment was going to be the lasting memory
I would use to get me through the darkness her death
would bring.*

"Here's to you, Stell," I say as I lift the bottle of whiskey up to the sky and take a long pull on it.

The circuit of thoughts that has etched a goddamn
groove in my mind starts again. Hell yes, I loved her ... in
my own way. I just wonder if her absence has made me
read more into that emotion than it really was. People
place those who die on pedestals, forget their misgivings
with a bat of an eyelash, and become more connected to
them since they can no longer tell them what they feel.
Is this what I've done to Stella and our friendship? Is this
why I've held tight to this last kiss we shared even though
it was a stupid move?

I've been through the seven stages of grief. You name
each one of them, and I've fucking done them more times
than I care to count. But when all is said and done, I'm
here and she's not. Guilt is a goddamn vise squeezing out
of me every ounce of emotion I never wanted to feel.

Plain and simple, I miss her. The easy banter, how we
could sit comfortably in silence, that I could predict her
remarks before she made them. We were a team and
now I feel lost, wondering why I pushed so hard to get
back here. So focused on getting out of my house, I didn't
think about how many damn memories were here waiting to haunt me.

I just need to get back in the game. Meet my photographer tomorrow and get back in the swing of things, use the hunger I feel deep down to propel me through the flashes of sadness that still come. Then I'll be better. Besides, it's not like I have any other option.

Plug and chug.

The memories continue to come, the good, bad, and horrific, and who knows how long it's been when I lift the bottle to find it empty. *Suck it up, Thomas. This will be the only fucking rooftop pity party you're allowed to have. You wanted back; now you're here.*

"Fuck," I say into the emptiness around me as I rise on unsteady feet and let my buzz filter through my limbs. Once the mattress is covered up by the tarp to protect it from the dust that blankets everything like an irrevocable stain, I make my way back downstairs.

I smell her before I see her. That subtle scent of hers, which seems so out of place in the air heavy with spices, fills the stairwell when I hit the eighth floor. She's coming up as I'm coming down. Our eyes meet and hold across the dimly lit concrete landing.

Anger fires within me. She's stupid for being here alone. Does she know how much fucking danger there is in this country? The disrespect that's shown to women simply because of their gender? Add to that, she's American. I think of how many times Stella and I went round and round on this topic before she just gave in and allowed me to be at her side most of the time.

And I don't want to care about this loose cannon of a woman, but my feet are glued to the floor as an indescribable current shoots through the empty space between us. I try to deny it, want to deflect it somehow, but we stand there, gazes held, and remain silent.

"Did you want something?" I ask, eyebrows raised, impatient.

"Hmm," she murmurs. "No. I thought I did . . . but now? Not hardly."

She starts to brush past me. Something about that haughty tone of hers with a subtle accent I can't place pushes buttons I don't want pushed, and I reach out and grab her upper arm. The force of my hold pulls her body into mine so that our chests touch, and the sharp inhale of her breath is unmistakable since it presses her breasts further against me.

Our eyes lock, breaths mingling over each other's lips, and that straight shot of lust spears to my lower gut and takes hold. We stand in a silent battle of wills. The same woman I was irritated at for wanting me earlier, I'm now pissed at for wanting to walk away.

Talk about a confirmation that my head is a cluster fuck of emotions. *Jesus Christ. Let her walk the hell away, Tanner. Bygones.*

But my fingers don't relax. They hold tight just like the invisible grip she seems to have over me.

The air thickens, and the sexual chemistry that I felt earlier at the bar—the zing I tried to avoid by leaving the festivities—sparks and lights up the space around us like an exposed live wire. The sad fact is I know I'm about to get burned but don't let go.

"Just for the record, Loose Cannon, I would have bought you a drink." I grit the words out, angry at myself for even saying them.

She eyes me with caution, trying to figure out what the hell I mean by Loose Cannon. "It's BJ, and I prefer to stay off the record," she says with that little fuck-you lift of her chin as she asserts her obstinacy despite her quickened pulse beneath my fingertips.

And fuck . . . I have to bite back the laugh on my lips because isn't that a fitting name for a woman with lips like hers. Images flash through my mind of what she'd look like staring up at me while her mouth is wrapped around my dick.

She pulls me from my lewd but damn fine thoughts when she tries to jerk her arm from my hold. My spine stiffens some because hell if I'm up for resistance right now. I'm emotionally drained, exhausted, and as much as I don't want to feel that grenade of desire sitting low in my belly, I still want to pull its pin so I can lose myself for a bit in the soft curves and sweet taste of a gorgeous woman no matter how fucking insolent she is.

I clench my jaw. A fleeting show of resistance before I give in to my need and the sexual tension. She gasps when I release her arm only to bring it up to her neck at the same time I crash my lips to hers.

And fuck yes I'm a dick for not letting her push me away, for letting my own need for this woman who will most likely move on by the week's end control my actions, for taking without asking, but goddamn her small display of independence turns me on something fierce.

I brand my mouth to hers, press my tongue between her lips as she parts them. Her hands push me away, but the movement of her tongue tells me she wants more. She's a clear contradiction in all meanings of the word. Soft and supple body, but I can feel the toned muscle beneath. Between kisses she tries to pull back, but a soft moan in the back of her throat when my free hand cups her ass tells me how much she wants this.

Her hands fist in my shirt at the same time my hand takes hold of the loose bun at the nape of her neck to tilt her head back and look into her eyes. But her mouth stays right where I want it because I'm nowhere near done with her yet.

"I don't like you," she claims through gritted teeth. Our hands run possessively over each other, but derision laced with defiance glimmers in her eyes.

"I beg to differ." I laugh at the ludicrousness of her statement, considering the predicament we're in. She tries to step back, but when she doesn't release my shirt, I know she still wants more.

And fuck, I'm definitely all in. I need this outlet more than I ever realized until I was in the thick of it. I've kept to myself at home, fought with my sister when she attempted to fix me up with one of her friends, punished myself, and now with the heat of a woman's body pressed up against me and the taste of her kiss seared in my goddamn brain, there is no way in hell I'm walking away now.

"I don't like you," she reiterates.

"Too bad," I tell her as I go in for the next kiss. One that's full of angry desperation and irresistible need with teeth nipping and tongues meeting and that ache deep in my balls taking hold of me. My hips pin her against the cold cinder-block wall behind her.

Her fingers dig into my shoulders as she tears her mouth from mine, our chests heaving. And then just when her protests stop and her tongue starts to dance with mine again, I pull back.

"You're arrogant and—"

"You don't have to like me to fuck me," I say, cutting her off. "You just have to want me."

She protests, and I cut her words off with my mouth on hers at the same time my hands grab her wrists. Even as I gain the advantage, I feel like she's pulling out the ground from beneath my feet. "Fuck you!" She manages to get the words out between fervent kisses.

I chuckle against her lips before pulling back and looking straight into her desire-laden eyes. "That's the plan."

Chapter 3

Thank Christ we're actually on my floor, because the minute the comment is out of my mouth it's like our desire overwhelms all sense, and we launch ourselves at each other, caught up in kisses tinged with greed. Her hands are in my hair while mine are fumbling with the door at her back as the need between us escalates to volatile levels.

We stumble through the stairwell door into the hallway without breaking physical contact. I keep moving her backward as her hands slide beneath my shirt and singe the bare skin at my waist with their warmth. We manage the few feet to my door, and I struggle with getting the key from my pocket because my jeans are stretched so goddamn tight from my dick, hard and ready.

I'm cursing between heated kisses, wishing this third world country had those credit card thingies versus an actual key, because my senses are so focused elsewhere that it takes a minute for me to get the key in the hole.

Once I get the door open and then shut it behind us, everything happens in flashes of time. Hands pulling our shirts overhead, feet kicking shoes off, my mouth kissing her exposed neck, fingers undoing her bra and tossing it to the floor. *Take, sate, taste* are the only thoughts on my mind.

The room's completely dark except for the light of the moon coming in through the open curtains. When she fists my hair in her hands to hold me immobile, I have no other option but to feast on the expanse of flesh from the curve of her neck down to her breasts. Her taste, her scent, the sounds she makes; I feel like I will never get enough of her.

"I still don't like you," she says, her quiet murmur turning to a gasp as I close my mouth over her hard nipple. The sound of the effect I have on her, the scent of her perfume in the dip of her cleavage, and the taste of her skin on my tongue are like a sensory aphrodisiac that grabs hold of my balls and doesn't let go.

The reverberation of my chuckle gets absorbed by her skin as I flick my tongue over her tightened peak before grazing it with my teeth. I don't care if she likes me or hates me right now because it feels like it's been so damn long since I've had sex. My only thought, my sole focus, is the heat of the moment and losing myself to the all-consuming euphoria of getting off. I know that makes me an asshole, but I've never pretended to be anything else in the whole ten minutes we've known each other—so at least I can't be accused of pretending to be something I'm not.

The bed's only a few feet from the door, and the back of her knees hit it. My body bent at the waist, my mouth continues to taste and tempt as she lowers herself to the bed so that she's sitting and I'm standing. And fuck, I thought I was doing pretty damn good on restraint until she unzips my cargo pants and her chilled hands slide inside. The contrast of her cold hands on my rock-hard dick paralyzes me momentarily because, damn, it feels fucking fantastic.

And shit, I'm a guy who's all about foreplay. I love teasing a woman with my fingers, tongue, toys, and anything on hand so that I can bring her to the brink of coming, then ease back some so that she begs me for more in that strained moan women have that calls to the animalistic part of me, before I dive back in to make her body tighten and pussy pulse. Only then do I usually jacket up and slide into the wetness I've helped create.

But right now? I'm all about the endgame. So when her hands begin to stroke me with a measured pressure that's equal parts strong and slow, I straighten up, let my head fall back, and lose myself in the sensations that are pulling me way too fucking quick to the edge.

The best part is this is a one-night stand. I don't have to worry about misconstrued intentions or even speaking at all because we both know what we're here for. And with my thoughts fractured a thousand different ways, this is perfect. Just what I need. A night of sweaty, gritty sex without promises. A hot and willing woman who will most likely evade my gaze when we pass each other in the lobby, and that's just fine with me.

I lose myself to her touch, but the tension builds so goddamn fast. It pains me to put my hands on my shoulders and stop her as I step back. "Fuck," I say, part groan from her stopping the motion, part verbal acknowledgment of what she's doing to me.

And if the smirk on her face, the flush of her cheeks, and her budded nipples weren't enough to taunt me, the laugh she emits does just that. I meet her eyes then, and it's a mutual exchange of our consent of what's about to happen despite her continued commentary on how much she dislikes me.

A split second passes, and then both of us are stripping off the remainder of our clothes in a riotous frenzy. I move to the cheap dresser in the room and pull out a condom, feeling like time is of the essence. When I turn around again, I'm staggered by the sheer beauty of the woman waiting for me. BJ is lying back on the bed, the lean lines of her naked body looking like an ocean of flesh and curves that I can't wait to sink into. She's let down her hair so that it fans in soft waves around her head like a black halo against the sheets.

"See something you want, Pulitzer?" I startle at the nickname. It throws me for a second until I refocus on her open invitation. Her confidence is so damn attractive and confusing all at once, but who the fuck cares because the trim strip of hair on her pussy calls to me so that my mouth waters and my dick begs for the feeling of her beneath me.

When I walk to the edge of the bed, I have the satisfaction of watching her eyes widen as they travel down to take in my cock, and while I'm above average, it's still a stroke to my ego to see her reaction. "I have a lot of wants, so right now I'm going to take the one thing I need. You think you can handle me?"

Her laugh is deep and rich and drowns out the sounds floating up from the street. It turns into an unexpected giggle that sounds like such a contradiction to her haughty remarks when I grab her ankles and pull her down in a sharp tug to the end of the bed. The heat of her pussy presses against my upper thighs and holy fucking hell, all coherent thoughts leave me because the sexual need within me takes over.

I grip her hips and pull her toward me at the same time I bend my knees so that our bodies meet in the most carnal of ways with her backside a few inches off the mattress. I grab a pillow from behind her with one hand while holding her up with the other and slide it beneath her ass. The minute she relaxes her hips, I line my dick up at her entrance and rub my head through her wetness, so damn turned on by her being aroused and ready that my balls tighten in anticipation.

My gaze travels up the length of her torso to where her hands are palming her breasts, the dark pink of her nipples visible between her spread fingers. Her teeth bite into her lower lip, and she looks up to me beneath thick lashes so that all I can see is the gleam in her eyes.

When I brush my thumb over her clit and stroke it a few times, adding friction as I push into her, the sensation of taking her is so intense, it makes the motion of my hand falter, and we each release a moan as we absorb that first-time connection.

"So good." My voice is a low moan, and I'm so lost in the feeling of her hot pussy wrapped tight around my dick that I forget the first part of the sentence, intending to tell her *you feel*, but at this point, fuck correcting myself because I can't think straight. She's wet, I'm hard, and I'll take this welcome back. I slide slowly all the way in, root to tip, and hold still so that she can adjust to me. My head falls back in ecstasy as her muscles grip me tightly, a silent urging to stroke her clit again.

And then I begin to move.

Desire roars to an inferno inside me with each slow withdrawal and then sharp plunge back into the depths of her pleasure. My God. Between the moan that falls from her lips, the way she lifts her hips up each time I thrust back in that squeezes around my cock, and the feel of her wetness at the top of my shaft that teases me . . . fuck. It's like a goddamn roller coaster of sensation that's climbing up to that inevitable drop I know is coming, but I'm trying to close my eyes and fight the release.

"Right there. Yes!" She draws out the moan in that throaty voice of hers that sounds like satisfaction.

I pick up the pace. My balls ache so damn bad and my dick swells to the point of pain. I try to hold back so that I can bring her there first. Make her writhe and moan and milk my cock to help me reach mine. But when I look down at my thumb on her swollen clit, her tits jiggling with each thrust I make, her hands at her sides gripping the sheets, and the mist of sweat on her chest reflected in the moonlight, the mixture of her beauty and the intensity of the act itself pushes me to work at this a little harder.

In order to please my partner, I usually try to hold out as long as possible. That's just not gonna happen this time. No fucking way, because the minute I hear BJ moan out that she's going to come, I lose sight of everything else in the room.

Usually I take pleasure in watching my companion ride that high that seems so goddamn intense for a woman, but this time I don't have the wherewithal for that. She tenses around me and pulls me to the edge hard and fast. My vision goes white, then black, as the ball of energy churns in my gut and branches out to my limbs like the beginning of a lightning rod. The combination of her crying out and me pressing her legs back so I can get as deep as possible drives me to the point of no return.

I climax with a hard groan as the electricity bursts through me, my nerve endings singed, my muscles tensed, and my body riding that sexual high. My dick is so goddamn sensitive that her muscles' contracting causes me to pull out quicker than usual.

As I gaze down at her lying on the bed, a blanket of hair framing her flushed cheeks, and her body still quivering, I smile shyly with awkwardness at her and get a smile in return, but it's the look in her eyes I can't read. She looks conflicted, guarded, like she wants to tell me something but isn't speaking up.

I shrug away the feeling because my fingers are still gripping the flesh of her thighs and my dick's coated from her pleasure, so does it really matter what the hell she's thinking? Maybe she's just uncertain what to say, because what's considered polite conversation when we've just fucked after meeting for a whole twenty minutes max?

We both startle when the ring of my cell phone cuts through the uncomfortable silence. And I swear I catch my sigh of relief before I blow it out; although I'm relieved to be saved by the bell, I want to mitigate any inevitable discomfort between us.

A gentleman would ignore his cell, and normally I'm just that. But in light of the situation and the fact that I'm waiting for a call from Rafe, I'm going to take the convenient out. When I glance to the floor where my phone sits faceup, I can just make out his name on the screen.

"Sorry. I can't not get this." I feel like such a dick, but it doesn't stop me, and I squeeze her inner thighs in a show of regret. "I'm sorry," I murmur again, meeting her surprised eyes as she unwraps her legs from around my waist. I take a step back, and I quickly avert my eyes as I toe the edge of embarrassment.

She murmurs something about understanding that I'm not sure I believe as I pick up my phone and head toward the bathroom to try and get some privacy in this tiny room.

"Dude. Do you have any clue what fucking time it is?" I ask the question to save face on why I sound winded, but then I look at my watch and realize it's two o'clock in the damn morning.

"No. No damn clue, but you picked up awfully fast, so I know you're not sleeping." His statement hangs on the line like a question, but I just ignore it.

"What do you need, Rafe?" I glance over my shoulder to see BJ lying on the bed but covering herself up with the sheet. Shit. Well, I guess I can look on the bright side; more sex might be in my immediate future. That's never a bad thing.

"Got your new photographer lined up. Name's Bo Croslyn. I set it up for you two to meet in the normal place," he says, referring to the hotel's one pseudo–conference room all of us correspondents have taken over as our place to do official business when we need privacy and we're not out in the field.

I knew this phone call was coming, knew I was going to get a new photog, but for some reason having it actually happen makes me feel like I'm betraying Stella. Ridiculous.

"Experience?" I ask as I take the condom off and toss it in the trash can next to the toilet. The line fills with silence while I turn the faucet on and clean up. "Rafe? What are you not telling me?"

"Nothing abroad just—"

"Nothing abroad?" My voice escalates. "Are you fucking kidding me? You're sending me a goddamn newbie? Some fresh-faced kid that's going to get himself killed . . . or better yet, get me killed. What the—"

"Calm down. That's not what—"

"This. Is. Calm." I grit the words out. The false calm from the whiskey and the orgasm that were like a salve to soothe the invisible wounds is now gone. "Jesus H., man. After Stella . . . after how that went down, you're gonna do this to me?"

"It'll be fine. You'll be fine. Bo's pictures are killer."

"That's what I'm afraid of." I catch a fleeting glimpse of BJ in the mirror, but I don't turn to look because I'm so damn busy being pissed at Rafe.

"That's not what I meant, Tanner."

"I know what you meant."

"Just wait. I think you guys will really click."

"I don't need you to bullshit me. I really don't. The only click I need from Bo is the damn camera's."

Rafe chuckles into the line, but I know he's just humoring me. I don't have a damn leg to stand on since I'm the one who begged to be back here.

"Oh wow. I didn't realize how late it was there. I'm so sorry," he says, feigning apology to change the subject.

"Uh-huh."

"Meet Bo at ten a.m. I'm late for a meeting."

"Rafe—" The rest of my comment dies on my lips when the line goes dead. Fucking hell. Seriously?

I slam my fist against the cheap bathroom counter, but I haven't even been here long enough to have any products on it to rattle. Something about the thought hits home. Why? Because I'm back and it's all so different but the same too. I toss the phone onto the towel there, brace my hands on the Formica edge, and let my head hang down for a brief moment to rein in my frustration.

"I'm sorry about that," I say as I walk back into the room. My steps falter when I take in the empty bed and my clothes as the sole items strewn on the floor. My immediate reaction is to stride toward the door, call her back, and apologize. Hell yes, it was a one-night stand, but my mother raised me to respect women.

Then I laugh at the thought, finding humor in the notion, considering what BJ and I just did: wham, bam, and not even a *thank you, ma'am*.

When I realize how stupid I am for almost chasing after her since I don't want anything more, I take my hand off the door, turn around, and stand there naked with my hands on my hips. I glance around my room to see if anything was disturbed. People are ruthless trying to get a leg up on a story in this industry, but shit, I've been here for less than a day; it's not like I have some big scoop worth stealing. Besides, I'm smart enough not to leave anything out if I did.

Look at me, paranoid already, and I've only been back in the game for less than twenty-four hours. *Just like riding a bike*. I sigh at my stupidity and make my way to the bed, but with Rafe's words still ringing in my ears, BJ's kiss still on my lips, and perfume on my sheets, I know sleep will be hard to find.

I sit on the edge of the mattress and lie back, scrubbing my hand over my face. What a fucking day. Back in this land I love and hate all at the same time with ghosts I need to let go. Except I fucking can't. Add to that how goddamn good it was to see all of the guys again and the unanticipated bout of sex.

The longer I lie here, the more I think about everything. I blame jet lag for my inability to sleep, but the problem is that no matter how much I try to pull my thoughts from BJ, they keep going back to her. It has to be her damn perfume clinging to my skin and the sheets, but I don't get up to take a shower.

Even though I need sleep to get a leg up on the wicked time difference that's going to hit me with a sledgehammer in the coming days, it doesn't come no matter how hard I try. So I divert my thoughts and make a mental list of sources I want to contact by week's end, military and locals, to try and get some information on what Pauly was talking about earlier, the rumored meeting of high-level opposition. But the moment I close my eyes to will sleep to come, I see BJ and her sexy-as-hell body laid out before me on the bed. I hear that little moan she made right before she came that was a plea to both move faster and to prolong things all at the same time.

And then my mind veers to the thought that we came

at the same time like in some goddamn cheesy romance novel. Why does that bug me? Why does our bodies being so in sync with each other throw me off, make me wonder if there is something more to it than incredible timing?

Shut it down, Tanner. It's been a long ass day.

Scratch that. Try a long ass few months.

Close your eyes.

Go to sleep.

Chapter 4

"Yes, I'm here and I'm doing fine, Ry," I tell her for the tenth time over the course of our conversation.

"I guess I have no choice but to believe you. And don't sound so condescending. I'm your sister—I'm allowed to worry about you. It's just . . ." Her voice fades off. "With everything that happened with Stella, I'm . . ."

"I'm fine. I promise. I'm not taking any unnecessary risks, but I've gotta go. I'll talk to you soon." I know never to give her a date or time because if I don't call by then, she'll get even more worried.

"'Kay. Love you."

"Love you too."

I end the call and look at the time on the screen. It's ten fifteen. So first day on the job and I can't say I'm too impressed with the new photographer they've assigned me, considering he's already late.

Add to that this room makes me antsy as fuck. The last time I was in here was with Stella. We'd fought. She stormed out. Goddamn ghosts.

So I pace back and forth for a few minutes, constantly

checking my watch, with my irritation growing each time I change directions. Ten more minutes pass and I'm pissed. I don't have time for an unprofessional person without courtesy. The world outside the window passes me by as I wait for Rafe to pick up the damn phone.

"So you've met?" There's amusement in his tone when he answers the phone, and my chafed nerves get even more ruffled.

"Nope. Didn't show. Glad to know you hired a real professional." Sarcasm is thick in my voice as I lean a shoulder against the window and watch a woman struggle to carry her wares from the market on the dirt-covered street below.

"What do you mean?"

"Just what I said. That's what you get for hiring a goddamn rookie, Rafe. This is—"

"I told you Bo's not a rookie. She has a great portfolio, security clearance for the base too. Just because she hasn't been—"

"Wait, what?" There's not a goddamn chance in hell I just heard him right. I close my eyes and shake my head. "You meant *he*, right? *Just because he ...?*" Silence passes through the line. I can picture Rafe leaning his hip against his desk, lips pursed, and the furrow in his brow that he gets when he's put on the spot. "Last night you referred to Bo as a *he*, so why today are you using the pronoun *she*?"

"No." He clears his throat. "Last night *you* referred to Beaux as he. Not me."

"What kind of name is Bo, anyway?"

"The kind that's spelled B-E-A-U-X," he says, amusement thick in his tone, and I'm not too thrilled about being mocked. Images of a rough-and-tumble tomboy come to mind, and I hate her out of reflex.

"Isn't that a guy's name?"

"I assure you, she's all woman, all right," he murmurs, shattering the image I've created in my head of her and concurrently pissing me off because he acts as if the fact she has tits and ass will ease the sting of what I feel is his deception. "And it's on you that you assumed Beaux was a male." His chuckle grates on my nerves.

"And what? You didn't correct me because you knew I was going to flip my shit and tell you to go to hell?" My pulse thunders and my hands shake with anger. "What the fuck, man?"

Snapshots of Stella flip through my mind. My promise to never let anything happen to her. Her body covered in blood while chaos swirled all around us. White flowers on her black casket. Having to look her parents in the eye and explain the circumstances and that ultimately it was my fault.

"What's your problem, Thomas? Male or female . . . The sex of your photographer shouldn't affect how you do your job."

Shouldn't affect me? He's crazy.

"That's bullshit and you know it!" I shout, fist pounding once against the windowsill.

"I beg to differ." His calm, even tone spurs my anger even further.

"A chick? I have enough of a problem keeping my own ass safe here. I mean after everything that happened with Stella . . . you're going to put me back in the same goddamn boat?" My voice hitches, and I hate that it fucking does, hate that after five months I'm still affected. I take a calming breath even though it does nothing for me. At least Stella knew the ground rules, the mistakes not to make—and yet she still ended up dead.

"You wanted to return and get back in the saddle. I told you I didn't think you were ready."

"So that's what this is? Some fucking proving ground?" Fire is in my veins and ice in my voice.

"Having a tough time there, are you? Been back less than forty-eight hours, and you're just starting to realize that whether you're there or here in your house, Stella's still everywhere. Not as easy as you thought, right?"

Is he fucking serious? I wasn't aware that he ever got a doctorate in psychology. I run a hand through my hair and then lean my forehead to the glass as I recognize that Rafe's trying to prove a point on which I really don't feel like being the test subject.

And yes, he's absolutely right, but hell if I'm going to admit it.

"I'm perfectly fine." I mutter the words with more conviction than I feel. Fuck if I haven't gotten good at repeating them over the past few months. I'm so damn sick of people asking how I'm doing. I'm alive. She's not. End of goddamn story. How do they think I feel?

He laughs loudly into the line, and the sound grates on every frayed nerve that I have. "Keep telling yourself that and maybe one day you will be. But the fact of the matter is that you're one of my oldest colleagues and friends, and I want to make sure you're okay. What better way to get you on your feet again than by throwing you right back in the fire you were burned by?" He pauses momentarily to let his comments sink in and burrow tiny little grappling hooks into my nerves, forcing me to see his truth through the pain.

"This is such a crock," I grit out between my clenched teeth, trying to figure out what's really going on here. "Since when do I have to prove shit to you, Rafe?"

"You don't." He sighs in exasperation. "I don't make the decisions, Tan. I just make sure they're carried out."

"How do those strings feel tied to your hands and

feet?" I ask, followed by a circus tune to reinforce my puppet reference.

"Dude, her portfolio is really incredible. Top notch."

"Uh-huh ... Remind me of that when you bitch at me for losing the story because I'm so busy holding her god-damn hand so she doesn't get us killed. I didn't come here to put my jacket over puddles to make sure some fresh-out-of-college punk doesn't get mud on her high heels."

"Shit, and I packed my Louboutins too."

The voice at my back has me whirling around, mouth lax, mind trying to catch up and put the pieces together. A sinking feeling hits the pit of my stomach when I see BJ standing with her shoulder against the doorjamb: Arms folded, she's wearing a tank top with faded blue jeans, an arrogant smirk on those expressive lips of hers, and shoes that are most definitely not of the stiletto variety.

I blame the jet lag for the momentary lapse as the situation hits me full force. Rafe's voice is in my ear bab-bling, and my one-night fling stands before me, but now she's so much more than just that.

How did I not see this coming from a mile away?

"Seriously, Rafe?" They're the only words I can form as I stare at BJ ... well Beaux, I assume. My body reacts viscerally to both the sight and memory of what she feels like, but common sense tells me I've been played on so many fucking ends of the field that I might as well sit on the bench and throw in the goddamn towel.

"Ah. She must be there. She's easy on the eyes, huh?" he asks, trying to use her beauty as a way to soften the blow as I walk back toward the window, not wanting to deal with her just yet.

"No. She's not hot," I tell him, damn well knowing she can hear me. She's far from fucking hot. She's drop dead gorgeous. Elegant. Sexy. All of the goddamn above.

Pissed off, I hang up on Rafe without another word. My mind reels, I'm questioning my judgment, and I find the world outside the hotel so much easier to focus on than our personalities clashing in here.

"I'm not hot?" The amusement laced with condescension in her tone causes me to roll my shoulders in discomfort, hating being played by her. "Glad to see Rafe makes sure looks are part of the job requirements."

"No, you're not hot," I repeat as I turn and walk toward the conference room door that she's blocking. "And if that's what he's looking at you for, that means your pictures are for shit. So . . ." I shrug. "Guess you can go back to freelance because you're not going to be partnered with me."

"I'm not going anywhere." As her glare meets mine, she crosses her arms over her chest in an innocent move that pushes her tits up, so of course I'm reminded of last night. Fool me once and all that. I'm not making this mistake again.

When I take a step toward her, she doesn't budge an inch. "Yes, you are," I inform her as I reach out to take her by the shoulders and physically move her to the side. It takes everything I have to force myself to ignore the damn jolt of heat that sears my nerves so that I can leave the conference room.

I've got to get the hell away from her. Just from one simple touch of her skin, my body feels like it's on fire. Her laugh reaches me as I start to walk down the hallway, and on principle, I turn back around, then stride with purpose up to her and get well within her damn personal space. And even though my blood is boiling, the only thing I can focus on is that fucking perfume of hers that tickles my nose.

"Just tell me one thing, *Beaux*."

"It's BJ to you."

I couldn't care less what she wants me to call her because it's not like I'll be speaking to her again anyway.
"Why play me like you did? *Because you did play me,
right?* You slithered up to me at the bar, used your sexy
voice and those come-fuck-me eyes to reel me in, and
then stayed long enough after I left to ask around and
see where I was. So were you waiting in the stairwell?
Biding your time until I came down so that you could get
in my pants and what? Ensure you'd get my blessing for
the position because you researched me enough to know
what happened with Stella and knew I was going to freak
the fuck out? And then when Rafe called last night, you
figured out who it was and bolted in case I put two and
two together?" I'm shouting now, hands fisted at my side,
and almost nose to nose with her. I don't care about goddamn protocol now.

Shit, we fucked that over last night the minute my lips
touched hers.

My breathing is labored and when I force myself to
step back, I can read the look on her face. I swear to all
things holy, she must be the best damn actress on the
face of the earth. Beaux's eyes are wide, her bottom lip
is trembling, and her eyes are welling with tears.

I love and I hate the sight of her tears all at once. I
love them because it means it just might have been a
coincidence, and I hate them because it means there is
no way in hell she's tough enough to survive the despair
here if she can't handle my chewing her out.

She wipes her palms on her jeans, and I focus on the
motion, because I'm always leery of a woman wielding
tears. When she doesn't speak but just stands her ground,
I look up and meet her eyes to find anger and disbelief.

"Rest assured, I knew who you were, Tanner Thomas . . .
but I didn't know until this morning that you were my
new partner."

I snort at the word *partner*, crossing my arms over my chest as I lean against the wall. "Yeah. Uh-huh. Convenient."

"Look, Pulitzer, I don't need your goddamn chivalry. I can handle myself just fine," she says with a sneer.

I reach out and grab her arm as she skirts past me. "You sure as fuck needed me last night." She wants to be a bitch? Well, I can be a grade A asshole. She has no idea who she's messing with. We already started this relationship with a bang, so why not keep it going that way, right?

"Wow. You forget all of your women that quick? Last I checked, you were the one who made the first move in the stairwell."

"Really?" My voice escalates with each letter of the word. "Parade that body of yours around and—"

"What? Be a woman? *The audacity*," she says, feigning horror. She stops trying to shrug out of my grip and instead surprises me when she steps farther into me. "Let's make one thing clear. Chivalry is dead. I wanted you. I had you. And I assure you, it won't happen again."

"You'd better come at me with better lines than that if you think I'm going to buy your bullshit lies. I believed them once. Not again, Beaux . . . or is it BJ?" We stare at each other in a silent standoff.

"It's both, but you have to earn the right to call me Beaux, and it seems you already lost that," she says as she lifts her chin in defiance. And shit, in less than twenty-four hours I believe I've met both Beaux and BJ. The funny thing is I'm not sure which one I like more. Or if I like either at all.

"Why'd you bolt last night? It's a little too convenient, don't you think?" I'm still feeling unsure about her motives and I hate it. I'm a man who survives by following his gut instinct, and right now my gut isn't telling me shit. So goddamn frustrating.

Beaux steps toward me, steel in her posture, and spite in her voice. "Did you think you were that special?" she asks, causing me to immediately bristle at the comment, male ego front and center. "Don't act so surprised. I found your bed easily in the dark, so why do you think I couldn't have found the door so easily afterward?"

Touché.

"I don't like being played."

"And I don't like being judged." She takes a step back. "Now that we got that out of the way, let go of my arm."

I keep my hand on her for a moment longer, wanting more from the answers than she's giving me. Still I'm aware we both had sex last night willingly. I didn't ask questions, didn't want to know more—and that's on me.

But I'll put a whole helluva lot of blame on her right now too. I think there's more to this story than she's telling me. I keep thinking about that look in her eyes through the darkness of the room last night, and I can so easily see that she was deceiving me. And that's sitting about as comfortable as a chastity belt on a hooker.

"Great, then I'll expect the call from Rafe shortly that you've changed your mind about the position."

"Fuck you." She yanks her arm back this time, and I let it go willingly, watching every nuance of her reaction to try and figure out the truth here.

"Do you talk to your mother with a mouth like that?" She's such a contradiction. Elegant with the mouth of a trucker and a body made for sin. No wonder I'm intrigued and pissed simultaneously.

"Shall I say it again? I don't have a problem repeating myself. And just so you know, I'm damn good. My candids earned me the spot." She starts to walk away and then stops. "Better yet, I will call Rafe. I'll ring him right up and let him know how emotionally unstable you are. How you refuse to perform the song and dance for the brass by taking me under your wing. We'll see how long you last before they yank you out of here for being the goddamn liability that they fear you are." That victorious smirk of hers returns with a vengeance, and she turns on her heel and stalks out of the office before her words hit home and take hold.

My feet remain rooted in place as I watch her ass sway from side to side down the hall until she turns the corner. Even when she's gone from sight, I can't move. My thoughts collide together with her words to shake the sarcasm from them so that I can really hear what she said.

And as much as it pains me to admit it, she's absolutely right. If I was pissed a minute ago, I'm livid now. I start to move on reflex, pacing without thought because I need to work off some of this anger while I process my thoughts.

The men controlling the strings are actually testing me. Making sure I'm not a liability because I refused to take the time off they requested. I believe *sabbatical* was the term they used. Well, fuck that.

Do they really think strapping me with some damn rookie and having to teach her the ropes is going to prove my stability? That it will keep me out of the trouble that they obviously believe I caused when everything went down with Stella? And if that's the case, they're contradicting themselves by saying I'm fucked up in a sense but meanwhile putting me in charge of teaching a newbie the minefield of reporting out here on what feels like the fringes of civilization.

Damn, it's like they're not sure what they want from me. They won't let me go to CNN because they're afraid to lose me and my reputation, but at the same time they think I'm about as stable as a fault line.

Yes, what happened to Stella and everything else that went with it messed with my head. She was my best friend, for fuck's sake. If it didn't affect me, then they should be worried. But just because I'm having a hard time with it doesn't mean I can't do my job effectively.

I went through their circus hoops to get back here. I retrained in all of the protocol I first did what feels like a hundred years ago when I started this career: captive training courses, first aid certification, ethics classes. I did them and then some. Even went to the fucking shrink they asked me to see so she could ask me the same question ten different ways from Sunday to just get the same answer I gave the first time.

Well fuck them. Fuck them and the horse they rode in on weighted down with all their asinine reasons for treating me this way. I'll prove each and every one of them wrong. I'll take this babysitting job and still get the best goddamn story out there. Break it first. Prove to them that I've still got my mojo.

Decision made. I can play the corporate bullshit game with the best of them. Now I just have to wrap my head around chasing after a woman I'd much rather let run out the damn door. She's sassy and haughty and she was a one-night stand, but damn it to hell, I'm a man with needs.

I just don't want one of them to be her.

"This is utterly fucking ridiculous," I mutter under my breath as I stride down the hallway to try to find the rookie.

I look in the obvious places first and can't find her. I'm about to walk up to the front desk of the lounge area of the hotel to ask if anyone knows where Beaux's room is so I can lay down the parameters of this partnership, when something catches my eye across the street from the hotel.

"Fucking hell, woman," I growl as I shove the entry doors open. The heat hits me like I'm in the center of a furnace, but I don't give it any reaction because in a few weeks' time I won't even notice it. Still, I grumble, pissed that I instantly feel protective of her. While I might try to shrug it off as being a good person, somehow I know it's more than that.

I'm playing right into corporate's hand by rushing out to rescue their new golden girl from making a huge mistake and getting into a car that looks like a cab but isn't one. The difference between the creeps here and the ones back in the States is that the ones here have ten times less regard for women. I know firsthand. I've reported on some scenes that made me sick to my stomach.

A sketchy-looking local has his hand on her upper biceps, and he's gesturing wildly over whatever he's arguing with her about. And the only thing I see is that she keeps trying to shrug out of his grasp, and he just holds on. I can't hear enough of the verbal exchange between the two of them to know what it's about, but rather can hear the frustrated pitch of Beaux's voice as she argues with him.

I all but run toward the yellowish taxicab with nothing more than a broken sandwich-board-type sign on the top of it. "Do not get in the car, Beaux!" I command as I come around the back of the car, causing her head to whip over to me in surprise.

"I'll get in the damn car if I want to!" she snaps at me, hands already on her hips and posture stiff. "Who the hell do you think you are? First, you insult me and my work upstairs, and then you chase me across the street and tell me what to do? Dream on, asshole."

The man she was talking to slinks around the hood of the car, far from inconspicuous, but shady nonetheless. "Everyone knows not to get in the cabs here if they're not—"

"I wasn't getting in the damn cab! I didn't come in here blind and wet behind the ears, so back the fuck off. You got me pissed off enough that I wasn't thinking, and I ran outside without my hijab," she says referring to the head scarf most women wear here. Her voice is a mixture of contrition and anger because I caught her making a mistake after I got her so flustered that she fucked up.

"Without thinking. Hmm. Guess that's something a rookie does. Oh wait, you're not a rookie, though, are you?" I hold her stare as I goad her, while the sun's heat feels as if it's burning through my clothes and straight into my skin.

She lifts her chin in defiance, a nonverbal *fuck you* that makes me respect her and dislike her all at the same time. The tough-girl routine is fine and dandy stateside, but out in this crude Wild West of a place, it can end up getting you killed.

"So where were you going in this cab that isn't really a cab, *rook*?" I ask the question to get a reaction, see if she's lying to me, and her quick intake of air and widening of the eyes is the one I was hoping she wasn't going to give me. She was really going to get in the damn car with this guy. Unfuckingbelievable.

I'm a reporter, not a goddamn nanny.

She huffs out a breath. "I'm a big girl. I was asking the guy a question. Is there a crime in doing that, *Pulitzer*?" Beaux takes a step toward me, irritation in her voice and defiance in her stance as the car idling beside us takes off.

"Nope," I say with a shrug, already pissed at myself for caring. "Go ahead and get yourself killed. No skin off my back. In fact, it's the quickest way for you to get out of my hair." I regret the words the minute they are out of my mouth. I feel like I'm bad-mouthing Stella, but fuck if I'm going to take them back.

I turn to walk away—from her, from this partnership, from everything—when her voice stops me.

"Nah. The quickest way for you to get someone to leave you alone is to fuck them."

Is she serious? It's the second time she's insulted my bedroom ability, and I'm not letting it go this time. I'm back in her face in the blink of an eye, hands on her shoulders so that I can give her a little shake. Even though right now I detest this woman, it's taking everything I have not to drag her up against me and kiss her senseless to show her just how wrong she is.

And what exactly she'll never get a chance at again.

"I must have mistaken your crying out loud when you came last night, then ... because last time I checked, a man's gotta have some skill and a large dick to make a woman come without any foreplay. And I know for a fact that you came," I say in an implacable tone.

The sounds of a flailing city erupt all around us, and yet all I can hear is that damn hitch in her breath. The one that tells me I've called her bluff and for now, that's enough to pacify my ego she tried to bruise, because I'm beginning to learn that touching her in any capacity gets my blood humming.

And I don't want it to hum when she's near.

"Rest assured, I don't need a man in order to come." She quirks her eyebrows up and purses her lips. "Now that we've got that out in the open, get your hands off me."

"Gladly. I assure you I won't touch you again," I mutter as I glare at her, the tension in my muscles from touching her relaxing fiber by fiber as we exchange silent *fuck yous*.

"I've got shit to do. I'm assuming you ran after me because you realized I'm right about the boss man." Her slight smirk and the gloating expression in her eyes are the only physical signs that she knows she's won this one. All I can do is stand and grit my teeth as I bite back how I really feel about it. I'm most definitely not admitting to her that she's right in any capacity. That would give her an advantage in a situation where she already seems to own the upper hand. She stares a beat longer before reaching in her pocket to pull out a small piece of paper with a number written in perfect penmanship. "Here's my number. Call me when you get a lead. Otherwise stay the hell away from me."

I take the paper as she walks past me. Out of habit, I turn to watch her and curse myself when I want to tell her she can't go that way. That there's nothing but a maze of alleys and a few unsavory characters I've been warned about by my own sources. I squeeze my eyes shut momentarily with my hands fisted at my side, telling myself it's none of my business where she goes or what she does.

So why in the flying fuck am I walking back toward her? I guess babysitting mode is in full effect, and I hate that I'm playing the part of nanny and putting the baby gate around her.

"Beaux!" Even when I say her name, I'm cursing myself for it. "Beaux!" She just keeps walking, causing my better judgment to win out over my obstinacy.

"I said stay away . . . and it's BJ to you." She stops and turns around, but a passerby on the sidewalk bumps harshly against her shoulder. Her small frame sways from the contact, and I'm beside her in two strides.

"You can't go that way unless you're looking for trouble." I decide to ignore her comment.

She just shakes her head and starts walking away from me, but at least she's moving in the direction of the hotel. I swear I hear her mutter something about always looking for trouble, but I miss the rest of it when a car passes in between us, the sound drowning out her voice.

My feet kick up the dirt on the street as I try to catch up to her. I lie to myself that I want to talk to her to establish some kind of ground rules about how we'll work together, try to restore a professional level, but I know I'm just making sure she gets back into the confines of the hotel safely.

The barely chilled air-conditioned lobby of the hotel meets us as we enter, but it feels like heaven in contrast to the stifling heat outside. If she knows I'm beside her, she doesn't acknowledge it, and that's fine with me. I just want to make sure she's nice and tucked away in her room where I don't have to worry about her for a bit while I try to drum up some leads.

The elevator doors open on cue as we approach. I step in right behind her, lean against the rear wall, and fold my arms across my chest to mimic her posture. The doors close, but neither of us moves in a game of chicken. Just when the doors start to open up again without the car ascending, Beaux steps forward and presses the button for the twelfth floor. She looks over to me and raises her eyebrows in question.

"My room, please. You remember where that is, right?" I angle my head, stare at her, and enjoy watching her cheeks flush with anger.

I wait for the snide comment to come, but she just turns and faces the doors of the elevator without pushing the button for the eighth floor. Tension is so thick in the car, you can all but see it.

"I don't trust you," I say evenly, but it cuts through the silence.

"Good," she says matter-of-factly as the car alerts our arrival on the twelfth floor. "Be careful whom you trust— the devil was once an angel, you know."

And with that she walks off the elevator without another word, her comment already replaying in my mind.

Chapter 5

The shrieks of mass chaos and the sound of desperate and injured people suffering ring in my ears, the scent of gunpowder and blood haunts my psyche as my own shout dies on my lips.

The nightmare slowly fades into the darkness of my hotel room as I wake, leaving me with nothing but the thundering of my pulse in my ears, along with memories I wish I could erase and a chest damp with sweat.

"Just a dream," I mutter into the silence, hoping the sound of my voice chases away the ghosts still lurking.

But it's no use. No matter how much time has passed, I can still hear that unsteady thread in her breath. The one I fixated on as fear and pain contorted her face because regardless of the false hope I clung to, that sound told me the truth I couldn't run from.

That Stella was going to die.

"Fucking hell." The words do nothing to abate the pressure in my chest, and frankly, I'm sick of feeling it. That's why I had to get back here. Get back to the one thing I can focus on. Ironic really, considering this is where it happened, but at the same time, I need this, need to be back in the thick of it all so I'm not scared by it. Because when nightmares and reality are the same, it's harder to fear them.

And you sure as hell can't outrun them.

I lie back on the bed and scrub my hand over my face. When I open my eyes again, they're drawn to the spider-web of cracks in the ceiling above me. As I will myself back to sleep to no avail, I try to quiet my head by tracing the cracks along their broken path through the darkened room. I know that the jet lag is going to kick my ass in the coming days and I need the sleep, but no matter how much I try, I'm wide awake. Sleep doesn't come.

The sounds of a drowsy city slowly stirring to life begin to float up to my room, and when I look over at the clock, I realize it is five a.m. and I've been staring at the damn ceiling for way too long. I give up hope that I'm going to fall asleep. Feeling restless despite the exhaustion deep in my bones, I shove up out of bed, knowing what to do to clear my head.

The clank of weights keeps me company. The cinder-block room is cramped and has two lightbulbs hanging by wires from the ceiling, but I don't care about the ambience because the physical exertion is exactly what I need right now.

The burn of my muscles as I squat down with the bar on my shoulder and focus on the proper form forces me to clear my head. I swear my laser-honed concentration on what I'm doing makes me feel every single rivulet of sweat that runs down my bare chest. And that's a good thing because if I'm concentrating on that, there's no room for anything else. Music blares in my earbuds, but my own grunt of strength to rise back to standing interrupts the sound.

I puff out a breath as I rack the weight bar, having

completed my reps and then some, before I drop to sit on a bench against the far wall of the room. My muscles are liquid fire, but God it feels good to work out the anger churning inside me. I rub my T-shirt over my face and hair to wipe the sweat away as I catch my breath for a moment, my body exhausted but in such a productive way.

The cold concrete wall feels hella good as I lean my shoulders against it and close my eyes. Beaux's face flashes in my mind, and I wonder if she's why I feel so restless. Maybe I just need to see her, set some guidelines for this fucked-up situation I've been forced into, and then maybe I'll get back into my groove a little quicker. What the fuck kind of way is it to start a working relationship when you've seen the other person naked and heard that sound they make as they climax? Talk about stepping out on the wrong foot.

I don't like her. Plain and simple. I had a moment of bad judgment, a lot of alcohol, and wanted some sex. Little did I know the woman I chose would be the new partner I don't want.

Fuck.

The quicker I rectify the situation the better. I need structure in my life—I thrive on it—to function in this tumultuous country where every day is something different and yet the exact same. But having Beaux here adds an unpredictability element, and so the quicker I let her know how I operate, the better off we'll be in the long run.

Maybe I'll even suck it up for the sake of calming the churning waters and apologize for the one-night stand.

Nah. Fuck it. She came with me willingly, left on her own accord. No need to set the precedent that I'm in the wrong when I know I've done nothing of the sort. Now I just need to decide whether I believe that she purposefully slept with me or whether it was purely a coincidence.

The jury's still out on that one.

I glance at my watch and figure it's okay to go knocking on her door since it is seven thirty. Maybe that's a little dick-ish, but at least I'll learn if she's a morning person or not; I can play it off like I want to make sure she can be up and ready if we get a call on a lead.

I'm winded by the time I leave the hotel's basement where the makeshift gym is located and jog up the thirteen flights of steps to the twelfth floor. Once I walk into the hallway, I realize I have no clue which room is Beaux's. Only one way to find out.

I grab my cell phone from my pocket and pull up her number, walking the short distance of the hallway as the ring fills my ear. It takes a few moments, but I hear the faint ring on my right-hand side and follow it until I'm standing outside room twelve thirteen.

My hesitation over having the wrong room is fleeting as my knock resonates through the empty corridor. Beaux's voice mail picks up, her throaty voice filling my ear at the same time the ringing on the other side of the door I'm standing at ceases. At least I know I have the right room.

I rap on the door again and listen for any sign of movement behind the door but hear nothing. I call again, almost determined to wake her up now, prove a point that she thinks she can handle this job but that she can't. Fuck yeah, I'm being a prick, but I don't care.

Her voice mail picks up again. I pound one more time and press my ear to the door. I tell myself I just want to wake her up, but unease begins to creep up on me. Why isn't she answering? Is she that dead-to-the-world tired?

Or is something wrong?

I fist my hand against the door to prevent myself from pounding it down as the same worries I always had over

Stella's safety in this godforsaken land come back with a vengeance.

She has to be asleep. No one leaves their cell behind anymore these days. Maybe she sleeps with earplugs in or music on or some other lame excuse for being unable to hear me. I accept the attempt at rationalization but can't ignore that feeling in my gut that tells me otherwise.

"Let it go, Thomas," I mutter as I turn away and head into the stairwell, despite all of the horrible images flashing through my mind of what could be wrong. And then I become angry. I'm not a worrier. I'm not some overdramatic guy who worries about people I don't care about. If I were, I wouldn't be able to do my job. I see death and destruction all the time in all sorts of unfathomable ways, so I've learned to not think about those possibilities.

So why the fuck am I thinking along those lines when it comes to Beaux? The last thing I want is to be thinking about her.

Shit. This whole thing with Stella has affected me. The thought pisses me off even further because that means the brass at work might just be right. And I won't let them be right. Now I'm pissed both at Beaux and myself, so it seems my little venture to set things right just put me back on the goddamn Tilt-A-Whirl.

I'm so lost in my thoughts that when I fling open the stairwell door to my floor, I collide solidly with another person going just as fast as I am. We both cry out as we stumble backward, and I know before I even look down whose biceps my hands are gripping. I push Beaux away like she's a hot coal.

We stare at each other, chests heaving, eyes guarded. Her hair is a mess and her makeup is smudged under her eyes, lips nude, but Christ she's still absolutely beautiful.

I shove the unwelcome thought away and manage to drag my eyes from hers to notice she has on the same clothes as yesterday, camera bag dropped on the ground behind her from our collision.

"Where the hell have you been?" She looks at me like I'm crazy for asking. Maybe I am, but I still want an answer.

"None of your damn business."

"Actually, it is." Still, I ask myself, why the fuck do I care? I shouldn't. I don't want to. But damn it to hell, this woman calls to me on all kinds of levels.

"Screw you." She pins me with a nasty look as she steps to one side, and I mirror her motions to prevent her from leaving. The truth is I'm looking for a fight, and she just walked headfirst into one.

"Well, you got the screwing part down pat." I make a show of looking up and down her body, connecting the dots I don't want to connect: same clothes, different floor of the hotel, a tired woman. She spent the night with someone else. "It seems you like to play with all the boys on the block, huh?" The words are out of my mouth before I can see through my disregard for her. Sure, I don't want anything more from her, but at the same time, my ego is bruised to think she didn't think more of me—or any other man for that matter—to at least wait a day before moving to the next warm bed.

I'm such an asshat. I was sitting up at her door worried that something was wrong with her because she wasn't answering, when instead she was busy ringing up her own bedpost tally. Serves me goddamn right for caring. Lesson learned.

Beaux stares me down, blatant derision mixed with embarrassment playing out all over her flushed cheeks, while my disbelief at my earlier concern skyrockets.

"I don't believe it's any of your business what I do or

don't do, Tanner. Now if you'll excuse me, I'm exhausted and want some sleep." Her gaze flickers down to my bare chest and the T-shirt bundled in my hand before reaching my eyes again. She raises her eyebrows as she waits for me to move, and the irony isn't lost on me how the positions were reversed just yesterday.

"What if we had a lead? What if I was just up at your room pounding on your door because you didn't answer your phone? How would you handle it then, huh?" Honestly I know I'm being a prick by baiting her with my questions, but I'm past the point of caring. "This isn't sorority row. It's best you start acting like the professional you claim to be instead of some two-bit—"

She's in my face so fast, the rest of the words don't have a chance to leave my mouth. "Who and what I am is none of your goddamn business so long as I do my job properly! It's best you start remembering that as well."

The heat of her body is pressed against my bare skin, and I hate the ache that stirs deep in my lower belly. Her breath mingles with mine from our proximity, and I want to step back from her, give us the distance I most definitely need to keep this on the professional level, but somehow I can't make my feet move.

"Good to know. I'll believe it when I see it." My gaze travels down to her lips and then back up to her eyes, a half-cocked smirk on my lips. "But I think you've forgotten one important thing."

"What's that?" she huffs out, and I love that I'm irritating her. Serves her right.

"If I can't get hold of you, then you can't do your job properly. It's best you start remembering that as well," I say, throwing her words back in her face.

"How long are you going to play the asshole card, Tanner?"

My only response is to raise my eyebrows and purse my lips. "Long as it takes."

"Lucky me." Her green eyes blaze into mine, but I just look back at her like I don't give two fucks. "This conversation has been absolutely scintillating, but I'm sure watching the back of my eyelids is much more exciting. If you'll excuse me . . ."

And there she goes again walking away from me, taunting me with what I most definitely don't want, but what man wouldn't enjoy watching her ass as it goes?

I'm dialing Rafe before she's up the first flight of stairs.

"Hey." He answers just as I unlock the door to my room, and I wait until I close it behind me before I respond.

"What gives? Where are all of the embed missions you said you were setting up for me?" I'm antsy as fuck to get out in the field, get that buzz again.

"It's only been forty-eight hours since wheels down, Thomas. Cool your jets." Rafe tries to placate me with exasperation.

"It may be only two days, but you had a few months to set shit up for me while you were making me jump through your circus hoops to get back here." He was so adamant that he be the ringmaster.

"Our military liaison is working on it, and—"

"Don't give me any bullshit lines, Rafe. You've got me fucking handcuffed. I know I'm being watched here like a goddamn dog to make sure I play by the rules . . . and I am, I assure you . . . but if you don't throw me a bone soon, I'm going to find one on my own, protocol be damned," I say, lying to him with ease.

"How's it going with you and Beaux?" The subtle change of subject tells me he heard me loud and clear and that he knows if he can't make something happen for me, I'll make it happen myself. We've worked together long enough that I know he can't consent to my going against company policy by entering the danger zone on my own accord.

It's my ass on the line. And I'm good with that. Too bad now my ass means Beaux's too.

I grunt a nonresponse. "Don't think I don't see the setup here. The babysitting job you guys dropped on me because you think I'm unstable. I'll do my job, Rafe, and I'll do it damn well."

"I never said that you wouldn't."

"You didn't have to say it. I'll be waiting for your call . . . and for your sake, she'd better be able to do her job." I hang up before giving him a chance to respond, the range of emotions from this morning making me more bitter than normal.

Tossing my phone onto my unmade bed, I strip down, the hot water of my shower calling to my sore muscles. When I enter the bathroom, I look in the mirror and flex out of habit to see whether this morning made any difference in the definition of my abs and biceps. But when I draw my eyes up from the lines in my torso, I take in my dark hair, worn a little long, and the stubble I sport when on assignment so that I can fit in as much as possible with the locals. I'm already missing my clean-shaven face and hair trimmed off my ears like I prefer when I'm at home. When in Rome . . .

I look like shit. My violet eyes are bloodshot from lack of sleep with dark smudges that look like bruises beneath them. I scrub a hand over my face and blow out a breath to shake away the ghosts I see hiding in the mirror and head for the shower. Productivity is my number one priority.

Chapter 6

"It's driving you crazy, isn't it?"

I look at Pauly through the steam of my coffee before answering him because his words are more true than I'd like to admit. "Of course it is ... but isn't that how it is here, always feast or famine? Weeks on end of waiting for something to happen and then riding that high when it does only for the boredom to hit tenfold until the next time. It's just taking a bit of time for all of my sources to know I'm back."

Pauly rolls his eyes and laughs. "Only you could think that you'll return to this shithole and things will start happening." When I raise my eyebrows with an unabashed shrug to remind him of all the times this has happened, he holds up his hands in surrender. "Forgive me, wonder boy. We all know you walk into a room and shit happens that only you know about."

"It's good to be me." I flash a smirk his way before taking another sip of coffee. We're sitting by the front windows of the hotel where we can watch life outside to pass time, but on the far left of us are some makeshift desks where a few reporters work on their laptops. To the right is the reception counter, and at the opposite end of the room, across from where we sit, is the bar. We've kind of commandeered that too—all sixty of us reporters and photographers from various agencies— and made it our second home since our rooms are so small and nothing beats boredom better than company.

There's a crappy pool table a few of the guys found abandoned somewhere in the early days of the conflict. It was broken and battered, but in between air raid sirens and being confined in here for safety's sake, they made it a mission to repair it with whatever they could find. It's a patchwork quilt at best, but it works, and we've all spent endless hours playing on it, trying to pass time during lulls.

Pool's not really my thing, though. Not enough action, enough adrenaline, not enough of anything really, but when I glance over to the table at the right of the bar, my pulse jumps. Because bending over the table, lining up a shot with her spectacular ass directed my way, is Beaux.

And even if I didn't have firsthand knowledge of how those curves look without those ass-hugging jeans on, I'd still guess it was her from a mile away because bodies like hers are few and far between.

The crack of the rack of balls breaking up rings out across the lobby, and it's only when she stands up to full height that her long mane of hair falls down her back. Damn it. I'm a sucker for women with long hair so when all of it falls to rest above the swell of her ass, I curse under my breath.

Visions of wrapping that hair around my hand and pulling her head back as I'm burying myself into her from behind fill my head instantly. It's one thing to push a woman out of your head when you wonder what some- one feels and tastes like, but it's almost impossible to do that when you know those truths from personal experience. Images from that night flash through my mind: her tits bouncing with each thrust, her lips parted with want, that small strawberry birthmark on her hip bone.

When Pauly clears his throat, the sound pulls me from my thoughts to realize I'm blatantly staring at Beaux. I turn my head toward him to find his eyebrows raised and tongue tucked in his cheek. "Must be a pain in the ass to look at that sight all day."

And fuck, I can deny it all I want, but Pauly will think I'm full of shit and assume more, so I might as well tell partial truths. "It's brutal, I tell you," I say as he groans when she positions herself perfectly in his line of sight across the table for a shot.

"I mean the lengths you go to for your job, Nanny Tanny . . ." His voice fades off as we turn our heads to watch her maneuver around the table.

I choke on my sip of water. There's no way I heard him correctly. "What did you just say?"

"Nanny. Babysitting . . ." He shrugs. "Nanny Tanny."

"Dude, that's so wrong." I laugh.

"You can be all kinds of wrong because I bet with a body like that, she'd fix it with all of her kinds of right. Man, I'd tap that in a heartbeat." He's all talk, but I laugh with him anyway. "On our next supply run, you should probably stock up on lube. . . . Wouldn't want you getting calluses unnecessarily now, would we?"

I just shake my head and laugh, grateful for the camaraderie but not willing to go into detail about how complicated the situation already is between the two of us. "Perfect in theory, my friend, but I don't quite trust her yet." And of course now I have his interest piqued. I should have kept my mouth shut.

"Why's that?"

"I don't understand why she came here telling everyone she was freelance when she had the job. Why not just tell the truth?" I hope my quick thinking pays off and Pauly doesn't sniff out my lie. What was I supposed to tell him? *Oh I slept with her and she didn't tell me she was my new partner, but she denies that she knew*?

He nods his head as he mulls over my comment. "Yeah but you weren't here yet. Wouldn't you have been pissed if you showed up and she was buddy-buddy with everyone and used your name as a way to get in with everybody?"

"You've got a point there," I murmur, hoping the resignation in my tone helps bring the topic to a close.

"But you're still going to tell me you don't like her, right?"

He knows me too well. When I glance over to the pool table, Beaux's chalking up her cue stick, but her eyes are on me. Her ears must be burning over the discussion I'm having. She stares for a moment, brow furrowed, but the minute she realizes I've caught her staring, she looks away.

"It's not that I don't like her per se, but it's the babysitting job Rafe's assigned to me that I hate. Since when does he get to judge if I'm *okay* or not?"

"So long as you do your job, it shouldn't matter."

"Mmm-hmm." I take another drink of my coffee. The scalding liquid burns a path down my throat at the same time my phone buzzes on the table in front of me. In a move so practiced it looks natural, I slide my cell off the table and rest it on my thigh just below the line of sight.

I comment to Pauly about something random, keep the conversation going so that he forgets the little vibration my phone gave, while at the same time it feels like an ember burning a hole in my goddamn leg. If there's a lead sitting here and I react, he'll know and want me to share it. We may be friends, but all's fair in friendship and getting the first wind of a breaking story.

Shifting in my seat, I glance down and see Omid's name on my screen. The ember becomes a damn wildfire at the sight of my most elusive but most trusted source's name. It takes everything I have to keep myself from pumping my fist in the air, because I feared he had disappeared on me while I was gone.

Or even worse in this land where someone who is your ally one day may turn on you the next, pledging his loyalty and allegiance to the terrorist just to save his own life. The possibility that Omid has been found out and turned against me is never far from my mind.

The familiar adrenaline rush hits me like a first fix to an addict. The rest of the message consumes my thoughts as Pauly drones on about nothing of importance.

"Ah, shit," I say as I make a show of looking at my watch, causing him to narrow his eyebrows. "I'm gonna get my ass chewed. I missed a conference call with Rafe." I scoot the chair back as Pauly laughs.

"Man, the jet lag fucks with your head."

"Catch up with you in a bit," I say as I start to walk away from the table.

"Not like I'm going anywhere."

The minute I turn the corner and walk into the conveniently open elevator car to go up to my room, I enter the pass code to my phone. The message lights up my screen: **Meet me at five. The usual place.**

I let out the fist pump I'd held back downstairs as the doors open at my floor. I reply to Omid that I'll be there, excitement ruling my thoughts and trepidation bringing me back down to Earth.

The last time I was out and about in everyday life here was the day of Stella's death. The fractured images of the events of that day move through my mind like a kaleidoscope, never far from the surface, and of course my discomfort clears the path for me to worry that Omid is setting me up somehow. It's a possibility with any meet, but I know his hatred runs deep for the terrorist faction that continually reasserts its stronghold in this country after losing his children to their brutality, so I try to shrug away the notion.

Stuck with the lie I told Pauly, I can't return too quickly to the lobby, so I decide to head up to my room and reward myself with some sleep. Yet within seconds of closing my hotel room door and stripping off my shirt, a knock sounds at my back.

Shit. Pauly caught on somehow. Before I respond, though, he knocks again.

"Dude, hold your horses!" I walk over to the door. Just as my hand grips the handle, I hear Beaux's muffled voice from the other side, and it surprises the shit out of me.

"Don't even think you're heading out without me."

How in the hell did she know something came up?

When I turn the handle and let the door fall open, we stand motionless as she stares at me with her green, assessing eyes. The damn woman is observant, and I'm not sure if I love that or hate that yet, but I have a feeling I'm going to find out one way or another because she doesn't seem to be a wilting flower in any sense of the word.

She enters when I take a step backward, and I like that the hard glint in her eyes goes hazy for just a moment when she takes notice of my bare chest. She stares a bit longer than is professional before dragging her eyes over my torso and back up to my face. Can't say it doesn't give me a small thrill of satisfaction to know she likes what she sees. Except there's no way in hell I'm letting her touch me again.

And then of course she opens her mouth and ruins it all. "Going somewhere, Pulitzer?" She stands with her hands on her hips and her head angled to the side.

"You stalking me or something?" I prop my shoulder against the wall and shove my hands deep in the pockets of my cargos.

"You didn't answer my question."

"Last time I checked, I didn't have to." I could volley like this all day if she wants to.

"So where are you off to?" she asks again, this time with a bit more impatience.

I gesture toward my bed. "I'm about to take a nap, actually. You're welcome to join me if you'd like, but for some reason I don't take you for the type who likes to spoon." I raise my eyebrows in a taunt as I wait for her rebuttal.

But she says nothing. She just stands there with arms akimbo, eyes reflecting her inner struggle over whether to believe me or not.

"I don't trust you," she says, throwing my own words at me as she steps backward into the hall.

"Good to know," I tell her as I shut the door in her face. Feeling like an ass, I stand there for a moment with one hand pressed flat against the door, the other on the handle, and indecision clouding my thoughts.

I'm not sure how long we both stand on opposite sides of the slab of wood waiting the other out, but eventually, I hear her feet shuffle away and the ding of the elevator. I run a hand through my hair and flop on the bed on my back, set my alarm on my phone, and find myself staring at the cracks in the ceiling again.

I can't help but question myself—technically she is my partner, so why am I keeping the information about the meet from her? For one thing, I'm not ready to have a partner again, not ready for some fresh-faced rookie to come waltzing into this position and fill Stella's shoes like she never existed.

But I signed up for this, right? Begged to get back here. How can I keep shutting Beaux out when I need to let her the fuck in so I can do my job to what the brass considers the best of my ability?

Add to that this is going to be my first time out in the field since the day Stella died. Do I really want to be so preoccupied with making sure that Beaux's okay when the last time I tried that, I failed miserably? Stella's blood still stains my hands.

Even with all of my reasoning, my justifications keep missing the mark. I doze off, still trying to grasp the concept that if I let Beaux come along, she's not replacing Stella.

And I'm not forgetting her either.

The sounds of the late-afternoon traffic on the streets travel up to my hotel room as I prepare for the meet. I know it's early, but I plan to get to the meeting location ahead of time and scope out the surrounding area to make sure no surprises await. My hands have a tremor with the adrenaline coursing through me as I open the bottom drawer of the hotel dresser and shuffle clothes around until my hand connects with cold metal. With caution, I lift the Glock 19 that Pauly has kept safe for me from its hiding place.

Taking a moment, I look over the gun again like I did yesterday when he returned it. I push the magazine into the grip and pull the slide to make sure the chamber is empty before tucking it in the back of my jeans. The weight offers a false sense of comfort but one that I find necessary nonetheless.

I pull on a baggy, button-up shirt that I can leave untucked to hide the weapon in my waistband before pick-ing up my San Diego Padres baseball cap. I should be focused on the task at hand, but the defiant look on Beaux's face keeps flickering in my mind as I tug my hat down and tuck my sunglasses in the neck of my shirt.

I start to walk out of the room but stop to take my wallet out of my pocket and empty it of everything but my reporter's credentials, two hundred dollars, and my driver's license. The cash is merely bribing money in case I should fall into trouble, which is quite possible, and everything else is to identify my body should something go awry.

Wouldn't Rafe be proud? All of that new training they gave me, and I remembered to empty my wallet. *Go team!*

And I don't know why all of a sudden I'm in a foul mood. I'm getting my first taste of action again; I should be ecstatic, but I'm not because I know that even against my own common sense, I'm not going to leave this hotel without Beaux.

It's a bittersweet sense of resignation. Having her with me means I have another set of eyes watching for danger, but it also means that I have someone to look out for besides myself.

And it's pretty obvious by what happened to Stella that I can't protect anyone from shit, so I'm not real thrilled with the prospect.

As I begin to walk out of my room, for some random reason I'm compelled to turn back and pick up a pad of paper. In a moment of indecision, I toy with the edge of the paper, thankful for the first time ever that our living accommodations are without housekeeping services, be-cause that means no one will ever see this unless some-thing happens to me. Moment of indecision over, I go with my gut and jot down where I'm going and whom

I'm meeting with. It's something I have never done before in all of my years in the danger zone, but after Stella's death, I feel a whole lot less invincible than I used to.

Maybe that's a good thing.

Maybe it's not.

All I know for sure is that it had better not interfere with getting the job done or I'm in for a whole fucking world of hurt.

Once I leave the room, my feet prove they have a mind of their own. Each step I take up the stairwell, I become more agitated with my obvious lack of follow-through on the promises in coming back here: first and foremost, to look out for myself and myself only. Knocking on Beaux's door proves I can't even do that.

How I guessed correctly that she's in her room, I have no clue, but when she opens the door, a visual sucker punch hits me square in the gut. An obviously just-awoken Beaux stands before me, eyes heavy, lips swollen, that curtain of hair covering her bare shoulders like a caress, and body warm like something I want to curl into. She has on a tank top and the tiniest pair of shorts that show off her toned legs.

If I thought coming up here was a mistake before, I know it for certain now. Every cell in my testosterone-driven body screams for me to back her up against the wall and see if her lips are as warm and inviting as they look.

And a distraction is exactly the kind of thing I don't need as I prepare to walk out of the hotel and into a possible lion's den.

So I shake the sparks of desire from my mind as I barrel past her into her room without being invited.

"Please, make yourself at home," she mutters under her breath as I take in her room. Same layout as mine, just reversed, but where my table and nightstand are covered with maps and notebooks, hers are lined with camera bags, equipment, and what looks like three laptops that I assume are needed for storage and backups.

I hate myself for what I'm about to do, but it's a hell of a lot more productive than sliding between her thighs again.

I don't like her.

At least I didn't want to.

I use my warring thoughts as a catalyst to purge the confession. "I'm meeting with a source."

The jolt of her body doesn't hide the surprise that her eyes try to play down. "About what?"

She gets minor brownie points for not saying *I knew it* like a gloating child. Very minor at that, but it's a step in the right direction.

"Need-to-know basis," I say, crossing my arms across my chest and leaning my ass against the dresser behind me.

"We're partners." Her forehead creases as she mimics my posture.

"No, we're not." She snorts in rebuke, but I don't play into her game, and I'm definitely not ready to bestow that term on us yet. "Here are the ground rules, so I suggest you pay attention because you only get one shot with me. You fuck up, you're gone—I don't care what the hell Rafe says."

We stare at each other for a moment in silence. For some reason I expect her posture to wilt from my authoritative tone, but she just stands her ground, shoulders square, and eyes wide, so I continue. "Bring a camera. A cheap one. Even though no one in their right mind would visit here on a vacation, we'll look like tourists to the outsider. When we meet up, your mouth is to stay shut and your camera is to remain at your side. You don't meet his eyes, and you make it known that I'm in charge. You don't question me, *ever*, in front of the locals, let alone a source."

"But, Tan—"

"Don't argue or I'll leave without you. Your choice, rook." I shrug my shoulders to reinforce my words.

"Glad to know you enjoy your power trip enough, you live in it twenty-four/seven."

She needs to take this more seriously. I take a step forward and close the short distance between us. "It's not a power trip. It's called trying to keep you alive. You got a problem with that?" Her comment grates on my nerves that are already frayed because she's showing her naïveté. I'm on the farthest thing from a power trip when it comes to this.

"Nope. Just a little confused. I'm not supposed to have your back?" She angles her head to the side and stares at me, the thin cotton of her shorts giving absolutely everything away beneath, and fuck if she's not doing it on purpose to distract me.

My eyes burn into hers—the darkest of emerald green— a slight nod of my head the only acknowledgment that she has a point.

"Get covered up," I tell her. "The last thing we need is to draw attention to us because . . ." My voice trails off as I gesture at her attire, but I silently complete the thought: *because you're so goddamn gorgeous you could stop traffic.*

She walks past me without a word toward the dresser and bends over as she rifles through the contents. And of course the movement affords me a very fine visual to add to the one I've already created where her hair is wrapped around my fist.

By the time I clear away the thought, Beaux is looking over her shoulder as she straightens up. "Do you mind?"

I've been caught looking but refuse to apologize. "It's not like I haven't seen it before."

She glares until I hold my hands up in surrender and walk toward the door to let her get dressed. Before I open it, I stop, facing the door with my head hung down, and give her a tiny little inch in that mile I'm holding over her head.

"My rules? They're not a power trip. I'm making sure we fit in and follow their cultural beliefs," I murmur in a tone completely devoid of any smugness. "Men must be in charge of their women here. If they see you lacking obedience, then they'll think I have no control and will be less responsive to me. And I have to have the locals' respect for them to think I'm honorable enough to give me information, risk their lives, and jeopardize their families' safety."

For some reason I have a feeling the obedience thing is going to be a problem.

Chapter 7

Sitting in the front seat of the beat-up Isuzu taxi on the way to the meet, with the smell of the dirt surrounding us, the motion of the car over the bumpy roads, the native music in my ears, I can't believe I actually missed this place. Normally I'd have my Worldwide News–appointed translator driving me, but I have a feeling his absence is another means through which Rafe is trying to confine me to the hotel, at least until I've been here long enough to prove my stable state of mind.

The familiar sights and sounds of the foreign country make it easy to slip back into things even though I've been gone a good while. I glance back at Beaux in the seat behind the driver, the constant sound of her camera shutter clicking an accompaniment to the squeak of the car's nonexistent struts. With her head scarf on, dark hair tucked beneath the fabric, and her caramel-colored complexion, she could easily fit in here in this society if it weren't for the camera plastered to her left eye as she documents life beyond the car.

I have the driver pull over a few blocks shy of the meeting place. As we exit the car, I flash the equivalent of one hundred U.S. dollars to him as a promised bonus if he sits tight and waits. You never know when the next cab will come along in this place, so I learned a long time ago that it's worth the money spent to ensure a return trip.

Beaux falls in step behind me, her head scarf draped over the lower part of her mouth, and her camera still resting against her cheek as she captures images of a destroyed city. We begin to walk, and I make sure that she stays slightly behind me and on the inside of the path.

Old habits die hard. Chivalry is definitely not dead in my book.

The closer we get to the old market, the more I scan my surroundings and notice little things that have changed in my absence. My eyes work the area, my mind and body completely alert and cautious of all movement around us, but the hustle and bustle of people heading home after work makes it that much more difficult.

We pass the market and circle back around it so I can check out the surrounding area, make sure everything looks okay. I grab Beaux's hand at one point, act like we are a couple when we walk by a crowded restaurant, but then release it after we pass it. I don't need the shit that happens to my body when we touch clouding my thoughts right now.

When my instinct tells me that everybody is going on with their everyday lives except to eye the out-of-place couple we make, we dart into a small alleyway that leads us to the rear of the market. With each step, my pulse beats faster and a sheen of sweat that has nothing to do with the heat causes my shirt to stick to my shoulders. A rush of nerves starts to rise up in my gut as I push past the memories I can't deal with right now. And just as the narrow lane opens up to a larger opening, I turn to face Beaux.

"Cover your face up," I instruct since her head scarf has fallen some and the last thing we need is to draw more attention to two Westerners in this part of town. She complies as my eyes dart over her shoulder to make sure that everything is still okay. Things change here at the drop of a hat, so I know to never let my guard down.

"Remember what I said?" I have to ask her again, have to make sure that she's not going to pose any risk right now because I've got enough shit to worry about and I can't have her be an added concern. She nods, eyes intense, and what I can see of her shrouded expression is serious.

"How do you know him? Have you met before? Is his information reliable? Can you—"

"You sure are full of questions for someone who is supposed to be keeping her mouth shut."

"I just like to know what I'm walking into, that's all."

I sigh, knowing I'd be demanding answers to the same damn questions. So I can't fault her for asking them. Just this once, I decide to break my own rules and tell her a bit of his background. "His name is Omid and—"

A familiar and unique-sounding whistle from across the common area interrupts what I'm saying. I whip my head up to see my source in the shadows across the way. I have sunglasses on, but he knows I see him because he motions for me to come across the space and toward him.

My stomach somersaults.

"You're not in Kansas anymore, rookie," I mutter under my breath, and notice her double take in my peripheral vision as I take the first step. I'm hyperaware of the sights and sounds surrounding us, including the unsteady pattern of Beaux's breathing behind me. If I'm unsettled even though I've done this hundreds of times, her nervousness must be off the charts.

As we expose ourselves in the common area and close

the distance, I'm conscious of everything around us, instinct giving way to education, and the weight of the gun tucked in my waistband offers a false sense of security that I know doesn't mean shit.

The moment we step into the shadows where Omid stands, he comes forward to meet me halfway. His eyes dart over to where Beaux stands behind me; his hand extends to shake mine despite the leery look he directs at me. And I know he hates that I've brought her because anyone new is a potential risk to his identity being uncovered, but I just nod my head to him and use hand gestures to tell him she's okay.

He stares at me and waits, and after a minute I realize that I forgot to remove my sunglasses, which has always been an unspoken rule between us so that we can read each other's eyes.

Once I've removed the sunglasses, we greet each other in mumbled phrases and wild gesticulations—his English is broken at best and my Dari is archaic—to tell each other we're glad to see each other again. We begin our awkward dance of communication, his eyes darting over my shoulder frequently to Beaux and then back to mine in an anxious cycle as we fall silent.

I wait out the quietness until he motions me to come closer, and I realize he doesn't want Beaux to hear. I step into him.

"Meeting organizing. Soon . . . like weeks. Village elders help." He interlaces Dari with his English, and it takes me a few seconds to catch up. "Your men . . . watching. Top secret. When happens, I get you close."

His words cause my blood to pump and adrenaline to surge. To be the only one on this story when everyone else is chasing their tails would be a major *I'm back* to the other reporters and a huge *In your face, I've still got it* to my bosses.

"Who else knows?" I murmur, hoping he says no one.

He shakes his head and puts one finger up and then points it at me. Sweet. "When?" I ask, pointing to my watch. "Who?"

He begins to speak at the same time I start to hear the click of the shutter. I'm so in my element, pumped with the promise of a killer story—one I know any military liaison would never let me embed on—that I don't question it because Stella used to click away at the world behind me when I was on a meet, and I never had to worry. It's almost as if for a moment in time, I forgot.

Concern washes across Omid's face, and I can see his struggle over telling me anything additional. "It's me, Omid. I'm not going to tell anyone else or get you in trouble." In my primitive sign language, I make the lock-and-key motion over my lips.

His heavy sigh fills the silence, and I hate that since we've started this conversation, his eyes have mostly been on his fidgeting hands. It unnerves me, makes me wonder if I'm being set up now with his lack of contact. But if that's the case, Omid deserves a damn Oscar because he looks just as nervous to be passing along this information as I am being here.

He finally begins to speak, stumbling over words that I can't make sense of, when over my shoulder, clear as day, I hear a feminine voice speak in perfect Dari. Omid's head whips up at the same time I turn around to see Beaux standing there, camera to her face, taking a picture of two little kids playing in another offshoot of the alley.

She lowers the camera, her head scarf falling off some, and looks straight at Omid, as if the fact that she speaks fluent Dari were nothing unusual. I swear I have to pick my jaw up off the ground, both surprise and disbelief fueling my unfounded anger.

Beaux is fluent in the native language and didn't tell

me? What the fuck? I'm partially thrilled because it means so many things will be easier with her here, and at the same time *she didn't tell me*. I can't give it much more thought, though, because of the riskiness of the situation. Things could go south at any moment.

I think Omid is just as caught off guard as me because when I tear my eyes from Beaux to look at him, I see the confusion and immediate wariness. He just stares at her, eyes flickering back and forth to me repeatedly. I put my hands up in an *it's okay* gesture — palms facing him at my chest level — and just when I think he is starting to believe me, I hear the click of a shutter and see his eyes widen to epic proportions.

I turn around to see Beaux clicking the shutter, lens angled directly at Omid. Her disobedience of my rules causes rage to erupt inside me because I know how skittish this contact is and she's now documented his face on record.

"What the fuck are you doing?" My voice is a quiet but harsh scold as the excitement over the information that was just promised me turns to disbelief. "Did you not hear a thing I said to you?" I don't want to draw attention to us by yelling, but it's pretty fucking hard not to when she just played every single one of her stupidity cards in a single hand.

Beaux's eyes are wide and her face must look similar to the way mine did when I heard her fluency, but I can't worry about her right now — I have to salvage Omid's trust in me. The problem is when I turn around, Omid is gone.

My hands are fisted and my temper is raging. I'd love to turn around and throttle Beaux for her lack of judgment, for her disregard to the situation, for not following my set of rules.

And because she's not Stella.

I take deep breaths, trying to calm the tumult inside me. It's no use even trying to find Omid—the man is a ghost in the wind right now—so I do the only thing I can. I leave. Without saying a word to Beaux, I walk right past her and head toward the end of the alley, not wanting to be in this dangerous part of the city any longer than I need to be.

As we emerge from the alley, I slow my pace and cautiously survey my surroundings before I walk into the flow of foot traffic and back toward our cab. I know Beaux is behind me. Only a deaf and blind man would not be able to sense her presence . . . or maybe I'm just a lesser man who has fallen under her goddamn spell even though I swore that I wouldn't.

Despite being completely irate with her, I can still smell her perfume over the stagnant scent of destitution that blankets things here and hear the shuffle of her shoes against the dirt-covered cobblestone sidewalks. Beaux tries to strike up a conversation by apologizing disjointedly while she follows me at a quickened pace through the crowded streets, but I refuse to acknowledge her.

I'm more pissed than I think she even realizes. I'm angry over so many things that it's better if I don't speak to her right now; otherwise I know I'll say a lot of things I'll regret regardless of how fucking truthful they are. With each step we take, my displeasure intensifies over the many reasons I have to be angry with her.

When we reach the cab that is surprisingly still waiting for us, I open the door for her to get in and say only one thing. "Get us home."

She scoots in and looks up at me, a thousand things running through her eyes, and the minute she speaks, I just slam the door shut, not wanting to hear her explanations. By the time I take my seat in the front passenger side, she's just finishing telling the driver where to go.

First of all, there's no way I'm attempting to communicate with the driver while she's sitting back there laughing her ass off while I make a fool of myself. Secondly, who the fuck is this woman? She comes on to me, we sleep together, and now we're in this predicament together and she just screwed me over with one of my biggest sources? I mean what kind of power play is she going for?

I'm all for dating smart women. Shit, intelligence is a major turn-on for me. But time and again I keep feeling like I'm being duped here even though her actions arc not really one hundred percent her fault.

Or they are and she's just smart enough to make me think they aren't.

Fuck! This woman is driving me crazy. What the hell? I never doubt myself, always trust that gut instinct of mine, and yet right now she's making me question so many damn things, it's not even funny.

And then there's her little show with Omid. First, shocking the shit out of both of us when she piped into the conversation in his native language so that even if he was trying to be quiet and only share information with me in the little bit of Dari that I know, she understood every single thing he said. Add to that she takes a fucking picture of him. A picture! My trust quotient with her just went down a whole helluva lot. She *was* freelance. Her stunt begs me to question if she still is, or maybe she's trying to chase the story too and will break it first, steal it right out from under me, and get the notoriety herself.

The more I think about this scenario, the more each bump along the uneven pavement lodges the idea firmly into my psyche. Pauly said she was freelance for a few weeks before I got here. Was she freelance as just a photog or as a reporter too? Was she just biding time to find some sorry fucking sap she could mooch off and steal what she didn't earn?

"Tanner." Her voice calls softly from the seat behind me, my name an apology and a question all mixed into one.

"Don't talk," I growl, my head spinning a mile a minute. The man who never gets rattled is fucking rattled, and not because of a goddamn mortar strike or IED but rather because of this woman. The only thing she has going for her at the moment is that at least she listens and shuts up.

This time.

We make it to the hotel without incident. I pay the driver and am out of the car and striding into the hotel without giving her a second glance. I know she's safe since we're at the hotel but couldn't care less what she does now. She thinks chivalry is dead. . . . I'll show her just how dead it is. Let her fend for herself in this godforsaken place.

Anger and theories fuel my every step as I stride into the alleyway at the rear of the hotel where I had the driver drop us off. We have to forgo a lobby entrance because making one would mean we'd have to pass by Pauly and the crew who would know something was up since we were out and about rather than locked in our rooms.

All I focus on is calming my temper, but the clipped sound of her steps behind me echoes off the walls around us.

"Tanner. Tanner." More footsteps. "Wait. Please. *Wait!*"

I ignore her, don't want to deal with her, but when she grabs my biceps, I'm primed for the fight and ready to unload on her. I whirl around and have her back up against the wall within a heartbeat.

"You want the fucking story, you work for it your goddamn self." My hands are on the sides of her shoulders, and my face is mere inches from hers. "You think you can waltz into my meet and take the fuck over?"

In an attempt to control my fury that's spiraling out of control, I release my grip and stalk away from her a few feet. I'm loyal to a fault, so to feel betrayed is something I don't take lightly. When I turn back around, Beaux's shoulders are pressed against the wall, her eyes are wide, and her mouth is slightly open—shock written all over her face—and the words I'm about to shout die on my lips.

She looks like a frightened child.

It takes me a second to see through the haze of my fury to realize I'm fucking losing it. I'm standing with fists clenched and more angry than I've been in some time, wanting to throw a punch like she's some damn guy. But I know beyond a doubt she's so far from that, it's comical.

I roll my shoulders and try to rein my emotions in because the woman makes me a goddamn lunatic. Add to that I don't know what to say or do besides shake the truth out of her, and that's not a fucking option.

I'm not sure if it's the look on her face or the memories dredged up in my mind, but I have a flash of clarity that causes me to take a step back. I'm out of control, my anger over what happened to Stella is being transferred to Beaux, and the certainty I had ten minutes ago that she was trying to steal my story now has more holes in it than a fishing net.

I begin to speak, but instead just shake my head, run my fingers through my hair, and blow out a breath as I turn on my heel and stalk into the hotel. All I can think about as I jog up the stairwell is how my always sure self is nonexistent these days and how fucking hard that is for a man used to being in control of everything—work, relationships, instinct.

When I shove the door of my room open, it slams into the wall behind it. I push it closed with my shoulder, but

I'm so distracted that all I can think about is hitting the gym to try and work this all out of my system before taking a scalding hot shower to wash away the day and the doubt that feels like a damn constant since I've been back here.

I forgo unbuttoning my shirt, grab hold of the back of my collar, and pull it over my head, tossing it to the bed behind me without glancing back. In a practiced habit, I pull the Glock from my waistband.

"You had a gun?" Beaux's quiet but surprised voice cuts through the tension pulling me so damn tight, a fucking breeze might cause me to snap.

I grunt in response but look toward her standing in my door anyway. Her head scarf is off, hair pulled back like that first night we met with little curls falling softly on those defined cheekbones of hers, and sincerity is reflected in her eyes that keep darting to my weapon on the tabletop beside me.

"Ever heard of knocking?"

"It was open." I hear the startled inhale of someone not used to dealing with guns when I release the magazine from the butt and set it on the dresser in front of me.

"Lots of places are *open* in this city that I wouldn't go inviting myself into, FYI." I slide an impatient glance her way as I double-check to make sure that the weapon is empty and safe.

"I—I just didn't realize that you could carry a weapon here."

"You can't. Next topic or get the fuck out because frankly you've used up about all of my patience, and it's probably best if you're not around me right now." I swear my anger must roll off me and slam into her, because she just stares with her mouth agape. "That's what I thought. Thanks for the chat. Now if you'll see yourself out . . . ," I say as I turn to the barely there closet where my suitcase is stowed to get some gym shorts, dismissing her and her surprised eyes.

"I'm sorry. I made a mistake." My step falters at the contrition in her voice, causing me to turn to stare and wait for her to continue. The silence between us stretches, and I can tell that my gun sitting out in the open unnerves her by the way her eyes keep flickering to it. Does she agree with the brass? Think I'm losing it too? "Tanner ..."

"You didn't tell me you were fluent in Dari." Screw waiting for her and her placating tone. I'm a man of action, and we need to get to the bottom of this right here, right now.

"You've been so busy holding a grudge against me, you didn't care to ask." She sets her camera down on the nightstand, and with her shield now gone, her posture changes and becomes more defensive.

"Don't you think that's something that was important for me to know?" I lean my hip against the edge of the dresser, but my eyes never leave hers. I'm trying to gauge her body language by her responses.

"Why didn't you—"

"I'm the one asking the questions here. Not you." I cut her off. I want answers, and I intend to get them. "Who are you working for?"

Her eyes widen slightly, and her brow narrows in confusion. "Worldwide News?" She answers hesitantly, drawing the words out as if asking me if it's the correct answer.

"No. That's who you're pretending to work for. When you steal my story, who are you going to report for and take the glory for yourself?"

Surprise flickers across her face instantaneously at the same time as she starts shaking her head back and forth. "You're a crazy asshole—you know that?" she says, voice rising as she steps toward me. "A neurotic, controlling one at that!"

"Get used to it, sweetheart!" I step into her space, welcoming the fight I see flashing in her eyes. "No one takes what I've busted my ass for, for themselves."

"Certifiable!" she mutters with a roll of her eyes, and the simple action sets me off. Who the hell is she to question me when she's the one trying to play me for the fool? "I screw up, and you think I'm trying to steal your story from a source I've never even met before?"

"Let's add it all up, because one and one sure as fuck isn't equaling two here." I need to pace, work through the anger eating me from the inside out. The space in my room is small, but I manage to find a path. "You hit on me in the bar, we sleep together, but the next morning you swear that you didn't know you were going to be assigned to me. Bullshit!" I cough the word out and hold up my hand to cut her off when she tries to argue. "You were freelance for how long before within the blink of an eye, my partner? Let me ask you. . . . As a freelancer, were you a reporter, a photographer, or were you both? Why be just one when you can have it all, right?"

"Fuck you," she spits out, and it takes everything I have not to be an even greater asshole than I'm already being and tell her, *No, thanks. Been there, done that.*

Just as she's about to say something else, I continue. "Then you miraculously know I'm on a possible story . . . how? By the way I walked out of the lobby? I mean how the fuck did you know to follow me up to my room and ask? And then of course being the good guy that I am . . . I bring you with me where you proceed to spook the fuck out of my contact when you bust out in Dari, and then . . ." I turn to face her, and she steps back so that her shoulders are against the wall. I can tell she's rattled, but I'm glad because I've learned that when you're rattled, your true colors show, and I'm waiting for hers to light up this room like a damn rainbow. "And then you take his fucking picture? A man who is giving me information about high-level meetings of terror officials and you take his picture?" My voice escalates with each word as I take another step forward to where I'm so close I can feel the heat of her body in the space between us even though we're not touching. "One and one is adding up to a whole bucket full of bullshit that seems a little hinky to me."

We stare at each other, eyes locked, jaws clenched, anger emanating off us in invisible sparks in the space between us that I can't see but can sure as hell feel. I'm so fixated on my spite and anger that she catches me off guard when she shoves against my chest to push me away from her. My hands close around her wrists and she tugs, only serving to bring us closer together.

"Let me go!" She struggles, but I hold tight.

"I want answers." I grunt out in amusement because even though she's so damn petite, she's also quite strong, and holding her still takes some concerted effort.

"Like I said, fuck off."

"It seems to me your mouth needs to be washed out with soap. Not real classy for a lady to keep repeating words like that."

"Oh, I'm a whole lot of classy. I just reserve all my fucks for assholes like you who deserve them."

"I deserve them if I'm wrong, and yet you are doing absolutely nothing to prove that point." She tries again to yank her hands away, and I just grip tighter. We keep brushing into each other, the physicality of it all setting off every one of my body's damn nerve endings. Still, I just want to tell them to shut up. I don't want her. No way in hell.

Not now. Not ever again.

But damn it is a hard thing to ignore when heart rates pick up speed, bodies are inching closer, and muscles are tense.

I know a perfect way to get her to stop. "Look, if you're into the whole rough thing, it's not really my cup of tea, but I'm sure I could bend my ways for you."

Bingo! She stops struggling immediately with a shocked expression on her flushed cheeks. She blinks her eyes rapidly as she processes what I've just said. "Ever heard of sexual harassment?"

With her wrists still in my hands, I lean in close enough so that I can hear her quick intake of air at my unexpected response. "I'm pretty sure we threw the idea of harassment out the damn window the moment we slept together and you walked out without a word . . . but please, feel free to call Rafe and explain how you were trying to get in good with me."

She holds her own in the glare department in our visual standoff. I can see so many emotions swim behind her eyes, but it's the one I don't expect, vulnerability, that throws me off. "I'll answer your questions. All of them. Just let me go." Her voice is so quiet and unexpected in the midst of her feistiness that I slowly release her and step backward.

"Well?" It's all I say because something about the look on her face causes me to shut my mouth.

She takes in a deep breath, steadying herself as she steps back from me so that her shoulders are flat against the wall. "I told you, I knew who you were. I mean who doesn't know of Tanner Thomas?" She starts to ramble and speed up her speech but stops when I hold my hand up.

"I don't want you to kiss my ass. I want the truth." She has another think coming if she believes I'm going to let her off the hook with flattery.

"I'm serious." She holds her hands up to emphasize her point. "I was in the bar celebrating having gotten a call for a job. Rumors were running all over the place about you, most of them saying that you had hopped ship over to

CNN . . . so when Rafe called me, he didn't specify anything other than to expect a text the next morning about when and where I'd meet my counterpart. I should have asked who he was teaming me up with, but I was just so damn glad to not be here on my own anymore . . . to actually be working for a company, that I didn't ask."

I don't want to believe her but once again find myself falling under her undeniable pull. I've been there before, when the draw to report was so damn strong, I grabbed my video recorder and my passport and took off to where the action was to try to make a name for myself. I can't fault her for that if she did the same thing.

A small part of me admires her right now. Her determination to be here out of pure love to tell the story. A woman in this tough career and even rougher country.

"So are you a reporter or a photographer?" I cross my arms across my chest as if the motion will prevent me from letting my guard down too quickly with her.

"I've done both." She looks into my eyes when she delivers the answer and doesn't waver in her resolve. There are so many things I want to say to her, but I want her to finish her explanations first before I give her my two cents. "I went to Dartmouth and focused on Middle Eastern studies . . . learned Dari as something to make me more valuable in the job sector, but then in my final year I picked up a friend's camera and fell in love with what life looked like through the lens. Shit started happening over here, and while my job with the local newspaper covering human interest stories was okay, it didn't call to me like this did. I applied everywhere." She shrugs as she sinks down and sits on the edge of my bed, eyes now concentrating on the nervous fidgeting of her fingers. "You know how it goes, though. Hundreds of applicants for a job that no one is giving up anytime soon. So I took matters into my own hands and started traveling and reporting freelance to try and build up a portfolio worthy enough to get me a job . . . and here I am."

She looks up and her eyes find mine. I want to believe her and what I think I see in the emerald of them but am so damn leery of everyone that I can't help but hold that close even now. Besides, for someone who wasn't giving me any information before, her data dump of facts seems a little too convenient. Add to that she still hasn't answered all of my questions.

I nod my head subtly as I digest her words, figuring out if I believe them wholeheartedly or not as her eyes flicker over my shoulder again, because certain things just don't jive.

"I want to see your phone." I hold my hand out as confusion flickers across her face, followed by her shaking her head from side to side as she tries to comprehend why I'm asking.

"Why?" She crosses her arms over her chest and lifts her chin in obstinacy.

"Because I want to see who you're sharing information with." I make the comment knowing full well I'd tell someone to go to hell if they asked the same of me. "Prove to me right now that you weren't in the back of the cab texting someone the information."

"Over my dead body. Who I text is none of your damn business," she says, her tone even with each word.

"I beg to differ."

"Differ all you want. This is a job, not a strip search, so if you have a problem with how I do it, talk to my boss."

"Strip search? And I thought we were leaving sexual harassment off the table." I can't help the sarcastic comment. I'll push her buttons all goddamn day if it ends up getting me the truth. "If you're not texting anyone, then it shouldn't be a problem to show me, right?" I step toward her, and she moves to put her hand on her back pocket where her phone is resting.

Fuck yes, I'm having an asshole moment here, but I hate that gut instinct that tells me there is something more to her explanation. It's the same instinct I've used to make a career out of getting the story no one else can get.

The worst part is, though, whereas I'd expect someone to shout at the top of their lungs how crazy I am at the accusation, she just keeps her voice soft, unbelieving. I want fiery denials and someone who fights against me to prove that they're lying to keep their cover. But she's doing nothing of the sort, and it's what I expected.

And I might live my life by the unexpected, but this time, I'm not too happy about it.

Beaux falls silent and just shakes her head. "Obviously you have trust issues. I'm not the one who screwed you over, and I refuse to stand here and have the shit verbally beaten out of me for whoever it was. You want another photographer? Call Rafe. You want to know why I took a picture of Omid? See for yourself." She reaches for her camera and opens a little door on the side of it. She messes with something momentarily as I try to figure out what she's doing.

When Beaux finishes, she looks me in the eye as she extends the memory card out to me. I refuse to take it, even though I'm curious because now I suddenly have a feeling that I'm going to end up being the royal prick when all is said and done. When I just hold her gaze, she purses her lips and gives a resigned sigh before walking back to the nightstand. She sets the card down and heads to the door, but stops before stepping through it.

"I quit." She announces the words in a quiet whisper, but they reach across the distance and hit me like a sucker punch as she leaves.

So I stare at the closed door for a few moments, completely at a loss for words over how the day turned us from partners to fighting to this, completely disassociated. All things considered, I should be happy; I just got what I wanted. The temptress who played me for the fool is now gone, and I can continue as a one-man jack-of-all-trades.

So why do I not feel victorious? Why do I keep glancing at the memory card, wondering what it is she wants me to see?

Don't do it, Tanner. Don't walk into another one of her mind games by doing what she intentionally left for you to look at.

Screw that. And yet curiosity killed the damn cat. Fucking cats and their nine lives.

Chapter 8

"She—she quit?" Rafe's stuttering tells me he's displeased with the sequence of events. And of course he has every right to be. "Is it that hard to keep your asshole tendencies to a minimum? Fix this, Tanner."

When I hear the dial tone in my ear, I don't even flinch at the fact that he didn't give me a chance to explain myself. Instead I'm transfixed by the photos on my computer screen. I keep the slide show running over the thirty or so pictures, mesmerized by what Beaux has captured in such a short time frame.

After I successfully ignored the memory card for most of the day, it sat there taunting me when I came back from my rooftop haven where I escaped into the memories there to calm down. And of course curiosity got the best of me, the need to know rooting itself into my thoughts until I couldn't resist any longer. When I inserted the memory card into the computer, I was shocked when my own image looked back. At first I was pissed that she took pictures of me. It took me a few seconds to realize she snapped them yesterday from across the lobby when I was looking out the window lost in thought.

And the anger and outrage that I'd usually hold on to with my type A personality dissipates when I look at the pictures again. I can't stay angry. She captured something in my eyes—more than just the expression on my face—that reflects everything I'm feeling inside but thought I was hiding so well: loneliness, anger, bitterness, grief, and temerity. You can't escape the truth in your own reflection—and everything she's drawn out through the curve of the lens hits me like an inescapable ton of bricks.

I can't stop staring at my image, for the first time really comprehending how other people see me, and when I'm finally able to tear my eyes from the lines and shadows of pain and loss written all over my face, I click the next set of pictures. The images depict the daily aspects of life here that we saw on the way to the meet but in a unique perspective. Objects are crisp but people are blurred; yet the images tell a story about each person with such a definitive clarity, I'm overwhelmed. It's eerie and beautiful and haunting and poignant all at the same time.

Each image is more compelling than the last. Each one holds my interest and engages my imagination. And it scares me that she can see through things so well, because that means she's probably seeing everything that I'm trying to hide.

I proceed through those images, and when I come to the picture of Omid, I'm staggered once again. Chills chase over my flesh as I stare at his face close up and see the exact same thing in his eyes and expression that she captured in mine. Identical.

We are two men with extremely different backgrounds and experiences in life, and yet it's unmistakable how similar our stories are. I stare at his picture for quite some time, wondering what atrocities he has seen, what life-changing events he has experienced, and can't help but feel ten times closer to this man whom I've only known from our limited forms of communication.

Clarity comes at me loud and clear: Beaux wasn't trying to steal my damn story. She was trying to capture a moment in time that relays an entire encyclopedia's worth of information in a single snap of her shutter.

For hours, I get lost in the images. Over and over I flip through them until I have to take a break, because you can only look at the truth staring you in the face so long before it becomes a sign of your own stupidity. Sighing, I lean back against the headboard and consider how I could possibly make this right. Because as hard as it is to admit, I was wrong. Beaux's an incredible photographer.

No one will replace Stella, and I need to come to terms with that right now before I waste more time fighting something that's not even in front of me. While Stella was an incredible photographer, she looked through her lens at the world in a different light than Beaux does. It feels silly to justify it this way, but it's so true.

Now, I need to figure out how to eat some crow . . . served right alongside a dash of praise. Problem is the very notion sticks in my throat like a blob of peanut butter. No one likes to admit they misjudged someone.

Especially a man.

For a while I debate my options, but eventually I figure straightforward is the best way to go about this; the least painful of all routes. I suck it up, knowing I'll need to go find her, but just as I close my laptop, my phone rings. The screen shows a random sequence of numbers that appears to be a satellite phone, which causes excitement to charge through me like a current, and I immediately pick up.

"Thomas here."

"Tanner, it's Sergeant Jones," the rigid voice on the other end of the line says as my hopes rise higher.

"Sarge! Long time, no talk." A smile spreads on my lips because it's been too long and oddly I've missed his stiff demeanor and dry sense of humor. More important, I miss the favoritism he shows me.

"You chose to come back to this paradise? Shit, why don't you just enlist if you want to put yourself through the punishment?"

"And steal your glory? Nah, I couldn't do that to you." I laugh at our long-running joke.

"Thanks for your humility." He chuckles. "So, uh, you want to tell me your source's name?"

And here we go, right back in the continual dance of him asking and me refusing.

"You know I can't do that, but I did let you know what I'd heard," I say as a means of an apology. I had to let Sarge know it's known to locals that his guys are privy to an upcoming meet, because if locals know, then possibly the opposition does too, and that puts Sarge's guys in danger.

"Thank you."

"No thank-you needed. A story is a story, but our guys' safety comes first."

"I'm sorry about what happened to Stella."

"Thanks." The line falls quiet and I hate the silence, so the next step of our dance. "So I have a favor to ask you."

"Ahhh." He laughs. "No, you cannot go out on the next mission."

"C'mon, Sarge. I'm bored to tears here. Help out your favorite journalist."

His sigh comes through loud and clear, and I know he's thinking about it. At a time when the military hates the post–Iraqi Freedom world where embedded journalists are allowed, the press are considered both a blessing and a curse. When things go well, our presence is a good thing for the men in office because they have an unbiased commercial to use to rally support for the millions of dollars they are spending to combat terrorism. On the other hand, when things go to hell in a handbasket, there's a documented blow-by-blow of the botched mission that can either turn public tide against the military objective as a whole or find a single person or unit as a scapegoat to blame the error on.

It's a fucked-up position to be in: to tell the truth and gain trust, all the while having the pressure from the public and the politicos to skew it to their liking. But I'm also aware I've earned a reputation with Sarge for not oversensationalizing situations and being fair to his men and their missions.

And I'll use this unique status to my advantage every chance I can get. He's required to have so many embedded reporters with him a month, and he prefers to use me over others. His silence tells me that he hasn't had anyone ride with him in a while, and that means I'll get my turn sooner rather than later.

"There's nothing going on but knock and talks right now," he says, referring to U.S. military knocking on neighborhood doors and talking to the residents to try and gain information on what the political undercurrent is in that specific area. "My guys are lying low." I groan because this means I'm going to be stuck in this goddamn hotel. "But, how about you come out, hit the range?"

"Are you throwing me a bone here? Something to get me out in the sunshine for a bit?"

"As long as you don't start humping my leg, we're all good."

I don't hold back the laugh, excited that I get to leave the confines of the hotel and the overly paranoid eyes of my counterparts. "Deal. But I have a plus one. My new photog. She has clearance and everything, but—"

"*She?* How come you're the only one who gets to score female photographers?"

"Because I'm just that good," I tease.

"Is she hot?"

"Sarge . . ."

"Ah. So you're humping her leg, then." I snort because his comment is pretty funny. "Dude, I'm stuck here in what feels like Hades. Can you at least tell me you're bringing me someone nice to look at to put in my spank bank? My stash of porn is getting old."

As much as his comment irritates me when I shouldn't care, it does, but I get it. I'm in the same boat most of the time when I'm abroad as well. Nothing but the same pool of women to look at.

"Yeah, she's no hardship on the eyes, that's for sure," I answer reluctantly before we firm up where to meet.

Beaux's shooting the shit with some other people in the lobby when I find her. And how in the hell does she manage to look hot in camouflage cargo pants and a tan tank top? I mean what female can wear masculine colors like that and have the word *gorgeous* come to mind when you see her? Obviously Beaux Croslyn.

Shut it down, Thomas. Just because you think she takes great photos doesn't mean you have to like her. Or like anything else about her.

I wait behind her, expecting her to sense that I'm there, and watch her hair ripple down her back as she moves her head. It's a bad idea, because that affords me the chance to take notice of every line of her body and how those ugly pants hug her as she talks to the group around her. The thoughts that flood my head are going to get me into nothing but trouble, so I decide to intervene.

"Hey, Chatty Cathy? Let's head out." I see her stiffen at my words before she slowly turns around to face me, one eyebrow lifted and lips pursed.

"You must have the wrong person. I quit. Remember?"

"Yeah well, Rafe refuses to accept your resignation and I was wrong, so let's go." I lift my chin over my shoulder toward the front doors. I figure it's better to say it and get it over with. Then we can move on.

The problem is, she doesn't move. Nope, she just crosses her arms over her chest and looks at me like I'm crazy. Even better, she's got an audience around her to witness the emasculation that comes with admitting I was in the wrong regardless of whether they know about the circumstances.

"I think I'm hearing things because that sounded sort of like an apology, but in no way did I hear the actual words *I'm sorry* fall from your mouth," she says, holding her hand to her ear in a childlike manner.

Shit. She's going to make me work for it. Then again, why would I think she'd just roll over and let it go since we've butted heads since day one? Or I guess I should say since the first orgasm.

I shift uncomfortably, but then recall the pictures she took of me and her undeniable talent. I've been a prick to her, doubting her skill when she obviously can hold her own. Man up, Tanner.

"I'm sorry," I offer at the same time I hold her memory card out to her as some kind of lame peace offering. She looks down at my hand and then back up to meet my gaze, her eyes asking me if I looked at the photos.

"You've got a good eye." It's not much, but I'm not

big on compliments and fuck if I'm going to start pulling off my jacket to cover puddles for her just yet.

She stares, hands on her hips, head angled to the side while her eyes measure whether or not I'm sincere. I guess she decides that I am, because her eyes flicker to everyone around her as she gauges what she can ask with an audience. "Where are we going?"

"I thought it was time that I show you the lay of the land." I nod my head toward the door.

"Okay . . ." She draws the word out, clearly unsure what I'm telling her. But it looks like she's on board.

The security at the base can be daunting the first time you experience it, but Beaux handles it like a pro. What she's not liking is how I'm not telling her why we are here.

As we're escorted via Humvee through the maze of tilt-ups and plywood barracks, I glance over and watch her take in the enormity of this military city for the first time. She leans toward the window to see better, eyes hidden by sunglasses, and when she finally looks over and meets my assessing gaze, she smiles softly before immediately turning back to take in the nonstop hustle and bustle of the base.

I stare at her a bit longer while her focus is elsewhere, allowing myself to get lost in the lines of her posture and wonder what she's hiding from, when she steps behind the camera herself. Stella used the device as a shield to protect her from the fucked-up reality of her life before she was adopted. I wonder what it is that Beaux hides from.

It's none of my business. Not prying is a noble notion, but I'm curious nonetheless.

Once we reach the outskirts of the base where there's

a secured shooting range, Sarge is already standing there, stiff and dressed in desert camo head to toe. I ignore the inquisitive look that Beaux gives me as we climb out of the transport, and I extend my hand to him in greeting.

"Good to see you, man."

"Likewise. Sarge, this is BJ Croslyn. BJ, this is Sergeant Jones . . . or Sarge for short." I catch her inquisitive look over my introducing her as BJ, but I don't plan on him knowing her well enough to use her full name.

Sarge extends his hand to Beaux.

"Nice to meet you," she says with a wide smile, but her eyes are still taking stock of her surroundings.

"The pleasure is mine," Sarge says with a nod before motioning to the empty range behind him. "Everyone must have found out you were coming today, because they cleared out."

"Funny. Very funny." While my tone is teasing, I hate that a part of me is pissed at the dig at my abilities in front of Beaux when I'm a damn good shot. It has to be my ego caring because I'm most definitely not here to try and impress Beaux. She's a colleague. My partner. A royal pain in the ass.

"You ready to prove me wrong?" Sarge asks as he walks toward the staging area.

I start to follow him, but Beaux grabs my arm and tugs on it. "What are we doing?"

"Target shooting." When her eyes widen at my matter-of-fact comment, I know my assumption was right, that the sight of my gun scared her yesterday. And if she plans on not flinching at the sights we will see on an embed mission, then she'd better get comfortable with guns. Hence the whole purpose of being here today.

"Have you ever shot a gun before?" Her lack of an immediate answer is answer enough. She just stares at me momentarily as she swallows, noticeably looking like a deer caught in the headlights. I continue before she can recover. "Look, you've got to get used to the sound of them if we're going out on a mission, so it's easier like this rather than by surprise outside the city's walls. C'mon. It's not as scary as you think. I'll show you."

She nods cautiously before following me over to where Sarge has a table set up with ear protection and a Glock resting there for our use. I'm not allowed to bring mine on base, so he's let me use his gun the few times he has granted me access to the range. This special privilege seems to be his way of thanking me for giving him information in quid pro quo fashion.

Beaux's nerves start to show as she stands there fidgeting while I check the weapon for safety measures. I know from experience with having a sister that if I feed into her fears, it will most likely only make them worse, so I don't glance at Beaux when I hand her the electronic ear protection. "Put these on."

The fact that she does as she's told without arguing tells me she really is nervous about the whole setup. I remove the gun from the table, then glance over to where Sarge is gearing up to shoot some targets. When I look back to Beaux, I motion with my index finger for her to follow me. Despite the hesitant look on her face and the fact that her eyes keep flickering down to where I hold the weapon at my side, she obliges without any attempts at resistance.

"Put your feet here," I instruct as I put my hands on her shoulders and turn them square with the target on the opposite end of the lane where we stand. So much for ignoring the desire to touch her. I guess I didn't think through this part of my plan very well; although I don't want to touch the woman, I'm going to have to do just that in order to teach her to shoot. Trying to put a bit of distance between us so that I can find my equilibrium again, I use my foot to kick hers a little farther apart into a wider stance. She turns to look at me, but I point to where the target is. "That's where you're aiming. I'm going to stand behind you and help you hold the gun the first few times so the recoil doesn't surprise you."

If she responds, I miss it, because I've stepped up against her, and the temptation of her body flanking mine, my front to her back, distracts me momentarily. I can feel the heat of her body, feel that electric jolt of chemistry between us ten times stronger than when it was just my hands, but I shove the thought away as quickly as possible.

"Put your arms in front of you like you're firing," I instruct, and she complies, lifting her arms in front of her at chest height with her palms together. I lift my own to mimic her, but I have the Glock in my left hand.

My chest is pressed against her back, my chin brushing just over the crown of her head so that the scent of her shampoo fills my head, and my arms frame hers so that we are literally touching in every possible way. And sure, my mind is focused on the task at hand, but in the silence from the headphones, everything my senses capture is magnified: her perfume, the warm breeze blowing so that her hair tickles my cheek, the feeling of her back expanding as she takes in a fortifying breath for the first time since we've been touching. And there's something about my touch causing her to hold her breath that takes hold of me and doesn't let go.

I lower my mouth to her ear so that the electronics can pick up my voice. "I want you to replace my hands on the gun." She hesitates momentarily. "C'mon, rook. Take it from me," I encourage her.

Beaux cautiously repositions her hands one by one, her arms dipping a bit when she first feels the weight of the weapon for herself, but I help reposition her hands before I close mine over hers. "See the little ridge right here? That's the guide, and you aim that where you want to hit the target." She nods her head ever so slightly. "Okay, so you're good. When you're ready, pull the trigger. There's going to be a recoil, but I'll help you so that it's not too wicked."

She nods again as I start to relax my muscles so that she can adjust the sight to her eye level. We stand like this for a few moments as I wait her out. I know she's about to shoot when I feel her spine straighten and arms stiffen. She takes a deep breath and pulls the trigger.

When the recoil hits, I hold her hands as steady as possible, but her body shunts backward into mine from the force before the sound even echoes around the range. My feet are planted so that I absorb the impact for her, but goddamn, it doesn't do shit to protect me from the feeling of her ass pressed against my dick.

Normally I'd give myself a second to enjoy the feel of her even though I'm trying to tell myself I don't like it because . . . well because it's her and I'm not supposed to like Beaux on principle, *but damn*. I'm supposed to be showing her how to shoot a weapon. The thought of sex with her should not cross my mind at all. . . .

Her laugh vibrates through her chest and into mine, pulling me from the physical thoughts that have no place on a shooting range. I focus on deciphering what she finds so funny and notice she didn't make a mark on the target at all.

"You've got to keep your eyes open, Beaux," I say in her ear, earning myself a laugh and confirmation that my hunch was correct. "It doesn't do you any good at all if you can't see where you're aiming." She reins in her amusement and nods her head in silent understanding. "You want to try again?"

"Yes."

So we go through the motions again of getting the right stance, and I swear a part of me feels like she's drawing out the time from when our bodies are pressed close to the time when she pulls the trigger. I know it's all in my mind, though. But having her so close is an unexpected seduction all its own.

And just when my thoughts begin to run through the memory of how her body felt wrapped around mine, she pulls the trigger and shocks the image from my mind. My conscience, guilty of nothing more than belonging to a red-blooded male, appreciates the jolt before my body starts reacting to the wayward sexual thoughts. I don't think Beaux is likely going to appreciate having my dick hardening against her ass.

I'm telling myself I need to step away from her at the same time she lets out a little whoop over actually hitting the edge of the target. It's the perfect distraction, and I release her hands to give us the physical space that I desperately need to prevent myself from acting like a prepubescent teenager.

"You hit paper!"

She looks over to me with a little bit of panic in her eyes. "What?" She turns her body, gun still in her hands, without thought, and I immediately step in and push her arms back toward downrange.

"Keep it pointed that way," I instruct. Her eyes go wide with panic as she realizes what she'd almost just done. "It's okay . . . Your turn to do it all by yourself. The kickback will be stronger, but you know what to expect now."

She looks at me with an expression of uncertainty, but my only response is to step farther away from her to emphasize that she can do this on her own. I watch her turn back toward the target, see her shoulders rise as she concentrates on what she's about to do, her small frame tensing just before she pulls the trigger. Her body jars with the recoil, but she does well holding her stance, and I have to say I'm rather impressed with both her shot and her form.

I retreat toward the staging area as she glances over to me, a smile spreading on those lush lips of hers, and there is something about her in the moment that causes my feet to falter. Maybe it's her regal beauty mixed with the rough elements around us: black hair against soft cheeks, cold metal in the hands I know are smooth, emerald eyes standing out amid the sea of camouflage netting around her. I can't pinpoint the exact nature of it all, but the excitement in her eyes combined with the softness of her smile has that familiar feeling dropping through me that I don't want to feel—not here, not with her.

In my head, I immediately hear Stella chastising me, telling me to step back from the ledge because my libido is leading the charge in a way that makes me want more from Beaux than just her photographs. It doesn't seem to help to remind myself this feeling is straight lust fueled by loneliness and desire. A total fuckup of a combination.

What sane man wouldn't be attracted to her? Shit, I fell for her ruse, so I can't feign innocence, but at least I learned my lesson.

"Damn, Thomas, she can pull my trigger any day," Sarge says under his breath as I pull my ear protection off. He has just proven my exact point.

"Nah, I think she bats for her own team." The comment is off my tongue before I can stop it, and thank God he laughs. I do too. The only difference is that I'm laughing at the ludicrousness of my knee-jerk response while he's thinking what a shame it is to waste that body of hers.

"Fair warning, I'll start to think less of you if you, the consummate ladies' man, can't make her switch-hit for just one inning." He whistles out in appreciation when Beaux sets the weapon down on the ledge in front of her and stretches her arms out overhead in a motion that gives us both a great profile view of her rack.

And as much as I want to audibly groan in appreciation of the sight, there's no way I'm going to draw more of his attention toward her. So many confused thoughts are running through my head by now, and the situation only feels more fraught when Beaux's smile grows wider and she holds my gaze a little longer than necessary.

"Ah, you just might have a shot, Thomas, if she keeps looking at you like that," Sarge teases, snapping me from the wave of thoughts that don't belong.

"What the fuck ever," I snort. "You got her for a bit? I want to go say hi to Maverick and see how he's doing." It's been months since I've seen him, so I know he's probably fine now after taking hostile fire, but it never hurts to recement connections here.

And now that I'm watching Sarge interact with Beaux, I realize what a bad idea it was coming here with the hope that he might have some time to babysit. Because bringing a gorgeous woman to a military base full of men who have been on deployment for months on end is like flaunting chum to hungry sharks. Someone is going to bite, and while chivalry may be dead, my ability to throw a punch to defend her honor sure as fuck isn't.

And that's the last thing I need, to cause trouble and bite the hand that feeds me.

"Sure. I've got time before my next briefing," he tells me right before Beaux fires another round, the pop drowning out all sound around us.

"Thanks." I stride out of the range with the hopes of letting a few more people know I'm back in action while she stays under the watchful eyes of Sarge. I trust that he'll take care of her without making a move.

Plus, he thinks she's a lesbian.

If he's watching her, that means I don't have to. And if I'm not watching her, then I can't keep getting irritated at how damn much I want to experience the feel of her body against mine again.

Besides, I don't like her.

Yeah, keep telling yourself that, Tanner.

Chapter 9

When I return to the range, there's no one there. At first, irritation flickers that Sarge couldn't stay put for a whole thirty minutes, but then I look at my watch and realize it was more like an hour. Shit. I glance at the service bars on my phone that are nowhere near consistent—ranging from zero to one—but that doesn't mean I'm any less irritated by their up and disappearing.

So where in the hell are they? I try to figure out the most logical place for Sarge to take her, but I come up with nothing. Add the fact that neither is answering their cell phone because their cell reception probably sucks as badly as mine.

But the more I start searching for them in places near the range without any luck, my mind keeps going to Sarge's comments about how attractive she is.

Hell yes, I'm an asshole for the suspicion that they could be off sleeping together somewhere, but my temper doesn't fucking care. I start poking my head into random buildings, half expecting to get my ass chewed out for it and frankly not really caring. Both of their numbers are on constant repeat on my damn phone and still no answer.

By the time I've searched a seventh building only to come up empty-handed, the temper I try so fucking hard to keep under control is boiling over. So I make myself stop for a moment and wonder why in the hell I am so worked up. . . . Why am I letting this get to me? First of all, I have no claim to her. Secondly, she's a grown woman, able to make her own decisions regardless of how wrong they seem to me. Like sleep with me and the next night turn around and sleep with someone else. I remember meeting Beaux a few mornings ago in the stairwell dressed in her clothes from the night before.

I stop in the middle of the street and blow out a breath as I rake my hand through my hair. I just plopped her on a base of horny men and walked away. What was I thinking? My anger turns inward as worry starts to take over. I search a few more bungalows before I hear her laugh behind closed doors followed by a man's laugh. In full big-brother mode I jog to the door, my imagination running wild in a way that adds fuel to my temper. When I pull the door open without knocking, what I expected and what I see couldn't be more different.

There's a room of about twenty soldiers, and Beaux is standing in the middle getting instructions from one of them on how to aim the dart in her hand properly at the dartboard on the wall opposite them. Her back is to me; her attention is on the fresh-faced kid while his hand is on hers, showing her the proper technique. The flash of jealousy that streaks through me instantly more than pisses me off.

"Okay, guys," she says, rolling her shoulders to make an innocent production of it all in a comical way. She garners a few chuckles from the men around her who appear mes-merized by her. It's not a hard thing to be, considering my boots are rooted to the ground as I watch the show. She shoots and misses, laughter falling from her lips as the guys stumble around her to help pick the dart up.

The guys reach out to touch her shoulders and arms—a pat on the back, a helping hand—all seemingly innocent; but I'm a guy. I know what's probably running through their minds, and a single touch is way too many for my liking. So when she lifts her head and locks eyes with me, I stop in my tracks even though I've got one foot out to move forward. There's something in the exchange that unnerves me: her soft smile, the fact that she's looking at me when all of these men are vying for her attention. I don't understand it exactly, but the minute it hits me, I hate it.

"You ready?" My voice comes out in an authoritative tone, causing the conversations in the room to die around us as my posture alone lets it be known that she's with me. Exactly what I want them to think.

She hesitates, the softness in her eyes turning to a defiance that causes me to grit my teeth.

"The lady's having fun," the private next to her says, squaring his shoulders to let me know that he'll step up to the plate for her. Little does he know I can throw a fastball with the best of them.

"It's time for the lady to leave," I assert.

He takes a step forward, two guys stepping up beside him, and I know a fight brewing when I see one. I'm definitely not afraid to take a hit, but causing trouble on the base is not a good idea when I need to stay in the military's good graces. More guys take notice of the showdown that looks like it's about to go down, postures stiffening and necks craning to catch a glimpse of the stranger invading their space.

I steal a look at Beaux and use it to tell her the words I can't say aloud: *Get your ass out the door right now before fists start flying.* And of course she fucking hesitates again, adding heat to my already boiling anger. She matches me glare for glare. I'm not sure what kind of game she's playing right now, but I'm definitely not in the mood for it.

"Sorry, boys," she finally says when the tension is so thick, it feels like I'm swimming in it. "My babysitter is right. It's time to go."

The soldiers let out a communal groan with some of the guys throwing out offers for their babysitting services. I don't find it amusing. *At all.*

Beaux takes her sweet ass time sauntering to the door, saying good-bye to a few of the guys as she heads my way before granting me a smug little smirk, and exiting through the door I hold open for her.

I salute the soldiers inside a farewell before shutting the door and following after her as she stalks off down the street. As I quicken my stride to catch up, I'm confused as fuck as to why she's mad at me when I did nothing wrong. With each step, my anger intensifies at her and at myself.

After all, I spent all this time worrying that I had put her in some bad situation when she was in fact sitting there flirting playfully with those guys. I wasn't rude, didn't act like a dick, but rather just told her it was time to go. And what do I get in return? I get her goddamn attitude and hips swaying back and forth, telling me to fuck off with each step.

"What's your problem?" I've gotten sick and tired of always being the one playing chase in whatever game of cat and mouse we seem stuck in. I'm not a man used to the idea of chasing, and it doesn't sit well with me.

"Go to hell, Tanner," she yells over her shoulder.

"Where's Sarge?" I ask, trying to ignore her melodramatics.

"Had to go to a meeting. You were late. He left me in good hands."

Good hands? Really? That's clearly what she thinks, although in my mind that was the farthest thing from it. "What the hell type of game were you playing back there?" She just keeps stalking away, and confusion riots inside me. Here I was worried sick about her, remembering what happened to Stella . . . and to think she was in there parading her ass around and getting the attention she must need to keep that ego of hers overinflated.

Jesus Christ. What the fuck is wrong with me? I can't decide whether I care about her or whether I can't be bothered to care. It doesn't really matter, though, because I've got so much pent-up fury when I catch up to her just as she turns a corner toward an alley. I don't even hesitate when I reach for her arm and whirl her around so that her back is against the wall behind her.

"Let go of me!" Her teeth are gritted, and there's spite in her voice that I still don't think I deserve.

"Babysitter?" I snarl, unsure why the term pissed me off so bad when it's exactly what I am in Rafe's eyes. Maybe it's because in front of all of those guys I wanted to be more than that.

"Yeah, babysitter." She tries to step into me, use that compact little body of hers to emphasize her point, but there's not much space between the wall and where I stand, so all she accomplishes is pushing her chest against mine, causing warning bells to fire off, but fuck if I care because the goddamn alarm's been sounding since I couldn't find her. "You think you can issue an apology, take me to the range, and you're forgiven? I don't hold grudges, Pulitzer, but I also don't forgive at the drop of a dime either—"

"Shut up!"

"You're arrogant and condescending and an asshole—"

"Will you be quiet?" My voice escalates with each word, bouncing off the concrete around us and coming back to me.

"No, because you—"

I don't know what comes over me other than wanting to shut her mouth, but it must be the feel of our bodies connecting, the heat of our tempers igniting the chemistry on constant spark between us, because without preamble my fingers are in her hair, and I crush my lips to hers. Savoring her taste. Goddamn it. It's everything I don't want but crave all the same because it tempts me and calls on me to have more.

But by the time I realize what I'm doing, and that she's kissing me back after the few seconds of shock pass, it's too damn late to stop. And I don't think I could if I wanted to. Anger and emotion fuel the kiss, plus adrenaline adds a bite of hunger that makes me not care if our lips are bruised when we part. Right now I need to answer the insanity this woman brings out in me.

So I let myself fall under the haze of the kiss with the heat around us and her soft body against mine. It's when she slides her hands up my chest and starts to respond with more than just her lips and tongue that the reality of what I've just initiated seeps through the desire ruling my body.

Then I break my lips from hers, feeling completely confused about how I can be so wrapped up in this woman and at the same time despise her. Our faces are inches apart, breaths warming each other's cheeks as her eyes tell me she's trying to understand what the hell happened. Just like I am. It's no use trying to explain, so I hold on to the only emotion that makes sense anymore, my anger.

"I still don't like you," I mutter as I turn on my heel to walk away but not before I see the shock flash through her eyes. I don't hear her footsteps follow behind me. "You'd best be following me, because I'm not going to save your ass again, rookie."

Two hours later, the bar is loud, the drinks are cold, and I hate that I keep thinking about Beaux. It doesn't help that she's sitting on the other side of the room, surrounded by men. And it's not her fault; the male to female ratio here is almost ten to one, so I get it.

But I don't want to wonder why exactly I care so much.

The more I watch her, the more worked up I get. She's flipping her hair, and several times she meets my eyes above the crowd around her . . . because, yes, she has a crowd. She just draws people to her, and it's annoying and understandable all at the same time. But the minute our eyes connect, that sneer returns to her lips and she averts her eyes from my gaze.

"If looks could kill, man . . . ," Pauly says with an audible exhale, and leaves the end of the sentence hanging.

"Yeah, yeah, yeah," I mutter, shaking my head when he pushes a glass of something amber in front of me. "No, thanks."

"What'd you do to piss off the princess?"

I snort at the endearment. "Nothing. She was being stupid, and I put her in her place. Now she's pissed at me."

"So in other words you were being an asshole? Or should I say you were being yourself?" He's grasping for clues and fuck, I love him, but I'm not giving him the details he wants. That means confessing we were with Sarge, and that's a Pandora's box that needs to stay closed.

"Something like that." I glance up and meet her eyes again, but this time she doesn't look away. She meets me glare for glare before standing and striding over to where we are sitting. Pauly whistles at the sight of her curves swaying and tits bouncing beneath her tank. And of course I groan in reaction, and as much as I appreciate the sight of her, I know she's going to cause a scene.

And a scene is not what I need.

When she's a few feet from where Pauly and I are sitting, I stand up with purpose, the chair grating against the tile floor, and I begin to walk right past her. She flashes her hand out and grabs my biceps in a move I'm not real thrilled with.

"We're gonna settle this here and now, Pulitzer," she says, her voice low enough that only I can hear her.

"There's nothing to settle." I raise my eyebrows at her before looking over my shoulder to Pauly. "You know where to find me if you need me." With that, I shrug my arm out of her grasp and walk out of the room. She mutters my name followed by a curse, and a part of me loves that I'm just as frustrating to her as she is to me.

The door sticks at the rooftop, but I welcome the chance to exert a little physical force to shove it open since it's either up here or the gym right now, and I'm sore from pushing myself too hard yesterday. What I'd give to go for a run. Feet hitting the ground as my eyes take in the world around me, but I'm a long ass way from San Diego and my favorite beach run along Highway 101.

Instead, I take the tarp off the mattress and take up residence in my spot just in time to watch the sun start to fall from the horizon. It slips ever so slowly as I try to ignore the nagging voices in my head telling me I'm being an ass. It's so damn easy to be an asshole with her, though, because I don't think I've ever met a more frustrating woman. Or a more beautiful one.

And that is saying a lot.

The scrape of the door to the rooftop jars me from my thoughts. I'm up and looking toward it in an instant.

Goddamn it. The fucking woman is invading my every thought, and now she's in the one private space I have here.

"Go away." Those two words are all I have for her as I sit back down and try to ignore her. Her footsteps draw closer, but I shake my head, close my eyes, and then lean back on the wall behind me. I can guess she's standing in front of me, giving me a nasty look when the scraping sound of her boots stops. "Just once I'd appreciate it if you'd follow directions."

Her laugh falls deep and rich around me. "Wow. I was right."

"Good for you." When she doesn't answer, I can't help my curiosity. "Right about what?"

"How far that stick's shoved up your ass."

Then I hear the clink of glass against glass, and my eyes flash open. She's standing in front of me, her body framed by the sunset's colors blazing across the sky, with a bottle of Fireball and a glass in one hand while the other is at her hip.

She's looking for a reaction, and I refuse to give her one. "It only seems to be there around you." I shrug. "What can I say? You bring out the best in me." I finally meet her gaze on the last word, and damn it to hell, she has this cute little smirk on her face like she knows my game.

"Here's how we're going to play this, Pulitzer," Beaux says as she kneels down on the mattress beside me, glass still clinking like a cowbell in a warning that she's here to stay. "I'm going to ask you a question, and if you refuse to answer it, you take a shot. Then my turn."

I slide a glance in her direction and see that she's leaning over, cleavage on display, as her proposition takes up real estate in my mind. Kind of ballsy on her end, and I like that. "We only get to ask the question once, right?" I need to make sure the rules of this game are clear before I agree, because in my line of thinking, she'll ask the questions she wants to know the most first, I can take the shot, and by the time I'm drunk and a little looser in my responses, the most pertinent ones will be off the table.

Plus, I make a living asking questions and then re-asking them in a completely different way after they've been evaded. This shouldn't be a problem for me.

"Agreed." She finally sits with her back against the wall with a sound of satisfaction. "You can go first, since I'm sure your ego's going to need nursing once I drink you under the table."

I snort. The amusement in her tone told me she knows there's not a chance in hell of that happening, but I respect that she can talk a good game.

"Thanks for the mulligan. What to ask … what to ask…" I make a production of coming up with something. "Where were you coming from that morning I met you in the stairwell?"

That's most definitely not the question I had planned on asking, and it sure as hell isn't any of my business, but the whole idea of her being with somebody else is driving me crazy. I stare at the night beyond us as the city begins to come alive, not wanting to see the look on her face and whether my question has surprised her. But the clink of the bottle's neck against the glass gives me the only answer I need.

She clears her throat from the sting of the straight whiskey and blows out an audible breath. "Your turn. What really happened to Stella?"

Knew that one was coming. I reach over and take the bottle from her without so much as a word and toss back the shot, welcoming the burn.

"Beaux versus BJ. Which one and why?"

"I used BJ for work. It was easier to get my foot in the door if people thought I was a guy. Show them my portfolio via a Web site, reel them in, then meet them in person. It's ass backward, but when you're up against the good 'ol boys club, sometimes you have to do what it takes. Beaux is the real me." Her voice softens, causing me to turn my head and watch her in the waning light. When she averts her gaze immediately, I'm intrigued. "Very few people get to know Beaux."

Something about the way she says the last sentence tells me there's more to the story.

"Beaux." I murmur her name, and for the first time she doesn't reject it coming off my lips. A part of me warms from the thought while the rest of me listens to those damn alarm bells ringing again. "Why do—," I start to ask, but she immediately reaches up and puts her finger against my lips. Her touch causes my body to stand to attention, my instincts warring with that first shot beginning to hum through my bloodstream.

"Be warned. Asking a follow-up question out of turn earns you another shot." She moves her finger away just in time for me to speak.

"You're changing the rules on me now that we've already started? I have a feeling you don't play very fair."

A smile plays at the corner of her mouth momentarily, and it takes a whole helluva lot for me to tear my eyes from those lips of hers. "There's no such thing as playing fair. Besides, playing dirty is a whole lot more fun," she murmurs, the suggestion in her voice as clear as damn day. "So what does your wife think about all of this?"

Her question takes me completely off guard and has me sputtering out a laugh. I swear she just mentioned playing dirty to throw me off track. "What in the fuck are you talking about?" There's nothing I can do but shake my head and stare at her like she's lost her damn mind.

She shrugs innocently enough. "It's the quickest way to know the truth. I thought maybe the stick up your ass was because you were feeling guilty about your wife back home, and so I just figured I'd ask . . . but now I have to keep trying to figure out why it's there."

"Gotta love a woman who's straight to the point," I murmur. "Let me be clear. There is no spouse at home."

"That makes two of us."

"Or girlfriend," I add on, and immediately question why I felt the need to clarify that point as well when she didn't ask.

"You and Stella weren't . . ." Her voice trails off as she leaves the question open-ended.

"Once upon a time . . . but no, we weren't. Not for as long as I can remember," I answer her, but that last night we spent up here on the rooftop flashes through my mind. The kiss. The promise. *The once-in-a-lifetime*.

And for just a moment I get caught up in the memory before I realize she threw me off my game. "Uh-uh. Don't think I didn't catch that you just asked me a question twice." I go to reach for the bottle, and she swats my hand away.

"In your dreams. You didn't answer the first question, so if I have to drink, then you have to too! Your call or your turn."

I just narrow my eyes and hold her stare, weighing my options and the shot ratio between us. "Rule breaker."

"Sometimes it's worth the risk," she says, the air electrifying with sexual tension. The silence stretches between us, her eyes darting down to my lips and then back up to my eyes. "Your turn," she whispers.

My body suddenly becomes very attuned to the proximity of hers along with that addictive scent of her perfume that calls on my libido. The memory of her lying out on my bed before me, tits jostling as we connected, hair like a wave of seduction, mouth parted on a moan, hijacks my thoughts. It causes my next question to die on my lips, and the one I tell myself I don't even care about comes out before I can stop it. "That first night . . . in my room—"

"I'll stop you right there and just save myself the embarrassment of answering whatever your question is." She takes the shot, and my mind spins with the possibilities of what she thought I was going to ask her. Over what question was so bad that she wants to avoid it.

If this shit keeps up, I have a feeling I'm going to be carrying her down to her room, because she won't be walking.

She shakes her head subtly to try and clear the alcohol that I'm sure is starting to warm her up some. "Why do you blame yourself for Stella's death?"

Her question smothers the air around me. It's a question I've asked myself a million times but one no one has said aloud before. And now that it's out there, hanging like a flag in the breeze, I hear the ludicrousness in it . . . but I still don't want to answer it.

"In case you missed it the first time you asked, what happened to Stella's off-limits." The steel in my voice is hard to miss. "Ask again."

I hear the stutter in her breath as she exhales into the silence. "Why were you being so nice to me today? I mean . . . why'd you take me to the range?"

"Because regardless of what you think, chivalry isn't dead, and I look out for those who are with me. Besides, that ass of yours is too fine to see something happen to it."

I hear her breath catch again, and a riotous ache settles deep down inside me at knowing that a simple comment like that affects her so easily. And I don't want to feel like this or to know my simple remark has that effect on her, so I stumble along to find a new question for her.

"Where are you from? What's your story?"

"Ha! That's two questions. Drink up, baby!" she shouts into the night as I cringe, realizing my mistake the minute the second question was out of my mouth. Beaux pours a shot of liquid and hands it over. I toss back the drink, and she immediately takes the glass from me and pours one for herself. This time she hisses when she downs it.

"Wait, you're not answering the question?" I'm a little surprised since the question was so innocent in nature, no hidden agenda other than getting to understand her background better.

"And there's another question!" She laughs. "Before you know it, Tanner Thomas, you are going to be putty in my hands."

"I see how you are. Trying to win this little game by default." I laugh. And it feels so good to laugh after all of the shit over the past few months. It feels even better to have someone next to me even if I'm not supposed to like her. When she reaches for the bottle and I shift it away from her at the same time so that she falls partially on top of me, it jolts me back to reality.

And makes me so very conscious of the heat of her body against mine, the scent of her shampoo as she moves her hair out of her face and angles her face up to meet my eyes. Her breath hitches and fingers grip tighter over mine on the neck of the bottle at our sides. Everything about her is like a high-definition television all of a sudden, so damn perfect you want to touch but know it's not real.

"Your turn," she murmurs, her whiskey-scented breath feathering over my lips. "Why'd you kiss me today?"

I stare at her, my free hand itching to touch her, drag her beneath me, and lose myself in every goddamn contradiction she has to offer—but I know that would only complicate things even further. But it seems that lately everything about my life has become complicated . . . so why should I care if I add one more thing to the mix?

"I think the question you should ask yourself is why did I stop?"

Her hand moves up the plane of my chest, teasing me with an unnecessary reminder of temptation because what she has to offer is already permanently etched in my mind. My muscles tense; the need to take and plunder those lips of hers that are in a devastatingly close range to mine is more than most men would be able to resist.

"You stopped because you hate how I make you feel. You tell me you don't like me, but I'm pretty sure what is pressing against my thigh tells me otherwise." She leans closer into me, her voice a seduction all in itself. "Admitting it is half the battle," she whispers before brushing her lips ever so softly against mine.

I don't respond, my body strung so goddamn tight that when she tries it a second time, my hand fists in her hair to prevent her from doing any further damage.

"I'm trying to do what's right here, Beaux." My voice is strained, the pressure of my restraint so obvious that I sound desperate for her.

"Rule breaker." She chuckles so the warmth of her breath hits mine. "Remember, sometimes what's right isn't always what's needed. Sometimes what's needed isn't always what's wanted. And sometimes you just have to live in the moment, take what's given, and sort out the consequences later."

"Fuck the consequences. They're rarely worth it."

"I'm worth it." Her lips brush against mine as she says the words, the whisper of touch almost more intimate than the kiss itself. "Wouldn't you rather be fucking me than the consequences?"

I clench my jaw as my control slips further. The mixture of her words and her proximity is too much to bear. My hesitation is fleeting before I give in to the desire waging its own war within me.

Within a heartbeat, my lips are on hers, tempting, tasting, seeking the combination of heat, comfort, and need from her all at the same time. Our mouths move slowly at first, asking questions that our words haven't: *What the fuck are we doing? Don't you want me regardless of the consequences? We don't like each other, so why are we doing this?*

And I really don't care about the answers to any of them because her soft curves and the enticing heat of her body draw me in and prevent coherence from being a priority. The memory of the feel of her beneath me has me deepening the kiss, taking what I want in the form of tongues melding and teeth nipping. Soft moans fall from our mouths as our hands begin to roam and rediscover each other's body.

The clink of the bottle hitting the glass when I set it down shakes me from the haze of desire. Reality comes crashing down around me as my thoughts start trying to align despite the sweetest of drugs, lust and alcohol, running rampant in my system.

My dick's hard in my pants, the taste of her kiss is on my tongue, yet again the niggling idea that she's playing me hits me hard and causes me to tear my mouth from hers. My hands frame her face, holding tightly as I stare through the moonlit night into her desirous eyes, and our labored breaths reflect the restraint that's nonexistent between us.

She came to me. She wanted a game. She kissed me first. Fucking déjà vu hits me and won't let go as much as I want to toss it off the side of the damn building and forget all about it! But I refuse to be the next in her line of men here, refuse to be the pawn in her rigged game of chess when I can't figure out the endgame.

"I want you," she murmurs, voice thick with need, eyes coaxing me to believe her as she leans forward and brushes her lips to mine again.

And fuck . . . I want to sink into her in so many ways, but I grab onto the slippery slope of my resolve, and my fingers tighten on her cheeks to push her away from me.

"I'd much rather fuck you than the consequences. And believe me . . . I will," I tell her, my voice strained, licks of desire snapping at my nerves trying to singe my senses into overriding my rational mind. "But it will be of my own volition. Not because you came to me with a bottle of whiskey in one hand and an agenda in your back pocket."

"I'm not—"

I use my lips to cut off her retort and to satisfy the loud voice in my head telling me that I'm fucking crazy for pushing her away. And I know it's a mistake the minute I taste her, but I don't care. As soon as I've branded my lips to hers, I tear them away just as quickly.

"Don't lie to me to avoid giving me more reasons to dislike you. I don't play dirty like you. I take what I want when I want it, and hell if I don't want you, Beaux . . . but not like this. Not with some deceptive pretense wrapped around us like the sheets I want to lay you down on."

"There's no agenda," she says, her voice soft and even with a tinge of disbelief that I'm reacting this way, yet there's something in her eyes that tells me differently.

"I call bullshit, rook." And this time I'm fully aware of the double entendre of her being a rookie and the chess game she's playing with me. "You want something from me, and it has to do with whatever you're hiding up your sleeve. So now we're playing this game on my terms from here on out. How's it feel to want something you can't have?" My gaze flickers from her eyes in time to catch the quiver of her bottom lip before she shoves back from me, the sting of rejection clear on her face.

"I understand more than you'll ever know," she whispers. And I swear in the short glimpse I have of her eyes before she turns on her heels and walks away, I see tears glistening.

Her footsteps resonate off the rooftop until I can't hear them anymore when she enters the stairwell. I'm left in the darkness of the night with my unsettling thoughts.

Alone.

Defeated, I flop back on the mattress behind me and put my hands behind my head as I try to make sense of what just went down. Was I justified in rejecting her? Because if the ache in my balls is any indication, they aren't too happy with my decision.

"Fuck." I blow out a breath as I scrub my hand over my face before staring at the stars above me. The certainty I had that she was playing me is no longer there. And I always trust my gut, so why is it twisting right now from pushing her away and accusing her of using sex when she's denied it over and over in regard to the first time we slept together?

And I think the part that's getting me the most—that little fuck-you lift to her chin, the one that says she's being defiant and defensive, never showed its face. Instead, I was granted a glimpse of a woman hurt from unexpected rejection with a touch of insecurity and vulnerability thrown in there.

The look on her face runs through my mind in loops, confusing me and calling to me all at once.

Guess it's time for this pawn to move past its zone of protection and face the queen.

Chapter 10

This is so fucked up.

Once again I find myself searching Beaux out to . . . what? Apologize? Make sure she is okay? Spend more time trying to figure out what's hidden behind that tough facade that I catch a glimpse of every once in a while?

Damn woman is going to drive me insane.

My knuckles rap on her door and the sound echoes in the quiet corridor, but this time I can hear music on the other side of it, so I know she's in there.

"Go away." Her voice is muffled, but I can still make out what she says.

"C'mon, Beaux . . . We need to talk."

There's no response this time, and so I rest my head against the door. I've got to try to fix whatever the hell I need to fix here, because not only have I gone from needing to break in a new photographer, but now I've added to that trying to figure out the irrefutable connection we have.

What's causing me to blame Beaux for tugging on

those strings inside me that at the end of the day I want left knotted and impenetrable because once they start to unravel, I can never seem to stop them? Even though I know that about myself, I can't seem to control it.

I used to try and convince Stella that it was this environment, as well as the experience of being on location for extended periods, that caused everything to be expedited: feelings, reactions, a sense of urgency. Adrenaline becomes a new aphrodisiac when you meet someone against this backdrop. She'd just laugh at me and call me a paradox: the alpha male who loved the thought of falling in love.

She was right . . . at least when it came to the first few months or so. Then it usually turned to shit because work always took precedence for me. Relationships had always been fun while they lasted, but no one, and I mean no one, has ever made me think for one iota of a second of hanging up my credentials. The day that happens will be the day I know love from lust.

In the life of a foreign war correspondent, chances to distance yourself from the harsh reality of the modern world are few and far between (if they occur at all), so it's not hard to recognize why it's so easy for me to fall for someone while we're ensconced in this self-imposed bubble. The lifestyle in the hotel where all the journalists reside is all about the status quo. It's not like stateside where you and the person you are dating go to work separately, hang with friends or have individual hobbies, and then see each other occasionally on the weekend. No, here on the fringe of civilization, you live, work, breathe, and socialize with the person you're interested in. It breeds an intensity between two people that's unrivaled, an acceleration of feelings equivalent to months of dating when you've only been together for a few weeks.

And the fact that I'm thinking all of this with my head pressed to her hotel room door because I feel bad I pushed her away and hurt her feelings proves all of my overly introspective thinking right.

My God this place fucks with your head. Although I'm sure the shots of Fireball don't help either.

Just as I get a grip on my rambling thoughts, I fall forward as the door opens inward. I stumble inside, and all I see is her back as she's walking away from me farther into the room. And fuck me, she's wearing short shorts that cling to her ass, highlighting every damn line of her legs, and a tank top so sheer in color, I swear I can see the bronze of her skin through it. Of course my mind immediately jumps to the thought of what the front of her tank looks like and if her nipples are pressed against the thin material.

I shake the thought from my head and kick the door shut behind me as she sits on the edge of the bed facing the window with her back toward me. "Save your breath, Tanner. I got your message loud and clear. I was only good enough that first night when you considered me disposable, but now that I'm here to stay . . ." She laughs derisively. "I'm no longer good enough for you."

I'm definitely the asshole for putting that hurt tone in her voice. "That's not it." My words come out on a sigh when I continue to explain. "It's a lot more than that, Beaux."

"It's BJ to you, Tanner."

That simple statement stings deeply, and now that the taste of the rejection is fresh on my tongue, I don't like it at all. I don't know how to explain—what I need to say and what I want to say are two different things.

"Beaux . . ."

"No, you don't get to Beaux me. You lost that right," she says as she turns to face me, and damn it to hell, the sight of her is like a one-two combo punch. First her sheer beauty with her face bare of any makeup and hair piled on top of her head and two, that I was right about exactly what I'd be able to see through the damn fabric of her shirt. "You kissed me today like a man who wanted more and then walked away the minute you realized you wanted more. You know why? Because I got to you. I heard what you said upstairs loud and clear. But it's the things you aren't saying that I think you need to listen to."

"You're so far off base!" I'm practically stuttering in my rush to deny it, needing to refute what she's said only because she's hitting way too fucking close to home.

"Keep telling yourself that." She stands and takes a step closer to me. "You like me and yet you can't admit it for some reason. You're so damn busy trying to keep me at arm's length because of your trust issues that you can't see what's sitting right in front of your damn face. As much as I want you, I won't be coming on to you again. No. Not after what you said to me upstairs." She pauses, and it's like her words have knocked mine from my tongue.

She walks toward the window, then stops and turns to look me in the eye. "There's something between us. You can't deny that, Tanner—a blind man would be able to sense it. . . . You're so quick to accuse me of playing games, and yet you're calling more shots than a bartender. Have sex with me and then get mad at me. Kiss me and stalk away like I'm at fault. I'm here to do my job, not get sucked into whatever this is so my head gets messed up and I can't perform. . . . So I think it's best that you leave my room."

With those final words she turns, slides into her bed, and turns the light off, effectively ending the conversation without giving me a chance to respond. And maybe that's for the best, because she's just unloaded so many truths on me that I don't even know which one to focus on first. I just stand there in the darkness with her comments suffocating the air around me.

I've never been at a loss for words when it comes to a woman, let alone an argument, and yet I am right now and it's unnerving. And exhilarating in an odd way to know that someone can see so clearly inside of you that you're not sure you want them to see. But I guess I should expect this from her after what I saw through the lens of her camera—she already knows all of this.

"Stella was my one constant over the past ten years." The confession is out of my mouth before I even realize it, and I instantly wonder if this is my apology in the form of an explanation, the comfort of the darkness around us allowing the words to come. She doesn't say anything in response, but she stills in bed, and I know I have her attention.

"We met when we were assigned together, butted heads instantly, but fell into bed not too long after we met." The minute the words are out, it's like my subconscious finally acknowledges the correlation between Stella and me and now Beaux and me. The similarities become clear for the first time. Is this why I keep rejecting Beaux one minute and then pulling her in the next? Damn. The thought staggers me. Because I've been so busy trying to figure out just what her angle is, I haven't noticed the parallels in the start of our relationships.

"And . . ." It's all Beaux says, but her voice has softened, and I'm grateful that she allows me the moment to digest this newfound revelation. It's one that should have been slapping me in the face, and yet I never realized it through my grief and obstinacy.

"It didn't last, obviously. We had fun during that getting-to-know-you stage, but it fell apart. Immaturity and stress from the job and from essentially living with each other from the first date on took its toll after about a year. We felt smothered, and that led to nasty fights. And yet we still had to work together." I lower myself to sit on the edge of the bed as the memories I thought I'd forgotten over time come back in bittersweet fashion. "Those first few months after we broke things off were brutal between us. It's never good to work with an ex . . . but somehow over time the situation that tore us apart as lovers made us stronger as friends and partners. I don't know. . . . It's hard to explain. She was my best friend for ten years. We were inseparable. . . ." My voice trails off as emotion clogs my throat.

"Losing someone that close to you is so hard," she murmurs, compassion in her voice.

"See, that's the thing," I say, almost feeling like I need to explain that the connection I shared with Stella went so much deeper than a normal friendship. "Out here . . . when you're forced into this situation, right away everything is much more intense. Relationships, bonds, friendships, all of those things are magnified and reinforced by the isolation of the job, so yeah, we were friends for ten years, but it's almost as if she were my twin in a sense. We had each other's backs, could finish each other's sentences. . . . We were a unit . . . so losing her is just . . ."

The silence consumes the room, but I allow myself to feel the grief for the first time in what feels like forever. And yes, I did the shrink thing for the brass, talked to them about everything, but right now with Beaux is the first time that I've talked about it voluntarily with anyone other than my family since it happened.

And for some reason it feels like a thousand-pound weight has been lifted from my chest.

"I'm not trying to replace her, Tanner." I don't respond, because I know she's telling the truth, but it sure as hell doesn't make me stop feeling guilty over the fact that if I accept her as my new photographer and anything else she becomes in my life, it's an eerily similar fashion to how Stella and I fell into lust.

Putting my hands behind my head, I lie back on the bed and find a strange comfort in having Beaux beside me beneath the blanket. What possessed me to lay all that information out there to Beaux of all people when I haven't done that to anyone before?

"I know you're not." I whisper the words into the room, telling myself to believe them and knowing it's human nature to not want to forget someone and to feel guilty when you begin to feel like you are.

"And I promise that I'm not trying to pull one over on you."

I just murmur in acknowledgment, fighting my skeptical nature but pleased that she said it anyway.

"So without the threat of another shot, I answered one of your questions . . . ," I say to try and break up the solemnity of our conversation. Her sigh in response is audible, cutting through the silence of the room. "Tell me something about you."

"I'd rather not." The disassociated quality of her voice pulls on my curiosity when moments before she was so full of compassion and intrigue.

"Let's think of this as us trying to get to know each other so we can start fresh again." I angle my head up so that I can see her face looking in my direction. And even though the room's only light is the one from the open bathroom door, I can see her dark hair against the white sheets and the softness in her smile. It looks like she appreciates my efforts to get off on a new foot.

"Well, if we're starting over, my name is BJ Croslyn. What's yours?" The warmth is back in her voice as she reaches down to shake my hand, and hell if my arm doesn't buzz like exposed live wires touching when our skin connects.

"Tanner Thomas. And *I'm the one*." Her laugh fills the room as she shakes her head at hearing me use her comment from that first night. When our handshake ends, she doesn't pull her hand from mine, so they rest on the mattress in the space between us. "Everyone has a story. I just told you some of mine . . . so tell me, *BJ*, what's yours?"

And because our hands are joined, I can feel the subtlest tension rise in her muscles from my question.

"There's a reason I chose to go on assignment, okay?" she says, the detachment returning to her voice. "Sometimes escaping behind my lens, out here in no-man's-land is better than the alternative. . . ." Her voice fades off, and images of scenarios I can't picture her in flash through my head.

What is so horrible she has to run from it? Bad home life? An abusive ex? I can't picture her putting up with either, and yet here she is. I hold on to her promise that she's not playing me, force myself to hear it for the first time so that I don't try to dig holes through her response to my question, and just allow myself to accept it for what it is, worry and all.

"Sometimes out here it is easier to create your own reality. Ironic as hell considering it's our job to report on the actuality of what's happening here when I also use it as a place to make my own . . . so I get it. I do," I confess as I roll on my side and adjust my positioning so that I can link my fingers with hers in a silent show of understanding to reinforce my words. And as much as I want to ask her so many more questions, my investigative journalist mode humming in full force, I don't.

"It doesn't sound like things have been easy for you either. I'm sorry for that. You want to talk about it?"

"No," I murmur, not ready just yet to rid myself of that guilt I carry over Stella's death. We've each shared a small piece of ourselves, and yet I'm not ready to delve into the rest of the shit in my mind. "I should get going." When I start to push up out of the bed, Beaux just holds tight to my hand.

"Stay?" And there's something in the way she asks that tells me she's not asking for sex, but rather for companionship, a warm body beside her in this place that leaves you feeling isolated from real life, good and bad, in more ways than one.

"You sure?"

"Mmm-hmm."

I rise from the bed, toe off my shoes, and pull my shirt over my head before crawling back up the mattress. Once I maneuver myself beneath the covers, I don't even think about what I'm doing when I scoot up behind her and pull her body into mine, her back to my front.

"No funny stuff, Pulitzer. We just met, you know."

I chuckle into the back of her hair, my breath heating it against my face as I settle into the welcoming feeling of her body snuggled up against mine, soft curves, warm skin, the scent of her shampoo, and the feel of her ribs expanding with each breath. I have a feeling it's going to be a long night on my end with temptation against me but with my chivalry wedged between us.

And as much as my ideal way to spend the night with a woman is not exactly with our clothes on, this is beyond nice. It's the first time I can remember in ages that I don't feel so lonely.

"Sleep sweet, BJ," I murmur as I press a kiss into the back of her head and pull her a little tighter against me.

"It's *Beaux*. And sleep sweet too, Tanner."

A ridiculous grin spreads on my lips at her correction and stays there as I slip into the clutches of slumber.

Chapter 11

Over the next couple of weeks, the days drag and tumble endlessly one into another until the boredom feels like one solid stretch of wasted time. I've reached out to every one of my sources to try and get something, anything, to give me an inside for a story, but they've got nothing to give me.

The lot of us in the hotel are on edge, keeping to ourselves as much as we can because we know from experience that this is when we start to get on one another's nerves. When there is something happening on the military front, this place hums with speculation, thrives with paranoia over who has a better story, and comes to life with excitement. But it's been quiet for a while now.

Even though I'm restless for action beyond the hotel's walls and the city's limits, I'm also antsy because something has me feeling like this is the eye of the storm. Something big is coming. I can feel it.

Let's just hope I get there first and report it better.

In the meantime we wait. Omid's gone back into the wind again. It's only been three weeks by the calendar, but it feels more like a lifetime. I'm not letting myself grow too concerned since I've seen this pattern from him before; nevertheless, I still worry after Beaux's error in taking photos of him that I've lost him.

In midafternoon I glance around the lobby at everyone keeping to themselves, heads down, earbuds in, and laptops open. I shift my gaze across the room and lock eyes with Beaux just as she's lowering the camera from where it was aimed in my direction. An unsettling feeling flickers through me as I wonder just what exactly she saw this time behind the curve of her lens.

A man who's finally settling back into the life he was meant to lead? One who's a little bit smitten with the woman snapping pictures of him?

Because . . . yeah, I guess I am smitten with her. Especially after the last two weeks where we've had easy conversation, numerous laughs over endless games of Scrabble to pass the time, and a few nights when we've fallen asleep together after talking late into the night. The funny thing is even with all this time spent in close quarters, I still feel like I don't know her at all and that I know everything about her in the same breath. We're comfortable together, feel safe with each other, and it's a welcome feeling after so much tumult over the past few months.

I don't have walls up when it comes to women. Never have. I didn't have a fucked-up childhood or any damaged relationships that have scarred me for others. But that doesn't stop Stella's voice from creeping into my mind in the silence of midnight to tease me about how easy it is for me to fall in lust with someone. And that has me stepping back some from Beaux and this newfound camaraderie, holding my emotions a tad closer to the vest, preferably protected by Kevlar, to prevent more ache in my heart already saddened by Stella's death.

But regardless of how much I tell myself to take that necessary step back, I can still feel myself slipping deeper into whatever this is between Beaux and me. I mean fuck, I want to have sex with her again—that's a given—but since that first-time buildup has already happened between us, we have this oddly fascinating connection now. It's like since we know how explosive the physical side of things is between us that we almost fear igniting that powder keg again unless we figure out if we can actually handle it.

And God how I want to handle it before I handle her, because I know the next time we connect, there will be no turning back. Both physically and where my heart is concerned. I know myself well enough that this feeling I have inside isn't going to allow me to stay behind the Kevlar for too much longer.

But I'm pulled from my thoughts as a soft smile turns up her lips and reaches her eyes. At the sight a warmth spreads through me. And with the quality time we've spent together lately, I feel like even though we are in this room filled with colleagues, we are having our own private conversation without speaking.

She slides her eyes over to the empty pool table, and when I roll my eyes in response, her laugh crosses the distance between us. She knows I detest pool just about as much as she hates Scrabble, but we've learned to compromise to pass the time. Shaking my head, I rise from my seat while she walks to the far wall and grabs the cues and the rack for the balls. Out of habit and because, shit, how can I not look, I take in the curve of her hips and the muscles in her shoulders as she grabs the sticks for us.

"Ready to lose, Pulitzer?"

"Someone has to let you win so you don't pout," I tease as she picks up a ball and pretends like she's going to huck it at me despite the smirk playing at the corners of her lips.

"You talk a good game. Too bad you can't play one." My laugh comes freely, our banter a reliable form of entertainment as we sit in limbo for the next story on the horizon.

We take our shots, and balls fall in the pockets while she hustles me like usual as we tease and walk that fine line of flirting without flirting: a brush of a hand on a lower back, a lean in with a comment in a lowered voice, eyes hungry for the next look from the other. All the while cautious of the eyes watching around us, ready to make assumptions that don't need to be made.

"You'd better watch your back, rookie," I tease as I glance at the table, well aware that there are a lot more of my solids on the table than her stripes. "I'm making a comeback."

Her laugh rings out above the chatter, echoing off the cheap tile floor in the lobby. "You couldn't beat me if you tried." She sits with her hip on the edge of the table, distraction at its finest because who cares about aiming my cue at little solid balls when I could stare at her instead?

"I'm in complete control here," I murmur as I line up my shot.

"Ha. I'll let you keep thinking that," she scoffs, knowing perfectly well that comment will rattle any man.

Our eyes lock, so many words exchanged without speaking as the sexual tension thickens between us. Want and need, desire and lust, reverberate through the air like our own private secret in this room full of people. I force myself to go through the motions, placing the chalked cue in the crease of my thumb and index finger as I prepare to strike the ball, except my eyes are on Beaux because, damn, how could I look away?

Her chuckle distracts me, her body calls to me, her

defiance is a challenge. And I blame all three of those things when I completely miss the cue ball like some chump. She jumps off the table, a hiss of "Yes!" falling from her lips as she dances around me with a taunt in her eyes and an arrogance to her swagger from being victorious in her distraction.

Out of the blue, music blasts through the lobby. At first everyone freezes, then turns to where one of Pauly's crew has plugged portable speakers into his laptop and is standing there looking back at all of us. Gus is his name, I think. I remember him because he always wears the most horrendous Hawaiian shirts that look like paradise got drunk and decided to throw up all over him.

"Let's liven up this joint! We're all bored stiff . . . so let's loosen the fuck up!" Gus waves his arms out to the side for everyone to get on their feet, and the minute he stops talking, the room erupts in "Hell yeah" and whistling.

The lobby transforms instantly as the music is turned up louder so that the speaker crackles from the volume. The necessity to break up the doldrums takes hold of all of us—even the sticks-in-the-mud get to their feet and bob their heads to the rhythm. I glance over to see Beaux's body sway to the beat as the familiar chords of a song by the popular band Bent begins to play.

Although I'm not normally one to dance, there's no stopping me at the chance to feel her body against mine. The next thing I know, she's walking toward me with her hips swaying and her body moving to the music. She sets down the cue and grabs my hand. We begin to move together in steps that don't match the beat whatsoever. I spin her out and pull her back in like I used to watch my parents do across the kitchen floor when I was a little boy.

On another spin, we lose our grip on each other. Beaux's

shoulder hits the wall, and we double over in laughter at how horrible we are, but my God the laughter feels good. The smiles remain as we get back into the rhythm again, losing ourselves in the song as we dance in the space around the pool table. She raises her arms over her head and shimmies her hips as she lets the music take over, and hell if watching her body move like this doesn't make me want to light the fuse to the powder keg.

I try to spin her out one last time as the final chords to the song hit our ears, and even though we are still laughing out of control — welcoming the stress relief from both the hours of waiting and the sexual tension that's slowly building between us — we actually manage to keep our hands joined. When I pull her back into me, I do it with too much force because she lands against my chest, our bodies connected from shoulders to knees, breaths panting in unison as she looks up at me.

And something happens in the moment when the song fades and a new one starts, because neither of us moves. We remain motionless, but the way she looks at me changes somehow. It's the craziest thing too, because as we stare at each other, chests heaving, the rest of the makeshift party going on all around us, my mom's in-finite wisdom chooses to flicker through my mind and take residence.

She used to always tell Rylee and me that she fell in love with my dad's eyes first and foremost and that was how she knew he was going to be the one. According to her, eyes are the one thing on someone that never changes, so if you can look into someone's eyes and see tomorrow, then you've found your forever.

Right here in this random moment with music fueled by spontaneity and the heat of her breath hitting my lips as she gazes into my eyes, I'm momentarily spooked by what I see there. And I think she feels it too, because even though we stay in the suspended state of inexplicable intimacy a beat longer, she pushes away from me seconds later, breaking the moment.

With enough distance between us, I can see the surprise I feel mirrored in her eyes. Right then there are so many things I want to tell her, and yet I have no clue where to start. It's like we've both been stripped of that false bravado we had last week when she said she refused to touch me again and I told her I'd control the reins. It's almost as if the moment were too raw, too real, and holding too much certainty that once we step over that edge, we won't be coming back.

Beaux takes a step backward, her head shaking ever so subtly, but her eyes never leave mine. "I've got to . . ." Her voice fades off as she motions with her thumb over her shoulder. "I've got some pictures to edit."

"Beaux?" Concern laces my voice as I ask her if she's okay.

"I'm gonna go do that." Her voice is anything but certain as she takes another step backward. "Now. Then bed," she says as she grabs her camera from the table, turns on her heel, and strides out of the lobby.

I begin to go after her, feeling energized that she just proved to me her emotions are running as haywire as mine are when it comes to *us*. When I catch Pauly's eye, my feet falter, and I know there's no chance in hell I'll chase her now and let him know that I care. He just nods once in understanding before throwing his head back and laughing over the beat of the music; then he approaches and pats me roughly on the back.

"Good luck with that," he says as he tilts the neck of his beer in the direction in which she left. "You lucky bastard."

Chapter 12

The sound of a car's horn shocks me awake and scares the crap out of me. I reach over to the nightstand and grab my phone with one hand while I place my other arm over my eyes to block out the harsh morning sunlight coming in through the curtains I forgot to close. I peek at the time on my phone and curse the early morning hour after staying up and shooting the shit with Pauly long after the lobby dance party subsided. There will definitely be a lot of hungover journalists in this hotel today, and thank God I'm not one of them.

Between talking with Pauly and the image of Beaux's face just before she'd gone upstairs, I decided to forgo the drinking. Besides, I had a hunch that if I drank, I'd be knocking her door when I promised myself I wouldn't do that again. And Christ how I wanted to do that again. But as I climbed the stairwell to my room last night, I hesitated before opening the door to my floor because every damn nerve in my body was begging me to keep going up a few more flights to her floor.

So now my dick is hard as a rock with thoughts of her

on my mind. And they're all indecent ones. I'm faced with a decision: hot shower and jerk off, or go hit the gym and work out this frustration in the hope that maybe I'll get the real deal sometime soon. It's sad that this is my dilemma of the morning, but fuck, I'll take it.

Maybe jerking off, then the gym and then the hot shower. It definitely doesn't hit the same pleasure spot, but at least something's getting hit. Besides, taking one for the team doesn't mean I can't still get lucky later.

Thoughts of Beaux are still front and center as I shove up out of bed and get ready to work out. I'm out of my hotel room and in the stairwell within twenty minutes of waking, earbuds in, and muscles tense with my mind running in a million directions, but sexual frustration front and center. When I'm three flights down, I turn on the landing and come face-to-face with Beaux.

Déjà vu hits, and although we're standing apart this time, I still feel as if my body has slammed into hers. And what knocks the air out of me is not just catching her like this when the images of all of the ways I want to fuck her have owned my thoughts. Not hardly. It's the look of shocked surprise in her eyes mixed with the realization that I've noticed she's wearing the same clothes as last night, camera slung over her shoulder, hair piled on top of her head.

Again.

Disbelief marries with hurt before it rifles through me. After that moment we shared between us last night, how could she have gone out and spent the night with someone else? I force a swallow to compose myself as I watch her eyes widen and her head shake back and forth rapidly as she realizes she's been caught. It's too much; I can't deal with this, with her, with the disappointment spreading through my system right now. It just doesn't make sense, and I'd rather feel the anger than the confusion.

And it's just the briefest of hesitations on my part as I allow myself a moment to feel stupid before I begin to rein my feelings in and turn to walk away. That slight falter gives her the opening she needs to reach out and grab my arm as I start to turn away. "No, Tanner! It's not what you think!" she shouts in the empty stairwell, the echo of her denials bouncing off the concrete walls and hitting my ears to reinforce her words.

The incredulity I feel at being caught in this same moment again on top of my mistrust toward her right now has me primed for an argument. "What the fuck do you mean, it's not what I think?" I growl as I turn around to face her, shrugging my arm from her grasp. "Because it looks pretty damn obvious to me. Guess the joke's on me . . . or whoever else you were with last night. You sure as hell have a way of making someone feel like you have eyes only for them . . . when in fact you give everything else instead."

I know it's a dickish innuendo to make, but it's true. What I don't expect, though, is the flash of hurt that flickers and then remains in the green of her eyes. When normally I'd be turning on my heel and stomping my ass down to the gym, that fucking look has me frozen in place.

"Just . . . ," she says, and then stops as she rolls her shoulders, a war waging across her features over the confession I can sec trembling on her lips. But the simple word and the tone in which she says it does its job, because I don't move. "All I'm doing is taking pictures." She holds her camera up in front of her as if its mere presence is proof. And of course the notion lingers that we've been here with the camera between us before and when I called her bluff, I was in the wrong. "When I feel restless, I go out and take pictures . . . I get lost in seeing the world through a filter, can distance myself . . . and sometimes it's not until the sun comes up that I realize I've been up all night long. I don't know how else to explain it, other than it calms me."

"What? Here? Are you fucking crazy?" And yes, I should really be reading between the lines, but fuck, I'm a guy. I react without thinking, jump to judge without hearing anything beyond helpless female all alone in the wild fucking West. "It's like willingly walking into the goddamn lion's den out there! I told you not to go out there by yourself! You promised that you wouldn't!"

"Yeah . . . well, I *unpromise*." And there's something about the contrast of the tone of her voice in comparison to mine—detached versus animated, defiance instead of compassion—that shocks me into realizing it doesn't matter what else I say because she's going to do it anyway. I search her eyes for a reason, a connection, anything at all, but all I find is disassociation and a complete lack of caring, and that only pisses me off further.

How can she pull away when all we've been doing is connecting, bit by bit, word by word, minute by minute, every day over the past week and a half? It's like she's slapping me in the face.

"Are you purposefully trying to push buttons to get a reaction? Because it doesn't take much to ignite my temper, and, frankly, knowing you're out there on your own is doing it already." I step closer to her, willing the warmth in her eyes to return. "What's really going on, Beaux?"

"It's how I deal, okay? End of discussion. Drop it." She retreats a step, and luckily the wall is at her back, because that means she can't run away now.

"Deal with what? Is shit that bad at home that you're

willing to risk your safety here so that you don't have to go back?" I immediately feel like a jerk for my original assumption that she's sleeping around, but now I'm worried about what she's withholding from me. And a small part of me cringes because I sound a lot like Rafe did to me when I wanted back here. I hate not knowing what has put this look on her face and the uncertainty laced with something else I can't quite pin down in her eyes. "What the fuck are you running from?"

"Nothing." She remains expressionless.

"Don't nothing me, Beaux. Or is it BJ now? Because I expect that kind of crap answer from BJ, not from you. Not from the woman who looked at me like she did last night before bailing out of the lobby like she couldn't get away fast enough." She holds my stare as my words punch her one by one.

"Like I said, I'm not running from anything."

"Nice try but I'm not buying it." I know she's going to try and run the minute she averts her eyes. Good thing too, because I reach out to grab her shoulders and keep her in place at the same time she tries to shrug past me. "Uh-uh. You're not going anywhere. In your words we're going to settle this right now. What's your story, then? We've sat for the last week talking about everything under the goddamn sun, and yet I know nothing about you."

Oh I've definitely got her attention now: the sharp intake of air, her eyes flickering left and right, the stiffness in her posture.

"Yes, you do!" She sneers back.

"I know you went to Dartmouth, your reasons for freelance . . . but I don't know the person you are at home without using that fucking camera as a shield in front of you. So tell me, *BJ*," I say as I step well within her personal space so that I can feel the heat of her breath on my lips. "Who the fuck are you, and what the hell are you dealing with?"

"Back off, Tanner." The warning sound in her voice is clear as day, but I don't care. I'm in big-brother mode now, and all I want to do is make sure that she's okay.

"No. You *know* me, right? Know how stubborn I am? It comes with my career choice, so I suggest you start talking." We stand there in a silent standoff that I sure as hell am going to win. "Is it your family? Are you running from them?"

"No. Don't have any."

"Everyone has family." I laugh in disbelief at her lie.

"Not me. They're dead."

I never knew you could get whiplash from words alone, but there's always a first for everything, and she's taught me a lot of those in the short time that I've known her. "Wh-what?" I stutter the word out as dread drops through my body for pushing her. I was sure she was going to look like the ass in the end, but it seems I'm taking the lead position in that race.

"My parents died my senior year of high school. Car crash. They were driving to school to bring me a project I forgot at home. Both were gone instantly. I'm an only child as were they, so there's no one else. I sold the house to pay for my college tuition. *My blood money*. So when you tell me no one understands the guilt you feel over whatever happened to Stella, you are so very wrong. I wear the crown most days."

Her eyes are steadfast on mine, her voice still void of emotion, but I understand her a bit better now that I know the why behind it. Detachment is a necessity, and yet I want more from her.

"Where are you from?"

"Doesn't matter. Podunk, USA. A black dot on a paper map. I'm giving you the answers you want, so the where is irrelevant."

Except to me it's all relevant when it comes to her. Every piece of information I can get will help me understand her, figure out the enigma of the female mind, and yet I don't push her any further. I know by the look on her face she's given me more than she ever expected to, so I'll take it and tuck it away and decipher it all later.

"I'm sorry. I don't know what to ..." I release her shoulders and step away from her, raking a hand through my hair and blowing a breath out as I try to digest everything she's told me along with the fact that she goes out at odd hours in this fucked-up place on her own. "So you go out at night to take pictures so you can deal with their passing?"

"No. I dealt with their deaths a long time ago."

And the whiplash strikes twice as I lower my hand from my neck and look at her like she's lost her fucking mind. She's dropped one confession after another on me, and yet none of them explains the reason she's being so foolish going out alone.

"Do you mind telling me what the hell is going on here? Because I thought we were past playing games and now you've sucked me right back there. You said you go out and take pictures to deal ... . What the hell has you so upset that you're outside the walls when for safety's sake you shouldn't be?" I'm all worked up, agitated, and annoyed, but all it takes is her single-word answer to knock every fucking emotion from me.

"You."

I snap my head up to meet her eyes, and the clarity in hers surprises me, engages me, confuses me. The air thickens in the small space, a blessing and a curse all at the same time because that means I'm breathing her in, and that in itself—her perfume, her shampoo—is addicting and distracting. My throat feels like it's being constricted as the silence stretches only to be interrupted by the stutter of our breaths. I clench my jaw and fists, restraining myself, from what I'm not exactly sure: from begging her to explain? From pushing her up against the wall and kissing her with the savage desire I feel until every carnal urge within me is satisfied?

Both are damn good options.

When I step into her and her breath hitches, I swear I can feel it deep down in the pit of my stomach. The anticipation of what we know we're about to do and can't take back connects us and defines the moment with such poignancy that as I reach out to touch her, I swear I'm moving in slow motion. Attraction sparks between us like a current when our skin touches, my palm to the side of her cheek. I lean forward, my eyes asking for consent and my lips already tasting hers.

As my heart races, I realize everything about me is affected by her proximity, and the next thought that crosses my mind staggers me. Why does this one woman get to me so profoundly?

Our lips hover inches from each other, our eyes still locked, amethyst to emerald, and bodies already on high alert when the sound of my telephone ring shrills in the small space and makes us jump apart like teenagers getting caught making out behind the gym. I swear as she laughs, the nervous energy between us has grown so palpable that I'm part relieved, part pissed off, and one hundred percent consumed by her as we both take a breath for what feels like the first time in minutes.

When I pull my phone out of its clip on my hip to dismiss the call, I glance at the screen only to find that I'm immediately pulled from the moment, my attention effectively diverted from what was about to happen with Beaux.

"Sarge," I say when I answer the phone, but it's a greeting to him and an explanation to Beaux all with a single word.

"Got a request for you to ride along. Boots down at ten hundred hours. Meet me at the usual."

Any adrenaline I didn't have flowing from Beaux and our almost kiss surges like a tidal wave through me, my thoughts whirling about what I need to do to get there before I even tell him yes. "We'll be there," I say, and before I even look at my watch to see how short we are on time, the line is dead.

"We're on?" Excitement edges her tone as she turns to follow me up the stairwell.

"We've got ninety minutes to get there. Let's go."

Chapter 13

We're jostled closer together as the windowless Stryker we can't see out of bumps down the road. I watch Beaux as she takes in everything about the confined space: the soldiers' faces, the gear they're weighted down with, their fingers resting loosely on their weapons.

I try to put myself in her shoes, remember how I felt the first time I did this, and yet all I can think of is the look on her face and the hitch in her breath in the stairwell. Hell yes, I'm pumped to be on this mission, but I use the image of her to settle the antsy feeling causing my knee to jog up and down and fingers to fidget with my gear.

When I glance over at Beaux, I take in the way her hair is braided under the advanced combat helmet, and visually check to make sure her modular body armor vest is on properly—items required by Sarge, but I would have made her put them on if he hadn't.

A harsh bump jostles us so that my elbow raps smartly off the metal behind me, and I know that if I've been thrown around, her small frame has to have experienced worse. Our eyes meet as the thought crosses through my mind, and although I see the grimace on her face, I also see the thrill in her eyes. And that thrill mixed with her flushed cheeks and devilish smirk tells me she gets this, gets me, in a way that so many others can't.

She feels this same buzz in her body right now, that razor edge of not knowing what's going to happen next, of the possible danger that lies just around the corner and rather than run from it, we're heading straight into it. It heightens everything—your senses, your instinct, your emotions—to the point where you're practically high on it like a narcotic. And hell no, we're nowhere near as brave as the soldiers who surround us because they are the ones going face-to-face with this beast, whoever it may be, head-on, while we are on the sidelines reporting. But at the same time, this is as close as any civilians can get.

"You ready?" I mouth the words to her since my voice would be drowned out by the sounds of this mass of metal surrounding us moving at high speeds.

A slight smile—part nerves, part excitement—spreads over her lips and her hands grip tighter to her camera bag, and it's a silly thought but I love that I get to share her first embed mission with her. I'm about to say something else to her when Sarge's voice from the right of me, loud and booming above the other sounds, fills my ears.

"So we have five units moving in. Different approaches. We're hitting a small town where we believe one of the couriers lives. He's delivering messages between the top officials to the midlevel. We find him, we get one step closer to knowing when and where the big meet is going to happen," he says, confirming my hunch as to why the mission is occurring.

"When we get there, you two will stay with Rosco over there," he says, pointing to the guy next to Beaux.

"He'll be your babysitter." He chuckles before carrying on about what is to be expected when we reach our destination.

"The military officials aren't really saying, Bob. The only information we are allowed to report at this time is that the mission was considered successful. What exactly we're looking at for measure of success is currently unknown, but they do believe the commanders have acquired the information they were looking for. Beyond that, details are slim," I report to the lead anchor as I juggle my notes since we finished in perfect timing to hit the tail end of the evening news.

The rush from being part of the military raid only intensifies since I know that my report is not only live on Worldwide News right now but since I'm the only journalist here, it's probably going to be picked up by other stations. *Take that,* I say silently to Rafe and the higher-ups questioning whether I could still do my job properly.

"Tanner, do we know if there were any casualties on the ground? Were any soldiers hurt?"

My eyes flicker ever so briefly over the top of my laptop screen from my Skype feed to where Beaux stands beside Sarge. They're both watching me, and it's ironic that millions of people could possibly be tuning in to my live feed and yet her eyes on me cause my stomach to somersault.

Rein it in, Thomas. Start showing that shit and the brass will definitely know your head's messed up.

The funny thing is, it would be over someone completely different than they think.

"Not that we've learned at this time, but as I said in my initial report, there appear to be a lot of moving parts to this mission, so that's not to say there aren't any injured at another location."

"Thank you. Tanner Thomas reporting live tonight. We'll have more on this exclusive story plus pictures on the late-night broadcast . . . ," the news anchor drones on, segueing into the next story before the Skype connection cuts off. My posture relaxes immediately as I disconnect my Globalstar satellite wireless Internet feed from my laptop and begin to pack it all up, making mental notes as I go about what I need to include in my written story that I'll turn in when we get back to the hotel.

"Great report." Beaux stands before me, camera held close to her face as she scans through the images on her Canon's LCD monitor. "I got some good shots to go with your filed report."

"Can't wait to see them," I say as I glance up toward her. All I can see is my own reflection in her aviator sunglasses, but the way her body is moving tells me she has as much nervous energy as I do right now after being bystander to that action-packed raid. It was most definitely the most intense embed mission I'd been on, but everything was so scheduled out, a testament to the military's skill level, that at no point did I have that uneasy feeling. I found myself more in awe of the sheer bravery of the soldiers kicking down doors and clearing houses in rapid speed, having to make judgment calls on the fly, so that adrenaline was my ruling emotion. "For your first embed, that was a pretty incredible one to be a part of."

"You're telling me. I'm still shaking from the rush," she says, holding her hands out so that I can see them.

While we talk, I watch a few soldiers speaking to a local across the street from us before I turn my attention back to her. "I call it the buzz. That rush is what keeps us coming back time and again." She snaps a quick picture of me before I can turn away. I give her a look behind my shades that I know she can't see but can feel.

"BJ?" Rosco interrupts. "I might be able to sneak you

over to get the pictures you asked for. The area appears secure, but let's get in and get out."

At hearing his words, I'm feeling the same shock that flickers over Beaux's features, but she hikes her camera bag over her shoulder. "You're on!"

"Beaux." Her name comes out in a warning tone so that she has to know I'm not thrilled with the idea, especially considering our discussion on the way to the base when I informed her I didn't want her out of my sight once we were beyond the city's limits. That rule fell right after the one telling her she must remain in arm's reach by my side.

"C'mon, Pulitzer. Share the glory with someone else, will ya?"

I know she's joking, but I also think a little part of her means it. All I know is that I want to tell her to wait up, to not go without me.

"If we're going to do it, it's got to be now before we move out," Rosco reiterates over her shoulder.

She flashes me a huge grin, excitement lighting up her face before she shrugs in my direction in an insincere apology and hustles after him while I'm left to finish packing up my equipment.

Sarge never willingly offers a chance to get pictures of a scene, so I know his bosses want this successful mission documented for propaganda. And shit, whatever the purpose, Worldwide News is the only news outlet here, so that's a huge positive.

It still doesn't mean I like having her out of my sight.

A few minutes pass as I finish packing my stuff up before a flurry of gunfire rings out through the silence of the village. Shots volley back from our position as soldiers scramble for cover.

For a split second I freeze. Memories collide with the present, and I swear to God I'm taken back to the frenzy of trying to find Stella. Sounds and smells and sights that don't exist fill my head, fuck me up, until another spurt of gunfire followed by men shouting breaks through the hold the memories have over me.

Instinct takes over immediately. The need to survive, overcome, and live fuels my movements. I duck down and run for cover on the other side of the Stryker parked behind me, while thoughts of Beaux commingled with frantic panic fill my head.

The need to find her consumes me. An eerie silence falls over the village, dust particles dancing in the air, and my ears ring. My heart pounds in my ears and my blood feels like it's mixed with jet fuel as it races through my body, causing my hands to shake, muscles to vibrate with fear-laced adrenaline.

Beaux.

I need to get to her.

She's my only thought, my only motivation. It feels like minutes, but it's probably only a few seconds of silence before I start to leave the cover of the vehicle to go and find her. As I step around the rear of the personnel carrier, I'm yanked backward by my vest and pushed through the open back doors of the Stryker at the same time the air around us erupts with more gunfire.

I scramble to get up and scurry back off, but Sarge is in my face, guys piling in around us. "Rosco's got her," he shouts, pushing me farther into the transport to make room.

And yeah, I believe him, but at the same time it's pure chaos out there. How do I know that Rosco really has her? How do I know she's not hurt and injured? My mind screams at me to shove the soldiers out of the way, get to her somehow, whatever it takes to make sure that she's okay. Before the doors are even shut, though, the Stryker is on the move, and my chance is gone.

I strain to hear Sarge on the radio. The words *unstable*, *insurgents*, *too open*, are being shouted, and with each bump over the rough terrain, the doubt lodges further into my psyche about whether Beaux is really okay. But I've got no way to interrupt him, to ask him to call Rosco and make sure he has her. Sarge is in charge of getting his unit of men to safety, and right now he's got no spare attention to pay to a reporter who signed on for the risk.

Each jar, each bump, and each mile stretches into what feels like an eternity as my mind races and my cell phone shows no signal, its eerie silence making me want to stomp it beneath my boots in frustration. My watch is not my friend either because each minute that ticks past, each mile that we put between us and the village, is more time and space from wherever the fuck Beaux is with her curiosity to take more damn pictures.

When my phone alerts a text, all of my panic and worry reach a boiling point as I glance down to see who's sent it. I sag against the side of the carrier in momentary relief before all of the tumultuous emotions inside me morph into anger.

> Are you okay? I'm worried. I'm with Rosco. We were under heavy fire.

> Yes. I'm okay.

I hit Send on my reply, but my signal fails again and I have no way of knowing whether it was delivered.

"She good?" Sarge shouts in my ear when he sees me looking at my phone. I nod, before resting my head back in exhaustion, the adrenaline still coursing through me, but at least I know she's safe.

For now.

*   *   *

I swear I'm going to wear a hole in the goddamn floor as I pace back and forth waiting for Beaux to get back. Not only were we separated during the flare up at the village, but then the convoy she was riding in had some mechanical issues. So now we're going on over an hour that I've been back safe and sound while she's out there. *Alone.* Without me being able to protect her.

And I'm not stupid enough to think that I could save her from all of the shit that can happen out there, but at the same time, the not knowing is killing me.

Pauly watches me from afar. Poor bastard was the first to greet me and congratulate me for the exclusive on the big mission. It also meant he was the first in line for me to rip into since I had no one else to take out my worry and frustration on. And thank fuck we've been friends so long he knows something's wrong, can assume what's bothering me given my history and that I came back without Beaux, and won't hold it against me. Shit. I know I'll feel bad later and I'll buy him a few rounds to apologize, but right now it's the farthest thing from my mind. Beaux is front and center.

Every time the doors to the lobby open, I look up, then curse when it's not her. I've been running the gamut of emotions, hating this feeling of unease that riots within me, knowing I won't settle down internally until I set eyes on her.

And then there's the anger I hold out like a shield around me. Of course she doesn't deserve it; deep down I know that, but I can't bring myself to care because if she hadn't asked to take more pictures, she would have been with me when shit went south, and she'd be beside me right now.

"Tanner."

I whip around at the sound of Beaux's voice saying my

name. And of course she's standing there in the lobby, looking no worse for wear, with her camera bag strap slung from one shoulder to opposite hip with her hair disheveled. In fact her cheeks are flushed with color and her eyes alive from the adrenaline rush. Even I can see it across the distance of fake marble floors between us.

Still, my feet are rooted in place as relief floods me, and the proverbial breath I never realized I was holding whooshes out. Neither one of us moves; our eyes lock and say so many things and nothing all at the same time. We're both guarded because there's no denying that what just happened made whatever that fucking stirring is deep down I have for her ten times stronger. And I think she feels it too.

"Knee-deep in chaos!" Pauly says, his enthusiastic voice booming through the room so that all of the other journalists take notice of Beaux standing there looking exhilarated and beguiling all at once. "Are you hooked now, BJ?" he asks as he approaches her and pats her on the back in welcome. "A goddamn rush, isn't it?"

Beaux smiles warmly, but all the while her eyes keep flickering to mine, and yet all I can see is Pauly touching her when I want it to be me. I let her have her few moments of rookie glory: being in the thick of an engagement, learning firsthand the rush that some of these journalists can only dream of experiencing. And I'm happy for her, but I experience the next moments as if I were an alcoholic in a liquor store; the craving to take what I can't have so bad it rules your every thought, your every breath, your everything.

I want to be the good guy, to let her taste the glory of being admired, but at some point soon, I want to be the one who has her attention. And enough's enough. I close the distance between us, working my way through the crowd.

"C'mon, guys, she needs to get upstairs and file her pictures along with my report ASAP. Worldwide is asking and wants it while the story's hot."

The group groans but backs off because they know I'm right. Within seconds, Beaux is following me across the lobby without a single word exchanged between us besides my name. The elevator opens as we near it, and although I usually prefer the stairs, I walk into the empty car, knowing that my body is so pent-up with need right now that I won't be able to make it more than a few flights up without giving in to the pull of desire on me.

"Whose room?" It's the only thing I say, my voice strained, my body vibrating from her proximity.

"Mine," she says cautiously. "All of my equipment is there so I can upload and—"

"Fine." I push the button just as the doors to the car shut, and I brace my hands on the wall in front of me, eyes closed as I concentrate on controlling everything that I can because I know the minute I have her alone, that restraint will snap.

The tension in the car between us thickens. The current of desire is so palpable, I feel like it kick-starts my heart every other beat. I blow out a breath as the elevator ascends, Beaux shifting her feet beside me.

"Did I do something wrong?"

I snort. Fuck yes. But where do I even begin to explain? *You made me want you? You made me worry when I told myself I wasn't going to put myself in that situation ever again? You fucking don't ever listen about not going off on your own? I want you so goddamn bad right now that the desire is so sharp, it's painful.*

The elevator dings, and I stride off the car to her door without looking back to see if she's following. My body just knows she is.

It takes her a moment to fumble with her bag, get her

room key out, and open her door, all the while casting curious glances my way.

"Put the camera down," I order the minute we're inside the door and it's shut.

"What is your problem—?" she asks, but the question is cut off the second the camera strap leaves her hand, my body crashing into hers and pushing her up against the wall behind her. My lips find hers instantly.

It takes her a millisecond for the shock to fade and for her to respond, but once she does, we meet in a savage union of frenzied hands gripping, mouths taking, bodies begging to join in every way possible.

Beaux weaves her fingers in my hair and holds tight as she tears her mouth momentarily from mine. "I thought you were pissed at me."

I kiss her fiercely, all tongue and teeth and possession, before I respond. "I'm furious. But I want you more." It's as true a statement as I've ever given, the moment stripping away any superfluous words. "You came back to me."

"I'll always come back to you," she says, her voice breathless but resolute. And a part of me feels a tiny iota of relief from her words before my senses are shaken and upended when a moan falls from her mouth as my hand finds its way down her pants and I use my one foot to knock her legs wider so that I can have better access. I may be completely consumed with her kiss and taken with the possession of her touch, but there is no mistaking her desire as my fingers run over the tight strip of curls. Her gasp fills the space between us as I part her cleft to find her heated and wet for me.

Jesus Christ. If I didn't want her enough already, feeling her push her hips into my hands makes that want turn into a need that somehow I feared wouldn't be satisfied anytime soon. We've built up to this moment for so long that I know as hard as I try to hold on to control, as much as I try to slow down, every nerve in my body is at such a riotous fever pitch that it's going to be impossible not to succumb to the urgency.

Then Beaux shocks me back to reality by saying, "I need you in me right now."

And that's what I want more than anything, to be buried in her. Yes, my hand is already between the lips of her pussy, but I need more of her, want all of her, naked and accessible.

"Tanner." My name leaves her lips as a plea, a moan, and everything in between when she releases her hold on me and moves to help tug her shorts down. But just her shorts aren't enough. I want all of her clothes off. She must feel the same way because, without a word, we begin an awkward dance toward the bed, an unspoken race to see which of us can get undressed quicker as we cover the few feet of distance. And just as she has her bra off so that we are both completely naked, I grab her from behind and pull her back against my chest.

As desperate as I am to bury myself in her, I also need to slow this down just a bit. Last time she came hard and quick, and as desperate as I am to do the same, I know that this will be our first second time that now holds meaning, and so I don't want to make it any less than it could be by making it quick. Our labored breathing fills the air as my hands cup her breasts and I scrape the stubble on my chin across the curve of her shoulder and up to her ear. The sound of her sighing out my name is so fucking hot, it's an aphrodisiac all in itself.

"Beaux." Her name is all I say before I lace open-mouthed kisses down the line of her neck, tasting salt on my tongue, while her perfume and the smell of her arousal assault my senses in an oddly arousing combination as I work my way to the other side of her neck. "I've had so many thoughts about what I was going to do with you once we had sex again. How I was going to slide between your thighs, tease you with my tongue until you were breathless and spent. Make you beg for more . . . but that game's on me, isn't it? Because right now I'm so god-damn primed, I'd beg, borrow, and steal to take you, and I think that's just what you want. For me to take without asking, because that's what you're used to. Well, think again . . . ," I murmur in her ear, and leave the last word hanging as my hands slide down her abdomen once again to the pleasure between her thighs.

The hitch in her breath and the voluntary lift of one foot onto the bed so that I have better access tell me she feels this too, wants this too. "How do you like it, Beaux? Do you like when I slide my fingers right here, rub a little harder . . . faster . . . or do you like when I bury my fingers in your pussy and stroke right here?"

And I do just that, dip my two fingers inside her so that she tightens around me at the same time as her hands dig into my forearms when the sensations swamp her.

And I love feeling the intense reaction, take pride in knowing I can make her stop everything, and break her concentration with just my touch. Then I curl my fingers and rake them over the interior patch of nerves again as my other hand slides around her waist just in time for her knees to weaken. There is something so intimate about the moment, so real, that it throws me momentarily and causes her to lean back so that my cheek rests against hers.

"More," she moans, and I begin to manipulate her sex again, fingers on the inside, thumb on her clit. Her head lolls back on my shoulder and her hips jut forward, a physical command telling me to give her more. I work my fingers in and out of her, desire growing, my thumb adding friction on her clit, her own writhing motion showing me just how she wants me to bring her to the cusp. With each thrust of her pelvis, she's rubbing her ass against my rock-hard dick in the ultimate temptation I'm sure as hell going to take advantage of.

Her fingernails dig deeper into my skin, an indication that she's almost there, so I keep manipulating her sex. "Argh. God," she cries, hips bucking against my hand, hands trying to push and pull my forearms all at the same time as the pleasurable pain overwhelms her body and annihilates her senses. The sound of her coming undone is enough to make every part of me ache like a man on fire walking knowingly into the flames.

And I was so wrong, it's comical. I thought I could take this slow, calm this ravenous hunger inside me, but the minute she comes, hips writhing, lips calling my name like a plea and a curse all at the same time, I lose it. Fuck slowing down. We can do slow all damn day later . . . but right now? Right now I'm a man desperate and ready to give in to the desire owning his every nerve.

She rides out her orgasm with my teeth nipping her shoulder and hands holding her hips tight so that she's forced to feel everything pulsing through her. But the minute I feel her body sag, muscles start to relax, I spin Beaux around in my arms and push her down onto the bed. She scoots back up the mattress, eyes wild with desire under heavy lust-laden lids that call to me, tempt me, dare me to come and take what she's offering. And there's no question, I'm definitely ready to take.

Lust and greed hit me in a potent combination as I stand at the foot of the bed and take her in. As much as I could stand here all day long and drink in the lines of her body, the dark pink of her nipples against her bronze skin, I'll savor it later. Much later. I'm already way past the point of no return.

So I kneel on the bed, which causes the mattress springs to squeak beneath my weight, my tongue darting out to wet my bottom lip in anticipation. As I crawl between her parted thighs, the urge to slide my tongue along her sex and taste her is so all-consuming, but at the same time, all I can think about is what she's going to feel like wrapped around me.

But what man can resist a pussy when it's framed by legs like hers?

On my hands and knees I give in to what I want and dip my head down so that my tongue slides just along the seam of her lips. There is nothing that turns me on more than the scent and taste of a woman aroused, and Beaux is . . . holy shit between her taste on my tongue and her moan filling my ears, I can't hold back anymore.

I lick my way up and down one more time with my hands holding her inner thighs apart as she squirms at the sensation of me dipping my tongue into her. And I'd stay here all night if I could, but as my rock-hard cock rubs against the mattress beneath me, my body reminds me how much it's being neglected in the moment. Giving in to my own needs, I rise up on my knees with my hands still on her thighs and meet her eyes.

And I know we've had sex before, but there is something that feels very different this time around. There is no alcohol, no ignorance over who the other is, no feigning that this is a one-night stand I will never see again. No. This time as I press her thighs forward so I can slide painstakingly slowly into her, I don't notice her lips part or her chest hitch from her slow breaths. Instead, I watch the pleasure wash over her as her eyes roll partially back in rapture before returning to mine with emotions swimming in them I'm not sure I want to process.

So I don't.

Instead, I bury myself all the way to the hilt, all trains

of thought overwhelmed by the physical sensations, and all sense of self lost because there is no me and no her; no, there's just *us*. A feral groan fills the room; even though it's my voice, I don't even realize I've emitted it when I start that slow, slick slide out so that just the tip of my dick is allowed the pleasure of her. Talk about torturing myself, but the little sound she makes begging for me not to stop is worth it. So I give her what she wants. I use my hand to hold my dick still, rub the ridge of my crest up with an added pressure over that sweet spot I can feel just inside her. I tease and taunt her like she's been doing to me since we started this way back on night one, but this . . . This is just so much more.

Once she starts lifting her hips and squeezing tightly around me, I have to hope my willpower will hold long enough so that I can give her what she needs. Because I know once I bury myself in her, I won't be able to stop the freight train of desire bearing down on me.

When I look into her eyes again, there is no mistaking it as she nears her orgasm. I watch her come undone — bit by bit, moan after moan, muscle by muscle. And I know she hasn't finished coming yet, but fucking hell, I feel like a vise is wrapped around my balls, that deep, sweet ache so damn intense, my fingers begin to dig into the toned flesh of her thighs to try and ward off the carnal need to plunder.

But it's futile.

Because the first time I look down and watch her pussy lips stretch around the thickness of my shaft as I slide out, the most delicate of flesh bringing me the most intense of pleasure, my control snaps. I press harder on her thighs to give me an unhindered view and the access to take as I please as I rear back and thrust into her until I bottom out. Then I groan out in ecstasy, balls buried so damn deep that I can feel her warm wetness coating me and turning me on something fierce. I grind against her, my dick as deep as it can possibly be, and it feels so good, I let my head loll back as I begin to really move.

The room fills with the sound of sex and pleasure, pleas and moans, passion unleashed and needs unfurled. And my God . . . talk about drugging a man into a coma. Everything about her forces me to concentrate so fucking hard on the moment that I'm losing so much more than a physical release to her.

Her muscles begin to pulse around me as the sounds of skin against skin heightens everything about the moment. I'm fixated on getting us both there, hips thrusting, fingers gripping her, and neck taut with my impending release.

And then the bed frame starts squeaking with each and every drive in to the point that even though I'm so pent up, so addled with need for release, it's so damn loud that when I look down and meet Beaux's eyes, I can see her laughing.

"We're breaking the bed," she pants out with a soft laugh that ends on a sharp mewl as I grind my hips into her again, sparks gathering at the base of my spine and readying for the onslaught of sensation just beyond the horizon.

But the bed's not the only thing that seems to be breaking; I think a tiny little piece of my heart just did too. There's no way in hell I'm telling her that, though. I hide behind the thought by flashing a devil-may-care smirk that lasts long enough to catch her eyes lighting up before I return to concentrating on getting us back in the moment, squeaky spring and all.

It doesn't take long to propel us onto that edge where lust and desire reign, want and need merge as one. With our bodies still connected in the most primal of ways, I lean down and slant my mouth over hers, the action driving me farther into her addictive pussy when I thought I couldn't go any deeper. And with my mouth on hers, her every breath mingling with my own exhalations, both my tongue and cock savoring and demanding all at the same time, I coax her over the precipice, swallow her moans as she falls, and enjoy the rhythm of her muscles as she contracts around me.

And then she does this little thing, this lift of her hips in a motion chock-full of greed that tells me she wants more to prolong her release as long as she can, and the action, the motion, of her gripping me in intervals pulls me into the vortex of ecstasy.

I crash over the edge, muscles tensing, dick pulsing, thoughts annihilated by the white-hot heat streaking through me and exploding in bursts of warmth. I can't weather the pleasure with my mouth to hers, can't handle the rush of fiery heat followed by drowsy bliss that courses on a pumped-up kick in my veins, so I rear up on my knees, eyes closed tight, and her name a broken cry in the air as I empty myself.

Our labored breathing is all I can hear when I look down at her, a half smirk on my lips at the satisfaction on her face—flushed cheeks, lips swollen from mine, eyes hazy—before pulling ever so slowly out of her, immediately wanting to do it all over again.

Well, after I recover some, because damn . . . all guys might need a recovery time but this, her, what just happened, have drained me in every sense of the word. And it's a new feeling, to be drained emotionally, physically, sexually, and not want to lie back and close my eyes and succumb to the exhaustion like usual. I don't want to at all. I want to lie down next to her, prop my head in my hand, and admire her, talk to her, and just breathe her in.

Shit. I think the paradox this time around is that, rather than my slipping down the slippery slope from lust to love, Beaux and I just experienced something unique to us. We bonded during the adrenaline-fueled action of the raid, the worrisome fear over each other's safety, and then the agonizing wait to see each other face-to-face. Hell yeah, we bonded, so I'm allowed to be a little in awe of her right now.

Then again, I also try to justify that it's just being with someone almost every waking hour that has me concerned with her safety, but I'm not real big on lying, so why lie to myself? That lightness in my head could be because of more than just great sex. It could be because Beaux's starting to mean something to me despite the mere month or so we've known each other.

But the time isn't right, so I push the thoughts away, shove the little pinpricks warning me to slow the fuck down away, and tell myself to enjoy the moment and the warm skin of the gorgeous woman in front of me. I settle down beside her, head propped on my hand, quiet my thoughts, and enjoy the moment.

Her hair is all over the place in stark contrast to the white sheets, but at the same time the fact that it's falling out of her ponytail softens the sharp lines of her face. She meets my eyes, and I love that even though she's so goddamn confident everywhere else in whatever this is between us, she appears shy right now. Her cheeks flush even more, and she averts her eyes before scooting into me so that the curves of our bodies fit perfectly into each other's.

It's a reflex that my arm wraps around her and pulls her tighter, our lips meeting in a soft sigh of a kiss that says the moment was so much more than solely physical, and yet neither of us wants to address it yet. Because physical attraction is acceptable, but feeling like this, the intensity with which I feel it, is extraordinary.

At least that's what I hope she's saying when her tongue meets mine in a soft dance of tenderness and acceptance. We cement our connection this way for a few moments, all hushed words and soft laughter. Hands smoothing over heated skin and heartbeats slowing down.

We settle into such a relaxed silence in the comfort of each other's arms—so very different than what happened after the last time we had sex—that it kills me when I have to bring up the inevitable.

"We need to work," I remind her softly, speaking of turning in the written reports that back up my live broadcast from earlier as well as the feeling I have that once I check my phone, there will be messages from Rafe about another live spot.

"I believe you just worked me perfectly fine." Her laugh is muffled, and I can feel the heat of it from where her lips are pressed against my sternum. The sensation sends a pulse of desire straight to my lower belly.

"And I have no problem working you again."

"Oh you better plan on it. Again and again," she says, and the suggestiveness that laces her tone is such a damn turn-on because it gives me that little ego boost to know she enjoyed what just happened as much as I did.

"I do like the again part ... but this squeaky bed poses a problem."

"Squeaky wheel gets the oil."

"Squeak all you want, because I have no problem oiling you up." My mind goes in pure male fashion from oil to dipstick to lube jobs and the correlation to sex.

"Hmm," she murmurs as she leans her head back to look into my eyes. "Maybe we need to change up the location. Does the bed in your room squeak?"

"I'm not sure. We can try it out ... but uh, I don't need a bed to have my way with you. There's lots of viable real estate: shower, wall, dresser, stairwell, rooftop." I love that damn hitch in her breath from the dark promise of my words. "I'm not picky so long as it's with you."

A part of me quickly realizes what I just said to her, the admission that I want there to be a *with you* when it comes to her, but I know she took it for what it's worth in the moment when she says, "You know what they say. . . . It's all about location, location, location."

"As long as the location is between your thighs, I'll take it."

Chapter 14

"Good night. This is Tanner Thomas, reporting live for Worldwide News."

As I wait for the connection to break, my body still rides the high from the raid today and the incredible sex with Beaux. I'm antsy and invigorated for the first time in what feels like forever here, and I sigh out in relief when the feed goes black so I can close down the Skype window on my laptop. Immediately my eyes focus on the iPhoto window open to the most recent downloads page, and I'm once again transfixed by the images Beaux took today that I had asked her to download on my laptop too.

And yes she got the action shots—great panoramas of knock and talks happening at the same time on three different residences, soldiers' backs with the muzzles of the M4 carbines visible over their shoulders—but she also got those kinds of pictures that make me stop and stare and read what's beneath the surface. A platoon of soldiers looking weary, the lines on their faces and looks in their eyes depicting both the fear and monotony of their

tasks. Villagers peeking out from windows, kids fasci-
nated to see soldiers, and adults leery of their presence.
Sergeant Jones giving instructions, the line of his posture
and angle of the shot reflecting his authority without a
single patch on his uniform in the image.

Then there's me. The few shots she snuck when I
wasn't looking where the rush I feel from being part of
the mission practically leaps off the page. She captured
the perfect image of what that buzz Rafe and I talk
about looks like, and it's hard to look away.

Beaux's muffled voice through the hotel room door
pulls me from my fixation on the computer, and I shut it
down, my thoughts now focused on her. The sex we had
earlier was mind-blowing, but I'm nowhere near satisfied. When it comes to Beaux Croslyn, I have a feeling
that no matter how many times she rocks my world, it's
not going to be enough.

So I close the laptop, scoot the chair back, and chuckle
at my on-air attire of button-up dress shirt and the khaki
shorts and bare feet that the computer camera couldn't
catch. One thing about fieldwork is I don't have to abide
by attire restrictions and wear stuffy suits like the desk
anchors. Well that and I get unpredictability and sunshine on a daily basis. Can't complain about that regardless of where that sunshine is located.

"How could this happen?" Her voice rises in a way
that causes me to go and make sure she's okay, because
it doesn't sound like she is.

The hotel room door is just barely ajar, and I can see
her through the crack in the doorjamb. She paces back
and forth as she listens to someone, hands gesturing,
head shaking, and words being cut off every time she
starts to speak by whoever is on the other end of the line.
I'm intrigued and don't mean to snoop, but the only
other time I've seen her this agitated is with me, so I

stand just inside the door and observe, curiosity getting the better of me.

"I told you . . . I can't. This is . . . ugh . . . Just know I'll take care of it somehow, okay . . . but please, no one else can find out. . . ." Her voice drifts off as she turns her back from me, something else being mumbled into the phone that I can't quite catch. Now I'm definitely all ears. "I know. I know. I call when I can—you can't be mad at that. It's not my fault and . . . Jesus!" She blows out a breath in frustration as she leans against the wall and puts her head back against it with her eyes closed. "He's going to kick my ass."

I can feel the tension radiating off her and am incredibly curious about what exactly is going on.

"We'll deal with it if it becomes an issue. Regardless I'm the one who's gonna get the blame. He'll come after me. . . . That's what—" Her voice cuts off when she opens her eyes and sees me standing in the doorway, shoulder against the doorjamb and hands shoved in my pockets. "I'm sure we'll get everything worked out," she says, her demeanor changing, voice softening, and I'm not sure if it's because she has an audience now or because she's trying to soothe whoever is on the other end of the line. Regardless, something is going on—that much is evident when she hangs up the phone without breaking eye contact with me or without saying another word.

"Nice broadcast attire," she says with a smile as she motions to my shorts and bare feet.

And I may be enthralled with the woman in so many ways I can't enumerate them all, but I know a change of topic when I hear one. At first I thought she'd just gone into the hallway to give me privacy during my broadcast— but now I'm beginning to think there was more to it than that.

"Thanks." I give her a nod of my head, trying to feel out where to go with this. "Everything okay?"

"Yep," she says as she brushes past me into the hotel room.

"Yep? Because it didn't sound like it. What's going on, Beaux?"

"Nothing."

I snort, can't help it because I wasn't born yesterday. "Uh-huh. He's gonna kick your ass over it? That doesn't sound like nothing to me." I challenge her to answer the question and dare her to meet my eyes because I hate the feeling I have deep down that something is off when things between us have just started to feel so damn right on.

When she finally looks at me, I witness her green irises swimming with conflicted emotion and her lips opening and closing without saying a word. I decide to let her have the moment, allow her to keep whatever cards she's playing close to her vest.

"Don't ruin this, Tanner. Please don't ruin this incredible night." She takes a step toward me and stops. "Today, tonight, has meant more to me than any day in a long time, and I can't argue with you over this right now. Please trust me when I tell you that things aren't always what they seem. That conversation, please just forget about it. I'm fine. Nothing is wrong. Just shit at home . . ." Her voice fades off, and I eye her warily, not believing a word she says. "Please don't make it something it's not and tarnish what happened tonight."

She steps into me as soon as she finishes speaking, both of us proceeding cautiously, as I start to process what she's said and she waits to see if I'll accept her request. Her eyes plead with me, reinforcing her words, and as much as I want to shake some answers out of her, I also want to fold her in my arms and erase the look in them.

The fact that I don't like the words I overheard or the fear I somehow feel emanating off her means I clench my jaw to prevent any questions from tumbling out, keeping them churning just beneath the surface. I don't deserve to know all of her deep dark secrets yet because we're still getting to know each other and still I feel the inherent need to protect her from whatever is haunting her eyes.

She must feel my turmoil because she reaches up on her tiptoes to brush her lips to mine in an attempt to ease the sting of the secrets she's keeping from me. And call me a sucker, but it does help a little bit. Well, until my phone rings — Rafe's distinct ringtone interrupting us.

Duty calls. Too bad everything within me wants to be focused elsewhere at the moment.

Like on her.

I know I'm dreaming, know this can't be real, but it feels so good to see Stella and the familiar smile on her face again, that I welcome the memory. I glance over at her and just shake my head. There's nothing else I can really do because she's just that damn funny.

"What? It's true." She shrugs, blond hair falling over her shoulders and a bottle of beer in her hand.

"It is not!" But I can't keep from laughing because she knows me too well.

"That's such crap. I've seen you do it. The minute a woman tells you she loves you, you get that knee-jerk re-action and say it right back."

"I do not." I feign ignorance when I know she's one hundred percent spot-on.

"Dude, she's right," Pauly interjects with the tip of his bottle before meeting Stella's hand in a high five. "You get pussywhipped and cave in to saying it back."

"It just comes out. I mean, what am I supposed to do?

Just ignore that the chick's said it and hurt her feelings because I don't respond?"

"Jesus," both of them say in unison as Stella slumps back in her seat and slides me a sidelong glance. "It's gonna hurt her feelings a helluva lot more when you say it and don't mean it, Romeo."

I blow out a long breath and swallow the smart-ass comment on my tongue with a sip of beer.

"You guys are too funny," Pauly says as he rises. "'Nother round?"

We nod and watch him walk off, and now that he's gone, I look over to Stella who's eyeing me once again. "What?"

"Nothing." Silence falls between us for a moment before she continues. "I think it's cute, you know. Most guys are scared of saying those three words."

"Well, according to you and Pauly, I say them too much."

"I'm just giving you shit," she muses, head on the back of the chair, eyes tilted up to the ceiling. "I like that it's easy for you."

"I guess the real question, though, is if I can say it so easily, how will I know when it's really real?" It's amazing the things you'll think to talk about when you're bored out of your mind.

"You'll know it's real when you hesitate."

I angle my head and meet her eyes. "What do you mean?"

"If the words are so easy for you to say when it's in reflex, then the first time you ever hesitate, when you don't say 'I love you' back immediately because you'll be so overwhelmed that she said it to you . . . well, I guess then you'll know it's real."

I stare at her, not sure if I believe her or not, but since I have nothing else to think about, the notion settles in as I lift the beer to my lips and rest my head on the back of the chair. "Food for thought," I murmur.

A noise in the hallway pulls me from my dream and the moment I'd completely forgotten. My dreamlike state lasts momentarily, and I hold on to the recollection of Stella since the memories are coming less and less frequently now.

Rolling onto my side to avoid the bright light that floods the room, I'm struck by how perfectly it frames Beaux's body in a halo as she sleeps. I visually trace the lines of her face and the sheet covering her body and take her all in. She's so feisty when she's awake that it's interesting to have a moment to watch her in sleep. And it's not like we haven't woken up beside each other before, but this time just seems so very different.

Good different.

The first time you hesitate . . .

I push the train of thought aside—how both Stella's wisdom and now Beaux lying beside me make me hesitate in so many ways—and try to redirect my mind to where I want my thoughts to wander: my family. I wonder how my sister, Rylee, is doing with her new husband and her band of motley boys that she loves more than life. I find myself guessing at how many times my mom has gone to pick up the phone to call me, only to hang it back up because she doesn't want to annoy me even though I tell her to call anytime and that I'll answer when I can. And then I get that little pang deep down as I wonder if my dad has found a new buddy to join him in sitting on the rocks of the jetty to fish since he'd gotten a little too used to my being home over the four months. We both found it therapeutic sitting there with fishing poles in our hands, him in having his only son home again for the longest bout in a decade and me in having his company. With my father, I didn't have to say a word, and yet he knew exactly what to do to help me deal with Stella's death.

Then Beaux makes this soft moan deep in her throat that tugs on every ounce of testosterone in my body. And it's not like I'm not sitting here with morning wood; I'd be more than willing to relieve the pressure and feed the ache, but at the same time there is something so perfect about just being lazy with her. Like we're lying together after an incredible first date instead of in the Middle East in some crappy hotel with squeaky bedsprings, waiting for the next story to hit.

Shit, even after leading into another morning broadcast in the States and not another mention of what happened in the hallway, we fell into bed exhausted but not too tired to go another round, a little slower, a little softer than the first time. And then complete and utter exhaustion took over, but damn, I'll take exhaustion when it comes at the hands and thighs of a beautiful woman.

She shifts in bed, my eyes taking in the span of golden skin that calls for me to touch it, and when I look back up, I meet her sleepy eyes and shy smile. "Mmm, good morning," she murmurs, shifting her pillow some so that she can lie on her side and look eye to eye with me.

"Good morning, sleepyhead."

She closes her eyes drowsily for a slow blink and yawns. I laugh at how tired she seems when I feel so invigorated after a killer story, great pickups by other networks, and, more important, the incredible night we spent together.

"Can we just stay here all day?"

"We could." I shrug, shifting the pillow partially covering my cheek. "I'm sure I could find some ways to entertain us."

"Ah yes. I forgot. Floors and doors and stand or sit—"

"You sound like a Dr. Seuss poem," I tease as I reach out and lift a strand of hair off her cheek. And damn. I don't know why I expected that zap of current I feel whenever I touch her to have dissipated since we've had sex, but actually it feels ten times stronger.

When she turns her cheek ever so slightly into the touch of my hand, the simple gesture speaks louder than the warning bells going off in my head telling me that slippery slope just became a full-on landslide.

"Nah, I'm just thinking of location, location, location," she says, making us both laugh before we fall quiet.

"Speaking of location . . ." I hesitate, not wanting to kill the moment but at the same time needing to address something while her tough-girl facade is gone, shed on the floor with her clothes. Because I don't have any doubts that the minute we leave this bed, her back will be up and she'll close down to what I want to say. "Yesterday. On scene. Can we not do that again?"

Her eyes widen slightly. "Sure. I'll make a point to tell the terrorists to stop shooting. I'm sure they'll listen to me. Not a problem." She looks at me like I'm crazy.

"You know that's not what I meant."

"Then what did you mean?" I can hear her irritation in her tone and know I need to smooth the feathers I've just ruffled.

"I meant, can we keep the picture taking of local interest things to a minimum, please? And at the least, can you warn me if you ask Sarge or Rosco for permission on an embed so that I can go with you?"

"Seriously? Now you're going to tell me how to do my job?" She starts to sit up, but I reach out and put my arm on her biceps to prevent her from pulling away.

"I'm not trying to tell you how to do your job, nor do I think I'm being unreasonable. . . . I just . . ." My voice trails off as I attempt to figure out how to say what I need to say without implying anything else. She's a woman, and women infer things, and not always the right things, so I take a moment to choose my words correctly. "I just don't want anything to happen to you. If I can at least be with you when you wander, then I'll feel better about it, I guess." And it's stupid really, like I'd be able to protect her from the shit that's out there, but it's a guy thing. Protect at all costs.

She just stares long and hard at me before finally speaking. "I'm not going to promise anything other than I'll try to keep you informed."

It's not exactly the answer I was hoping for, but at least it's better than her telling me to go to hell, which was what I expected. I nod in cautious acceptance because I don't have a leg to stand on after witnessing how incredible the shots she got yesterday were. "What exactly is it that you're looking for when you take the pictures? What is it that calls to you?" She leaves in the middle of the night to take photos, she braves a war zone to get shots, and I want to understand why so that maybe I'll get to know her better.

"Life." She answers in such a matter-of-fact way, but her eyes have a daydream quality to them that reminds me of when I first started this career and felt the same exact way. And I still love my job, still am consumed by it, but it's that fresh-faced wonderment that I see in her eyes that makes me hold off on telling her it's going to change. I should let her enjoy this period.

So long as it doesn't get her killed.

"What about life in particular?"

"I enjoy watching people, documenting their lives, seeing the things that others don't see in the looks in their eyes and lines of their faces."

"And you're good at it—your eye is exceptional, but let's try to keep it to a minimum, please," I tell her. "Life is harsh here and dangerous, and you never know who is or isn't your friend, so I'd prefer—"

She stops my brotherly speech by pressing her lips to mine. I resist at first, try to talk through her sensory on-slaught, but after she keeps at it, her lips vibrating against mine from her laughter, I allow myself to slip into the kiss. And it's the farthest thing from a hardship, to let her pull me so handily from everything outside of these ho-tel walls with a single kiss. Damn does it feel good.

There were so many other things I wanted to say to her, so many questions I wanted answered about where she goes at night and how in the hell she plans on de-fending herself if she's scared at the sight of a gun. So how does this singular woman make me lose my need-to-know attitude that I've built a career and a reputation on? It's almost as if I'm blinded by her—and that's never a comfortable place to be when you've lived your life trying to see for everyone else.

And yet, I'm completely content with it.

Our kiss softens to brushes of lips while her fingers weave into the hair on the nape of my neck where her fingernails scratch gently, and my body wants so much more than what she's offering. I start to deepen the kiss, my hand finding her breast beneath the sheet so that my thumb rubs back and forth over the peak of her nipple.

She slides her hands down to my chest and hot damn, just when I think she's gonna have her way with me, she pushes against me and tears her lips from mine.

"While we're making requests . . ." She raises her eye-brows, and I love that her breathing is labored because it means she's just as affected as I am.

"Mmm?"

"I'm really enjoying whatever this is between us . . . but in order to keep up my credibility, that I got this job on my own merit, can we please keep this on the down low?" She averts her eyes, cheeks flushing with embarrassment over a request that's completely valid. And she's so damn adorable, giving me a glimpse of vulnerability in her otherwise badass facade.

"Never mind." She shakes her head, and I realize that I'm so mesmerized seeing her like this that I didn't respond. "Forget that I—"

"No. I'm okay—"

"Just drop it—"

She's so damn flustered that I can't get a word in edgewise, so I do to her exactly what she did to me. I grab the back of her neck and bring her mouth to mine to shut her up. She resists at first, but I love how it's only fleeting. And just when we fall so deep into the kiss that we're almost to the point of no return, all greedy hands and needy sighs, I pull back from her and look her in the eye.

"I'm okay with down low," I murmur, and brush a gentle kiss against her lips. A soft laugh turned moan falls from her mouth as my hands find the wetness between her thighs. The arch of her hips calls to me, and I'm more than willing to be pulled under her hold. "I especially like your down low."

Chapter 15

"Smitten, huh?" I must be, because it's been almost two weeks since Beaux and I fell back into the sack together, and she's all I can think about.

"Yes. You definitely sound smitten with whoever she is," my sister says, her voice holding a trace of amusement.

"It's just different here. Same people day in, day out. It's—"

"Six weeks' time? Hmm, I'd call it accelerated dating." I chuckle into the phone at her assessment of the situation that's correct in a sense. "Well, I'm right, aren't I? When there's nothing to do but get to know each other and waste time together, it's like a relationship on speed."

"I wouldn't exactly call it a relationship," I start, but then stop to think about the notion, because in a sense that's exactly what Beaux and I have together.

"Uh-huh," Rylee says, and I can tell she's having fun with this, enjoying questioning me about whom I'm dating because I've never really cared before. I mean yeah,

I've dated and fallen in what felt like love at the time, but no one has ever made me feel like a giddy teenager at the same time as we've shared such an intense connection. "Have you spent the night together?"

"Jesus Christ, Bubs." I choke on my nickname for her because I am not discussing my sex life with my baby sister.

"Don't Bubs me. That's not going to get you out of this conversation."

She's got my number. Fuck. "You really want me to answer that?" My voice cracks on the last word.

"So that means yes." She laughs thoroughly, and I picture her ticking off the first question on one of her always handy task lists. "Do you have a pet name for her?"

I swear silently into the empty room. "No, not a pet name. Just a nickname. And who are you to ask these questions, huh, little Miss Married?"

"And that's another yes," she says smugly. "Are you seeing anyone else?"

"Well, considering the options are slim here, what do you think?" She's starting to get on my nerves. I love and I hate this inquisition from her all at the same time.

"True." She snorts.

"Are we really doing this, Ry? I'd rather hear about home. How are Colton and the boys? Is the project still full steam ahead?" I attempt to change the topic and ask about the endeavor to build more houses for underprivileged boys; the project itself brought my sister and her now-husband together in an amusing set of circumstances.

"He's good, the boys are great, and the project is challenging and incredible all at the same time. We can talk about them later. Don't think for a minute I'm going to pass up the chance to make you squirm." Her laugh is maniacal at best.

"You're getting back at me for all the times I put those rubber snakes in your sheets, aren't you?" The memory of her shrieking and throwing them at me brings a smile to my face some twenty years later.

"Paybacks are a bitch, aren't they?" she says, her voice dripping in false sympathy. "Have you taken her on a proper date yet? I mean that's super import—"

"Hey, Ry, I don't mean to cut you off, but I have to go. Work's on the other line," I tell her as I glance quickly at my phone's screen and see Sarge's number.

"Convenient." But I know she's not really mad.

"Love you."

"Love you too. Be safe."

"Always," I tell her before ending the call and accepting the new one. "Sarge? How goes it?"

"It's going, brother. Another day in paradise, right?" he snorts, a sarcastic laugh following the noise.

"What can I do for you, man?" The hair on the back of my neck has started to stand up in anticipation as I hope for the holy grail here. Another embed mission where we can report in the thick of the action versus going out solo on our own to the safe and approved locations where you get the same old shit day in, day out.

"Just giving you a heads-up that things have gotten awfully quiet this week. Chatter is nil, so we're thinking the meet's going to happen soon."

"And . . . ?" I respond, knowing he's asking something of me but wanting to make sure it's exactly what I think it is. Need to know what chips I hold and how to play them to my advantage in the future when I need them.

"Just making sure that you pass along any information you may get from that source of yours. We wouldn't want to get caught with our pants down."

"Mmm-hmm." It's the only response I give him, my mind going a hundred miles an hour. Wondering if their intel has gone dry and now he's fishing with me to see if I know something I'm not telling him.

"Hope to be talking to you soon, Thomas."

"Sarge." I know that's his way of saying good-bye and giving me a warning all at the same time. Something's going on, and now I just need to figure out what.

I sit on the edge of my bed and then lie back, eyes trained on the ceiling and the cracks I've memorized as I mull everything over. I guess the military is pretty desperate if they're calling me up, trying to get information. It's flattering and fucked up all at the same time. And not knowing what to make of it all other than Sarge is grasping at straws to get more information, I decide to do something that I never do. I text Omid.

Usually I wait for him to make contact with me; I don't want to cause him any trouble should someone see a text, but I take the risk. The minute I hit Send, I wince and wish I could take it back, as my need to know doesn't feel as strong as the need to not cause him trouble; in this place, that could mean the unspeakable. I don't expect a response right away, and know if I lie here much longer, I'm going to go crazy.

Restless energy hums through me as I enter the lobby and look for Beaux to tell her what's going on, but I can't find her anywhere.

"Hey, Pauly?"

"Yeah. What's up?" he asks as he looks up from his laptop with a cup of coffee in one hand and a Cup Noodles in the other.

"You seen BJ?" He twists his lips momentarily as his eyes try to gauge whether I have some hot story and I'm looking for her so that we can sneak off to cover it without anyone knowing. I don't say anything further because he won't believe me anyway.

All's fair in friendship and reporting.

"Last I saw her was about two hours ago." He sets his coffee down and glances at his watch. "Everything okay?"

"Yeah. She's been begging me to get out and do some human interest shots. And, man, I'm getting bored and antsy. . . . Thought that maybe getting out in the city a bit would help some."

"I hear that, brother. I hear that. If you go, just make sure one of us knows where you go . . . safety and all that," he says with a wave of his hand.

"Thanks, Pauly," I say with a smile, appreciating his friendship as I stride from the lobby.

By the time I reach Beaux's floor, my texts to her have remained unanswered. A lick of panic creeps its way into my thoughts, but I shove it away, knowing she's probably safe and sound in her room, in the shower or something.

But when I knock on her door and don't get an answer, I immediately turn the handle. And the door is locked, but when I push against the door, it opens because the latch never clicked into place. I hesitate momentarily, the door a few inches open, deciding whether I should enter.

"Beaux?" I call out into her room, knowing damn well if she doesn't answer I'm going in because it's not like I've never been in her room before. Shit, I've slept in here on and off over the past few weeks, but it's more the invasion of privacy factor that causes me to hesitate.

When she doesn't respond, I enter cautiously and yet hopeful that she's just so dead to the world asleep that she doesn't hear me, but the bed's made and the room is completely in order. I hate that I immediately worry, hate that for a split second I wonder if she's with one of our other male colleagues.

Telling myself to calm down, that she's perfectly fine and more than capable of taking care of herself, I wage an internal war over whether to leave the room and search the hotel floor by floor until I find her or slow the fuck down, take stock, and sit here and wait her out. Make her come to me so that I don't look like some sap losing his shit when I have no reason to feel so concerned about her safety.

But holding on to your dignity is a hard task when worry rules your mind. It'd be ten times easier if I were foreign to this environment and hadn't seen the atrocities and disrespect shown to Westerners, let alone their own people. So I sit and wait. Bide my time by watching the world below outside her hotel room window as I sit in a chair next to a table cluttered with cameras.

Minutes stretch into what feel like hours although very little time has passed. My elbow hits a camera beside me and draws my attention. My original intention when I turn the Canon on is to pass time. See if there are any photos on the memory card that will allow me to get lost in the world as Beaux sees it until she gets back. Save myself some worry by looking at the beauty she's captured.

And I do for a moment. I scroll through pictures of dirty-faced children playing ball in a dirt parking lot, of women at the market with their arms around small children while armed soldiers stand nearby. Groups of shots of men gathered around a table, playing a card game, and wasting away the afternoon.

She focuses on eyes and facial features, wrinkles etched in skin that tell a story all on their own. I get so lost in the images that I forget to question when she took them until I notice in the background of one of the images a minaret a few miles from the outskirts of town. The picture was taken near dawn, the sun rising over the mountains behind it and a group of men kneeling on their prayer rugs.

At first I notice the unique perspective of the shot; then I swipe the digital touch screen of the camera to get more details on the picture. And when I see the date is from two days ago, I immediately think the camera must have the wrong time stamp. It has to.

And then I become almost obsessive, going through the pictures on the camera card again to look at the time stamps. Again I see the wrong date that can't be right. Once I'm done with the pictures on that camera, I pick up the one beside it and start the process all over again. Normally I'd get caught up in the new images that are just as incredible as the ones the first camera held, but this time around my mind is running a million miles an hour.

By the time I'm done, I've noticed that the time stamps on all of these images fall on the nights that Beaux didn't spend with me. I'm immediately taken back to how I felt day one with her, like I've been played—and yet I know she isn't playing me. She's explained this all to me . . . but then in the same breath she promised she wasn't going to go out on her own anymore.

What the fuck?

My temper is rising. The restless energy I felt earlier after Sarge's call returns with a vengeance so that the minute I hear the key in the lock, my posture is stiff and I'm primed for a fight.

Beaux pushes open the door and startles when she sees me sitting in her room with a look of complete disdain aimed solely on her. My elbows are on my knees, hands clasped in the center, and my eyes are laser focused on hers.

"Argh!" she yelps. "You scared the shit out of me!" I remain still as I wait to see how she's going to play this because all that worry I felt is still there, but the anger and frustration are a hundred times stronger.

"Sorry," I say, my voice lacking all emotion.

"Did something happen? Do we have a story? Why do you look so upset?" She asks the questions in rapid succession as she sets her key on the dresser and takes a step toward me.

"Don't." The one-word warning reflects so many things I feel inside me right now. *Don't* come closer. *Don't* bullshit me. *Don't* think you can lie to me. *Don't* make me feel like this: angry, confused, worried, conflicted, wanting to pull you close because now I know you're safe and wanting to hold you at arm's length because I don't want to get hurt by you.

"Tanner?"

The cautious nature of how she says my name tells me she knows I'm pissed, but the confused look in her eyes and parted lips tug on the sucker side of me. And no one likes to be a sucker.

"Where were you? And don't tell me you were downstairs in the lobby."

"I was ... out. I went for a walk, needed some fresh air."

"Was the fresh air so thick that you couldn't hear your cell ring?" Her eyes widen, but her mouth stays shut. Smart woman. I lower my head for a moment, stare at my hands as I try to rein in the urge to shake the truth out of her, but I know it won't do any good.

"Whose idea was it to take nights off?" I ask, referring to our agreement to not spend every night in each other's bed as I lift my head up to meet her eyes again. I see that the change of direction in the conversation throws her by the furrow in her brow.

"I don't remember. It just kind of came up, didn't it?"

"You tell me." I honestly don't remember because my brain was probably fogged up from the incredible sex we'd just had when the topic arose as we lay spent and panting a few weeks ago. But right now, I have a deep, unsettling feeling that she's the culprit of starting the conversation. That she created a way out to have nights to herself to get away and do whatever the fuck she does.

"I don't know. Maybe I did. I honestly don't remember."

"Convenient," I snort.

"What's so wrong with not wanting to smother each other? With knowing a damn good thing when I see one and not wanting you to get sick of me? Of wanting to keep this thing between us healthy for both work reasons and for whatever this is between us? I don't understand where you're going with this, Tanner."

"Where I'm going with this?" My voice rises in volume for the first time since she's entered the room although it feels like I've been screaming in my head the entire time. "Where am I going? How about where are you going? That's a more fitting question." When she just stares, her eyes blinking and fingers hanging over the edge of the dresser where her hips lean, I continue. "You promised me you weren't going to go out anymore at nighttime."

"Yeah . . ."

Letting the silence hang between us, I give her a chance to fess up even though I know from her eyes there is nothing to tell because she thinks she did nothing wrong. I gesture nonchalantly to the cameras on the table beside me. "The pictures on the cameras . . . they're good. When'd you take them?"

C'mon, Beaux, don't lie to me. I need her to be up front with me, need to know that I mean enough to her to come clean now even though she lied to me when she left to take them. It's screwed-up logic at best but something I need to hang on to.

"When I was out."

"Can you be a little more specific?"

"About?"

"Well I sure as hell wasn't with you when you took these pictures."

"True." She raises her eyebrows and crosses her arms over her chest like she's losing patience with me, and all I can do is chuckle at the irony in her body language. "Why don't you just come out and ask what you want to ask, Tanner?"

"Did you go out by yourself to take pictures?"

"Not since the last time you told me not to," she lies as she makes a show of looking at her watch, "which was two minutes ago."

Her sarcasm infuriates me even though a part of me admires her all at the same time. It's a fucked-up mix, and that I respect her for standing her ground makes me even more pissed. The goddamn woman is going to be the death of me. "You're a horrible liar."

She just lifts her eyebrows in a "yeah, so what" gesture that causes me to grit my teeth.

"And I believe you promised me you weren't going to go out by yourself anymore, let alone at night, and yet the time stamp on these pictures says you did just that." I wait for a reaction, wait for her to disagree with me, offer an explanation, but she doesn't. She just stands there and ever so slowly nods her head in agreement with my statement. "What the fuck are you doing, Beaux? Trying to get yourself killed?" I can't contain my frustration anymore. I push up out of the chair, shove my hands through my hair in a useless gesture, and pace the floor in front of her to abate some of the restless energy that feels like it's eating me alive.

"Tanner . . . you're overreacting."

"Don't Tanner me, and don't you dare make light of this! It's not like you're out on some goddamn Sunday stroll." I stop walking and square my shoulders to her with my face inches from hers. And she just continues to hold my stare but doesn't give me an inkling of what she's feeling on the inside and damn it to hell I want to know. "This isn't some city back home, rookie, wherever the fuck you're from that you aren't telling me about. Not by a long fucking shot. Do you have any clue what . . ." I stop midsentence as I realize what I just said to her. As everything comes clear over why I'm so pissed at her disappearing into the night by herself in this dangerous city. That it's not just her going out by herself, no, but rather having these feelings like I did from when Stella disappeared churned up in addition to everything Beaux's still keeping from me after all of this time we've spent together.

How I still feel like I know so little about her since she continually changes the subject any and every time we talk about home.

My anger collides with my insecurity and makes me realize just why I'm so upset. No one likes to be made to feel like a fool, and right now it's exactly how I feel. My life, my past, my everything, has been completely opened to her, and while I don't expect her to give me a blow-by-blow of her past, shouldn't she at least offer more than the generalities that I do know?

I run a hand down the back of my neck while I stare into those deep green eyes of hers, needing to step the fuck away from her so that I can gather my thoughts and figure out where my heart and head are, because obviously they are a hell of a lot more invested than hers are.

"Just forget it," I tell her in a voice eerily similar to her emotionless tone.

I walk from the room without another word and head up the stairwell, needing my space to clear my head, take stock, and be by myself. Too much, too damn fast.

I can't help but laugh, though, the sounds dying in the heat of the day as I shove open the door to the rooftop and make my way to my sanctuary. Stella was so damn right, it's comical. I sure as hell feel a lot more than just lust for Beaux right now, and even though I refuse to say the L-word that Stella was so damn fond of using, it doesn't mean my head doesn't see it lurking on the horizon.

"Fuck!" I bark to no one, knowing it's going to be hotter than hell up here right now and not caring, because I just need a few moments, some time not to feel so fucking scattered.

First of all there's Beaux and her lack of emotional investment in this. And the minute the thought crosses my mind, I reject it just as quickly because that's a total bullshit statement. I know she's invested in what's between us. I can see it in her eyes, feel it in her touch. I just wish I knew what the fuck it is that's keeping her from opening up to me. Whatever it is that's holding her back is so damn strong, it's almost tangible.

Maybe I'll call Rafe and ask him more about her. It's not the first time the thought's crossed my mind, but I keep telling myself I need to wait her out, let her tell me in her own time. The question is, how much longer do I wait? At what point will I have to step back to prevent myself from getting hurt?

Except I have the sinking feeling I'm pretty much all in at this point, or else I wouldn't have just reacted like I did.

I scrub my hands over my face. This emotional overload like I'm a damn teenager can stop anytime now.

Fuck. I close my eyes and lean my head against the wall behind me as I take refuge in the tiny bit of shade from the wall the mattress is pushed up against. I haven't been this worked up in a long time, and I feel stupid yet validated in my feelings.

"Tanner?"

"Go away, Beaux."

"We need to talk."

My mind flashes back to the last time I was up here with Stella and the talk we had that led to the kiss.

"No, we don't. You're stubborn, clearly going to do whatever you want without any worry for your own safety, and I just . . . I've already lost one person I cared about because of that lack of caution, and I can't go through that again. Simple as that."

Silence settles around us as if she really heard what I said and recognized the sincerity in my tone. "Is that what this is all about?" She lowers herself beside me on the mattress, yet I refuse to glance over at her.

With so many emotions churning within me, I shouldn't be surprised that I just gave her an insight into Stella's death. And I recognize that was just the tip of the iceberg in a sense, because it's time I finally talk about it. How can I expect her to want to be open with me when I can't be with her?

"This is about you wanting to be partners, but you shut down anytime the discussion turns to you. This is about you promising me one thing and then going out and doing the opposite. This is about losing my best friend because she got caught up in an idea and never saw danger coming until it was too damn late." I shake my head, needing to purge all of my explanations at once, and yet the last one is harder to readily admit than the others. "This is about the fact that you mean something to me and yet you have no regard for your own safety."

Once I've finished, I appreciate that she remains silent, but the hitch of her breath tells me that she heard me loud and clear. She reaches over and laces her fingers with mine, her touch bringing comfort and a little more security in the midst of the sudden isolation I've felt.

"I'm from a small town in the Midwest. Let's see. . . . There's not much to tell really. I had a Norman Rockwell type of upbringing, nothing spectacular, and then my parents died and my world turned upside down." Her voice cracks, and I squeeze her hand, hating myself for asking her to speak about her past and at the same time needing to know, to hear it so that I can connect with her. "I've never been back. I left that town because there were just too many memories there, too much pain in the idea of walking down Main Street to see where my dad used to take me for ice cream or where my mom and I would meet for lunch. Or the place where the drunk driver hit them head-on and they died. So to me it doesn't exist anymore because it reminds me too much of the loss, and I'd rather keep those memories sacred."

I exhale slowly in response to the grief in her voice; it's so raw that I sense that she understands how I feel about Stella, that even after all of this time, she still hasn't fully dealt with the losses in her life either.

The heat makes me sweat and causes my shirt to stick to my skin as I prepare myself to really talk about it for the first time.

"It was my birthday." Those first words are the hardest to get out, namely the admission that I was the cause of Stella's death. "I told Stella not to make a big deal about it, that we'd have a little celebration at the bar later. I told her that I wanted to Skype with my family and have the party downstairs and I was more than happy with that. She agreed. . . ." My voice trails off as I recall the look on her face, the sound of her voice as she promised me that she wouldn't do anything else because the city had been in some major unrest with the opposition making a few daring assaults in the city to make its power known.

"There were a few new freelancers, all eager beavers to get out there and pop their break-the-story cherry. From what I could gather after the fact, Stella was hell-bent on getting me a birthday present. She wanted to get decorations for the bar and pick me up something else. I didn't know any of this obviously, or else I would have stopped*. . . It wouldn't have all happened."

I pause for a second, the memory coming back to me clear as day. The party in full swing in the bar just as dusk fell. Stella snapping picture after picture, telling me, "Pictures make memories last forever," every time I balked when she pointed the shutter my way. I can still feel the way her arms slid around my waist and how she looked up to me as Pauly took the picture that sits on the memory card in the camera on my dresser at home—I've never looked at it, but that image is forever burned in my memory.

"Halfway through the party she disappeared. I couldn't find her. I guess she'd told some of the newbies that she was upset that I wouldn't let her out of my sight long enough for her to surprise me with a birthday present. The new guys didn't know me for shit except for my reputation, and so they wanted to get out in the city, experience the danger they'd come here to witness. She agreed. Said as long as they'd be out and back within thirty minutes so I didn't notice she was gone."

"Oh, Tanner." It's all Beaux says as she shifts her body so she can lean her head on my shoulder, but it's just enough to tell me she knows what's coming next. Understands the guilt that weighs so heavily on me.

"At some point I noticed that the camera was gone. I'd had enough to drink by then, but I remember thinking, *Thank God Stella's not taking pictures anymore*. One thing led to another, and I found out what she was doing when I questioned another reporter who'd overheard them talking. I went apeshit. Ran out of the hotel, sobering up with each step because I swear, Beaux, it was like I knew I had to get to her, sensed something was going to happen to her . . . but it already had by the time I got there." I clear my throat, trying to use my training as a journalist to tell the story, except it's utterly impossible to keep my emotions out of it.

"I guess Stella wanted to get me this satchel thing she'd seen when we'd passed by the market earlier in the month. Nothing big, just *something* to make me feel like I was a little more at home having a normal birthday. Apparently some of the opposition had targeted the location, thought the shopkeeper had turned information or something over to the standing government here from what we can make out. They opened fire on the market when she was paying. Three people were inside. I got there a few minutes after it happened. Tried to save her." I stop talking at that point, can't say anything else for a moment as I turn my head away from her, not wanting her to see my eyes well up.

I use the back of my hand to wipe the tears away before they spill over as she runs her free hand up and down my arm. "I'm so sorry, Tanner. I don't even know what . . . I'd tell you that it's not your fault, but I know more than anyone those words are useless when you feel guilty anyway."

"Yeah," I agree, and turn to face her. "She promised me she'd never go out alone. It was one of the very few times she did. . . ."

"And look what happened," Beaux says, her eyes telling me she gets the correlation I've made between her and Stella, that every time she walks out without me knowing about it, I worry the same thing will happen to her.

We sit in silence, the temperature rising as the sun moves higher in the sky, and I come to terms with the fact that I feel better having told her about Stella and what happened and that maybe, just maybe, she'll feel the same way and tell me her history someday.

Chapter 16

"This is Tanner Thomas reporting live for Worldwide News."

I wait for the Skype connection to end like usual, make sure the feed is dark, before I shut down and close my laptop. I find myself staring at the world beyond as I take a deep breath, wondering where exactly Omid is in that mix. Is my number one source gone for good now that his face is on record? My texts to him saying the pictures have been destroyed have gone unanswered.

I just hope my relationship with him isn't gone too.

"That went well," Beaux says, pulling me from my thoughts so that I turn to watch her as she exits the bathroom, hair wet and robe knotted with a tie around her waist.

I snort. "Thanks. It's the same boring shit, though," I say, scrubbing a hand through my shaggy hair that's starting to drive me crazy. "I'm here to report conflict, action, not repeat the same repetitive crap," I groan to her. "I'm getting antsy. It's been what, a little over two weeks since Sarge called and still nothing."

"Lest you forget the Scrabble tournament. I mean that was scintillating entertainment," she teases, drawing a chuckle from me over one of the lame ways we tried to pass time last week with an impromptu Scrabble challenge amongst all of the journalists. "Who knew *qwerty* was a legitimate and legal word?"

When I meet her eyes, I've got a lopsided smirk on my face over our first real fight over nothing. Every relationship has to have those, and the fact that we hit that milestone makes me feel a little more like we're a normal couple despite this crazy-ass set of circumstances. There is supposed to be a war going on and it's my job to report those events. And not having anything happening makes me feel useless, even though I don't appreciate the evils of combat. Despite the company I get to keep nowadays, I'm feeling bored.

Although that company is definitely not a hardship to look at. I glance back as Beaux walks toward me and take her all in: ebony hair wet and falling over her shoulders making a dark mark on the fabric of her robe, her toned, tanned legs making me wish the thigh-length robe were even shorter, and the press of her nipples through the thin fabric.

"Nothing from Omid?" she asks as if she's been reading my thoughts—and like it's perfectly normal to be talking about sources when my libido is thinking about everything that's beneath the light blue fabric of the robe.

"No." I sigh loudly, my frustration audible. "Not from him or any of my other sources. It's complete radio silence. I think that's part of the problem. I know something is in the works. I agree with Sarge. Everyone is lying low, waiting to see who makes the first move. I know Omid knows something. . . . That's why he's lost in the wind again. If only he would text me back, then I'd feel so much better knowing that there isn't some huge meet going on that we're going to miss, you know?"

"Mmm-hmm," she murmurs as she walks up behind me, presses a kiss to the crown of my head, and runs her fingers through my hair, playing with it where it curls over the tops of my ears.

"That's my story. I've been tracking it for months, worked my ass off to get the contacts to ensure that I'm there when it goes down, and now I feel like it's going to slip through my fingers."

"I understand why you think that . . . but you're just antsy from being stuck in this damn hotel. Maybe you need to get out. Take a walk. It helps me when I do."

I snort out a laugh. "Yeah, I know it helps when you take a walk," I say sarcastically, aware that she's probably rolling her eyes right now. But at the same time I know those solo walks of hers are nonexistent now since I've made a habit of being with her each and every night.

And being smothered never felt so damn good. Especially when it's the weight of her body on top of mine.

"He's probably just playing it safe. He seems totally loyal to you. I'm sure if there was something going on, he'd tell you about it."

"Yeah," I murmur, leaning my head back against the warmth of her belly, while part of me worries about Omid, hoping that he really is okay and nothing has happened to him. "I spoke with Rafe when you were in the shower. He reiterated what he said to you about how much the brass really loves the pictures you're turning in." For some reason I need her to know how incredible they are, especially after all of the shit I gave her in the beginning about not being good enough.

"Thank you," she whispers softly as her fingers thread through my hair, nails scratching my scalp in the most hypnotizing of ways.

"He asked me how we were getting along."

I love the throaty laugh that follows with that hint of the unique rasp of her voice to it. It sounds almost as if she's holding a secret and I'll be the only one she's going to tell. It also causes that slow burn of desire that's always on low flame to start to simmer inside me.

"And what did you tell him?"

"Hmm . . . that we were managing one day at a time. That I still found you irritating and a know-it-all. That it was a real feat for me to sit hours on end with you and not want to strangle you. But that at least you were good at taking photographs because you can't play Scrabble for shit," I deadpan as her hands still in my hair and I wait for her reaction.

"Irritating, huh?" She removes her hands from my scalp and steps in front of me. She lifts an eyebrow in challenge as I try to figure out just where she's going with this.

"Yep. And a know-it-all," I say with a nod and a smart-ass smile on my lips as my eyes flicker down to the deep V of where her robe parts. Only about a foot-long section is closed now, affording me a killer view of her cleavage down to just above her belly button and a lot of leg, and damn if I don't suddenly lose all train of thought.

"Well, Pulitzer, I'm so sorry that it's so taxing for you to have to sit with me all . . . day . . . long," she says in the breathiest of voices, drawing every single word out at the same time she steps forward and stands so that her legs straddle both of my thighs. I slide my eyes ever so slowly from her legs up her torso to meet her gaze, my hands itching to reach out and touch, but shit, I'll let her take the reins for a bit to see just where she takes this because I'm liking the direction already.

"It's a *hard* job, but somebody's got to do it," I say with emphasis. And of course at that same moment she lowers herself to sit astride my lap, ass on my knees, placing the enticing heat of her pussy right atop my cock. I have to hold back the wave of dizziness that threatens to assault me from the downright mind-rattling sensation.

"I like *hard* jobs," she whispers as she leans in and brushes her lips against mine so that I can smell the toothpaste on her breath and the lotion on her skin. I lean forward to try and deepen the kiss, but she pushes her hands against my chest to keep me still in my chair while her hand snakes between her parted thighs to cup me.

And while damn those fingernails felt incredible on my scalp, the muted sensation of them scraping over the fabric hugging my nuts is Heaven. I groan, a man wanting his woman and not ashamed to show it. "Beaux . . ." My head falls back as the feeling of her more-than-competent hands on me shifts my train of thought from one frustration to a whole different type.

"Don't speak, Tanner," she says, causing me to snap my head forward and catch the taunt in her smile and desire in her eyes. "I'm annoying." She slides backward off my lap. "And irritating." She drops to her knees before me. "And while I may suck at Scrabble, I can suck other things much better."

Yes. Please.

Our eyes hold, her lips twist with humor, and as I look at her on her knees before me with her hands running up my thighs, her thumbs stroking over my khaki-clad cock, the only thought I can process is what a lucky man I am.

We never break eye contact as her hands push my knees apart so that she can wiggle her way in between them and her hands begin to work the button and zipper on the shorts. In perfect sync with her, I lift up as she tugs my clothes down, and my dick springs free.

I love watching her eyes light up at knowing I'm hard and waiting for her without much if any foreplay. Shit, she could blow a cold breeze my way and I'd be ready for her. Even better than the look in her eyes is watching her have to make the conscious decision to tear her eyes from mine and look down at what's waiting for her.

And call it male ego, call it machismo, I don't give a fuck, but it's such a turn-on watching her eyes widen and her tongue dart out and lick her bottom lip when she looks down. Every part of my body feels like it is standing at attention, waiting for the next touch, her mouth to take me in, the enticing visual of watching her suck me off.

Her eyes dart up to meet mine one more time as she lowers her head and puts my dick in her mouth. And it's not like she teases me, puts the tip in and licks her tongue around the head to taunt me with promises of what's to come next. Hell no. She lowers her mouth onto my cock and keeps going all the way until I hit the back of her throat.

"Goddamn," I moan brokenly.

The sensation is so damn overwhelming that I want to close my eyes and savor it and at the same time don't want to miss the sight of her working me in and out between her lips. One hand cups my balls, fingernails teasing the sensitive skin there while the other wraps around the base of my cock, following her mouth up and down with an added pressure that drives me fucking insane. She takes me all the way to the back of her throat again so that I can feel the vibration of the moan she emits against my dick. Her green eyes flutter up to meet mine as she holds still there.

And the sight of her cheeks hollowed and lips stretched around me, stuns me motionless. Something passes between us. Something more than just the desire coursing through us or the act we're engaging in. And it's fleeting, but it's unmistakable.

The mix of sensations, tight grip followed by soft lips, her quiet moans of desire mixed with my harsh grunts of pleasure, my hand fisted tightly in her wet hair, and the endless pleasure of going deeper and deeper in her mouth catapults me to the edge of reason so damn fast that I'm holding her head still and bucking my hips in natural reflex.

I come fast and hard; my pants are harsh, my heart is lost, all sensibility thrown out the damn window as the grenade of sensation explodes within me, streaking up and back down in a fiery flash of everything and nothing all at once.

And she's so fucking incredible as she rides out my orgasm, her mouth sucking me dry, her fingers becoming more gentle as my muscles contract and my dick becomes hypersensitive. My muscles start to relax, and she must sense it because the vibration of her chuckle around my cock still in her mouth is like a little aftershock of sensation that breaks through the fog of my climax.

She pulls back and just looks at me with a cat-that-ate-the-canary grin. "How are we going to explain that one to Rafc, huh? That's all you, my wordy friend."

It takes me a minute to get my wits about me, my mind still reeling from the unexpected but completely welcome blow job at the hands of BJ Croslyn. The irony.

"Up to me?" My voice sounds drugged and drowsy, and fuck if I'm going to apologize for it. "I seem to think you have journalist in your title too."

Her laugh is low and seductive as I reach out and pull her back up to sit astride me, my hands working on undoing the knot of her robe, needing to feel her skin on skin. "Oh but you forget, I report with pictures, so I don't quite think we're going to document what exactly just happened."

"Mmm, probably not." I look up to her, our positions allowing her face to hover slightly above mine so I can see her eyes widen as I slide my hands inside her robe, my rough palms against the smooth skin of the undersides of her breasts. "But I might want to document a few things myself with your equipment of what's going to happen next."

"Oh really?" she asks, the words starting out strong but then ending in a sigh as my thumbs flick over the hardened tips of her nipples. I love watching her like this, eyes hazy with desire and her lips fallen lax from the pleasure I can bring her. "What's going to happen next?"

Without saying a word, I reach down in the space between our thighs, brush my fingers over her pussy, and find it slick with desire. And the fact that she's wet from sucking me off has my own libido already stirring back awake, her ability to make my body expedite my recovery time almost frightening. She gasps at the feel of my fingers just barely touching her as they find the tie of her robe and place it between her legs with one hand so that it falls through the opening that both of our parted thighs make. I grab it with my other hand so that one hand holds the robe tie at her back while the other holds it just above the front of her pelvis.

"Uh-uh," I command as she looks down. "I want to watch you, want to see in your eyes what I do to you. Keep your eyes on me."

And a quiet hush falls around us so that the anticipation thickens, our eyes locked, her mind wondering exactly what I'm going to do next. Drawing things out, I take the sash and press it against the cleft of her sex. Her legs tense at the feel of it there, but when I slowly start to rub it back and forth, I work it between the lips of her pussy so that it rubs with perfect friction over her clit. The first time her eyes widen and her breath hitches at the newness of the sensation before her head falls back for a moment to absorb the unexpected feeling. But then as I continue to move the tie ever so slowly back and forth and watch the sensation swamp her as she fights to keep her eyes from closing with the pleasure of it, the moan that falls from her mouth tells me she likes it.

Her hands flash out to grip my shoulders, and her hips slowly begin to move opposite the pull of the sash as she tries to chase the release. The strained moans she makes, the bite of her fingernails digging in my flesh, the heat of her ass rubbing back and forth on my bare thighs—all of it and then a thousand other things I can't even put in words make me fall for her ten times harder than when her lips were wrapped around me.

Because there is something so damn powerful in making a woman come. With men, an orgasm is basically a given, but with women? As a man you have to work at making them climax, have to know where to stroke and just how hard to rub. It usually takes communication, a lot of trial and error before you learn each other's bodies enough to not have to speak other than to praise and enhance the moment.

But with Beaux, she doesn't have to instruct and I don't have to ask. Our bodies just know, just respond and react without so much as a word exchanged between us.

I vary the pressure and speed as I pull and rub the sash along her body, my mouth closing around the peaks of her breasts as she arches her back when the pleasure starts to become too much for her body to absorb. Her legs tense over mine as her head falls forward onto my shoulder. Her control begins to give way to pleasure and incoherency. We remain like this for a single, powerful heartbeat of time with her teeth nipping my shoulder and my hands working her into a fever pitch.

And when she comes, her strained voice calling my name, her hips bucking wildly against my body, her wetness evident on my own thighs, the only thought that remains in my head is it doesn't get any more powerful than this.

Physically.

And emotionally.

She's my little piece of Heaven in this land full of Hell,

Chapter 17

The heat has my clothes plastered to my skin from sweat as the sounds and scents of the city around me permeate my pores and all five senses. It's a feeling you think you'll get used to the longer you spend on-site but never do. *I'm pulling a Beaux,* I think to myself with a smile as I walk through the city's dilapidated streets, venturing out without telling anyone.

I needed the fresh air, the time to myself to sort some shit out in my head while finding a few things to complete the surprise I have planned for Beaux, because as much as it pains me to admit my sister was right, she was. Beaux and I are in a relationship. We may not have verbalized it, but I think I silently erased that fine line between dating and relationship a while ago and just pretended like I wasn't looking. And as for the three words that most people hang their hat on, we may not have said them, but it doesn't matter. When you spend almost every waking minute with someone — with as much time in the sheets as you spend talking and getting to know each other out of bed — over a several-month period, you're in a relationship.

And since that's the case, I figured I ought to up my game some in the boyfriend department. It must be a miracle, because for the second time in a day, I'm caving in to something Rylee said . . . I'm trying to manufacture an out-of-the-ordinary night for Beaux without anyone knowing.

She needs it. We need it. Something simple in nature but special at the same time. We've both been climbing the walls with boredom as we wait for a story, any story, even a human interest story. Anything besides rehashing the same shit ad nauseam, because as much as I don't long for international conflict, there is no denying it prevents people in this instant-gratification day and age from flipping the channel to find something newer and more spectacular.

So I've got most of my night for Beaux planned. I've bribed the hotel manager with cash to help get the rest of the items I don't have the ability to get myself. And now I'm just searching for the final few things while Beaux is back at the hotel sleeping in my bed with strict instructions for Pauly to interfere should she wake before I get back and wander downstairs to the lobby.

There is definite irony in the fact that I find myself sneaking out to wander the city's streets at night.

But I'm so lost in thought, so consumed by Beaux's and Ry's comments, that when I look up, my feet falter when I notice where I've unconsciously veered. My breath catches in my throat as I stand in the one place I've yet to come since being back, the place where Stella died.

The market front looks so benign, nothing like the horrible nightmares that flash through my sleep every so often now. The smell of death is gone, the dark stains of blood nonexistent, the fear riddling through my soul absent. All I feel is a bone-deep sadness when I take in the open windows with wares hanging all around the canopy and the cart out front displaying random items—there's not a single thing to commemorate the loss of someone so damn important to me.

Immediately, I long to walk away and quiet the images that keep coming back into my mind, but at the same time I can recognize that I need to face this for a moment, allow myself to say good-bye one last time in the one place where my world was turned upside down. Maybe then I can finish finding a bit of the peace that being with Beaux has allowed me to start to feel.

So instead, I take a step forward, my fingertips running over the woven bags and childish trinkets on the table, my eyes searching for any sign that Stella existed here. I know it's stupid and that it won't prove anything, but I feel like I need something to be here, to validate my grief in order to help lay it to rest. I begin rifling through the bags hanging off the canopy in front of the crumbling walls of the storefront. I tell myself I need a bag like this for Beaux's surprise, but there's no denying I'm reaching for an excuse until I find what I'm looking for.

Then I move closer and lean over the table, my hand reaching out so that my fingertip fits in the bullet hole that's been left unrepaired in the store's facade. My finger stays frozen there, the nightmares of that night colliding at a ferocious pace with the good memories of the ten years Stella was in my life until they crumble to pieces, falling with the guilt laid at my feet.

I inhale deeply through a clenched jaw and face all the emotion that's overwhelming me right now, good, bad, and irrevocable. I shake my head softly, a soft smile on my face as I remember our last full night together. Our kiss. Our promise. That smile of hers and the friendship we had for so long.

"Good-bye, Stella," I whisper, my words carried away in the sounds of the streets around me and the music coming through the store's window before me. I hang my head for a moment and close my eyes. *I'd be your once-in-a-lifetime, your goddamn everything if you'd come back.*

But I know she can't.

And I know that she was one of the most incredible people I'll ever meet. I know that I'd live the lie if given the chance to make her happy even though I know now that she wasn't my once-in-a-lifetime in return. I'd have been cheating the both of us of that chance to find it. Our friendship was the strongest one I've ever had the fortune to experience, but that sexual chemistry wasn't strong like it should be.

Not like the way it is between Beaux and me.

So maybe that's why I'm here. Maybe I'm saying good-bye to one woman so that I can give myself completely to another. And yes, Stella and I were more like siblings than a romantic couple, but when you're that close to someone for so long, you still feel like you are cheating on them in a sense when you start to move on with someone new, sharing a friendship, your confessions, your laughter, your comfortable silence.

Once I've had my moment with her memory, holding on to the image in my mind of Stella laughing from behind her camera and shedding the horrible ones of that night as best as I can, I'm determined to leave the pain here and move forward with the happy memories.

With my head still angled down, I open my eyes, and something about the sight in front of me makes me smile. There is a bowl on the table filled with small bottles of bubbles. Although it's amongst a hodgepodge of items, it's such a welcome sight nonetheless because it brings up memories of Rylee and me growing up. Her theory at eight years old that blowing bubbles makes everything better because you can't say the word *bubble* without smiling. How when the bullies in third grade picked on her when I was home sick from school one day, I brought out a bottle of bubbles to where she sat sniffling on the swings in the backyard and made her blow bubbles until she smiled. And then of course I went to school the next day and earned some detention for persuading them with my fists to not pick on my little sister again.

Or how, years later, after her eighth grade formal when she came home upset that no one had asked her to dance, I brought out a bottle of bubbles, again to the swings that hadn't been used in years, and made her blow them until she laughed.

With a huge smile on my face, I immediately know that even though Beaux doesn't know the significance of bubbles to me, she'd love them and the small piece of normality that they represent.

Besides, who doesn't love bubbles?

With the bubbles and a colorful tote bag stuffed into my backpack so Beaux won't see them, I leave the shop, the weight of grief a little lighter in my heart for the first time since Stella's death. Glancing at my watch, I realize I need to get my ass back to the hotel before Beaux wakes up and discovers that I snuck out.

Just as I'm crossing the street, my phone alerts a text, and I cringe in fear that I've been caught. My mind is already scrambling for the excuses I'd prepared, but suddenly my feet falter as I look at the name lighting up my screen. It's Omid with a text: They are here. Many in my village. I think the meet happened today. Sorry. Did not know.

My heart sinks as soon as I read his message. Mostly because I didn't come through for Sarge and the good guys but also for the lost opportunity of reporting on a meet that no one else knew was happening. Fuck. That single word sums up how I feel and then some so much that it bears repeating. *Fuck*.

I stop in my tracks on the sidewalk and type out a text as fast as I can: When? How many? Where? Meet me. I could go on endlessly with the questions, but the language barrier would make it impossible to persuade him to give me any further information. I need to see Omid face-to-face; I need to have Beaux there to translate if there's any hope of having this situation not be so damn fucked.

"Answer, Omid," I groan into the night as I stare at my screen with the hope fading that the harder I stare, the quicker he will respond. After a few minutes I realize that standing here is not going to help anything, so I start hurrying back to the hotel when at last I get his reply.

Not now. Dangerous. Trust gone like I said last week. No more.

My mind races as I try to figure out the text. Last week? Did he text me last week and I didn't get it? Trust is gone? From Beaux taking a picture? Yes, but what I don't get is I didn't speak to him last week. What the fuck? I growl out in frustration. Fucking cell phones and their limited service in this godforsaken land. What did he text me that I didn't get?

And *no more*? *No more what?* I want to yell. No more people there? No more information? No more being a source? *What?*

I'm frustrated and disappointed and just disheartened at the missed opportunities all around. Defeated, I look at my screen one more time before picking it up and dialing a number. The phone rings several times, and just as I'm about to hang up, he answers.

"Hello?"

"Sarge. Here's what I've got . . ." And I tell him what I know.

Chapter 18

"Tell me again why we use your room for reports?" I ask Beaux as I look over to her and laugh when she shifts on the bed and the springs squeak.

"Location, location, location," she says, and I join in on the last repeat of the word with her. And really she is right. At this time of day, the early evening's natural light through the windows is soft enough that I can file a live report and not look like I'm cordoned off in some darkened cell like I would if I were in my room.

"I'll give you location, all right," I tease as I turn my computer off and hold my hand out to her. "Come with me." I love the little surprised tilt of her head.

She stands cautiously, squinting her eyes as she tries to figure out just what I'm doing. And it's nothing really, nothing except realizing Beaux deserves a little something special, something girlie in this land where we're faced with so much harshness.

The rooftop door sticks like usual until I thrust with my shoulder on the right-hand edge to get it to fling back. Beaux laughs as I play up my demonstration of strength by pointing out the dent in the metal that's always been there. With fingers crossed that all of my preparation and bribes have worked perfectly, I put my hand on the small of her back and usher her over the threshold first.

She walks from habit around the one rooftop vent that blocks the view of my spot, and the minute she clears it—the moment I hear her sharp intake of air, my name in a surprised tone on her lips followed by a hand flying up to her mouth—I know the past week's preparation has paid off. Beaux turns to face me, tears welling in her eyes before looking back to the scene before us as she walks slowly toward the mattress.

When I can force myself to look away from her, I'm filled with relief to see the scene set to perfection by some of the hotel staff that I had paid on the side. A small canopy made with local fabrics from the closest market has been rigged to hang above the mattress. Scattered across the ground are glass votive candles that create a soft light against the skyline. The mattress itself has a new cover; the colorful tote I bought sits on top of it.

Beaux takes in everything, her hands smoothing over the fabric, moving past the flame of a candle, and running over the mattress. All the while her eyes flicker back and forth to me to make sure all of this is real.

"You did this?" The incredulity in her voice tugs on every damn heartstring I have. "How? Why? I . . ." Her voice fades off as she shakes her head.

"It's not much, but—"

"It's perfect!" There's appreciation and so much more woven in her tone. "Just perfect."

And the repetition of the word mixed with the break in her voice tells me that this was the right thing to do, that my sister was right: Every woman needs to feel like she matters regardless of how many hours you spend together a day.

"I won't take all of the credit. I had some help." Her eyes whip over to mine, but I just smile at her. "Relax. Hotel staff that don't know us from Adam. It wasn't anyone who works with us."

When her smile softens as she turns to survey the scene again, I reach out and grab her hand, tugging her body so it lands firmly against mine. As she looks up to me, her eyelashes flutter, and her eye color is such a sharp green in this vast backdrop of tan landscape. "I just wanted to give you a real date like you deserve. Something more than sex in a hotel room . . ." I pause when we both laugh. "Which is kind of the only way we can have it here, considering the circumstances, but . . ." I have to stop myself from rambling, because even though I am never unsure of myself around women, for some reason, right now, I am nervous.

I don't know if it's the look in her eyes or the fact that this is the first time in forever that I really, truly wanted to try to make something special for someone, but the sudden sense of insecurity that I feel is foreign and oddly welcoming. Yet at the same time the feeling is a pain in the ass.

And I think she senses my conflict, sees me falter over the words that I can't form, because she steps up on tiptoe, uses her hands on my shirt to pull me down to her, and presses her lips against mine. The kiss lingers over the next several minutes, tongues fluttering as we drink each other in, before she leans back and looks at me. "It's the nicest thing that anyone has done for me in as long as I can remember. Thank you. It means more to me than you'll ever know." Tears glisten in her eyes as I pull her into my chest, wrap my arms around her, and just hold on.

We stand like this as time moves slowly amid the glow of tiny flickers of light and colors illuminating the sky on the horizon. And then, I begin to sway back and forth with her, stepping side to side, dancing to the beat of our heartbeats in rhythm together. I twirl her out at arm's length, her gasp of surprise turning to a laugh that causes her head to fall back and her hair to hang farther down her back. She spins into my arms again, so that our chests touch and our hearts are connected once more.

"I guess I could play some music on my phone," I say in a pseudo apology, suddenly embarrassed that I forgot such an important element of the evening. But when I start to let her go, she just holds on tighter.

"No. Don't. It's perfect just like this. Everything is . . ." Her voice trails off as emotion thickens it.

So we dance for a few more minutes, spinning around the rooftop and laughing until our bodies home in on the need to be close again, before we sit down on the mattress. Beaux looks at me over the bag, and her face lights up when she pulls out a bottle of wine followed by cheap plastic glasses and some cheese, crackers, and chocolate. "Oh my God, this looks like Heaven!" She takes a bite of the gourmet cheese that I had to pay an arm and a leg to get here, but for the look in her eyes and the smile on her face, I'd have paid double.

"I pulled out all the stops. Even the fine china," I tease, thinking that in a way this date is beyond silly but still perfectly fitting for the two of us. In the life we lead chasing stories, it comes down to the little things that mean so very much—and tonight I'm glad to know by her reaction that she feels the same way.

"You did!" she says as she leans over the food spread between us and presses her mouth to mine. "When did you do all of this?"

"You're not the only one who can go wandering the streets all by themselves, rookie." I give her a quirk of my brow and receive a head shake from her in return.

"Should I give you the same lecture you give me?"

"It's different."

"No it's not!" She swats my arm.

"I'm a guy. It's totally different," I repeat.

"And I'm a woman," she says, crossing her arms over her chest in mock irritation.

"That you are," I murmur, a suggestive smirk turning up the corners of my mouth. "A mighty fine one at that, and I most definitely am not complaining."

"Good to know you approve."

I trace my fingertips up the bare skin of her thighs. "Oh I approve, rookie. I definitely approve." Desire stirs in an atomic bomb of need curling in the pit of my stomach.

"Later, Pulitzer. You'll get to approve a lot more later." She laughs as she pushes the bottle of wine against my chest to fend me off.

"That's cold!" I take the bottle, though, and start to open it.

"Do you actually think you are going to hand a woman who has been deprived of indulgences a bottle of wine and a bag of chocolate and who knows what else is in here and think you're going to distract her with sex?"

"Did I just get denied for food?"

"It's not just food. *It's chocolate.* That's like the holy— Tanner, what is . . . really?" Her voice escalates in excitement and then laughter as she pulls two kid-sized bottles of bubbles from the bag.

She glances over to me again, and I can feel the look she gives me along every single inch of my skin causing the part of me that second-guessed the bottles to vanish. The look is raw and real and vulnerable and accepting and so many other things I stop trying to analyze because right here, right now, I have an absolutely gorgeous woman sitting beside me, enamored with the silly little touches I added to the date, and so there's no need to question a damn thing. I'm just going with it.

"Bubbles," she says softly. "I haven't opened a bottle since I was a kid. But I used to love to sit in the front yard blowing them and watch the breeze take them up in flight, and see just how far they could go before they popped. Do you have any idea how cool it is you bought these for me?"

"I wanted us to take tonight to enjoy the little things." I shrug as she reaches out to squeeze my hand. "Besides, no one will ever regret the time they spend blowing bubbles."

"Never," she whispers softly before breaking the moment and looking away, almost as if she's afraid I'll look too deeply inside her and see the feelings written all over her face.

She opens the bottle as I finish pouring the wine, and by the time I've handed her a glass, she's blowing a blizzard of bubbles around us. We dig into the cheese and chocolate, all smiles even though we are in a fierce battle, first over who can blow the biggest bubble and then who can get a bubble to travel the farthest before it pops.

"Yes! See! Mine is definitely bigger!" I raise my arms in triumph as her laughter booms around me.

"I guess I'm a lucky woman then since yours is the biggest," she says sarcastically. Glancing over, I spot a small bubble still on the top of her hair.

"Lucky you," I murmur as I reach out to cup the side of her face, my thumb brushing over her bottom lip. But deep down I know I'm the lucky one. Hands down. I lean forward to show her just that—that her being here with me is so much more than a mere consequence of workplace attraction that will fade when the assignment ends—and brush my lips against hers.

Our kiss deepens, then lingers as we pour all of the emotions we feel into it. I lean back some, prop myself up on an elbow, and brush the hair away from her cheek as I stare into her eyes. There are so many things I want to say, so many things I want to confess and need her to know, but the words die on my tongue because all I can think of is, how in the hell did I find this incredible woman in this hellish place?

"Tanner?" she murmurs with lips swollen from my kisses and with a desirous expression in her eyes.

"Hmm?" Her body is so warm and inviting that I'm more focused on the feel of her against me than on what she's going to say next.

"I've fallen in love with you. How are you going to handle that one?"

All I can do is stare at her as my heart tumbles in my chest and every nerve ending in my body reacts viscerally to her words. I don't know what the fuck this feeling is, but I know the sound of those words being said to me scares me and exhilarates me like never before. I just sit there, my face inches from hers as a slow, smug smile tugs up the corners of my mouth. The words to echo her admission stall on my lips.

"Hmm, I think we need to blow more bubbles," I say with a resolute nod of my head, and I flash her a smile.

"Bubbles?" she says, obviously taken aback by my response.

"Yep, bubbles. Because that means nothing has changed from a few minutes ago except now I finally know this is real between us. That what I see in your eyes and how you look at me is real. That what I feel is real." I drop my head down for a minute, totally blown away by the moment, by the surge of inexplicable emotions within me. "Beaux . . . I . . . I . . ."

My voice fades off because for the slightest of seconds

Stella's comment flickers through my mind. About how when the love I feel is real, I won't be so quick to say the words back to someone. It turns out that she was absolutely fucking right. When you really mean it, you don't want the other person to think you said it out of obligation.

As I continue attempting to speak, to untangle myself from the asshole I feel like while I'm stuttering and falling flat, I need to make sure she doesn't take my reaction the wrong way. It's not that I don't feel the same, because I do. It's just that I don't even know what to say or how to react, and it's pretty damn hard to figure out when your heart is racing out of control and your mind is thinking of possibilities.

But she doesn't let me talk. She just presses a finger against my lips and shakes her head. "I don't want you to respond. I just want you to kiss me," she whispers.

So I do the only thing I can. I kiss her. But not just any kiss. I take everything I feel inside and try to express it with the tenderness and reverence of my touch. And just as her fingers thread through my hair and my hand finds its way beneath her tank top, my phone disrupts the rooftop's silence.

We both groan, but at the same time the distinct ring tells me it's Sarge, and a quick glance at the face of my phone tells me my assumption is correct.

"What is it with him and his awful timing?" I mutter as I lift my phone to my ear, recognizing that it's the second time he's interrupted us. "Sarge," I say in the way of hello to also let Beaux know I didn't break the moment up between us over something unimportant.

"Be at the usual meeting place tomorrow. We move out at sixteen hundred hours." His voice is clipped, all business.

"What's going on? Yes, of course. We'll be there," I respond, my words trying to catch up when I'd felt like

I'd lost this story and now here's a chance to report it. "Was my source—"

"Wrong. Very wrong. No questions, Thomas. You and BJ are on the mission, but you will be removed from the action. We're coming in for cleanup after air support moves out."

"Can—"

"I said no questions," he snaps, not letting me get a word out. "It's this or nothing. I'm sure Pauly would kill for the ride if you have a problem with the terms."

I'd say he's under a bit of stress right now since I've never heard him like this.

"Ten-four. We'll be there at sixteen hundred hours."

As the line disconnects, I look up to meet Beaux's widened eyes before dropping the phone on the mattress beside me. "We're in, baby!" I exclaim, completely confused over the information that Omid gave me but reeling because that buzz is back with such a vengeance that when she raises her arms in the air and lets out a whoop, I tackle her playfully until she's on her back and my body is flanking hers.

"I thought we were going to blow more bubbles?" She giggles, and it's the best sound.

"Bubbles can wait. I've got more pressing things to do," I tell her as I push my hips forward before smothering her laughter with my own mouth, to try and take advantage of the moment and the high of being with her tonight and what promises to be a kick-ass exclusive tomorrow. She responds without hesitation, hands hooking under my arms and over my shoulders, and actions speaking without words.

I lose myself to the moment under the cover of this desert night with the star-riddled sky above and a woman who loves me beneath me.

Chapter 19

I replay Sarge's phone call from last night in my mind and try to piece everything together. The crux of what I can't figure out is why Omid would tell me the meet had happened when it hadn't. Was he found out? Was he trying to protect me? Or more likely himself from a threat?

I remind myself I shouldn't care because we're getting to ride along and get the story and that's what we are here to do. But it still bugs me to the point that I'm wasting time surfing the Internet.

But when I raise my eyes above the screen of my laptop, I stop worrying simply because it's much more interesting to watch Beaux while she works. She's methodical and precise and double-checks everything as she moves through her camera bag to make sure each compartment is properly filled, adding extra batteries, memory cards, lenses, and filters.

She's in perfect silhouette against the sun's rays behind her that are somewhat muted from the sheer panels on the window. And she's not doing anything fascinating, yet I can't keep my eyes off her.

Perhaps it's the words she expressed last night that I can't get out of my head nor stop thinking about. The ones that made me realize how very meaningless everyone else before her has been. I mean, yeah, I loved Stella, but not this way. Not the kind where I start to look at the future stretched out beyond the next assignment, the next country, or after the hard beat's over.

I wonder if this is how she'd look on the deck in my backyard with the ocean behind her: wisps of hair dancing around her face, a drink in her hand, and the freedom to do as we please without the danger that hinders and plagues our every movement here. Could we survive as a couple in the everyday world? With real life and the problems it creates?

The thought makes me shake my head, because of course we could. We've spent every day together for weeks on end in the tight confines of the hotel. Sure our relationship—because yes, I can most definitely admit that this is a relationship now—is still in the proverbial butterflies-in-the-stomach stage, but we are under a constant pressure here that doesn't normally occur in the real world. We've gotten annoyed with each other, figured out how to give each other space, and passed the ever-important phase of don't-push-each-other's-buttons-on-purpose.

Suddenly I scrub a hand through my hair, completely and utterly shocked at my train of thought. The no-go compartment of my mind opened without the crowbar I thought I might need someday to even begin this thought process.

Then my fingers run back and forth on my keyboard, lost in thought momentarily before I lift my phone without her knowing and frame her in the lens of the camera.

"Do you ever think you'll quit this life someday?" The question comes out almost on a murmur, my thoughts spoken aloud as I click the shutter on my screen.

Beaux's hands fall still, half-submerged in her camera bag, when she turns her head to look at me. Her eyes narrow as I click another photo.

"What are you doing?" She smiles shyly.

"Ah, the photographer doesn't like to be the subject, now does she?" I tease as I click another one, a shot that turns out blurry since she's walking toward the bed.

"Never." She laughs softly, angling her head to the side as she takes a step toward me where I sit on the bed in my boxer briefs, one hand behind my head against the headboard, the other holding my phone. "Gimme."

"No way." I laugh as she crawls her way over my legs, picks up my laptop to move it off my lap, and takes its place. At the warmth of her pussy resting right over where I want her the most, I have to bite back the hiss I want to emit. "Are you trying to distract me, Croslyn?"

"Nope. I just wanted to add you in the picture."

I stop fighting immediately at the comment, my eyes meeting hers and loving the coy smile that spreads over her lips. She leans forward and brushes a kiss to my lips before causing me to groan when she slides off my lap to sit beside me with her head resting in the crook of my arm.

"Smile," she says as she holds the phone out and captures us together in the small square window. "See? Perfect. Now what were you asking me?"

I'm reminded immediately of my question that had slipped out, but I refrain from repeating it. "Nothing. Forget about it. It was nothing."

"No it wasn't. Nice try, though." She shifts her body so that her head is on my chest and one hand runs idly up and down my midline. "You asked if I'll ever quit this life."

"Mmm-hmm," I murmur.

"Will you?" she asks, and I'm so mesmerized by the

surge of desire I feel at her touch that I don't immediately realize I'm answering my own question before she does.

"Someday when my career has run its course ... This life isn't fair to kids, and I definitely want to have kids someday."

"How will you know it's run its course?" she asks, pressing a soft kiss to the underside of my neck.

"When the buzz is gone," I say matter-of-factly. "Then I'll know that I'm too complacent, too cautious, and not worthy of this job anymore."

She's quiet for a moment, and I can sense her collecting her thoughts, trying to figure out what I mean. "The buzz?"

"Yeah. That adrenaline buzz you get from getting a story or for you the perfect shot. The one that—"

"Lights your blood on fire and makes you fidget with the unexpected anticipation of what's to come next," she finishes for me, and causes my breath to hitch because she gets it. Gets me. That's a rarity.

"Exactly." I press a kiss into the crown of her head. "The day I no longer feel that from the first phone call on, I need to hang up my credentials." I laugh halfheartedly. "But I don't see that happening anytime soon. I love what I do too much. Am addicted to that buzz in a sense. It's what drives me on a story, and the promise of it is what keeps me patient in the lulls between them."

"I feel the same way, in a sense. I always told myself I'd do this job until I met *the one*," she says, reminding me immediately of that first night we met, the "You're the one" that fell from her lips, and I immediately clear away the thought, knowing that isn't exactly what she was referring to. "And then I'd have to domesticate myself, and my only clients would be babies and brides." She mock shivers. "So in other words I'll be doing this for a long time, because I don't feel that urge coming anytime soon. What would you do, though, Tanner, if you didn't do this?" Curiosity infuses her tone, and for the first time ever, I don't feel stupid telling someone besides my family the answer.

"I'd like to write a book." I wait for her to make a sarcastic comment, but none comes.

"You'd be good at it," she muses in a way that warms me from within. "Some people like to create storms and then complain when it rains. You, on the other hand, like to stand back, watch the storm move in, churn, and affect people, and then document the fight and fallout. You're able to separate yourself from the emotions of it all in self-preservation, and yet you can still explain and express what happened so that people feel like they were there. It's an incredible gift."

Frankly, I'm a little shocked by her assessment. Flattered by it really. "Thank you," I murmur to Beaux. It's all I can say as a comfortable silence falls around us, and I wonder if her thoughts are as foggy as mine on the topic right now. I shift my weight so that we are lying face-to-face on our sides with my hand on the side of her neck; I'm enjoying this moment and completely ignoring the hornet's nest we will be walking into later today on the embed.

She responds instantly when I brush my lips against hers, her body fitting into mine perfectly as I deepen the kiss.

I lean back and look into her eyes, knowing that my period of hesitation is over. I've let the emotions churn and swell within me long enough, and I'm ready to tell her. "Hey, Beaux? I l—"

"Open up, Thomas!" A fist pounding on the hotel room door knocks the words from my mouth. As soon as she recognizes Pauly's voice, Beaux scrambles up from the bed to grab for a pair of jeans resting over the back of a chair.

"Hold on!" she calls out, but looks at me with a mixture of unease about getting caught in a relationship—as if Pauly didn't already know since he's knocking on the door of her room—and confusion over why in the hell I'm not getting some clothes on myself. I snicker as she does the hop-around-to-get-into-her-jeans thing and then succumb to full-blown laughter when she falls over to the ground in the process.

I rise calmly from the bed and pull on my own jeans and slip a shirt over my head as I walk to open the door, still laughing at what just happened. Once I know Beaux is clothed and doesn't look like we were just rolling around in the sheets, I open the door.

"What's up, man?" I open the door for him to come in and head back to stand near the table, sliding Beaux a glance and trying not to laugh.

"Nothing. I was just curious if you'd gotten wind of anything, because word on the street is you might have gotten a mission to tag along on," he says as he leans a shoulder against the wall, eyes flicking back and forth between Beaux and me, lips pursed, expression leery.

Fuck. Now I have to lie to my friend on top of being mad at him for interrupting us and the perfect moment for me to tell Beaux I was in love with her too.

"Possibly. I'm still waiting to hear from my contact." I figure a partial truth is better than a complete lie.

Still, the moment he asked, I knew Pauly was on the scent, and he'd follow us in his own transportation if necessary in order to get the story he thinks we have for his own, which means we need to figure out how to leave in the next few hours and do so without him finding out.

Chapter 20

The scent of destruction is one you never forget and one you can recognize at the first whiff. It also helped that for the hour-long ride to the village, we could hear the F/A 18 fighter jets overhead followed minutes later by the squelch of the radio and then Sarge relaying to us that a direct hit was made.

Sitting in the back of the armed transport carrier in the dim light, one thigh pressed against Beaux's and the other against Rosco's, I could feel that buzz humming through me, that rush that had been missing while I sat for hours on end in the hotel, watching the insects fly in endless circles around the lobby.

As the rocky terrain jostled us around, our combat helmets hit the metal of the transport behind us more times than we cared to count, but that only amplified the anticipation of what was going to greet us when we got our boots on the ground. Being packed like sardines in the Stryker, shoulder to shoulder, made it impossible to turn and meet Beaux's eyes, to make sure she was okay without speaking aloud and giving away that I might care a little more than I should about my colleague. But I tried to ascertain her comfort level in other ways. With my hands flat on my thighs, I ever so subtly moved my pinkie finger to brush over the edge of where our thighs met. Just enough to let her know I was there, next to her, looking out for her.

But that was all I could do. The words I wanted, no, needed, to say, were lost for now in a lack of opportunity between when Pauly interrupted us and we were forced to slip out of the hotel on the sly, to the crazy cab ride where Beaux was stuck giving turn-by-turn directions to the driver in Dari until we arrived at the meeting location. Surrounded by soldiers geared and amped up on the adrenaline of the big raid stretched out before them, their excitement was palpable. In order to do our job, Beaux and I both needed to be in the right mind-set.

I never got the chance to tell her: either the moment was not perfect enough, my timing was off, or my courage gave way due to other circumstances.

Once we start making our way on foot to the bombing sites, the click of Beaux's shutter accompanies the background noise of the soldiers' boots crunching over cobbled streets, and the intermittent conversations between stern voices in English and confused villagers speaking in Dari to the American soldiers. The air feels thick with dust, plus the smell of nitrates and the scent of fire grows with each step we take closer to the epicenter of the bombing campaign.

Although I'm making mental notes as we walk so that I can commit things to memory, I also keep my ear attentive to the conversations Sarge is having a few steps in front of me. In between commanding soldiers to clear houses, check for hostile or retaliatory activity, and to hurry to the main site to help where the SEALs have already moved in and are looking for intel that might be left over, he's also talking to commanders looking at the scene through drones flying overhead and discussing mission success.

"The situation seems stable," I can hear him say to his next in command, "but this isn't a friendly zone. I want you guys clearing houses. I want all military-age males in the village square so that we can make sure we have any threats contained until we clear out."

My eyes wander as we walk. The many women I see peering through windows, eyes shaded by their burkas, make me wonder what they are thinking right now. Do they look at the uniforms of our armed forces and think savior or enemy? Their eyes express nothing. Barefoot little boys sit on thresholds, eyes wide as saucers with both fear and curiosity as they watch the brigade of desert camo uniforms stomp through their town. A constant keening sound has become white noise to my ears, but I can see women and kids bent over at the waist in certain courtyards, mourning whomever they think they've lost. I force myself to put up my fourth wall, shut my own emotion off so that I can report objectively and not be affected by the sights and sounds of devastation around me as best as I can. It's not as easy as it looks, but I know Beaux is documenting everything: the emotional destruction in candid shots now, and then the physical destruction for Worldwide when we reach the epicenter.

I glance over at her as we walk, taking in her hair braided down her back beneath the helmet, camera bag slung over her shoulder and Kevlar vest, and the black Canon an extension of her hand as she snaps the shutter over and over, changing the angle to get a new shot every few clicks. She must feel the heat of my stare because she lowers the camera momentarily, her vibrant green eyes meet mine, and a soft smile forms on her lips.

The thought flickers in my mind again how she is this little piece of Heaven in this land full of Hell.

"Remember the rules," I tell her, which earns me an even bigger smile.

"Yes, Mr. I'm-in-control," she teases, adding a little bit of lightheartedness to this oppressive atmosphere. "I won't leave your side. I'll listen to you. I won't leave your side, and I won't leave your side. Satisfied?" She shrugs, her smile turning into a lopsided smirk as she raises the camera again.

"Smart-ass," I murmur, although I feel a tad bit better hearing that she knows how important it is not to wander off.

"You wouldn't know what to do with me if I was any different," she fires back, causing me to just shake my head.

When I move to adjust my backpack, the weight of all of my reporting gear heavy enough to cause discomfort, I can't help but think how Pauly's going to kick my ass for once again getting the story first. I'm sure the other news agencies will be here inside of sixty minutes of my first report due to travel time. No doubt some are already en route, sniffing their way here after hearing the Hornets overhead and subsequent explosions.

But we got here first, and I can't wait to get set up and go live. I have Rafe on standby waiting to patch me in.

My mind wanders to Omid and how his intel was wrong. I wonder whether he was protecting me or playing me for the opposition, except I can't give it much more thought once the edge of the bomb zone comes into view. Beaux and her camera are back in action as we step into the scene of destruction, the steady sound of the shutter click a reassurance because when I hear it, I know she's okay.

Piles of concrete rubble with trickles of smoke ascending from them lie before me. American soldiers comb through the piles, putting items I can't quite make out into sacks to bring back to base and turn over to the CIA. Black bags are laid out here and there to signify deceased victims who appear to be high-value targets waiting to be DNA tested and identified. Such a mechanical set of procedures for the manmade loss of life.

And no matter how many years I've been on the job, how many scenes like this I've come to report on, I've never gotten used to the sight or the scent of lost lives. Quickly, I turn to look toward Beaux, to make sure that she's okay; she doesn't have many situations like this under her belt, and I know how tough it can be to process it all. She stands a few feet beside me, camera up to her cheek as her shield to make the reality seem far away even though, in all irony, it brings her closer to the destruction.

She seems as fine as one can be under these circumstances, so I turn my focus back on Sarge's communications, all the while getting more perspective on the enormity of the operation. I begin to work out the wording of my report in my head, ears tuned in to Sarge's voice and Beaux's shutter, and eyes darting at the debris field stretched out in front of me.

I collect as much information as possible—the destruction of buildings, the emotional devastation on civilians, gauge the hostility versus the willingness to help the soldiers, anything and everything to add to my report and allow the viewer to understand the magnitude and importance of this campaign. I take it all in, filter through the things I have to be vague on now and details to clear with Sarge later before I can give an in-depth report. All that matters is I find a place to set up right now, get the feed up live, and file a story before anyone else gets here.

So you're the one.

I chuckle to myself, my mind flashing back to the first night I met Beaux and the comment she made that's never been more true than right now. Yep, I'm the one that every reporter hates and wants to be all at the same time. I find a setup that I think will work to report from just as loud shouts break out across the square. Soldiers are physically coercing three men from a house who are not cooperating. The soldiers have their guns drawn on the locals as shouting escalates from both sides, hands gesticulating wildly to try and bridge the language barrier in an attempt to mediate an already volatile situation.

"Thomas?"

I look up to find Rosco bearing down on me. "Yeah?"

"We know it's not your first rodeo, but Sarge wants to make sure you're vague. No location. No confirmed hits on high-value targets. No—"

"I know the routine, Rosco. I'll play by the rules," I confirm, irritated he's even saying anything as I look back down to my computer to finish setting up my connections.

It's a split second that lasts a lifetime for me. So many things happen simultaneously, but at the same time feel like they are their own individual moments: I swear I hear "BJ" called somewhere behind me at the same moment I realize the constant comforting click of Beaux's shutter is gone. I snap my head up just as Rosco's eyes widen at something over my shoulder.

And I know in an instant that it's something to do with Beaux. That gut instinct I've spent my career honing picks up on something, and my heart plummets to my feet.

"Beaux!"

We both call her name as I whirl around to make out what he's seeing. She doesn't hear us, too damn preoccupied with her camera in one hand and that big heart of hers that she wears on her sleeve. She's walking toward a dog lamed by something wrapped around his hind quarters. He whimpers, tries to walk, and stumbles.

Everything clicks into place at once for me. Snapshots that play together to show what's about to happen minus the sound of her shutter.

Pure, unfettered terror steals my voice as I move on instinct—fight-or-flight—and knock everything over, my only thought to get to Beaux.

Rosco's shout rings through the chaos around us and adds to the riot of fear screaming in my own head.

Beaux stops a few feet from the dog before her body jerks at the absolute commanding terror in Rosco and my voices even though I swear no sound even came out of my mouth.

Her face. I know before anything further happens that the look on her face will forever be scarred in my mind. At first it's confusion, parted lips, widened eyes, as she ever so slowly lowers her camera.

One second. All it takes is a split second for the confusion to morph into a perfect visual of her panic-stricken fear that is like a vise grip on my heart.

My feet feel like they are wading through concrete, legs seizing up and not moving nearly fast enough to get to her.

She drops her camera. I don't know why I focus on that, the sight of it falling and then stopping and recoiling back up like a bungee jumper when the strap around her neck loses slack.

Her body contorts, arms pumping, legs pushing, eyes locked on mine pleading with me in an apology I never want to accept.

C'mon, rookie, I call to her silently, urge her, beg her to put as much distance between herself and the dog caught in the improvised explosive device.

C'mon, baby.

The explosion rocks me to the core. The earth beneath my feet is nonexistent as I'm thrown into a spin cycle of smoke and sound and the complete unknown before my shoulders end up finding the ground again.

I'm stunned, shell-shocked, paralyzed. Unable to speak, can't think, can't hear anything except for a high-pitched ringing in my ears, and I am terrified to see.

Beaux?

Beaux.

Beaux!

My mind screams with fear; the horrific images of war in my memory mix with the thought of Beaux producing visuals I don't want: her small body impossibly contorted, soft skin marred, long hair matted with blood. I hear the sound of Stella screaming in pain, but I'd swear it's Beaux's voice this time around.

Then the pain that radiates throughout my body and the sensation of my skull feeling like it's beneath the wheel of a car rolling at an excruciatingly slow pace drown out everything else.

So you're the one, huh?

Panic ricochets, and my head swims in a viscous haze that grows thicker by the second. My body is so heavy, and all I want to do is roll onto my stomach and crawl to find her. But I can't move, can't think beyond the dust and particles raining down around me, the staggering scent I winced at earlier now becoming a part of me.

"Tanner! Tanner!"

Voices shout from every direction, hands touch me and minister to my injuries and wave in front of my eyes. Sarge and Rosco and a soldier. A medic, I think. But I don't know anything for certain because my focus wanes, fades to black momentarily before coming back, a little fuzzier, a lot more confused.

I don't know much, can't make anything I see stay still, but I do know one thing: There are people around me, trying to help me—everyone but the one I want to see there the most.

Bubbles. I close my eyes, my head feeling adrift like the bubbles we were blowing last night. Was it last night? I can't pinpoint anything because I'm fading. Slowly. *I welcome it because when it pulls me under, the pain stops momentarily.*

"He's in shock!" someone I can't focus on shouts over the deafening ring in my ears.

Well, no shit. The observation is so odd that I want to laugh, want to tell them to stop looking at me and get to Beaux. She was closer. She was closer.

I couldn't get to her.

I couldn't save her.

Beaux.

My world spins, blackness seeping into the fringes of my consciousness and bleeding from the edges in, closer and closer, darker and darker.

Until there is nothing left.

Beaux.

You promised you'd always come back to me.

Chapter 21

I struggle to swim above the water. I claw my way to just beneath the surface with lungs burning, the sky in sight, only to be yanked back down. And I struggle against it less and less because when I'm swallowed by the darkness again, I can go back to the rooftop with Beaux, blowing bubbles, making love. It's so much easier to be here in the warmth of the hot sun and the sweet taste of her kiss than to endure the ache in my head when I try to open my eyes.

I can't keep track of how many times I resurface, but the penlight in my eyes and the cool burn of something like ice being injected into the top of my hand are annoying enough that I promise next time I'll wake up.

Next time.

But then the minute I'm firmly ensconced back in the depths of my subconscious, the look on Beaux's face as she realized what was happening flashes before me.

I never told her I loved her. It's on constant refrain in my mind when I come to and the only thing I know for sure before the darkness steals my thoughts from me once again.

The void of sound and pain is so soothing that when I reach the surface the next time, the beeping that's muffled in my ears confuses me for a moment. The bright light that hits my eyes as I break free from the weight of the water holding me down causes me to squint and then blink rapidly as I try to focus on the room around me.

"Tanner? Can you hear me, Tanner?"

I feel like I'm on the wrong end of a megaphone, sound siphoned through a pinhole, but at least the roaring pain in my head has dulled to a nagging ache behind my eyes and at the base of my skull. My eyelids are heavy, wanting to droop back down, but between my name being called again and my sudden awareness of everything, I force my eyes open as confusion gives way to worry.

And dread.

"Beaux. Where's . . . ?" My voice breaks as I try to make the question sound as urgent as it is in my head, but I know at best I sound groggy.

Patient brown eyes assess me as I look around and place myself in the military combat hospital on the forward operating base. "Tanner, do you know where you are?" I start to nod and stop immediately as the pain radiates through my head. "Don't move. The pain will ebb slowly. You took a pretty big hit to the head. Have a slight concussion. So much better than we'd expect with the blow we were told you took," he says as he writes something down on the chart in his hand. "You're a lucky man. We gave you some sedatives to allow your brain to rest for a bit, so it may feel like you're having a hard time waking up."

I *don't care about me,* I want to yell. *How is Beaux? Where is she? Tell me she's okay!*

"You've been here a little over a day with a concussion and some minor scrapes and stitches. You're likely to be sore with how close you were to the blast zone, but you're lucky those are your only injuries."

I try to process that I've been here over a day. At least twenty-four hours. A lot can happen in twenty-four hours. And while his words are delivered in a soothing Southern accent, they make me even more upset because if I'm lucky and I was that close to the epicenter, what the fuck does that mean for Beaux? Emotions riot through me, so many of them that I can't pinpoint one to grab and hold on to other than my need to know that she's all right.

"Where is she?" I ask, trying to sit up. All I can focus on through the stabbing pain in my head from my sudden movement is that I need to see her.

"Whoa! Lie back down, Tanner," he says with his hands on my shoulders, pressing me back down as I continue to resist, unable to accept that he's not answering me. "You need rest."

"No, I *need* to know where she is." It feels like I'm asking for the umpteenth time and this only adds more panic to the fear lying deep down in the darkness I just broke free from. The one I think I intentionally left behind because it can't be true; she can't be dead.

And when the actual thought crosses my mind, when I allow myself to think the worst for the first time instead of wrestling against it, all of my fight leaves me. I let the doctor push me back to the pillow as I search the expression on his face and his eyes that won't meet mine for the answer I most fear.

"Tanner!" Sarge's voice booms into the empty space, and the relief in his voice and concern in his eyes are a dead giveaway of how serious the situation is. "Doc told me you were coming around, so—"

"Where's Beaux?" I demand, not caring or wanting to talk about myself. The fact that his steps falter gives me enough of an answer.

"She took a big hit," he says softly. The man I've always known to have a stiff upper lip doesn't have one right now. That doesn't sit well with me.

"Where is she?" I grit out, wanting to shake him and tell him to tell me something I don't already know. I may feel like I've been knocked around by a baseball bat to the back of the head, but I'm not stupid, I know stalling when I see it, and I don't think he gets that internally I've been shredded to pieces waiting for an answer.

"She's on her way to Landstuhl," he says, voice quiet, tone grave.

I hang my head for a moment and close my eyes as I absorb his answer. The single comment brings me unfathomable relief because *God, yes*, she's alive and then uncontrollable fear, because if she's on her way to the largest military medical center outside of the United States, then she's most likely critical. The U.S. military doesn't just fly people there for scrapes and bruises. Let alone nonmilitary personnel.

The air whooshes from my lungs from the elephant-sized amount of pressure sitting on it. I try to process the situation, come to terms with possibilities I don't want to face again.

"Get me on a plane to Germany." As I make the demand, I start to rip leads off from under my hospital gown, making the machines around me beep with obnoxious warnings. The doctor whose name I don't even know yet steps forward and tries to stop me. Despite the pounding in my head and how my muscles feel like I just went a hundred rounds in the gym, I grip his biceps and hold him at arm's length. By now I'm running on pure adrenaline.

"We need to monitor you, sir. You—"

"I'm alive, right? That's all you need to know." I dismiss the doctor without a further thought, loosening my grip on him before I turn my eyes back to Sarge. "How is she?"

He visibly works a swallow down his throat. "You guys are lucky you were wearing armor."

"That's not telling me shit, Sarge." No one can mistake the warning tone in my voice.

"She's critical. Unconscious. A few broken bones. They were mostly concerned about brain injuries at first, but after a few scary moments, they got her stabilized here before putting her on a transport to LRMC."

I hang on to the few positive words I can, hold them close to my vest, and don't let go. "You said stable."

"No, I said she was critical but stable," he says as I stare at him, my jaw clenched and heart racing as I try to figure out what exactly that means.

"We were concerned about the possibility of a traumatic brain injury at first. Her brain was swelling from taking the brunt of the blast. We got her broken arm taken care of, wrapped up her ribs, took some scans of her head, and once we saw the pressure inside was ebbing off, we opted to transport her to Landstuhl where they can give her the treatment she might need since we're limited in our capacity here."

I try to wrap my head around the one term that scares the fuck out of me. "Brain injury?" I swear my voice sounds like I'm scraping it from the back of my throat; it's that difficult to find the words.

"Yes, but that can refer to many things, so let's hold off on jumping to conclusions. She was responsive to stimuli, which is huge, and the swelling stopped, so that's the biggest positive. We were just concerned about a few things and thought we'd better be safe than sorry, put in a request to send her off, and got the okay, so we did."

There's an iota of relief from the constant worry that floods me, but it does nothing to abate my need to see her, hold her hand, breathe in the same air as her. "Thank you," I whisper with an acknowledging nod, "and I'm sorry about . . ." The doctor waves his hand in a never-mind gesture in regard to my apology for how I struggled against him.

When I eye Sarge again, the look on his face says he already knows I'm not going to back down. "Tell me you've got some way to get me to her or else give me a goddamn phone so that I can manage it."

A war of wills happens between us before his eyes flicker over toward the doctor and then back toward me. "I'll see what I can do, but I'm not doing shit until the doc clears you to leave." Then Sarge and the doc meet each other's eyes in a silent agreement. They'd better not be fucking with me right now or I'll walk out of this sterile prison on my own accord and get to her any way I can. I have to see her. It's the only way I think I'll be able to stop this ache in my chest that has nothing to do with the blast.

"You've got twenty-four hours to get me there," I demand even though I know I don't have a single leg to stand on. I'm not military personnel. He is under no obligation to get me to Germany to see her, and yet I feel so fucking helpless right now that I do the only thing I can: boss him around with the hope that it will work.

"You need to rest now," the doctor says as he looks up from his clipboard, the stern warning reinforced by the look in his eyes. Shit, now that I know Sarge is going to work on getting me to Beaux, that she's currently stable, I realize just how fucking much my head is pounding.

So I let my head fall back against the pillow and inhale a deep breath as I close my eyes. I instantly feel better without the bright light of the room, but my mind still wanders.

Still worries.

Still relives that look on her face as she ran toward me, knowing I wasn't going to make it to save her in time.

Chapter 22

There's a lot of time to think on a seven-hour flight.

A lot of time to look at the same five photographs of Beaux from the morning of our embed mission over and over. Her silhouette against the sky, her cautious smile, and the selfie we took together that shows two people in love.

Except only one of them knows it.

I try to sleep to escape the pain in my body and the more prevalent ache in my heart, but the deep rumble of the C-17 Globemaster III transport vibrates through my chest in a way that prevents me from getting any real rest. I feel like I've been in the center of a tornado, both mind and body battered and bruised and heart put through a wringer. Thank God that Sarge was able to pull some strings so I could hitch a ride on a plane of medical evacuees heading to the Ramstein Air Base in Germany just beyond my twenty-four-hour time frame.

From my tiny little jump seat at the front of the plane so that I'm out of the way of the critical care team taking care of wounded soldiers, I can overhear the medics relaying to one another they need to buckle up for landing.

I owe Sarge big-time. I'm sure he's breaking every rule in the military handbook to get me on this flight, but I think he blames himself a bit for what happened. And he shouldn't. It's not his job to watch Beaux or me on an embed. It's not his responsibility to know Beaux has a soft spot for dogs and that she was going to see a wounded animal and want to help.

No. That's my job. And once again I failed—and I have berated myself over it left and right in the past thirty hours. I've gone over the entire chain of events and blame myself for getting caught up in my conversation with Rosco without looking around more, not that that would have solved anything. Beaux made it clear on more occasions than I care to count that she's stubborn and has a mind of her own.

I just have to hope she uses that obstinacy right now to fight like hell to overcome her injuries.

The frustrating part is that I don't even have enough energy to be mad at Beaux for not following the rules, because all I want is to see her. The measly bits of information I've gotten haven't told me shit.

Sarge got me on the transport but hadn't been able to get me any other information beyond that she was stable. And stable doesn't mean shit to me. Stable could have so many variations that my mind has gone over and rejected every single one of them while the minutes have crawled by without any updates on her condition.

When the wheels touch down, the jolt makes me wince as my head gets jarred from side to side and my sore muscles ache as they tense up. My knee jogs in anticipation from the fact that I'm minutes away from Beaux now, and the pressure in my chest has intensified now that I'm here.

And for some reason as I sit in this beast of a plane as we taxi across the tarmac, I begin to question myself. Am I making more of my feelings for Beaux because of everything that happened to Stella? Am I overly attached to her, considering how long we've known each other? Has the coincidence of what's happened made me marry the feelings for both women together?

What in the fuck am I thinking? I swear to God it has to be nerves along with the hit I took to the head that's making me think crap like this. Because I know how I feel about Beaux without a doubt. I go to scrub a hand through my hair and stop when I remember how sore my scalp is, settling for running my hand gently over my stubbled and scratched-up jaw to try and knock some sense into myself.

I knew how I felt about her on our rooftop date when we blew bubbles together. I knew how I felt about her as we walked side by side into the destruction of the village bomb site. It's never been more clear to me than right now, even with the anxiety over her condition and doubt trying to weasel through the cracks all of my fears have left in my psyche.

What I feel for Beaux isn't that lust-to-love crash course feeling that Stella used to tease me about. Fuck no. This is so completely different, and yet I can't even explain it to myself. When I think of Beaux, there's an ache in my chest, a warmth in my gut, and a fear in my heart kind of feeling like someone used Super Glue and it just won't let the hell go. It's like even if I wanted to rid myself of her, I don't think I could.

Love. It's an incredibly euphoric and unbelievably scary feeling all at once. I think the only thing that could make me feel more vulnerable is if I'd told her I loved her and she didn't say it back.

Like I did to her on our last date.

Holy shit. How fucking stupid was I? Trying to be cool and play by old-school rules when I knew all along that things were different with Beaux. The never-say-I-love-you-back-or-it-doesn't-mean-the-same-thing philosophy didn't apply to her. Damn it to hell, if I say it, I mean it, so why did I ever hesitate? Is it because I thought that it was too quick to feel this strongly about someone? Well, I do.

Now she's lying in a bed somewhere, not knowing how much I care about her. There's nothing that's going to stop me from telling her I love her now.

Nothing.

The ride to the medical facility feels like it takes the same amount of time as the flight: forever. The minute I step foot in the lobby of Landstuhl, I forget all of my aches and pains from the blast, the stitches in my shoulder, and the gash up the back of my calf—all of it— because my body is running on pure adrenaline from the thought that she's here.

After the rigmarole of the front desk, checking in, getting a visitor's clearance sticker, it takes everything I have not to scream at the lady behind the desk who I'm sure is sweeter than sugar to just hurry the fuck up because I have a woman upstairs I need to see.

And time is of the essence.

Impatient, I can't wait any longer as she turns around to call and inform the intensive care unit that Beaux has a visitor. Time is wasting. I ignore the dull throbbing in my head and jog toward the elevators, knowing that I get to see her in mere moments is the only thing I can focus on, each moment overshadowed by the anticipation of the next.

The ding of the elevator as I reach the third floor causes my heart to skip a beat and lodge in my throat as I all but run off the car and toward the nurses' station in the center of the hallway. As I rush to the desk, my heart thunders in my ears, and my eyes dart all over as the sounds and sights of the ICU ward assault my senses: the sterile smell, the steady beeps from the monitors in the rooms around us on a constant barrage are an immediate reminder of the gravity of the situation.

Yes, I'm going to tell her I love her, tell her I'm sorry, tell her I'm not going to leave her side until she's discharged, but for the first time, the thought hits me that she might not ever hear it. And then that blinding panic I felt when I was trying to get to her and again when I woke up two days ago hits me with blunt force. My eyes dart furiously around the unit, but the room numbers are obscured by all of the medical carts and paraphernalia. All I want is to see her to clear up all of this unsettled bullshit. Once I can touch her and be reassured by the sight of her chest moving up and down telling me that she's breathing, then I can ease all of the discord I feel within and deal with concretes.

I'm good with the concrete. I may live a life that thrives on the spontaneity of others' actions, but fuck if I like to live in that suspended state of limbo when it comes to my personal life.

I approach the nurses' station, smiling warmly at the petite woman behind the desk. It takes me a minute to find my voice as urgency and anxiety collide in a ball of turmoil within me. "Beaux Croslyn's room, please?"

"Your name, please?" she asks as she picks up a clipboard toward the side of the desk and flips a page up, her eyes lifting to meet mine.

"Tanner Thomas." My body vibrates with so many emotions that I find it hard to stand still as I wait for her to look for my name on the approved list. And then when her brow furrows, I immediately start to panic. "I'm approved. I know I am." I pound a fist on the desk, an action that jolts up my shoulder and causes me to wince.

She puts her hands out in front of her in a "calm down" gesture. "I'm sure you're on here. Just give me a moment please, sir." Her eyes meet mine, trying to calm me just like the soothing tone in her voice. I don't think she gets the only thing that is going to calm me down is seeing Beaux.

But I turn around and walk a few feet away from the desk, my hands kneading the back of my neck as I try to contain the frustration while I wait yet again to see her.

"Mr. Thomas?" Eyes wide, I'm at the desk in a second, leaning forward and ready to take off in whichever direction her room is. "Sorry for the wait, but since you aren't immediate family, I had to make sure you were approved by the chain of command." My audible exhale of relief fills the space between us. "Ms. Croslyn's room is three hundred seven, and I—"

I don't hear anything else she says because I grab my bag and am already taking off, searching for her room number. And when I finally find it, in my mind I hesitate for the slightest second before barreling through the doorway to face what I fear head-on.

The immediate sight of her staggers me. She looks ten times worse than I ever imagined and a hundred times better than my fears had her looking. I expect my feet to falter when I see her bruised face, the cannula in her nose for oxygen, her small body dwarfed by the white, imposing bed, but they don't. And I don't pay an ounce of attention to the two doctors off to the other side of the room as I take her in because nothing and no one matters right now but her.

I'm at her bedside in a second, bag dropped to the floor, and my hand immediately finds one of hers while my other hand reaches out to cup the side of her face. And ironically I don't know which of us I'm trying to reassure more with the rub of my thumb over her cheek. And Christ, even like this, that zing when I touch her skin ripples through me in that indescribable and unmistakable connection between us.

I can't help myself, even though a small part of me worries I might hurt her more, but I sense that I won't. I lean forward and press my lips so very gently to her forehead, tears stinging the back of my closed eyes as we stay like this for a moment, allowing myself to feel the warmth of her skin, know she's still alive, still fighting, and that I haven't lost her now that I've found her. I draw in a shaky breath, my heart at an uneven pace, and my lips needing to tell her the one thing I can't hold back any longer.

When I draw in a deep breath, despite the medicinal scent of the room, I can still smell the underlying scent of her shampoo, and I hold on to that little piece of normalcy as I lower my mouth to her ear with my hand still on her cheek. "I'm here, rookie. I'm here and you're going to be okay and we're going to get through this. I'm so sorry I couldn't get to you fast enough. I . . ." My voice breaks as I'm overcome with the emotion of everything that has happened, especially finally being with her again, skin to skin, heart to heart. "I fought my way to you, Beaux, and now you'd better fight as hard as you can to get back to me because damn it, I love you. Did you hear me? *I love you.*"

Leaning my head against the side of her face, I draw in comfort from her as I let my heart hope for the first time since the ricochet of the blast froze it with fear. "I was stupid and didn't tell you that night on the rooftop and I'm sorry and regret it but I'm saying it now. And I'll say it to you every day until you open those eyes of yours and hear me say it to your face. I love you, Beaux Croslyn. You'd best get used to that."

As I press one more kiss to the side of her cheek, my heart feels a little lighter after my confession, but my soul is a bit wary of the road ahead. When I lean back, my eyes still trained on hers, I become cognizant that one of the doctors who'd stood in the corner of the room is now on the opposite side of the bed. But when I switch my focus from Beaux to him, ready to ask a zillion questions about her status and prognosis, I realize he's not a doctor at all, not even in uniform as are most of the people in this hospital. My gaze trails up the Levi jeans, muscular arms crossed over his wrinkled T-shirt, unshaven jaw, and then stop when I meet tired but demanding blue eyes.

"Name's John," he states.

Unsure why the man feels like a threat on my testosterone radar, I rise to full height to meet his eyes, pissed that he's ruining this moment between Beaux and me. "Is there a problem, John?" I ask, irritation prevalent in my voice because I'm more concerned over finding her actual doctor so that I can get an update on her condition than wanting to deal with whoever this guy is. He's already rubbing me the wrong way before he even says anything of relevance.

He clucks his tongue before pulling his lips tight as he nods his head, eyes never leaving mine. "Yes, I believe there just might be," he says in a slow, even drawl.

It immediately gets my hackles up, and I feel like I'm back on base with Beaux when she was surrounded by all the soldiers who were teaching her how to play darts. "How so?" My gaze flickers momentarily to the doctor in the corner of the room whose attention we've piqued before returning to the man across from me.

"Because I believe you just told *my wife* you loved her."

It takes me a few moments to hear what he's just said. Well not really. I hear what he says immediately, a confused chuckle on my lips, but it takes a few seconds for it to sink in. Shock, disbelief, then indescribable confusion flicker through my already fucked-up head. I just stare at him, jaw lax. The ability to form a response is not even a remote possibility as I slowly pull my hand off Beaux's and take a step back to physically distance myself although I already feel like I've been carried a thousand miles away from her.

This isn't possible. Not at all. She said she loved me. She . . .

"What do you mean *your wife*?" I must look shell-shocked, because the bomb he just dropped on me was ten times worse than the one that exploded in our faces days ago.

"I really don't think you have any right to ask the questions here." He raises his eyebrows at me as I shake my head, the staggering pain in my chest only intensifying as I try to process some of this, but I just keep coming up empty-handed. "Were you sleeping with my wife?"

What the fuck am I supposed to say to that? I can't even wrap my head around the fact that the woman I just professed my love to is married. Like silver-ring-on-his-left-ring-finger type of married. How can I answer him when I don't even understand what's going on here? I was just so absolutely blindsided that I'm still trying to find my feet after being knocked on my ass with one clothesline tackle.

"Yes." It's all I can say to him. I can't lie to the man, can't take back the words I said to her even if right now they taste like bile on my tongue. His revelation doesn't change that I love his wife. *Oh my God, what the fuck is happening here?*

I step farther away from the bed and bump into the

wall behind me because I haven't been able to tear my eyes from the sight of Beaux bruised and broken in the hospital bed. I need her to open her eyes and talk to me, need her to explain what the hell is going on . . . that what was between us was real and that what this guy is saying is all a joke.

But she's not.

And neither is he.

John rounds the bed, teeth gritted, shoulders squared, and I know what's coming next, but still I stand there like a deer in the headlights. "Then you deserve this," he says as he cocks his fist back lightning fast and connects with my cheek.

My body crashes into the corner where the walls meet, my arm flying out and knocking over something on the bed tray that clatters loudly to the ground, causing the doctor to drop his clipboard and run to get between us. But there's no need. Absolutely none.

I'm not the kind of guy who takes a punch without scrambling back up and landing a few myself. No one coldcocks me and walks away unscathed. And yet right now, I have absolutely no fight left in me. It's not just the pain radiating in my already scrambled brain, but the fact that I deserve a whole helluva lot more than one punch because just like I don't let anyone coldcock me and walk away; I also don't sleep with someone's wife. That's not the type of guy I am.

But fuck, man . . . I didn't know. I did not know. And I still fucking love her. How is that even possible?

I rest my head against the wall for a moment with my hands pressed on either side of it, the doctor and John at my back, to try and gain my bearings. I feel like I'm drunk and am trying to get the room to stop spinning out of control around me.

I need to leave, know I need to go, but can't bring

myself to walk away from her just yet. "Is she going to be okay?" My voice doesn't even sound like mine, but I need to know the answer before I walk away and sort the shit out in my head that's throbbing like a mother-fucker right now. It's rivaled only by the ache in my heart.

"Not your business, now is it?" John says as I turn to face him. The doctor stands between us in the small space at the same time security arrives in the room. "He needs to leave," he tells the guards as the doctor takes my arm. I shrug out of his grip, my only show of resist-ance.

For a moment when I start to walk from the room, John and I are shoulder to shoulder, emotions raw and tempers escalating on both sides. I pause to contemplate their relationship for a second. Shit, I didn't even know there was a relationship, but I speak the one thing I know deep down for certain. "You don't deserve her."

I may not have thrown a punch, and I may be one hundred percent in the wrong since I'm the one sleeping with his wife, but fuck me, I know he doesn't deserve her. The Beaux I know would cheat on her husband only if the situation was bad, if she had reasons.

And now I just need to wait until she's recovered and stronger to find out what those reasons are.

Chapter 23

"Can I get you anything?"

I look up at the sound of the voice, surprised to find the petite nurse from the ICU station peeking her head into the waiting room. Glancing around, I notice there is no one else in here and realize she's speaking to me. "Not unless you can tell me how she's doing," I murmur. The clock on the wall tells me that I've been sitting here for six hours without a single person talking to me except for my family via cell phone. I'm the pariah, the asshole who slept with a married man's woman, and now I'm banned from the third floor with no hope of getting another glimpse of Beaux.

Without returning my eyes to the nurse, I sink back in my seat because every other person I've asked this question has left and never come back. I lean my head against the wall and scrub a hand over my jaw, surprised when I hear the chair next to me scrape across the floor as she moves it. I snap my head forward, my hope building that I might get some kind of answer here.

She stares in silence with sympathetic eyes that flicker

toward the door every few seconds before she starts. "I could get in a lot of trouble if anyone found out I'm giving you this information," she says, emphasizing how much she's risking by being here. All I can do is nod. "Ms. Croslyn is stable. She had some swelling of her brain due to her proximity and the force of the blast. After the medical team successfully stopped the swelling, they were able to determine that she has what is called a diffuse axonal brain injury." She pauses momentarily because yes, I knew coming here that Beaux had a head injury, but hearing the technical term scares the crap out of me, and without my computer open so that I can Google it and see all of the details, I need more.

"What does that mean?" I plead for more information even when she's giving me more than anyone has thus far.

"Once she arrived here, the neurologists were able to do some more intensive testing and believe she's incurred a stage one injury, which is the least worrisome of them—"

My audible exhale cuts her off, the pressure in my chest abates some, so that I lean forward, elbows on my knees and head in my hands as I try to rein in the rush of emotion that thunders through me like a freight train. And the nurse hasn't even explained what an axonal whatever it is called means, but that it's stage one is enough for me to hold on to until I can look it up myself.

"Now please remember that it's still a brain injury. Until she wakes up, we won't know the extent or if there will be any long-term damage, but compared to some of the injuries that we see here from the same scenario, I'd say luck seems to be on her side."

I swallow over the lump in my throat as I nod my head because the diagnoses I'd imagined were so much worse and daunting. "How long until she wakes up?"

"That's up to her body and the doctors. They did give

her a mild sedative to allow her body to settle some, so they'll probably bring her off that later today and then it's a wait and see . . . but she's a fighter. Has been responsive and seems to be struggling to wake up."

All I can do is nod once again while tears well in my eyes before I blink them away as relief and hurt surge through me. "Thank you for talking to me," I whisper as she scoots her chair back and nods in kind to me before walking away. She's almost to the door when I speak without thinking. "I didn't know she was . . . That's not the kind of person I am. . . ." I'm not sure why I feel the need to explain to her that I didn't knowingly fall in love with a married woman, to let her know I'm not *that guy*. Maybe so she doesn't regret her decision.

The nurse falters in her footsteps, keeps her back to me, but nods her head. "I figured as much by the way you came barreling into the ward. A man acting like that doesn't know. I'm sorry for you too." And with that she exits the room and leaves me alone with my thoughts.

I slump back in my chair and close my eyes as I let my thoughts war against one another. I'm the fool here. I should leave and never look back since the woman played me like a damn violin, but I can't find it within myself to leave just yet. A small part of me hopes that there is some huge misunderstanding, that she's going to wake and clarify everything, because I can't comprehend that she doesn't love me. If I was watching someone else go through this, I'd tell them they were a sucker, to cut their losses and leave with some of their dignity intact.

But I just can't bring myself to put one foot in front of the other and walk out of the hospital. Only I know the passion in her kiss, the raw honesty in her eyes. *God, I am a sap. Honesty?* It seems that word doesn't apply to Beaux Croslyn at all.

The longer I sit here, the more I hold on to that fact,

shoving away how much I care for her, and try to focus on the anger I feel—at her, at John, at the whole fucking world. But then as the reality of my situation comes crashing down on me in this solitary waiting room, the eddy of my thoughts whirls back to the fact that there has to be a reason why she'd let me fall in love with her when she was committed to someone else.

Her explanations about her past filter through my anger, make me recall my fears that she had an abusive ex or a bad situation at home that she was escaping. Could that still be true? Is John one of those missing pieces that Beaux purposefully left unexplained? And if so, how does it all fit together?

Further, why the fuck do I care? If that was the case, then she should have just told me. Wouldn't she at least have told me there was someone else and that it was complicated?

Stop making excuses for her, Tanner. She played you from the get-go, made you believe her time and again until you fell for her. Fell for her? Shit, more like yelling "Timber" at the top of my lungs in a forest-full-of-falling-trees type of fall for her if I'm being honest with myself. And yet through everything, rooftop confessions, afternoons spent making slow and sweet love, trying to teach her the lay of the land, none of it mattered because in the scheme of things, I was being played on every level imaginable.

Now I know I should walk away while I can. Grab my bag and go the fuck back to my reality where the possibility of being hit by opposition fire seems ten times more appealing than having my heart toyed with by a woman like Beaux and an angry husband in a hospital room that I don't even belong in.

But I can't. Not until I know she's going to be okay. Call me a pussy, but I can't turn off my feelings for her. I just can't.

Instead, I shove up out of the chair, needing a change of scenery, some fresh air for a bit instead of this depressing waiting room with artificial light and waning hope. On the elevator ride down, I tell myself that I need to let this go, but I know for sanity's sake that I need to make sure she's okay before I can go back to the life I knew without her.

The minute I exit the doors of the hospital, I feel like I can finally breathe again, clear my thoughts, and am dialing my phone instantly. The phone is picked up on the third ring.

"Everything okay?"

"What do you know about Beaux, Rafe?"

"What do you mean, what do I know? Are you not in Germany with her?" Rafe asks, confused about where I'm coming from.

"I'm here. I want to know about her background. What do you know about her?"

"What? Whoa? What's her status? What aren't you telling me, here?"

I clench my fist at my side as my feet eat up the sidewalk outside of the facility. I need to slow down, know it's important to tread lightly considering Rafe is my friend but also my boss who might look down on co-workers who sleep together. Especially when my stability is already being closely watched after Stella's death.

The last thing I need is for him to see that as misplaced grief over Stella, and that I fell for Beaux with misguided feelings.

After a deep breath, I relay what the nurse told me about Beaux's status. "But when I arrived, her husband was here. She never mentioned having a husband, Rafe. She just referred to a bad situation at home...." My voice trails off, and I let him infer what he will, hoping it's what I want.

"And your point is what, Tanner?"

"My point is that my gut instinct is zinging here that something's off, and I wanted to know if you knew she was married." I'm toeing the edge of mistruth with my friend, hoping he doesn't see right through me.

He blows out an audible sigh that hangs on the connection while I wait him out to hear the answer. "Man, I'm her employer. . . . I can't give out that information."

I harden my jaw in frustration because I knew this was going to be his answer. "Throw me a bone here, Rafe," I groan into the phone, sick and tired of being railroaded. "How about if I ask this way instead: Does her job application have something written in the spot that says maiden name?"

"Damn it, Tanner." He sighs, and I can tell he's conflicted over professional versus personal obligations. Silence stretches for a moment before he continues. "But if you were concerned for her safety, for instance . . ."

"Yes. I might be," I tell him without hesitation. I'll take any out I can to get information to validate my feelings or justify hers if there is any such thing.

"That's not really a question I can ask in an interview because it implies that I can discriminate if she is or isn't married, but I did ask her if being away for extended periods of time for work would cause any problems. She said no and didn't elaborate."

"What about a wedding ring?" I ask, unable to give the topic up.

"Kind of hard to see when the interview was done over the phone. She was already freelancing. All I had were her bio with her picture, her portfolio, and an urging from the bosses to hire her."

"You're not giving me shit to go off. . . . Can't you look at her file, see what it says?" I hang my head back, my feet stopping as I come to the edge of the grounds lined with huge trees.

"I can't. It'd flag HR, and they'd want to know why I'm looking at her info. Personal data is kept under lock and key around here since you guys are in the public eye."

"Guess I shouldn't expect anything less from you, should I? You used to break rules with me left and right to get what we needed. I guess when you slipped on that suit, you gave up your personality too."

I end the call without another word and lean back against a short retaining wall behind me, not caring at all that I just hung up on my boss. My finger slides across the screen to those damn photographs again. When I pull up the one of the two of us together, I just stare at it as frustration builds inside me because there is no way in hell that moment was fake, that the happiness in our eyes and the smiles on our lips were not authentic. It takes all I have to tear my eyes from my phone and at the same time not throw it away from me in anger.

Instead, I sit there for a moment with my face up to the sun, enjoying the warmth since the heat here is so different than in the Middle East.

My phone rings again and I'm immediately pissed. I don't want to speak to anyone, but when I look down and see it's Rylee, I have to answer it.

"Hey, Bubs." Shit, I sound like a dejected puppy dog.

"How are you feeling?" she asks with concern in her voice. It's only been twelve hours or so since we talked last, since I reassured her and my mom and dad that I was completely fine, just a little worse for wear, but I know she's a worrywart and is going to call me often. And in a sense I'm okay with that because everyone loves to know that they are loved. On the other hand, I'm not home much, and so I'm not used to her being in my business.

"I'm fine. Nothing I can't handle."

"How's Beaux?" My hesitation must clue her in immediately, because before I can respond, she continues. "Tanner, is she okay?"

"Fuck, Ry." My breath comes out in a whoosh as I try to find the words to tell my sister, the one person I've always tried to be a good role model for, that I fell in love with a married woman. What is she going to think of me now? "They think she'll be okay.... It's gonna take some time but not as bad as I feared ... but ... my head's all messed up. ..." I let my words trail off, anguish as prevalent as the uncertainty in my voice.

"Well, of course it is," she says, misunderstanding my comment. "You just took a blast—"

"That's not what I mean."

"Talk to me." Her simple statement means so much to me right now since I feel so very alone.

"How did I not know she's married?"

"What?" I can envision from memory the look that's probably on her face.

"I got here to the hospital, professed my love for her as she's lying there, and then her husband's fist met my face."

"Oh shit," she murmurs, those two words expressing what I feel perfectly. "You had no clue?" The shock in her voice fires so many emotions within me because of course I don't want my sister to be pissed at me for something I had no control over.

"No, Ry. None. And a part of me thinks something is hinky here. Like she took this job to escape him."

"Tanner ..." She draws my name out in disbelief.

"I know, but I fell for her, Ry ... and not just because she was there. We fought like cats and dogs at the beginning, but I really fell for her. She challenges me and makes me laugh and is a really good person and ... damn ..." I sigh because even as I'm telling my sister these things, I know she already hates Beaux for hurting me. "She was so closed off about her past, so adamant that it was bad and you know me, you know what a good instinct I have when it comes to people, so I'm just . . ." I force myself to stop rambling and try to hear myself through Rylee's unjaded ears.

"Telling the truth is easy. It's deceiving someone that's hard work." Silence fills the line as her words resonate with me. "Trust your gut, but just don't be blinded by love when it's founded on mistruths from the start."

"When did you get so wise?" It's my attempt to stop the advice I need but really don't want to hear.

"The same time you got so handsome," she says, a line we've exchanged a hundred times over the years that brings a small slice of normalcy to me right now when nothing seems normal.

"Ha. So that means forever."

She laughs, but I can tell she's trying to do me a favor in doing so, to lighten the mood some so that we hang up on a good note. "Tan?"

"Yeah?"

"I believe that you didn't know," she says softly, understanding how important that is to me. "Love you."

"Love you too."

Once we hang up, I wander the grounds, unable to sit any longer in a waiting room and unwilling to walk away without some answers. Although I'm not sure how I'm going to get any since I've been banned from the third floor. I'll find a way. Somehow.

Next I buy some coffee from a cart on the grounds but don't even taste it as I sip it, my mind lost in turbulent thoughts and my chest aching from so much more than the blast. Rylee's words come back to me occasionally, drag me back to reality when I'd much rather be lost elsewhere. I ignore Rafe's texts and his apologies that he can't give me more, and his questions about why I'm so invested when I hated her from the get-go.

I can't speak with him right now or he'll see right through my transparent emotions.

At some point night falls and forces me to realize that my nomadic wandering has pushed me to the point of mental and physical exhaustion, my body still recovering and needing to rest. As I trudge toward the main building, I realize for the first time that my doubt is winning out over hope. The whoosh of the entrance doors greets me as I head on autopilot to the elevators to take back my chair in the second-floor waiting room.

A part of me wants to waltz onto the third floor like I don't give a fuck who's there and see her again. The idea finds purchase in my mind as more and more people pile on the elevator around me.

"Floor?" an elderly lady asks me since I've been pushed on the opposite side of the car from the controls.

"Three, please," I respond without hesitation, because sometimes you just have to fight for the girl. I was blindsided before, didn't tell John to go to hell, and right now I'm primed to do just that, because until I hear from Beaux's lips that she doesn't want me, I'm not going anywhere.

I exit the elevator car with several other people and walk with them right past the nurses' station where the same nurse is still on duty. I keep my head down when I approach Beaux's room, yet I notice a flurry of activity that makes my heart fall because I immediately fear that she has taken a turn for the worse. Not caring about anything but her, I rush to the doorway, only to be met with the sound of her voice.

"Beaux?" Her name falls from my lips, relief mixed with anger, and I must say it loud enough because I catch a very fleeting glimpse of her before John and two other men are in my face with hands on my arms pushing me out of the doorway. "Beaux!" I struggle against them.

"She doesn't want to see you," one of the guys says harshly in my ear as they start to pull me away.

"Not until I hear her say it!" I shout, my muscles burning and head pounding, but my resolve is stronger than ever. We're causing such a scene that staff are starting to come out of other rooms, and a nurse at the station picks up the phone to dial for more security, but I just can't let this go. "Not until she tells me herself!" I shout, hoping she'll hear me and call out to me.

"Fine!" John says, which makes the men cease their forceful advance, but their grip on me remains firm. He walks over to me with a fuck-you smile on his lips and fists a hand in my shirt. I try to jerk back from his grip, but the men have too strong a hold on my arms. "You want to hear it yourself? Go right ahead before you're escorted from the hospital for good." I match him glare for glare. "Hey, Beaux, do you want to see your lover?" he says toward her open door. All I can see from my position is her feet beneath the sheet, but his mocking tone and his knowing chuckle hit me like a knife in the back.

"No. I don't care if I ever see him again."

If John's words were a knife in my back, Beaux's soft but steady voice is equivalent to her twisting the knife over and over in the open wound. And that sliver of hope I was hanging on to—that when she woke up, she'd want me, choose me, and not John—dies a quick and horrid death.

I'm escorted from the hospital grounds by the base police after the military clearance I need to do my job effectively is threatened if I don't go peacefully. I follow their orders without resisting, my head and heart trying to wrap themselves around the fact that the worst part about Beaux's lying to me isn't the lies themselves.

No, it's the fact that after everything the two of us shared, she didn't think I was worthy enough to warrant her telling the truth.

Chapter 24

"Rafe." It's the only greeting I have for him because frankly I don't want to speak to anybody right now.

"It's a miracle. You actually called me back."

"There's been shit reception since I got back." I grunt the lie as I look around the chaos in the hotel room.

"Convenient, don't you think?" I greet his sarcasm with silence. "So you got my messages, I take it?"

"No." I sigh as I run a hand through my hair, not wanting to get into it with him about how many times he's called. And luckily he's filled my voice mail with unlistened-to messages, so at least I know there will be no more.

"No? What's going on with you, Tanner? Pauly says—"

"We've got a problem here." I cut him off as I look around the destruction of Beaux's room. Dresser drawers tossed through, cords left plugged into outlets but unattached to the cameras and laptops they were charging, her things upended all over the place in the careless robbery.

"You're right, we have a lot of problems . . . especially if you don't get back in the saddle."

"That's not what I'm talking about, Rafe." I wave a hand at the chaos in the empty room around me; tears of frustration that I don't even understand are forming, burning the back of my eyes. "Someone broke into her room."

"What in the hell are you talking about? Beaux's room?"

"Yeah, Beaux's room," I answer, irritated that he has to even ask. "Who else did you think I was talking about?"

"Wait. . . ." He exhales slowly in obvious frustration. "Why are you in her room?"

"Because—"

"No. Don't answer that!" he says, cutting me off. "For someone who told me that nothing was going on between the two of you, you can't seem to let anything about her go."

"Someone broke into her room and stole all of her shit," I say, completely ignoring his comment, not having the wherewithal to go there right now. It's been almost seven days since I left her in the hospital in Germany. Seven days where I sat in my damn hotel room in an attempt to avoid every memory of her and move the fuck on because I'm a guy and that's what guys do. That's what I do.

But I can't.

Shit, when I returned after Stella, sure there were ghosts I had to face, but this time was different. This time when I walked through the lobby and up the stairwell, I wasn't only assaulted with the recent memories of my time here with Beaux, but I was also overwhelmed with questioning whether every memory was in fact real or fueled by deception.

Her panties that were tucked between the sheets and

the bedspread, the game of Scrabble sitting half-completed on my table waiting for her to finish it with me, the bottle of her shampoo in my shower. It was like she was everywhere, and that simple notion made it so much worse.

So I threw every reminder of her out. All of them went into the trash can with an amazing flare of melo-dramatics that did absolutely nothing to make me feel better. My initial theory was that I needed to wipe her away, act like she'd never existed.

But memories are a bitch sometimes. They haunt you in the middle of the night when nightmares jar you awake with her name on your lips because you didn't get there fast enough. They sit in a trash can you refuse to empty because if you do, that means she wasn't real and therefore your feelings weren't either.

And just when I thought I was getting a handle on it all, on the deception and the heartache because yes, call me a sap, but there's no other word for that burning pain in my chest that feels like it's eating me apart, I got the call from the hotel staff about her room. The one place that I refused to venture because if I did go in there and snoop around, I just might find something that would mess me up further: a love note to her husband or a jour-nal entry about how much she loves me.

Not worth the goddamn risk when I'm trying to get her the fuck out of my head. And of course the minute I walked into her room, where her perfume was still haunting the stale air and her bed was unmade from when I'd propped the pillows under her hips as we'd had sex, was like a cruel assault on my senses from every possible angle.

The funny thing was, I thought I didn't want confirma-tion that she was madly in love with her husband, but now seeing all of her equipment gone—laptops, cameras, lenses—it's almost as if I need to know. To the hotel staffer who supposedly stole the items, the equipment had a monetary value, something they could sell. To me it was the intangibility of her absence, when something—possible e-mails or photos from back home—could exist, something that could answer my questions.

"Tanner? Tanner?" Rafe's words break through the disbelief that's deafening me and draw me back to the present.

"Yeah?"

"We'll deal with the stuff in her room in a minute, okay? For right now, though, I'm going to talk, and you're going to listen. *Capisce?*"

And here comes the lecture. Probably similar to the one Pauly gave me last night. I lie back on the bed and the damn mattress springs squeak in a bittersweet sound that makes me want to jump off the bed and at the same time shift my body so that I can hear it again. One more thing to solidify in my mind that what we had was real.

And since we didn't tell anyone, it's not like I can admit to Rafe his assumption is true. Everyone here thinks I'm moping around because I'm upset that I couldn't protect her from the IED and that the déjà vu of not being able to get to Stella in time has fucked with my head even more than they thought.

Too bad my head is fine. It's my heart that hurts like a son of a bitch.

"I can't wait to hear your words of infinite wisdom," I say, not really caring that I'm pushing the boundaries with my boss. "Lay it on me, Rafe."

"We're on a strict don't ask, don't tell policy right now. I'm not going to ask and you're not going to confirm what I'm asking without asking because it's none of my business and one hundred percent my business all at the same time. You guys built a bond as partners, she got hurt, so now the bond is stronger. So strong in fact that you caused a serious scene at Landstuhl, risking your security clearance. There's only one reason in my mind why you'd react so strongly, call me up and ask me questions about Beaux's marital status, and then get pissed when I don't give you answers . . . but that's all supposition from the outside looking in. That and the fact that I've never seen you act like this before, even after . . ." His words trail off, the implication of *after Stella died* left hanging on the line like a goddamn white elephant, and I bite back every smart-assed comment on my tongue because it's just not worth it.

The only response I give him is a low "Mmm-hmm."

"So you hoof it back to your assignment, and have been there for what, a week? And you're still desk jockeying the shit out of recycled material instead of following up on the story. Can you tell me what's wrong with this picture?"

The buzz is gone, I almost say but catch myself. I got back here and I had no desire to get back in the game. Zilch. Zero. I had no desire to contact Omid or to get on an embed mission with Sarge despite his calling me about exactly that to assuage his own unfounded guilt over the blast. Nothing. That live by the sword, die by the sword buzz I've used for over ten years to propel me to become the top foreign war correspondent is nowhere in sight.

"There's most definitely not a picture, Rafe. None whatsoever, considering I don't have a photographer to take one until she comes back," I state evenly to try to hide from the fact that he's absolutely fucking right.

"Is that what this is? Are you waiting for her to come back, Tanner?" He sounds so much like my father giving my teenage self a lecture that it's comical. "Screw her stuff that was stolen. It's insured, and I'll have the hotel staff pack up what's left. She isn't coming back."

The breath I didn't even realize I was holding whooshes out in a deceptively even draw as the wind is knocked out of me. There goes that stupid little thread of hope that I had held on to for some reason that she'd come back, see me, and we'd be good again. It shatters me.

"She's not?" I ask, making sure my voice is calm although my insides are screaming.

"No. Her condition is improving. She just needs some more monitoring and to take it easy, so she was moved stateside."

Silence fills the line as a part of me breathes a sigh of relief. "When?"

"Yesterday."

"Where?"

"I'm sorry, I can't give you that information."

"What do you mean, you can't give me that information?" My voice escalates on the question.

"Not your business."

"What the fuck, Rafe? What's your problem? I just want to make sure she's okay."

"She's okay. Hear me tell you that. And now hear this: You're too close right now, so what's going to happen next is you're going to pack your shit up and come home. I have—"

"No." I spit out the refusal, but there's not a single ounce of conviction behind it. First Stella, now Beaux . . . I couldn't save either of them, and the one that's still here doesn't want me. How's that for a blow to the male ego? Even scarier, though, is the will to fight for her was left behind at the hospital. It's no use fighting for someone who doesn't need your fight.

"I have transport coming to get you in one hour," he

says evenly, ignoring my outburst. "You're either on that flight home, Tanner, or you can look for another job."

"This is bullshit!" For the first time I feel fire blazing within me, and maybe it's because I don't want to leave the only thing that's connecting me to her now.

"No. We can talk about bullshit all day, Tanner, but it'd start with you. I'm worried about you. You took a big knock, physically, emotionally, and I know you hate me right now, but I'm just looking out for your own good. You'll see that someday."

I blow out a breath and start to pace the room. My foot hits something under the unmade bed we abandoned when Pauly interrupted us. The sight of the empty bottle of bubbles that bounces against the dresser when I kick it is like a knife wound to an already ailing heart, reinforcing the truth I just can't face right now: This was all a lie. One more final *fuck you* from Beaux.

The bubble has burst.

"I'll be on the flight."

There's nothing more I can say.

Chapter 25

Rafe's words still ring in my ears as I sit at home in the dark. Even though my name's on the title, the place feels so much more foreign than a hotel. The shades are drawn, I've got a beer in my hand, and my thoughts are still back on a woman I should let go but just can't.

I've made a career living on gut instinct, and my instinct is telling me that something is off here. But isn't that the same feeling I've had since day one when it comes to Beaux?

I ignore the knock on the front door. The only people who know I've touched down on U.S. soil besides those at work arc Rylee and my parents. And I bit the bullet and saw my parents yesterday, faked my way through why I came home, blamed it on needing some recovery time—because let's face it, you don't really tell your parents who have been together since they were in their early teens that you fell in love with a married woman. It's not exactly a crowning moment of their parenthood regardless of whether I knew she was married or not.

So the persistent knock on the door has to be Rylee.

And of course if it is her, she will have driven the two hours south from Los Angeles to San Diego, so that means she won't go away easily.

Besides, she has a key.

I sink back farther into the couch and close my eyes only to immediately open them because damn it to hell, Beaux's there too. She's fucking everywhere. And nowhere.

The rattle of a key in the lock tells me I was correct in my assumption about the visitor's identity. "Tan?"

"In here," I say, not eager for company.

"You becoming a vampire or something?" she asks at the same time as blinds start opening in my kitchen and the telltale sounds of the ocean crashing on the cliffs below filter in once she's opened the windows.

"I hear it's all the rage these days," I snort as she snaps open the blinds in the family room where I sit, causing me to wince at the brightness even through my closed eyelids. I track her movements through sound, know she plops on the love seat catty-corner to me by the squeak of the leather, and then feel the weight of her stare as she waits me out. I don't budge.

"You look like shit."

"Thank you," I say with a nod, finally opening my eyes and meeting hers, which are identical to mine in their amethyst color. And shit, she's my sister and I'm in a crappy mood, but it doesn't stop me from shaking my head at how beautiful she is. She always has been, but since she married Colton, she has this newfound confidence that makes her radiate. It's cool to see on her and frustrating as fuck to me all at once, because it makes me remember what I've recently lost.

"Well that's sugarcoating it, but I thought I wouldn't kick you while you were down." There's humor in her voice as she rises from her seat and sits down next to me and cuddles into my side so that she can rest her head on my arm. It's a simple gesture, but just feeling her here next to me makes the emotions well up in my throat. She reaches out and pats the top of my thigh. "So how are you doing? I mean you at least have pants on ... That's a good sign. Colton told me that if you were sulking in your underwear, I should just back out quietly and let you be."

"He's got that about right. Good thing I got up a few hours ago and pulled some jeans on." She laughs low and rich, a sound from my childhood that brings back so many memories of backyard forts and riding bikes until the streetlights came on.

"So talk to me. Tell me where your head's at, what's going on. . . . I'm here to listen and shut my mouth."

I snort. "That's pretty comical. You? Quiet?"

"Shh, I can listen with the best of them—just don't spill that secret to Colton. So, anything new?"

I shove up off the couch, toss my beer bottle in the trash, and get an unsatisfactory clink as it hits the others inside before I look out the kitchen window to the neighborhood beyond. "Anything new? Well, Wendy had her baby while I was gone, cute little boy named Timothy," I say, referring to my next-door neighbor. "And what else? It seems that William down the street bought some black eyesore of an SUV that he won't park in his damn driveway, so it sits on the curb over there blocking the view some. And then there's Mike on the other side who—"

"Tanner," she says in warning to let me know that she's not amused by my sarcasm whatsoever.

"I don't want to talk about Beaux," I say with a firm look even though she's all I want to talk about because I can't get her out of my fucking head despite having been back home for almost two weeks.

"Your place looks nice. You look good."

I grunt in response because I know she's lying since I

look like shit and she's already said as much. "Not much else to do besides clean a place no one lives in and take long runs on the beach to fill time because . . . well because I can, seeing that I'm not in a war zone with land mines and such." There's a bite to my words that I didn't intend but don't apologize for. She gets it, I know she does, but that doesn't mean that she deserves this treatment or that I even deserve the effort she's putting forward to try to connect with me.

I walk toward the patio door to the backyard that Rylee opened, see the ocean, feel the sun in the sky, but I'm completely indifferent to it. My phone alerts a text from where it's pressed into the cracks in the sofa cushions, and I choose to ignore it, knowing it's yet another from Rafe or my parents. I don't want to speak with anyone right now since my hand's being forced as it is with Ry here.

"All I've done is think about her, about us. Run back through our conversations and the time we spent together over and over in my head to try to search for the clues I missed . . . but there's nothing concrete I can pinpoint. I mean sure there're things she kept private, certain things she didn't address, but isn't that how all relationships go?" With her behind me, it's easier to talk for some reason.

"Yeah. It takes time to open the closet of skeletons . . . but married, Tanner? Tanner, that's not a skeleton in a closet. That's a ring on your finger. That's the person you look forward to seeing every morning even when they annoy you or you're fighting. It's your other half. Marriage is made—"

"Marriage is made in Heaven," I say, giving her one of my favorite Clint Eastwood quotes, "but so are thunder and lightning."

"What's that supposed to mean?" she asks, and I can hear the annoyance in her newlywed voice.

I walk outside and take a seat in a lounge chair where I know she'll follow me. "It means that we grew up with Mom and Dad's marriage as an example. You have Colton. Not all marriages are like yours. What if there's something wrong in hers? What if she's trapped and can't get out of it? What if he's abusive and—"

"That's a long stretch, Tanner. It sounds like you're just trying to justify her actions." She takes the chair across from me, her face toward the ocean, but her words are sharp. "Love makes you more of who you are, not less . . . and right now, her lies? Are definitely not making you more."

I let her words sink in, tell myself I'm reaching for something to hold on to when I just need to let go and free-fall into the pain. Take the rough landing and broken heart in one fell swoop so that I can heal all at once instead of piece by piece where hope ties each one together with the thinnest of strings.

"You know, Ry," I finally say, "I can handle being dumped for someone else. I'm a big boy who can handle rejection just fine . . . It's this schizophrenic feeling that's driving me crazy." I run a hand through my hair and sigh. "How come I am so fucked up over this? How can I feel so strongly for someone after just a few months together? I mean one minute I miss her like crazy and feel like such a loser because I can't let this go . . . and then the next minute I hate her guts and never want to see her again even if I had the chance to."

She leans her head back against the chair and laughs before turning to meet my eyes, a knowing smile on her lips. "Because it's love."

"Do you care to elaborate since you think this is so funny?" I snip, not amused at all.

"It's real love," she says with a shrug that makes me uncomfortable instantly even though I could have assumed she'd say as much. But saying it aloud and feeling it in my own miserable silence are two different things. Once it's out in the universe, you can't take that shit back. "Real love messes you up no matter how long you've been with someone. Believe me. I've been there with Colton. We butted heads from day one, but there was something there I couldn't deny no matter how hard I tried. Sometimes no matter how hard you fight it, it's just there." And of course my back immediately goes up that my brother-in-law made my little sister feel this way at some point. But at least I have comfort in knowing they obviously worked things out. "I can see you longing to work the Prince Charming angle, Tanner, but you can't. Bad marriage or not, it's her situation to deal with. You can't go charging in on a white horse to save the day."

"Why not?" I ask with more conviction than anything else I've said today.

"Do you love her?" I look at her like she's crazy, because I definitely wouldn't be this fucked up over a woman I didn't love. "How do you know you love her, though?"

"Really, Ry? Are you going to treat me like an idiot now?" I'm getting more irritated by the minute.

"No," she says, backpedaling. "You've loved lots of girlfriends, so why is she the one that you're *in love* with? How do you know it's real?"

"She knocked me on my ass, Ry." The comment comes out before I can stop it, and I know I sound pathetic but don't care because if I can be dead honest with anyone, it's with my sister. "Because my heart races out of control at just the thought of getting to see her again. Because she's all I—never mind." I stop, knowing how ridiculous I sound.

"I get it. Believe me, I get it. You may love her, but unless she gives you something to go off now, unless she contacts you, then you have no right to be in her business. It sucks and it's brutal and I know that feeling when your chest aches so damn bad you can't breathe . . . but that's love. It makes you crazy insane and doesn't always work out."

The flip side of being so comfortable talking to my sister is that she's just as honest with feedback even when I don't want to hear it. Like right now.

"You're making no sense," I mutter, not having expected her to solve my problems but at least wanting something a little more clear to go on.

"How so?"

"Well in one breath you say that it's real love and imply how rare it is, which makes me think it's worth fighting for, and in the next you tell me I can't fight for it unless she gives me a reason to. Talk about fucking confusing."

"Exactly."

"That's all you're going to give me?" I groan through the smile that graces my lips for the first time in what feels like forever. "You suck at this because you're deliriously happy."

"Yep on all accounts," she says as she scoots to the edge of her chair. "This is so hard for me because I'm trying to be objective, to tell you that if you really feel how you feel and if she gives you a single opening, you need to fight like hell for her, and at the same time I hate her because she did this to you. She doesn't deserve you, Tanner. You know what Mom says, 'Cheating on a good person is like throwing away a diamond and picking up a rock.'"

"The question is, am I the diamond or am I the rock?" I murmur as she steps forward and presses a kiss to the top of my head.

I watch the ocean for a long time after she leaves, lost in my thoughts and not sure if I want to hold on or to purge the memories that are still so vivid I can taste them. I wander into the house, grab a beer, and settle down on the couch, Rylee's comment about me not being Prince Charming on constant repeat for some reason.

Maybe it's by the third beer in that I realize she's right. Completely right. I'm the farthest thing from Prince Charming. I'm a reporter who rides an adrenaline rush instead of a horse. I have nothing to offer someone long term except for constant worry for my safety, missed birthdays, lonely anniversaries, and middle-of-the-night phone calls due to time zone differences. Dating casually is one thing, but there is no room for happily-ever-afters in my world. Look at Pauly and the number of wives he's lost count of because they couldn't handle the loneliness.

And even if I did rush in to try and save the day, who exactly am I saving her from? A husband who flew thousands of miles in a heartbeat because his wife was injured? Yeah, because that screams, "I'm a husband who doesn't care." Not.

Suck it up, Thomas. You were played. Now man up and get over it.

"Fuck," I sigh out into the empty room, feeling so out of place in my own home. Setting my empty beer bottle down, I shift on the couch so that my head is on one armrest and my feet are on the other. The problem is when I look up toward my ceiling, the cracks I'm so used to tracing as I work through my thoughts aren't there. Restless, I move onto my side so that I can look elsewhere, when something jabs my rib cage. Shifting again, I reach down to find my cell phone there, but when I pick it up to toss it on the table and glance at the screen, my heart stops for a beat.

It was all a lie and none of it was a lie.—Rookie

It takes me a moment to really believe that the message could be from her, but I can't deny she's the only person I've ever called that nickname. I slowly exhale the breath I'm holding. Just when I've decided to get the fuck over her, she comes and slaps me in the face. No, not a slap in the face. She's given me something to go off, and in Rylee's book that's a sign I can start fighting for her.

Damn. I guess it's time for Prince Charming to learn how to ride a horse.

Chapter 26

Several times in my career I've heard the saying, "Ideas pull the trigger, but it's instinct that loads the gun." Until the moment I walked through the Kansas City International Airport, I never thought it would pertain to me. Or have led me to this moment.

I was disappointed but not surprised when I called the cell phone number that texted me, only to find that the call went unanswered and there wasn't a voice mail. A quick Internet search told me the number was most likely from a disposable cell phone, meaning it was untraceable.

And even though my gut reaction was to immediately call her back, I was still confused. If she didn't want me to come after her, why did she text me? Why send me a cryptic message instead of just letting me be?

I'm a reporter, someone who asks the tough questions in situations that are not easily answered. She had to know I'd go apeshit over having a clue to something that I couldn't figure out. Was that her point? Was she in trouble and needed help, or was she just trying to tell me she was sorry in some fucked-up way? Or even worse, was she toying with me again to see if I'd come running and play right back into her hands?

I hated wondering as much as I hated thinking she needed me but was playing me at the same time.

The whole thing didn't sit well with me. So after I had spent days calling in favors and being put on the back burner, one of my old military liaisons turned federal agent turned source took pity on me. Well, pity mixed with the delivery of a rare bottle of aged Macallan for the Scotch aficionado. Regardless, he attempted to trace the cell phone number for me.

And three days later I may not have had much more than that it was a disposable cell phone with no contract or traceability, but there was a single ping off a cell tower that occurred when the text went out. A single black dot on a map that gave me a triangulation range and let me narrow down a general location of where she was: the Kansas City area.

Something about it fit for me. The funny look on her face that first time we met up with Omid when I said, "We're not in Kansas anymore," tells me that I'm in the right place. But my problem is that I don't have much more to go on than intuition, a determined heart, and a pocketful of hope. On top of that, the pocket has a hole in its bottom, an hourglass of sorts, and I've promised myself that this time around, when the hope bleeds out, I'm done.

My gut tells me that I need to visit the hospitals, need to work that angle because she was transferred to a U.S. hospital and will need to continue with her care even if she's been sent home already. It's a long shot at best, but she gave me an opening, and if I don't follow through with it, I'll always wonder what if. I'll always question whether she was my once-in-a-lifetime and I passed her up.

*   *   *

By early evening I'm wiped out and feel like I've exhausted every existing avenue. I've been to all of the hospitals—Saint Luke's, University, North Kansas City, Select Specialty, and even Kansas Heart—trying to leave no stone unturned. But not a single person recognizes her picture; nor will anyone confirm or deny that a Beaux or BJ Croslyn has been or is a patient. I'm so desperate to find her that I'm willing to try Children's Mercy just to make sure that all of my t's are crossed and i's are dotted.

With my head back against the headrest of my rental car, I debate what to do next. Should I just say fuck it and catch a flight home? I mean really, what the hell am I doing here, looking for the pot of gold that doesn't exist? Desperation doesn't look good on anyone, least of all on me, and I reek of it these days.

Sitting in the parking lot of a strip mall, I glance at the map in my hand with the circles around the hospital icons as I set it down, unsure where to go from here. I was so gung ho when I got here and now just feel pathetic. The radio drones on, and I switch the station out of boredom, stopping when I come to a Cardinals baseball game and just leave it on for background noise as I debate my next move.

The smart thing would be to get a hotel, wait for shift change, and then head back to the hospitals, flash her picture, and try with the different employees. If I'm here, I'd better satisfy my need to be thorough when investigating a story, because that's how I'm trying to treat this, like it's a story. It's the only way I can approach the Beaux situation and consider the possibility I might not get the outcome I want. Put the filter up, turn the emotions off, treat it like the hard beat I had in the Middle East.

I start the car and turn out of the parking lot with thoughts of heading to a hotel, grabbing a quick shower, and then heading back to the hospital circuit. "And Ramirez hits one hard." The announcer from the game breaks through my scattered thoughts. "It's going, going, and it's gone! A home run for the rookie to tie the game."

It takes a few seconds for the words to sink in, but the minute they do, I flip a U-turn across the double yellow line and head back to the hospital because an idea has seated itself—and I swear that I know it's going to be the break I've been looking for. Within minutes, I'm at Saint Luke's, where I buy flowers in the gift shop, and then head to the front desk to greet the new person manning the desk.

"Hi there, what can I do for you today?"

I fidget back and forth as if I'm antsy, a nervous smile plastered to my face so that I can play the part, but at the same time I am nervous. "I think I'm at the right hospital. I just . . . I just need to see her." While I speak, I dig in my pocket to make sure my boarding pass falls onto the desk between us.

"Calm down, sir," she says sweetly, her head angled to the side and her eyes wide behind the lenses of her glasses. "Who are you looking for?"

"My girlfriend. I've been in the Middle East, and she was hurt. Brought here or University . . . I can't remember which one because it was such a whirlwind, but I was able to get leave from my unit and I got here as soon as I could and I came straight from the airport and now I just need to find her to make sure she's okay," I ramble on as her smile softens.

"Of course you're flustered. Thank you for your service, sir," she says, and I nod at the assumption she makes about my being in the military, hating myself for implying it but at the same time, a man's got to do what a man's got to do and everyone loves a man in the service. Especially a middle-aged woman who could have sons of her own and can appreciate a man trying to get home to the woman he loves. "Now what's her name and I can look her up for you, see what room she's in?"

"Thank you so much." I set the vase of flowers down and keep up the act to look scattered by collecting my boarding pass and stuffing it in my pocket. "Her name is BJ or Beaux Croslyn . . . but she goes by Rookie, Rookie Croslyn. So I'd try that," I say, my hopes lodged in my throat as I spell out the last name for her.

"Just give me one second, sweetheart," she says. Her fingernails click over the keyboard as I watch the reflection of the screen in her glasses, the blue hue an easy thing to see, but it's the slight frown on her lips as her eyes flicker back to mine that has my heart stopping in my chest. She knows something. The hesitation, the pause in her fingers, and furrow of her brow tell me more than any words could. "I'm so sorry. There's no one by that name," she responds, shattering any hope I'd had. A defeated thank-you is on my lips when she murmurs to herself, "Only a Rookie Thomas."

"That's her!" I all but shout as I'm overcome with emotion. There's no need to continue my Oscar-worthy performance because my heart leaps into my throat when I hear the name. It can't be a mistake. Beaux used my nickname for her and my surname—the thought that she's kept a part of my feelings for her alive knocks me back a step.

She has to be telling me something. What it is, though, I have no idea.

The receptionist's face smiles broadly, all trace of the hesitancy I saw moments before gone. "Well good news, Mr. . . . ."

"C-Clint," I stutter, her comment giving me an instant

high, that buzz that's been nonexistent since I left Germany running rampant for the first time.

"Clint." She smiles again when all I want to do is tell her to spit it out. "Rookie was discharged three days ago, so I guess that means she is doing much better."

I contain the stab of disappointment that rifles through me because as much as my hunch that she was here was right, it does me no good now. We've just passed like ships in the night, the only thing left being the ghost of memories. The problem is that I can't let the sweet receptionist know my disappointment and realize that she's just been duped.

So I use the think-on-my-feet tactics that have propelled my career over the years and only have a split second to hope that this works. "Oh that's such a relief to know she's okay!" I say as I bring my hand up and *accidentally* knock the vase of flowers over.

She shrieks and jumps back as water and flowers spill across the desk and toward her keyboard, which she quickly pushes to the side. "Shit! I'm so sorry!" I round the U-shaped desk in an instant. "I'm so clumsy. So excited she's doing better. Oh my God. I'm so sorry!" I repeat the comments over and over, making sure I play up the bumbling boyfriend, all the while hoping this act is all worth it and that what I'm hoping to find is actually there.

The minute I breach her space behind the desk, my actions reflect a contrite man, head down, hands busy helping to push the water away from her paperwork and electronics, but my eyes are laser focused on the computer screen. It takes a heartbeat for my eyes to find the name Rookie Thomas and to not sag in relief when I see the address listed below her name.

That damn buzz? It's full-blown electric shock right now.

I read it several times to etch the street and numbers into my head. "Let me go get some paper towels," I offer once most of the water has been pushed to the floor so that nothing on the desk is compromised. "I'm so sorry. I don't—"

"Towels. Please," she says, her patience wearing thin, and I'm perfectly okay with that. I rush over to the lobby restrooms. Once inside, I immediately pull my phone out and type in the address so that I don't forget it before grabbing a handful of paper towels and heading back to help pick up the mess I made.

Chapter 27

So many emotions course through my veins as I get out of my car and walk toward the quaint little clapboard house on Elm Street. And I can't help but feel now as I did last night sitting and watching the house that it doesn't fit the Beaux that I know. None of it. She's all hard lines and fiery edges and not a postage-stamp-sized patch of grass in the front yard in need of mowing, petunias in the planters, and a porch swing that sits a tad crooked.

Even though I sat parked on the street for a few hours last night, watching as the lights in the front windows went dark, it took everything I had not to knock on the door. But I knew I had to wait. I had to be patient until the morning to see if John got into his manly little Prius and went to work. Because a good husband goes to work every day, right?

So after a restless night of sleep when all I could do was think about what I was going to say to Beaux when I came face-to-face with her after almost three weeks of wondering and hurting and missing her, I sat for three hours this morning, waiting to watch John amble out of the house and into his car, briefcase in hand, with a wave hello to the neighbor before driving slowly away.

And then I waited—just to make sure he didn't forget anything, didn't come back for one last kiss from his lovely wife—before getting out of my car. As I walk down the quaint, tree-lined street, everything I've felt over the past few weeks comes back with a vengeance, and for some reason it's anger right now that I hold on to the most. Now that I'm seconds from seeing Beaux face-to-face, the hurt of her deception hits me the hardest.

I knock on the front door with my heart in my throat and venomous words ready on my tongue, each second I wait making them even more poisonous.

And then she opens the door.

The startled gasp she lets out does nothing to rival the freight train of emotion that bears down and slams into me. Every single word I had ready to say dies on my lips now that I'm face-to-face with her. Her perfume, her hair pulled up with pieces hanging down, the startled O of her lips, all of it hits me like a battering ram, but more than anything it's her eyes. That flash of utter surprise quickly followed by pleasure before it's smothered out by what looks like anger. Or fear. I can't tell which she's feeling, because the sucker punch of seeing her after all of this time clouds my ability to reason.

But it sure as fuck doesn't cloud my ability to feel.

"Tanner . . . what? What are . . ." She leans her head out of the door and looks back and forth quickly before grabbing my arm and pulling me into her house. In complete contrast to her actions, she says, "You can't be here. You have to leave!"

And my God, the feel of her touch on my skin is like connecting jumper cables while standing in a puddle of water. That connection between us is still there, stronger than ever, and I know she feels it too, because she jumps back the minute I'm inside her house.

Inside another man's house.

Eyes locked, we stare at each other, leaving words unspoken as we let the invisible current between us die down some.

"You can't be here, Tanner," she says again, and for the first time I notice the cast on her left forearm before looking back to her eyes full of concern. And the question I ask myself is whether the apprehension is because she hurt me or because she's more concerned about hurting her husband.

"I think you lost the ability to tell me what to do the minute you forgot to tell me you were married."

"We can't do this right now. It's not safe, Tanner. It's just not safe," she says, backing up until she hits the wall behind her, almost as if she forgot where the walls in her own house are. And her words, the look in her eyes, eat at my anger.

"Why is it not safe, Beaux? Does he hit you? Does he hurt you? Tell me the word and I'll have the cops here in a second and I'll take you away so that—"

"No! No. It's nothing like that. I can't explain. I can't," she says, her voice rising with each word, and I stare at her, shaking my head back and forth because I don't understand. And I don't know if I believe her. Why would she be telling me to leave when our connection is still so irrefutable?

"Help me understand!" I shout, shoving a hand through my hair because if it's there, then it's not on her, and God, how I want to be touching her. "Why didn't you tell me you were married? Why did you tell me you loved me? Why did you lie to me?" I could ask about a hundred more questions, and yet no more come because all I can feel is anger when all I want to feel is her.

"It's complicated," she says softly, her voice even for the first time and her body stilled.

"Fuck complicated because I'm worth complicated. Jesus Christ!" I grit out as I take a step away from her and try to hold on to the sanity that she is stealing from me with each and every word. How frustrating is it to have the one thing you want so desperately right at your fingertips? Beyond that her behavior is making me feel like she is a million fucking miles away. I don't know what I thought was going to happen once I showed up. That maybe she was going to open the door, see me, and then profess that she chooses me over John. And clearly that's not happening. So the only thing I allow myself to feel is anger; the acrid taste of rejection is already churning in my gut, and I have a feeling that I'm going to have a long time to taste that because the reaction I'd hoped for from her definitely isn't happening.

"You are worth it, Tanner. Worth every bit of it, but not from me. I can't give you what you need."

"That's bullshit!" I yell as I get in her face, needing to do something to expel the ache in my chest. "Then why not leave well enough alone, huh? Why send me the fucking text? Why give me false hope?"

"Because . . . because . . ." Then she stops with her eyes welling with tears I don't want to see. I fell for them once. Believed them once. I won't be as quick to fall again. Our faces are inches apart, and it takes everything I have to keep from pulling her to me or pushing her farther away. "I wanted you to know that how I felt for you was real."

"Goddamn it, Beaux!" When I slam my hand on the console beside me, the sound resonates through the empty house just like her words do through my heart. "Tell me what he does to you! Tell me so that I can try to make it better. Tell me so that I'll stop going fucking insane trying to figure out why you told me you loved me when you were married to another man!"

"Tanner—"

"Don't Tanner me. Don't anything me!" I yell, my mind spinning from her mere proximity.

"You need to go," she says again.

"No! I won't go until I hear you tell me that you don't want me. I know what we had was real too, Beaux. Why do you think I've tracked you down and am fighting like hell to get you back?"

"I've never been yours to fight for."

Her words leave her lips and die in the space between us, and yet she never says what I need to hear to force me to walk away. I step closer so that she's backed against the wall, and my body presses into hers. And even through the anger, I can still feel the snap of the live wire of our combustible chemistry when we touch.

"Tell me you don't want me." I grit the words out as our breaths mingle and lungs breathe like one.

"I don't want you," she deadpans. For a second I believe her. For a moment I hesitate, plan to step back and walk away. But I know her. I know how feisty she is and how she doesn't back down until she's won, and I don't see that right now. Not a single ounce of the fire within her that I've come to love, and so I take one last chance to win back the girl that by now I don't think I ever really had.

"Bullshit," I sneer at the same time my mouth slants over hers and takes everything I've been wanting and then some for the past three weeks. The kiss is horrible and wonderful all at once because it's like coming home and being shown what you're going to no longer have.

She struggles against me, pushing against my chest as our mouths fight a savage dance of denied desire and frustrated passion, shifting into resistance and acceptance, as our tongues meld and teeth nip and throats moan with want.

She drags her mouth from mine, her eyes drugged with desire beneath heavy lids, and lets her words slash out at me. "I don't want you."

"Don't you fucking dare lie to me again! I deserve better than that. Tell me! Tell me that again!" I shout at her with one of my hands gripped in her hair and the other digging into her hip.

She doesn't say a word. She just stares with tears filling her eyes until she whimpers. "I can't, Tanner. I can't." But afterward she leans forward and presses her lips to mine in the most tender of kisses. It's like a drug and a poison to me, pulling me further under its haze and hurting me all at the same time.

"You can," I urge, my own voice thick with emotion when she brushes another kiss on my mouth, but this time I can taste the salt of her tears on her lips, and my chest constricts at whatever is going on that I can't comprehend.

"I can't," she says again, but her words don't match her actions because her hands find their way beneath the hem of my shirt, her touch branding my flesh so that I know even when I walk away it will be like a tattoo there, permanent and painful.

I know before our lips meet again, before my hands slip beneath her shirt and skim up the linc of her spine, before I let her undo the buttons on my jeans and slide her hands inside my waistband, before she tells me she "can't" again that this is such a very bad idea. That I'm going to end up hurt and reeling with one more memory to cling to and to be haunted by simultaneously. That this time around I'm just as guilty as she is because I'm knowingly cheating with a married woman.

But I can't stop myself. It's impossible to hold back.

With the taste of her kiss on my lips and the scent of her perfume in my nose and the feel of her skin against mine, I hope that if she can just feel me again, remember what we have together, if we can have just one more moment, then she'll know it's me who she wants.

Me who she'll choose.

Me who will keep her safe and her eyes dry from tears.

Our breaths are shaky, our kisses are bittersweet, and unspoken emotion swells between us as we help each other undress just enough so that we can race with unsteady hearts toward the ultimate pleasure that I'm pretty sure will result in more pain. But I push the rational thought away, quiet her lips telling me she can't over and over with my own.

We move in hurried but meaningful motions: my hands pushing her pants down, her hands stroking my dick. My fingers spread her open, the groan in my throat when I find her soaking wet. Hands skimming over warm flesh, the weight of her breasts in my hands, the creak of the console as I lift her hips up and she parts for me. The adamant repeat of "I can't" morphing into a soft sigh of need when her muscles tense as I push into her.

And that singular sensation, my hard cock sliding into her resisting muscles undoes me. Consumes me. Blinds me from seeing the truths that I don't want to face. That this is a good-bye to rival all other good-byes. Our kisses have communicated it all along, and now our bodies do the same through slow strokes, the tilt of her hips up to meet mine as I grind into hers, the bite of her nails in my shoulders, our unsteady breaths as we break momentarily from a kiss only for her to repeat her mantra before I kiss her again to stop her protests.

I move my hips slowly at first, the emotion and sensation almost too much to bear because how can we be this close and yet so far from how we used to be? But I find as much comfort as I can in the familiar little things: the gasp she emits when I brush my thumb over her clit, the texture of her tightened nipple against my tongue, the tensing of her thighs around my hips.

She won't look at me, though. And I can't have that. Can't have her trying to shut me out now, so I still my hips when I'm buried to the hilt in her, leveraging her weight against mine, and bring my thumb and forefinger to her chin so that she's forced to meet my eyes. Only when she holds her face steady, emerald eyes drowsy with lust but glistening with tears, do I continue the slow withdrawal from her body and then the bittersweet thrust to join our bodies again.

She comes in a violent shudder, her muscles tensing around me and my name on her lips for the first time since we started, but her voice sounds thick from the tears lodged in her throat.

"Beaux." I groan her name as a blinding flash of heat surges through my body and possesses my movements so that when I grind into her one last time, I lose more than just my orgasm to her. Oh fuck. I lose so much more, but thank God I'm blinded by my climax so that I can't think about it just yet.

We remain motionless for a moment, our bodies connected in the most intimate and carnal of ways, our arms wrapped around each other and our heads resting on opposite shoulders as we try to come to terms with what just happened and what I feel deep down I know is going to happen next. I'm afraid to speak, afraid to move, because once I do, I know I'll never get this moment back.

"Beaux," I murmur into her shoulder, "please . . . I need to understand."

"We shouldn't have done this," she whispers. "You need to go."

"How can you say that? How can—"

"Just please go. Forget I ever existed."

I snap my head up painfully, eyes searching hers for answers she won't give me as I try to dredge up the promise I made to myself before I walked onto the flight: to walk away and never look back if she rejected me. The hard thing is my feet are rooted in place, just like my heart.

"I could never forget you. Never." I grit out words that have never been more true in my life. My hands come up to frame her face tenderly, her bottom lip trembling with the emotion I feel but don't think I can show her because then I'd just give her another piece of me I'll never get back.

And she already holds too many pieces of me as it is.

"I'll walk away, Beaux. I'll walk away and never look back if you ask me to . . . if that's what you want. It'll kill me because I don't understand, but I'll do it for you. God, I'd do anything for you right now," I plead as my voice breaks with the weight of what I'm saying to her. "Just please tell me this wasn't all a lie. Please tell me the nights we spent on the rooftop and the laughs we shared and the sex we had wasn't just a joke to you. I need to leave knowing that what was between us wasn't all in my head."

"Tanner . . ."

"Can you give me that? Can you answer me so that I have something to hold on to?"

In an unexpected move that startles me, she takes my hand and places it on her chest over her heart with hers on top of mine. "Can you feel what I'm thinking?" she asks as her heart beats an erratic staccato beneath my palm. When she looks back up, her eyes are filled with tears, and one slips off her cheek and hits our connected hands. I bend my knees so that we're face-to-face and she can't escape from answering me with words. "I meant what I said about everything," she whispers, and it makes my mind whirl.

About loving me? About not being able to be with me? About what? I want to shake her shoulders and insist that she answer all of my questions, but I know it's no use. I know how stubborn she is, know how she'll close down. Well at least I think I do, because I thought she loved me too and now she's pushing me away.

My jaw is clenched, and my pulse is pounding a useless tempo because I've lost her. I close my eyes for a brief second to gather the wherewithal to walk away, angst slowly giving way to anger and resentment that she gets to make all the decisions here. "Don't do this, Beaux," I whisper more for myself than for her.

"If you ever loved me, you need to do this for me. Walk out the door and don't look back."

"I lov—"

"Shh! Not now. Not like this," she says as she puts a fingertip to my lips, her head shaking side to side. "You need to go."

There are so many words I want to say to her, so many things she needs to know, but as I start to lower my hands from her face, disbelief burns like a cannonball in my stomach. I grab her cheeks without warning and press my lips to hers in a kiss teeming with need, want, desire, desperation, and good-bye.

Once I break off the kiss, hoping it tells her everything I haven't said, because I know I could keep at it forever, I stride from the house, heart on my sleeve and a hole in my chest. All without meeting her eyes for a last time or saying another word.

Let her think about that kiss on the nights when she's lonely.

My feet eat up the sidewalk. Then finally I slide into

my car and bang my fist against the dashboard. It would be so much easier to walk away if the sex had been savage and carnal and full of spite. A quick fuck to work each other out of our respective systems so that we could move on. A little piece of physical satisfaction to mask the anger and hurt vibrating beneath the surface. It would have screamed that we weren't meant to be together. That we were a fucking flare of desire that had already hit the high point and was crashing to the ground, burning itself out.

But it wasn't. Not in the least. We made love. It was slow and emotional and so real that I can taste more than just her kiss still. So it's that much harder to walk away because you can't fake that. You can't connect with someone on every level like that and have it be a goddamn farce.

It gave me hope. A false hope. And false hope is the worst kind of all.

I made a promise to myself to walk away if she pushed. Well I pushed back when I shouldn't have, tried to help her, love her, be with her, anything with her, and now I have to walk away and never look back. So I choke back all of the emotion within me that threatens to come bubbling out. I won't allow it.

As I drive away from the perfect little Stepford house growing smaller in my rearview mirror, all I keep thinking is that looking back is all I want to do.

Fuck the popular theory that if you love something, you should set it free; I came back and look how that turned out.

Whoever said love is like war, easy to begin but hard to end, knew exactly what he was talking about.

For the next couple hours I drive aimlessly, losing my way and not caring if I find my way back because frankly

I have nowhere to go. I vacillate between thinking what a huge mistake it was coming here and knowing that Beaux does love me.

How in the hell can I walk away from her without more of a fight?

When my phone rings, my hopes surge that it's her calling me to come back. Seeing Rafe's name, I ignore the call, in no mood to speak to him. He calls one more time. Then my phone alerts a text. When I look down, my curiosity is piqued when I see the code 9999, the one that we've used over the past five years for him to tell me that a story's about to break and he wants me on it.

I stare at the screen for a few minutes. The fact that I'm interested but the buzz of adrenaline I thrive on is thready at best tells me that my head is elsewhere. I contemplate ignoring the text and heading back to Beaux's house, but know I'll kick myself later if it's something huge that I passed up for a woman who'll no doubt reject me again.

Even though my heart's not in it, and my head is warring over whether I'm giving up too easily on Beaux, I dial the phone to return his call.

I was raised to fight for what I believe in and to not give up until I get it, so what do I do now?

"Tanner." Rafe greets me, his tone curt and his impatience more than obvious.

"What gives?" I ask before realizing this is the first time we've actually spoken in more than ten days, and a part of me cringes at the sound of his voice.

"What the fuck are you trying to pull, Tan?"

Whiplash hits me full force because I have no idea what he's talking about. "Come again?"

"You're in Kansas?" He yells into the phone as my hand falls off the steering wheel and into my lap while the shock and confusion over how he knows I'm here rifles through me. "You couldn't let it go, could you?"

"What in the fuck are you talking about?" I shout back, my mind coming up blank on how he knows I'm here. I didn't tell anyone where I was going or what I was doing.

"Don't try and play me for a fool, man. Beaux. You tracked her down? What in the hell were you thinking?"

I open my mouth and close it before something I can't take back comes out of it. "Rafe ... you don't understand. I'm just—"

"You're just getting a restraining order filed against you is what you're doing."

My head whips up in complete bewilderment because there's no way he just said what I think he said. "What are you talking about?" I feel like we're having two completely separate conversations, and neither of them looks promising for me.

"I just got a call from Beaux. She's filed a restraining order against you."

"What?" I feel like the word screams through my head in a tornado of bewilderment, but my voice comes out even and quiet.

"Yeah. She wanted you to know that if you show up at her house again you'll be arrested because she's already filed one against you."

I laugh long and hard, the edges of the sound tinged with hysteria that I won't even deny as I sag against the seat, my head dropping back as I attempt to fathom how we went from the intimate murmurs in the foyer of her house to the tearful good-bye after sex to me being threatened with arrest. I'm at a complete loss and in utter shock.

"She did what?" I finally say into the phone as I try to

piece together what in the fuck she's trying to prove here.

"I'm not joking, Tanner, and I don't know what's going on with you, but you're scaring me. Forget what I said before when I was talking as your boss and ordered you to come home. Listen to me right now as I speak to you as a friend. Dude, you're losing your shit. You just tracked down a married woman, visited her house when she didn't want you there, and did who knows what, but whatever it was is bad enough for her to spend the last few hours taking legal action to prevent you from doing it again. It's called stalking, Tanner."

"Stalking?" I say as I run a hand through my hair. This entire conversation is comical on so many levels, considering I believe I accused her of the same exact thing those first few days after we met when she was everywhere I turned. The irony is just too good to be true. "Oh that's rich." I'm dumbfounded as the laughter won't subside. "She's out of her damn mind."

"Yeah, well maybe you should knock it the fuck off. Honestly, dude, I think you're way off base here. Not acting like the person I know at all, but what do I know? Maybe she's the crazy one. Maybe you need to get the fuck away from her. What if she accuses you of something worse?" he says.

"Not Beaux. No way. She wouldn't do that." I reject his implications immediately. He wasn't there, doesn't know what just happened . . . but then again I was, and now she's filing a fucking restraining order? I pinch the bridge of my nose, welcome the pain of it as I try to wrap my head around the incredible highs and staggering lows of the day, and shut out the thoughts that he's planting.

"I sound like a broken record, but you need to get on a plane and get home. She's banking on the probability that you'll be rational and listen to me. That you'll leave

Kansas and her alone or else she'll go to the boss men next time, and you know what that means." He blows out a frustrated sigh.

"I'm trying to figure out when it became your job to manage my private life, Rafe."

"Well when you keep risking your job for a piece of ass who's obviously playing you and going to get you fired, then it's my job."

"Are you threatening me?" I shout incredulously, purposefully ignoring the first part of his statement and the need to defend that she was so much more than just a piece of ass.

"If she goes to the brass and it comes down to it, man . . . I'll have to fire you."

"Then fire me," I challenge. The buzz is already gone for me anyway.

"Really, Tan? You're going to throw away all of your hard work and killer career for a woman who doesn't want you? Who lied to you?"

"She does want me, though." I cringe when I realize I spoke my thoughts aloud. "Something's off here, Rafe. My gut instinct tells me that—"

"Stop! Please just stop and come home. It's one thing to throw yourself into the fire when you're trying to save something, but there is nothing to be saved here. Do you really want to be burned at the stake for nothing?" he rants as I fall silent and try to digest everything and question parts of my own sanity. How long am I going to chase a woman who loves me but obviously won't let me into her life? "Tanner?" Rafe's concerned voice breaks through my musings.

"I'm on sabbatical, remember?" There's resignation front and center in my voice as I end the call without another word. Let him worry about what I'm going to do next since it's none of his damn business. *Fuck.* I blow out a breath and rest my head against the steering wheel to try to come to grips with my warring thoughts and what he said.

Nothing makes sense, and yet I gave it all I've got. I can't keep throwing good after bad no matter how much it hurts to walk away.

But that's what I'm going to do. It's what I have to do. I'm not a man who grovels. I'm a man who falls in and out of love at the flick of a switch, a paradox as Stella called me, and so I'm just going to get my shit from my hotel room, hop on a plane, and leave everything I thought I wanted behind so that I can force myself to fall back out of love.

It can't be that hard to do. I've done it a hundred times before.

Even I don't believe my own lies this time.

Chapter 28

"Are you seriously going to pass up that wave, Thomas?" the voice calls out behind me in a tone that has me rolling my eyes and raising my middle finger to my brother-in-law when he paddles up behind me.

"It wasn't good."

"That's what you said about the one before that and then the one before that. That photographer still have your dick in a twist?"

"Humph." Even two weeks after my visit to Kansas, I still don't understand things any better than I did that night. I can't tell if the whole situation is killing me or making me stronger, but I know that the hurt's turned to anger and the disbelief to resentment. The one thing I know for sure is that the unknown still looms like a weight in my chest that I'm slowly ignoring more and more, bit by bit, day by day.

But that twist? It's still there.

"So more like kinked than twisted now?" he says, earning a smile from me.

"Something like that." I exhale loudly, not in the

mood to talk, not in the mood to surf either now that I think about it. But there's nothing like getting out in the water to clear your head. The sun feels good on my face, and the water steadily lapping over my legs on the board unwinds me bit by bit. I almost don't even care if I catch a wave or not because for the first time in forever it feels like I can relax—ironic in itself since I haven't gone on a story in almost two months.

And usually that's the only thing that can relax me.

"Kink can be good, brother," he says, and lifts one eyebrow with a smirk.

I flash him a warning look. "I don't want to know," I say, drawing a laugh because I sure as hell don't want to even remotely know anything about my sister's sex life. Our eyes hold for a minute, and I can see him trying to figure out how to get to whatever he wants to say. "Just lay it on me, man," I finally tell him. As much as I'll take a day surfing at Trestles, I also know that Colton had an ulterior motive when he asked me to meet him here.

His was the same motive my sister's had with every phone call she's made in the two weeks since I've been back from Kansas: to see how I'm doing or try to get me out of the house. To make sure I'm not wallowing in whatever it is I'm supposedly wallowing in.

Oh yeah, heartbreak. That's what it's called.

"Lay what on you? Your brother-in-law can't invite you to go surfing without a reason?" he asks, and earns a long, disbelieving laugh from me.

"Look, any excuse to get out in the water is a good one, especially here of all places," I say as I look toward the renowned Southern California beach before looking back to him. "But remember, I grew up with my sister. I know from experience how well she can assert her will to get you to do what she wants."

Colton throws his head back and laughs and doesn't

need to say a single word to tell me that I'm right. "Ah, God, she's a trip, but I love her to death," he says, making me smile because I feel the same way. And it's good to know that he does.

I debate how to play this, wondering if he's really going to go to that place men don't go, to talking, and yet it feels good to be out of the house and hanging with someone I like since everyone else I know is still on assignment somewhere. "You don't have to do this, Colton. I appreciate you inviting me to meet up, but if Ry wants to fish and see how I'm doing, she doesn't need you to do her dirty work for her."

"I know," he says, and ruffles a hand through his hair to shake the water from it. "Look, it's none of my business, but what the fuck, man? You're a good judge of character. . . . Didn't you see crazy coming from a mile away?" he asks incredulously with a half laugh.

"I don't know what to believe anymore." I shake my head, still at a loss over everything but slowly moving on.

"Dude, we are talking about women, right?" he jokes, and garners an *amen* from me. "When it comes to women, what you believe gets thrown out the window and whirls around in a little eddy I call the estrogen vortex. It sucks you into their crazy and spits you out completely dazed, confused, and questioning why you ever stepped close enough to begin with . . . well besides the tits and ass and curves. . . ."

"You can say that again."

"It's the mythical blooming onion."

"The what?" I question.

"You know. . . . She's got all kinds of layers you can't wait to taste, but then once you peel them away, your gut feels like shit and you're left with a bad taste in your mouth."

I snort and roll my eyes while we fall into a comfortable silence as the set of swells on the horizon dies down some.

"Bad taste is right. Shit, I didn't see any of it coming, Colton, not at all. I feel like a fucking chump. No idea she was married. Didn't realize the sneaking away in the middle of the night to take pictures was a cover because she was calling her husband. Not the text she sent me where I tracked her to Kansas, thinking she was leaving me a goddamn clue to come and save her. Not the sex we had when I found her that she used as a final good-bye before filing a fucking restraining order against me . . ." My voice trails off, incredulity in my tone and frustration reflected in my posture.

"That's cold, man," Colton says with a shake of his head. "I had a woman do that to me once. Have sex as her way of saying good-bye."

"What did you do to get over her?" I'll admit I'm surprised the infamous ladies' man Colton Donavan was played like I was. Makes me feel a little better.

"I married her," he deadpans, causing my head to whip over to meet his eyes as he throws his head back in a laugh.

"Rylee did that shit to you?" I ask, completely surprised by the ballsy move on my sister's part. "You probably deserved it, though."

"Yes, I did." He smirks at a memory, but the way his face softens tells me that it was a good one and that he wouldn't want it any other way because he got the girl in the end.

"For some reason, though, I think the restraining order tells me that I won't have the same ending." I laugh at myself because there's not much else I can do.

"Would you really want one, though? Legal action is kind of an extreme move to play in the game of hard to get."

"True," I murmur.

"What's her deal? I'm assuming you dug into her background."

"Couldn't find anything. Not even mortgage records for the house, nothing. So either they have a friend on the force who buried their information, or I'm getting rusty. I've got to be careful, though. Don't want to get caught snooping between losing my job at Worldwide and the restraining order . . . so who knows. . . ."

"You should have checked the asylums." His comment earns a snort from me in response. "I mean the only advice I can give you is the next time you fall in love, make sure that you're the crazy one."

My laugh comes out long and deep. Such a typical comment from the former playboy himself. "Well some say love is a serious mental disease," I say with a shrug. "Guess that proves something I've spent a lifetime trying to prove."

"What's that?" he asks.

"That my sister is crazy," I state matter of factly.

He laughs and shakes his head before staring out to the ocean around us. "Look, man, I know how hard it is . . . but everyone's life is like a story. Maybe that chapter of your book is closed . . . ," he says, his voice fading off. "Then again, maybe you need to open the damn book back up and rewrite the shit you didn't like. Don't accept it, Tanner. Some people say you can't change your fate. I'm living proof that you can. If you don't like the ending, change it," he finishes with a shrug before duck-diving under a wave as I'm pushed toward shore, my mind toying with the truth in his words.

Colton's analogy rings in my ears but brings a smile to my lips as I make the drive home down the coastline. My mood is the best it's been in a while, so I'm glad I took the offer of a day on the water to get away from my doldrums right now. After the guy talk, I feel like my head is back on straighter than it has been in the last month, an affirmation that I need to hold on to the anger a little tighter and let go of the want a little more, because what I need to do is forget all about her.

My cell rings through the Bluetooth as I exit the freeway, and for the first time in two weeks I decide to pick up Rafe's call.

"You're finally talking to me again?" he asks with a chuckle, and I feel the smile tug at the corners of my mouth.

"I'm slowly forgiving you."

"For what? Saving your ass? *Thank you* is what you should be saying."

I sigh into the line. "Don't press your luck."

"Regardless, you sound good."

"I feel good," I answer as I try to figure out where he's going with this.

"Feel good enough to head back into action?" he asks, which stuns the hell out of me so much that I miss my own street.

"What do you mean?" There is a cautious tone to my voice, and I'm not sure exactly where it's coming from. Maybe getting back on assignment is just what I need to distract me from the temptation of seeing her again.

"You haven't seen the news today, have you?"

"What do you mean?" I ask as I turn down my street, noticing William finally moved his beast of a car because I can actually see my house when I turn on the road. Thank God. At least some other neighbor was the asshole and told him to move it before I did.

"The U.S. embassy was bombed. On your old stomping grounds. An ambassador and an agent lost. Figured you'd want a chance to report—"

"When?" Immediately I'm sitting taller in my seat because it's been a long time since this has happened; it's usually a precursor to a military campaign of some kind. And a military campaign means I have something to occupy me overseas to avoid the temptation of knowing where she is and that she doesn't want me. Somehow distance seems like it will help.

"A few hours ago. There's a briefing first thing in the morning in D.C. with intelligence officials to explain the objective of the mission, make sure it is spelled out and not misrepresented," he says.

"So basically the government's inviting the press to handle the image we'll portray in regard to what's happening," I say, discouraged and frustrated all at the same time, but I know my reputation precedes me. If Rafe's calling me, he knows the story he'll get from me, that I won't bow to the pretty wrapping of the package they are trying to tie up for me. "I'll go. No one is going to tell me what I can and can't report, though."

Rafe chuckles. "That's exactly what I was hoping you were going to say. You know my rules — report the truth; I'll worry about the rest. When can you leave?"

For the first time ever in my life, I hesitate before answering him. And that I don't know why makes it even worse. Is it because I've gotten the longest taste of normal life that I've had in forever? Or is it because a small part of me is still hanging on to the hope that regardless of how much I tell myself that whatever was between Beaux and me is dead, I still have the slimmest margins of hope that she'll call?

And that thought alone spurs me to respond immediately.

"I'm turning down my street. Give me two hours tops to pack my shit and take care of a few things, then I'll head to the airport. I'll start making calls with my sources on location while I'm waiting for my flight. See what I can dig up to get ahead of the story," I say as I turn into my driveway.

I hang up the phone, my thoughts running faster than my mind can process as I grab the bag of stuff Rylee gave Colton to give me, get out of my 1976 restored Bronco, and pull my surfboard from the open back. I quickly hang my wet suit up in the garage and rinse my board off, acting as if I won't be coming back for a while.

The funny thing is, I'm going through the motions of things I've done so many times in my life, and yet they seem so halfhearted compared to normal. There is no urgency, no hurried movements, just more a quiet resignation that I've never felt before. My mind travels to thoughts of clapboard houses on quiet streets and teaching a little girl with long dark hair and amethyst eyes how to ride a bike without training wheels. Shit, I never thought it would happen until much later in life, but for the first time ever, I find myself wondering how much I'm missing, how many memories I'm missing out on making, because of my career choices.

Sure, the rush of getting the story first is such a fucking high, so then why don't I feel anything close to that right now? Why isn't my blood humming and my mind already back in the dirt and dust of a foreign country that doesn't seem inviting right now?

I enter the house from the door in the garage and toss my shit on the table, cursing when the bag from Rylee falls on its side, the contents spilling out. A card, as well as some random get-well presents from the boys that they made me after the blast that are so sweet they make me smile, tug on those heartstrings a tad more, but it's the bottle of bubbles that rolls to the edge of the table and falls to the floor that causes my bittersweet smile.

As soon as I pick them up, memories of Rylee using them to work out her life's disappointments and then the laughs Beaux and I shared on the rooftop that last night when everything seemed so crystal clear assault me. Too bad I didn't know it was all murky as fuck. Without thinking of the bags I have to pack, the phone calls I have to make, the task of emptying my refrigerator so that nothing spoils in case I'm gone more than a couple of days, I open the bubbles and blow a few into the empty space of my living room. Perfectly round, they float in a mix of colors, before they pop, each memory, good and bad, disappearing with them.

There's something about watching them that brings some kind of closure, one that's tinged with sadness. Stupid in the grand scheme of things when I should be packing, but it's there nonetheless.

I stand from the couch feeling like an idiot, a grown man blowing bubbles and not wanting to let go of the woman he loves. "God, Thomas. You're acting like a schmuck. Get over it. Get over *her*. Pack your shit and leave her behind."

But I don't want to leave her behind. The bubbles make me think of Beaux. Of rib-hurting laughter and sigh-worthy sex. Of her undeniable feistiness contrasted with her incredible tenderness. Of just how much I want to rewrite the last chapter or the whole fucking book if that's what it takes, because I want her in my life.

I blow out a breath, knowing I have so much shit to do and I've wasted a fair amount of time with a childish novelty, but I have to do one more thing. I pick up the phone and dial.

"Hello?"

"Hey, I just wanted to let you know that I picked up a story and am gonna hop on a flight. Should be gone a couple of days, but you know what?" I say to my sister, so amped up by my decision, I know by that alone that it's the right one. That I'm being true to myself.

"Tanner ... A story? So soon? I thought you were taking a break. What's going on?"

"Never mind the story. It's not important, because I figured it all out. Bubbles. It was the damn bubbles." I'm rambling and don't care if she thinks I'm losing my mind. I've lost it and found it, and everything is so damn crystal clear to me for the first time in far too long.

"What in the world are you—"

"I was blowing—never mind," I say, speaking ahead of my thoughts that are running out of control. "Look ... You were right. I've never walked away without a fight before, so why am I walking away now?" Rylee starts to speak, and I just step right over her. "I love Beaux. Like I'm whipped, want to do anything to make this work."

"There's a little thing called a restraining order," Rylee says cautiously, trying to hide the sarcasm mixed with the need to protect me from her voice.

"My gut tells me that there's more to it than what's going on. I just need to get a handle on what it is." I pace the length of my hallway as I agree with my own self-diagnosis that I'm crazy. "You told me you fight like hell for what you love. . . . Colton told me to rewrite the chapter and—"

"Rewrite what chapter?" she asks, confused.

"Ask your husband," I tell her, not wanting to waste any time. "But I love her like no one else I've ever been with before, and I know she feels the same way and damn it, I'm going to fight for her."

"Well, okay." She laughs. "But wait! You can't tell me all of this, get on a plane, and leave on that note!"

"I'll be back in a few days, Ry. The way I feel isn't going to change, and neither is my determination to win her back. You said love's crazy. Well now it's my turn to be crazy, but this time? This time, crazy is going to get the girl!"

Her laughter fills the line. "Go get 'em, Tan!"

I hang up the phone with the incredible feeling that

everything is falling into place. I'm going back to work, gonna do my job, get the story first, do it better than anyone else. Because like Beaux said, I'm the one. Then I'm going to fly back to Kansas and fight for the girl. Get her out of whatever situation she's in with John that puts that constant worry and fear in her eyes. I may be the farthest thing from the white knight, but I sure as fuck can save the day.

But right now I need to get ready to leave.

I get everything packed, clothes, electronics, passport— all of the shit that sits in the closet waiting for the word go on a moment's notice—but when I turn to take one last glance at my bedroom to make sure I've got everything, my feet falter as my eyes fall on Stella's camera collecting dust on the top of my dresser. Conscious that time is limited, I walk over and reach out for it, my finger wiping away a streak of dust.

It's been a little over nine months since I last saw her smile, heard her voice, laughed with her. For the first time since then, I think I'm ready to see the images from that night. I'm ready to face them.

Not to forget her, but just to say good-bye.

Because for the first time in forever, I can admit that guilt held me hostage from doing it. And not guilt because she was out buying me a birthday present when she was killed but instead for not protecting her long enough for her to find her once-in-a-lifetime. God yes, I loved her. Loved her company and her corny jokes and so many more things about her, but I wasn't that person for her. It's taken me the longest time to realize that. And maybe, just maybe, when the hurt fades from all of the shit with Beaux, I'll be able to be thankful to her for that because learning that I loved Beaux, feeling the intensity of that connection, made me realize what that once-in-a-lifetime might possibly feel like.

And even though it still feels like a spilled beaker full

of acid in my chest at times, I know it's possible. And at least I know that I wasn't cheating Stella out of that by not trying to rekindle what we might have had.

When I pick up the camera and turn it on, I'm surprised that the battery is still charged enough that when I click over to the slide show of pictures, it responds. The first image that pops up causes a lump to form in my throat but also a smile to come to my face. Stella has her arm around me, a silly cone-shaped party hat on her head, and her tongue stuck out at the camera while I'm beside her, an exasperated look on my face but a smirk on my lips. And of course the first picture captures us perfectly—our friendship, our partnership, everything— so much that it's just what I need to see to know I'm right and at the same time to be able to say good-bye.

I flip through the rest of them quickly. Pauly dancing on the tabletop, Bob's Pee-wee Herman dance that I'll never forget, the shots lined up and down the bar top, the disaster of a birthday cake they made me, but none of them compares to the one time that Beaux stepped out from behind the camera for the picture of the two of us.

Feeling less burdened, I stare one more time at the image of two people lucky in friendship, carefree, and lost in the moment before I look up to catch my own reflection. The lines around my eyes are a little deeper now and my eyes a lot more weary, the curve of my mouth still holding on to the bitterness some. Reflections don't lie. They magnify the truths you want to hide from, the reality you don't want to face, the shit you need to get over.

They also make you want to punch the mirror so you don't have to see anything you don't want to.

Well, at least I've dealt with one of the two women who fucked me up. It's still best if I don't think about the other one too much.

Restraining order, my ass.

Chapter 29

When I enter the conference room, I'm already late. My plane landed on time but then was delayed on the tarmac due to airport traffic. Once I make it through the security checks at the meeting facility, sign my life away to confidentiality, and open the door, I'm not quite sure what to expect. The tiered room is medium in size, with the back portion filled with people sporting their press credentials and the front of the room a sea of military uniforms ranging from fatigues to dress blues to the more subtle suits and ties usually typical of intelligence officials.

I work my way as close to the front as I can, but since the press person leading the meeting is speaking already, I don't want to draw too much attention my way. The whole flight here, I questioned the justification of this meeting, its overall purpose, and then as I'm seated and tune in to the speaker, I realize it's just what I thought— a dog and pony show. A propaganda fest promising numerous embedded missions to ensure that we report in a positive light all of the action that we will see once we get boots down on the ground.

I'm not a rookie. I'm irritated that I have to even be here when I've proven time and again that I'm not going to bad-mouth U.S. military tactics for the sake of television ratings. I could be on a plane right now to ensure I'm the first one at the scene instead of here wasting my time.

My head's down as I doodle on my pad, taking the names of the people who are speaking although I'll never use them when I'm in the middle of dirt and dust and gunfire, but it's something to do rather than let my mind run away with thoughts of once again touching down without a photographer.

Especially the one I want the most.

The speaker begins to finally talk about the one thing I have interest in, the terrorist bombing at the embassy. And as explanations begin, I look up to the screens flashing images of the on-site devastation: twisted metal, concrete rubble, smoke, and dust. Then she moves on to the deaths incurred. When the image changes, everything in my body freezes as Beaux's image appears on the screen.

The image changes before I can process it fully. Before I can believe it. I laugh out loud like this is some kind of joke, my eyes looking around for the hidden cameras, but as I meet the appalled gazes of those around me, the bottom drops out from under me. All I can do is look back at the screen in front of me and wait for the image to appear again in the series of photographs.

I'm staggered. Confused. Broken. Disbelieving.

I struggle to draw in a breath, fight incoherency as I try to process thoughts, wince as the pain in my chest constricts so tightly, I feel as if someone is pulling my heart out and not letting go of it all at the same time.

There's no way she's dead. Can't be.

My thoughts run rampant as I slide to the edge of my

seat, willing the picture to appear again. And when it does, I blink my eyes rapidly and wish the image away.

Because it's Beaux. There's no denying it. The picture may be older and of Beaux dressed in a business suit, but it's her, the woman I love, raven hair, green eyes. I hear her laugh, see her smile, smell her perfume, and miss the sound of her voice.

The projector turns off, the screen goes black, and yet I still stare.

This can't be happening. Fractured thoughts break free and crash around in my head, but the one that sticks the most is that *I'm too late*. Through the fog of emotion, that's the only thing I can process right off the bat. I never even had the chance to fight for her again, win her back, tell her I love her. . . . Once again I'm too late.

The vise grip of disbelief squeezes tighter as the speaker drones on, and I hear nothing, see nothing, except for the look on Beaux's face the last time I saw her. Conflicted, compliant, flushed, beautiful, and still *mine* despite being married to another man.

Shock numbs me at first. Doesn't allow me to accept the truth of what I just heard, that Beaux's gone. That I've lost yet another woman to this violent lifestyle I've chosen to live.

And even though it feels like a lifetime, I'm sure only seconds pass as the second what-the-fuck moment hits me like a wrecking ball. Only tiny slices of reality are able to slip through at a time, but all of a sudden I realize that I didn't lose her because she was a photographer in the wrong place at the wrong time. No. I lost her because she was with the CIA, an intelligence officer, Special Agent BJ Croslyn.

Disbelief wars with grief, and a whole shitload of con-fusion in a matter of seconds as I realize Beaux was a spy. *A fucking spy.* At first I reject the idea despite where I'm sitting and what I'm hearing in the briefing, because there's not a chance in hell that she was an agent. She was small and naive and didn't even know how to shoot a gun for Christ's sake.

But as soon as that thought hits me, a dozen others flicker and fade in my mind's eye and neutralize the bitter taste of rejection on my tongue: her fluent Dari, the pictures she'd take at night when she'd sneak out time-stamped for proof, secret phone calls in the hallway, keeping her past a secret, so many things that appeared unrelated at the time. But now this common denominator blinking like a huge arrow overhead makes the truth seem so obvious.

But more than anything is the feeling that from day one I was being played somehow, some way. That notion she wiped away with her defiant nature and addictive body. The one she made me forget all about with words like *I love you* and *I can't.* She used me, used false emotions in a real world.

Except my emotions weren't fake. They were real. Still are real.

She's gone.

This can't be real.

But they are saying it's real. The woman at the front of the room is telling me she pretended she couldn't shoot a gun when I knew her. That she was faking it and used it as a perfect way to play someone like me and make sure that I believed she was this naive little thing in this big bad far-off land.

I'm completely disengaged during the rest of the briefing, overwhelmed with memories that won't release me. With feelings on my end that were one hundred percent genuine that now make me feel so ridiculous and yet hurt nonetheless. She wasn't some little inexperienced freelancer. She was a spy who came overseas, used me for cover, and then when she was done, came back home to her husband and everyday life until it was time for her to leave again on another mission.

An agent who was playing me at every turn. And I had no idea.

I thought I knew her. Thought the love I felt in her touch and saw in her eyes was real. How did I misread every single fucking moment when they were so damn perfect, so sincere, just so much more than I've ever allowed myself to feel before?

Dropping my head in my hands, I try to comprehend how I was willing to go back on every single principle I've ever held. How was it just hours ago I was more certain than anything I'd ever felt in my life that she was the one? When I got back from this assignment, I was planning to show her I was willing to give up my career for her, take a chance at getting arrested considering the restraining order, and fight like hell to prove that even though she was married, I was the right one for her. Not John. Not anyone else. Just me.

Because it was that fucking real.

But obviously I don't know shit, least of all what real love is, because every single thing was a lie. A big fat lie.

Why couldn't she have done her job and been my partner without luring me in? In time I'm sure I'll understand that maybe she was protecting her family and John back home by saying she wasn't involved with somebody, but why do this to me too?

But she's gone. I wish I could ask her, wish I could shake her shoulders and demand an answer, and then I wish I could kiss her senseless and feel her pulse race beneath mine. I'd give anything to get the chance to be mad at her, fight with her, tell her how much I hate her for putting me through this and then leaving me to sort through it all, but I'll never get the chance.

Rage burns through my veins, leaving ash piles of heartache and disbelief behind. That staunch determination I walked in here with to get the story first, then get the girl and make a life with her is gone just like she is. I have nothing left to hold on to, least of all confidence in my own judgment.

I don't know how long I sit in the meeting room with a broken heart, an aching soul, and a damaged psyche, but when I break from my thoughts, I realize the conference room is almost empty with a line at the door as people wait to file out. And I really don't care, because a huge part of me that prefers the dark places I've learned so well to hide in after Stella's death knows that the minute I leave this room, I fear she'll cease to exist. As much as I'm hurt and angry and devastated, the notion still stabs deep within me because fuck yes she played me, made me fall in love with a woman who didn't really exist, but the emotions I felt for her were incredibly real to me.

So a small part of me worries that if I step out of this room, I'll then have to admit it was all a fake, and I can't do that just yet because, call me a fucking sap, but I still love her. None of this takes that away.

The hand on my shoulder startles me. I'm on my feet and turning around in an instant and without a second thought when I see John's face before me, my arm is cocked back, my fist flying. I connect with his right eye with a satisfying reverberation traveling up my arm and into my body but abating none of the emotional distress I feel.

"You son of a bitch!" I yell as bone meets bone again, every ounce of emotion I have fueling the impact of the

punch. I hate him. I hate him with everything I have because he didn't protect her. He had her when I didn't,
kept her when I couldn't, and he failed as a husband to
do the one thing he was supposed to do, keep her safe.
And I know I'm being irrational and there's no way he
could keep her safe when she was off doing God knows
what, but it feels good to unleash my confused fury on
someone else for a change rather than let it eat me apart.

"You didn't keep her safe! I loved her! I loved her!" I
shout as flesh gives way to force, my voice breaking, my
body vibrating with everything that I refuse to accept.

People in the room move, gasp, and I can't even process how many punches it takes for one of their hands to
grip my shoulders and pull me off him at the same time
I realize that John isn't resisting me. He isn't even flinching with each punch I land, and all of a sudden it regis-
ters that he might be in the same boat as I am. He may
have never known Beaux was a spy. He may have just
lost the love of his life too.

I can't hold on to the thought for more than a second
because all I can hold on to is the grief that owns my
every action and reaction right now, robbing my breath,
stealing my tears, and annihilating the very idea of fate.

I fight against the hands pulling me off John, and then
I just give up and roll onto my back atop the broken
pieces of a chair that we just obliterated. My chest is
heaving; the sound of my labored breathing is the only
thing I can hear besides my heart breaking as I lie there,
John battered beside me, and despair stretched out in
front of me.

"She loved you." I freeze at the strained words coming from him lost in the shuffle of feet moving around us
now that the show is over. I blink several times as I lie
there, trying to make sure I've heard him correctly, because they were the last things I ever thought I'd hear

come from him. I open my mouth to speak but shut it when I'm not sure exactly what to say. "We need to talk in private."

And the way he says it has my curiosity piqued, my mind clearing some to briefly wonder how a civilian could be in on this meeting, but my thoughts are lost to the feeling deep down that I want nowhere near him right now. We may have loved the same woman, but that doesn't mean that I have to like him. In fact, it is completely opposite from the way I feel. As soon as I catch my breath, I want the fuck out of here because I can't breathe. Can't think in here. I don't want to believe the lies I was just told in this room . . . because they are lies. She can't be gone. This can't be happening.

How can her own husband make that statement? That would mean they've talked about me.

But he said she loved me. It's the one thing I've wanted to hear more than anything, but at the same time right now, I'm not sure I can handle it.

"Go to hell," I grit out between breaths, starting to push myself up because I have a plane to catch, and if I catch it, then I can run away and pretend like this meeting never happened and that she's still alive and I'm still going to come back in a few days and fight like hell to win her over. To make her understand that what we have is real and true and worth it.

"We weren't married," John whispers ever so softly. I stop midway to standing and look over to him for the first time as my heart stutters in my chest. His eyes mirror the grief in mine, the loss burning bright, but they are also saying something else that I can't quite understand. "Can we talk?" he asks, using his chin to indicate a doorway over to his right.

I stare at him, wanting to know and yet afraid to know more. But I follow John inside and shut the door behind us, leery, uncomfortable and overwhelmed because so many things have been thrown at me that I can't comprehend any of them.

"Sit?" he asks, and I just lean a shoulder against the wall. I've had enough things knock me to my knees right now; I don't think there's much more that can. Besides, I fear that once I process this all, once it all sinks in, I won't be able to move anyway, so sitting? No, thanks.

"What I'm about to tell you is classified and could get me fired and you in trouble, but you deserve to know the truth." I just stare at the ground, my eyes shut, and fingers pinching the bridge of my nose because I'm so afraid of hearing what's next and at the same time a small part of me holds on to some hope that he's going to tell me that was all a farce out there. That Beaux's alive. That when I open the door, she's going to be standing there with that smirk on her face and green eyes looking for me. "I'm Dane Culver. Nice to meet you."

My head whips up at his extended hand. What the fuck? "Wha . . . ?" I don't even bother finishing the word or shaking his hand.

"Beaux was my partner. I'm an agent too. Our marriage was a cover."

"Wait a minute, so—"

"So that means how she felt for you was real. She loved you." His voice is soft, sympathetic, but all I can hear are the words "She loved you."

I sag against the wall, another tsunami of emotions hitting the wave that's already ebbing because I can't focus on anything, my thoughts splintering into a million pieces as the questions try to bubble up to the surface. My hands are cradling my head as I double over because if I thought the news of her death was devastating before, it's crippling now. Because now that I know she wasn't married, hadn't cheated on her husband, it's like the veil of guilt that shrouded around the love I felt for her has been lifted and those feelings are a hundred times more intense and a thousand times more devastating.

"Oh. My. God." They are the only words I can say, and I repeat them over and over as all of the things I doubted and questioned and berated myself for dissipate, so that what I thought I really lost, I really did lose.

And after a few minutes of trying to breathe underwater, all of a sudden it's like I can draw in a breath for the first time when my thoughts line up together. "So this is part of it too, right? She's really alive. The bombing wasn't real either?" Even I find the hope lacing the incredulity in my tone pathetic, but I am holding on to threads here, and when that's all you have, you don't care how bad they cut you as your grip slips so long as you're still holding them.

When I stare at Dane, I know my hope is fleeting, because his eyes well up with the tears that won't come for me. He shakes his head slowly, sniffing his nose and clearing his throat. "I'm sorry. . . . Goddamn it!" He pounds on the table and shoves up out of the chair he's sitting in as he swallows back the emotion threatening to overwhelm him. "I was supposed to be at the embassy with her, might have been able to save her," he says, unable to look at me, "but I wasn't slated to leave for a few days while I made sure her cover remained intact."

I swallow over the lump in my throat, hating him for not being there to protect her once again, because if she was his partner, that was his job, and at the same time knowing that this is my anger speaking, because there's no way to protect someone from a bomb blast you didn't know was coming.

"I'm so confused," I confess, using the wall for support because it's taking everything I have to concentrate on his words and not on the pressure in my chest.

"Beaux wasn't just a photographer. She was an agent sent to gather intel for the agency on the high-level meet. Her job was to document figures in the game, watch their comings and goings, where they met up, who they spoke to. Cause some confusion amongst some of the local contacts so that we could make sure to take the targets out without them knowing."

"Omid." His name falls from my lips as I recall the look on his face the first time he got a good look at Beaux.

"Yes, Omid," Dane says. "He was sharing info with both sides. Beaux called me one night, afraid that he had recognized her when they came face-to-face in enemy territory when she was out gathering intel. She wasn't sure if he had or not, but—"

Dots connect for me. Her phone call in the hallway that night and how upset she was. Was that all about Omid? "He sent me a text about not trusting her that made no sense at the time. I just thought it was because she was a woman." All I can do is shake my head at all of this.

"She wasn't sure."

"The photos with odd time stamps, the late nights out by herself, the—"

"All missions to gather information and meet with sources," he says as pieces start clicking into place. Now things make so much sense, and yet I feel so stupid for not putting them together sooner, but how could I? This is like a Tom Clancy novel. Who would think this shit exists even though I live in its world on a daily basis? "We cleared her room out of all of her info while you were on your way to Germany," he explains as I just sit there and shake my head in disbelief.

"So her cover was blown?" I ask him, trying to draw connections that still aren't clicking solidly into place.

"In more ways than one," Dane says, and stares sternly at me in a way I can't read. "She called me one night while you were filing your report and told me she broke her cover with you. I was so pissed at her, told her she was risking everything, including her life. It was so hard having her there with you when I couldn't be there to protect her," he says, and for a moment I sympathize with him because I know that exact feeling, have failed twice in fact in doing just that. "She said you guys were talking and she forgot for a moment where she was, what she was supposed to be doing, but that she told you about her parents, her past. . . . Fuck man, that's like rule number one, know your backstory like the back of your hand, and she completely disregarded it."

I blow out a breath as a small part of me grabs onto his comment because that means that I have something more of Beaux to hold on to, that regardless of the reason she was there, she still showed me the real her. I fell in love with the real person on the inside, not something she wasn't.

"It was right then I knew something was going on between you two. She denied it fiercely, but I knew her well enough to know she was lying. I got her to admit in a roundabout way that there was something between you, but she told me that you guys weren't telling anyone, that you'd honor the promise because the integrity of your work was so important to you and so if push came to shove, her cover would hold. . . ." His voice fades off, allowing me to absorb what he's said to this point, and while I still feel like I'm drinking the information from a firehose, at least I have information to drown in. And heartache. There's definitely no escaping the weariness that assails me from finding this all out too late. Everything is just too late.

"The IED," Dane says, pulling me from the riot in my

head and heart. "Both Rosco's and Sarge's reports stated that they thought they heard someone call Beaux's name. We intercepted radio chatter congratulating over a takeout. We couldn't be positive they meant Beaux, so we immediately went into protective mode, because if someone called her name, that meant she might have had eyes on her, a bounty on her head for playing both sides."

"So if her caring husband shows up at Landstuhl, makes a scene—"

"And she goes home with him and has a domesticated life in a house that they suddenly moved into and a fake background to reinforce it, then there's no way she could be a spy. Eyes and ears everywhere, making sure that—"

"Jesus fucking Christ!" I say to no one as something dawns on me. "You guys were fucking listening to us that day?" The look on his face tells me what I don't want to know, and now it's my turn to pace the floor. The one last memory I have of her, the bittersweet and intimate moments between us were documented by who knows what kind of devices and the perverted fucks on the other end of them.

"They were turned off when we realized what was happening," he murmurs, but the admission does nothing to stop the anger that eats at me. "She wanted to run after you, you know. . . ."

"No, I don't know!" I yell, at him, at her, at everyone because I feel so fucking in the dark right now, and while I don't want to know another thing, I need to know everything. Then I can leave here and try to comprehend so that I can mourn the loss of her even though I still can't believe she's gone.

"She wanted to run after you," he repeats, but this time with more compassion, "but we couldn't let her. We were afraid for your safety too. Afraid that if your source was the one who ratted her out, they'd think you were spying too. So we had eyes on your house from the moment you got home."

"William's black Suburban blocking my view ..." I say more to myself than to him. The believability factor of this whole situation has become almost too far-fetched, cloak and daggerish for my own liking. So much so that if I weren't living it, I'd say it was a bogus story.

He murmurs in agreement. "You left the house in Kansas, and she was beside herself because she knew how much she was hurting you. I made her promise just a few more weeks to make sure everything was kosher before she could come to you, that the intercepts still weren't clean of chatter yet. If you two had seen each other again, then she'd have been putting you in danger. She said you were going to come back, that you don't give up without a fight," he says, followed by an audible sigh, my own heart swelling despite the pain to hear this and know she was as tormented as I was. A misery loves company sort of thing.

And then I remember she's dead. And now it was all for nothing.

"She filed a restraining order, called Rafe to warn you so you wouldn't come back and be at risk. . . . She just wanted you safe because she loved you. In all the years we worked together, I'd never seen her like this, Tanner. You have to know that. She really did love you." He rests his shoulders against the wall and leans his head to look up at the ceiling. "She was going on a quick mission to the embassy to deliver some information and confirm a few things for a source we have there. She told me her return flight was going to be to San Diego so that she could tell you everything, beg for your forgiveness, and have a real life for the first time. . . ."

I wince at the words, cringe at the realization of what

will never be. He walks up to me and puts his hand on my shoulder and squeezes it momentarily while my eyes look down at my shoes. I know I should apologize for punching him, since he lost his partner and probably feels much like I did when I lost Stella, but I can't bring myself to say anything at all. Absolutely nothing because every single thing ricochets around in the numbed void inside me. I just can't believe it all yet.

"I'm so sorry, Tanner. For everything . . . I couldn't let you leave without your knowing the truth."

I just nod my head ever so subtly, my eyes still focused on the floor. And I stay like this long after Dane leaves the room, reality slipping through my fingers like sand as I try to hold on to it.

At some point the walls feel like they are closing in on me, suffocating me with the memories I have to hold on to but don't deserve, the love I feel that can no longer be returned, and a connection with a woman I'll never be able to touch again. I have to orient myself in the fog of disbelief, and once I do, I grab my bag and soon I'm all but clawing my way out of the private room followed by the meeting room in search of fresh air.

I shove through the exterior doors to an empty courtyard. I must make it only a few yards away from the exit before I drop my bags without thought and fall to my knees as the emotion catches up to me and hits me like a sledgehammer to the heart.

My huge gulps for air turn into body-racking sobs as the tears that I thought had dried up come out in a temper tantrum of visible emotion. Shoulders heaving, head falling forward, and mind accepting that my reality has just changed forever and I didn't get to have a fucking goddamn say in it.

I was so worried about protecting her that it never once crossed my mind that she was protecting me. And the idea that I could have suspected any of it is ludicrous at best, but it doesn't make the notion sting any less. Through blurred vision, I look at my hands and know that even though she's gone, her hands will always hold my heart.

"I'm sorry, Beaux," I sob out loud because I am so sorry, sorry I didn't go back to her house that day. Maybe if I had, she would have confessed, never gone on this ill-fated mission, and would still be alive. And then of course the idea of the mission takes hold, and the images of the press briefing flash through my mind. The notion becomes a reality that somewhere in that twisting metal and demolished building was my *once-in-a-lifetime*.

I'm a man falling apart amid the hustle and bustle of life around me—the click of high heels, the ring of a cell phone, someone's laughter—but time stopped for me in the devastating blink of an eye.

Chapter 30

Somehow I make it back to the airport.

Make it to the one place I've always relied on to escape everything. To the one place that I knew would take me away after Stella died, back into the thrill of the pursuit, the adrenaline rush of being first to report a story. But right now as I stand before the departure board, how I got here is all a blur I don't even recall because I was too busy keeping my shit together. I can't remember ever feeling so lost in my life.

I just need to get on the plane, do my job, and then get back home and figure out the life that eight hours ago seemed crystal clear but now is a fucking shattered mess of glass.

And then it dawns on me that I can't get on the plane because deplaning means that I'm going to be rushing to and reporting on the story that took Beaux's life. If I feel paralyzed now, seeing the devastation in person, knowing her blood has been spilled somewhere in the rubble, would make it more real than I can fathom.

Even if I could gather myself to do the report, use the

numbness to get the story out before the journalistic fourth wall crumbles, I don't want to. I can't face it.

I'm done.

The buzz I've lived my life by is gone. I don't feel a single zap of it, and the last time I did was telling Rylee that I was going to fight for what was mine. For Beaux. The inexplicable draw to the hard beat has died for me. I stare at the electronic boards, a man who finally found what was missing in his life only to lose it before he could fully recognize it. The destinations blur before my eyes, running together, and I have no idea where I'm going, what I'm doing, but there is one thing that is crystal clear.

It takes me a second to realize my cell is still turned off, that I was so fixated on getting to the meeting and then with the aftermath that I never turned it on. When I do, texts from Rafe come in a flurry, and I know that he's found out somehow about Beaux's death. As much as I don't want to talk to him, don't want to share my misery, I dial and wait for him to pick up.

"Jesus Christ, Tanner. I had no idea," he answers. But his words aren't enough for me. What did he have no idea about? That she was killed in the embassy bombing or that she was a spy?

"Did you know?" I grit the question out, needing to know more than ever if he knew about the setup, was in on it. When silence hangs on the line, my instinct tells me that he doesn't. He's not a good enough liar to play me that well, and if he was, he's not going to tell me anyway. He remains silent for a moment. "Put Pauly on the story."

"What . . . what's going—"

"Pauly deserves it. Give him a shot to make the headline."

"Talk to me, Tanner. What are you—"

"Thank you," I say, cutting him off again, my eyes still

trying to focus on the digitized cities on the screen in front of me. I don't know where I'm going, but the only caveat is that there won't be a desert. "This time it's for real."

"What is? What are you talking about?"

"I quit."

Chapter 31

One week later

She's so beautiful, it hurts sometimes to look at her.
I glance up from the bed to see Beaux standing at the edge of it, hair down, eyes on me, a soft smile on her face.

"Tanner," she whispers as she sits down beside me. The mattress springs squeak, and we both laugh at the memory. She leans over, her hair tickles my face as it falls down to my chest, but I forget all about it the minute her lips brush mine. Her kiss tastes like her, like everything I've ever wanted, like forever.

I startle awake from the dream. Just like I do every morning, every night. Every time I close my eyes. And the vivid imagery of it and the way it leaves me feeling is so real, so tangible, that it takes me a minute to remember she's gone.

And then the ache comes roaring back with a vengeance. The pain still radiates in my chest, the grief still weighs down my soul, the loss still runs my life.

This is my good morning. Has been every day since she's been gone.

I walk down Main Street through the two-bit town I'm playing recluse in. The plane touched down in Billings, Montana, and I drove until I couldn't see from exhaustion and found myself in this tiny little town of Freeman, population one thousand.

The bartender at Ginger's greets me by name as I walk in, and my beer is pulled from the tap and slid alongside the shot of whiskey that she's had waiting here every day since I've been in town. It's easier to numb yourself with alcohol. While the drunken haze makes the memories that much sweeter, it also makes your heart that much more hardened.

"Hey, handsome," Ginger says.

"Hi." I nod my head and then lower it, keep to myself, like I have since day one. My mind's still a mess, and I need this solitude and the noise in my head simultaneously to come to grips with everything.

"So let me guess, you're nursing a heartbreak?" I cringe when she starts to pry, because I keep coming here because no one has asked me shit besides the general curiosity questions. And now she just went and ruined it.

"Something like that," I murmur into my beer, my eyes looking up to catch the baseball game on the television on the opposite wall. My lack of interest in any conversation should be more than apparent.

"I have a few ideas how we can cure that for you," she says, and I can hear the smile on her face even though I'm not looking at her.

"Whatever you're looking for, I assure you I'm not him," I tell her, and immediately startle as my mind shifts back to the first time I met Beaux and said something similar. I lift the beer, my eyes focusing on the bottom of the glass as I drain it before sliding some cash across the bar top, scooting my chair out, and walking from the bar.

"You okay?"

"Yes, Rylee. I'm getting there."

"I just wish there was something I could do or say to—"

"There's nothing to say, Bubs," I tell her as I sit on the steps of the back porch of the little cabin I've rented on the edge of the woods and lift a beer to my lips. It's amazing how cash can get you anything, including anonymity and seclusion. "I just need some time to sort my shit out, you know?"

"No, I don't know. I'm worried about you. I've been through this before," she says, referring to her fiancé who died years ago, "so I understand this more than most people do, but I didn't take off to the edge of nowhere and disappear. I needed people, Tanner. Needed to be around people to cope."

"And I don't. I need to reevaluate my life. The things that I thought were priorities just might not be anymore, and that's a tough thing for a man to come to terms with," I say, not trying to be a martyr but at the same time finding it hard to focus on the outside world when the one around me has crashed down. "Who knows, maybe I'll write that book I always wanted to write. You never know what might happen."

"Knowing you, you'll write it and win the Pulitzer," she says with a laugh, having no idea what that term does to my insides. It's the first time I've heard it in forever, and it stuns me momentarily, silence filling the line as sweet memories collide with sadness. "Well, I love you, and I hope you come home soon."

"I love you too." The words come out barely audible as I hang up and close my eyes. It's always much easier to sleep than to be awake.

Sleep means I can hide from the grief for just a little bit longer.

Sleep means Beaux.

Chapter 32

Two weeks later

She's so beautiful it hurts sometimes to look at her.
    I glance up from the bed to see Beaux standing at the edge of it, hair down, eyes on me, a soft smile on her face.

"Tanner," she whispers as she sits down beside me. The mattress springs squeak, and we both laugh at the memory. She leans over, her hair tickles my face as it falls down to my chest, but I forget all about it the minute her lips brush mine. Her kiss tastes like her, like everything I've ever wanted, like forever.

I startle awake from the dream. Same dream. Same heartache when I wake to find her gone and my reality colder than the mountain air coming in through the French doors and slapping me in the face.

I lie there, contemplate the possibility that I'm making my feelings for her out to be more than they were. That the loss means I've put her up on the pedestal where people put those they've lost; where all of their wrongdoings are erased and good deeds are considered saintly.

But I know that's not the reason. I know it's because deep down this is how I really feel. It just took me too long to realize it, too long to tell her, too long to not be so damn scared of real love and fight for what we both deserved, a chance at a future together.

I prop my hands behind my head and mentally go over the beginning of the story that I started on my laptop last night. I looked at the blank page for well over an hour, unsure what to write until I clicked over and got lost in Beaux's images I had downloaded to my hard drive.

They made me feel close to her for a bit. Sounds silly since it's technically only been ten days since she died, but for me it's been months since I've held her, seen her smile, heard her laugh. So I clung to the images, looking at the world through her eyes when the story hit me: tired reporter meets a fresh-faced photographer. Definitely not the sort of material a Pulitzer is awarded on, not even the type of book I had planned on writing—a romance of all things—but when I finally fell asleep at the computer after a few hours of type and delete, type and delete, I felt the best I'd felt in a few days.

Almost as if I'm preserving her memory somehow, keeping her alive, keeping her close to me.

I roll over in bed, look out to the forest of trees beyond the cabin, and contemplate falling back asleep so that I can see her again. Just one more time before I start my day.

"Afternoon, Ginger," I say with a tip of my ball cap as I slide onto the same stool at the same time I do every day.

"The rugged thing looks good on you," she says with

a nod as she slides my beer and shot glass in front of me, pointing to my face where I opted not to shave today. "Pretty soon you're going to look like a local."

"Huh," I say, my eye catching something behind the bar. "What's that?"

"What's what?" she asks as she glances along my line of sight before laughing. "Oh those. A lady was in here earlier, just passing through town ... forgot them on the counter. Cute little thing."

I angle my head to the side, the sight of the bubbles making my throat close up some. Just when I start to feel like I'm doing better, something dredges up the raw emotion hiding beneath the surface.

And then of course a part of me has to ask. "What did she look like?"

"You think your heartbreak's coming looking for you?" Ginger asks with a lift of her chin, an excited smile spreading on her lips at the possibility of anything to gossip about in this one-horse town.

I shake my head and fight the burn in the back of my throat. "Nah. My heartbreak can't come back." I lower my hat down farther on my head to hide the emotion in my eyes that I don't really feel like showing her.

"Sorry," she says quickly, realizing the meaning behind my words and maybe understanding for the first time why I occupy this stool every day. "She was petite, dark hair, little pregnant belly. Boyfriend was waiting in the car while she was asking for directions and truth be told having a little morning sickness." I swallow over the lump in my throat as she slides the bubbles down the counter my way. "Go 'head and give them a blow. Something about 'em always makes me feel like a kid again, and you look like you could take a moment to forget."

My fingers fidget with the bottle in my hand because she has no idea that this little yellow container does anything but make me forget. "Thanks," I all but whisper as memories of the rooftop come back to me. Of hearing her say she loved me for the first time.

And for the last time.

Thank you. You'll never know how much it means to us to have this. I stare at the text from Stella's mother with a bittersweet smile. On my directive, Rylee had sent them Stella's camera along with the final images on her memory card. Since her last personal effects helped me be able to say good-bye to her, I thought they might add some sort of closure for them as well.

My finger hovers over the text, reflex taking over so that I'm pulling up the photos from that last morning together. Broad smiles and genuine happiness. And no matter how long I stare at our picture, I can't seem to find any closure when it comes to Beaux.

When the phone rings, it startles me from the trance the image holds over me.

"Rafe."

"Hey, man, how you doing?" he asks in that sympathetic tone that reminds me of wilting flowers after a funeral: pathetic, what people deem necessary, but something the person they're intended for doesn't need.

I wish people would stop asking me that. I've only spoken to my sister and parents and now Rafe, and every single damn conversation starts out this way. "I'm doing."

"Good." An uncomfortable silence fills the line while I wait out the purpose for the phone call.

"Did you need something?"

"Nah. Just wanted to check in with you," he says.

"Thanks." Quiet falls again, and even without him saying it, I know why he's calling, glad that he knows me well enough that even though I said I quit, I might not have really quit. "I'm not ready yet. May not ever be, to be honest."

"Mmm-hmm."

"Might be ready, but for domestic stories. I don't know," I answer his unspoken questions.

"Good to know, but I really was just calling to make sure you're okay."

"I'll get there."

We talk a bit more, nothing of any importance, no mention of where I am or when I'm going home, but when we hang up, I find my mind wandering to the bottle of bubbles on my makeshift desk in this little cabin beside my laptop. I debate writing, but there are just too many memories today, too many things that have made my chest ache and my thoughts wander to what ifs. And the only way to fix that is to sleep so that I can dream again. Grief may change shape, but it never ends.

Chapter 33

Three weeks later

*S*he's so beautiful, it hurts sometimes to look at her.

I glance up from the bed to see Beaux standing at the edge of it, hair down, eyes on me, a soft smile on her face.

"Tanner," *she whispers as she sits down beside me. The mattress springs squeak, and we both laugh at the memory. She leans over, her hair tickles my face as it falls down to my chest, but I forget all about it the minute her lips brush mine. Her kiss tastes like her, like everything I've ever wanted, like forever.*

The dream should end now. It always does, leaving me wanting more of everything—her presence, her kiss, her perfume, her warmth—but this time it keeps going. I know I'm dreaming. I tell myself not to wake up and ruin it, because this is more than I've ever had before, and therefore it's one more thing to hold tighter to, one more thing to coax me to sleep and wake me up every day.

Our kiss continues with soft lips and murmured moans as her fingers thread through my hair, and as much as I want to remember every single nuance of the dream, also *want to lose myself to the moment, to feel her love one more time.*

"Beaux." *I say her name between kisses, so many things I want to say and confess, but at the same time I'm afraid if I push my own agenda, the dream will end.* "I miss you so much," *I murmur against her lips and can feel hers turn up in a smile.*

"Tanner," *she says again, trying to pull away and look into my eyes, but I don't let her because the silk of her hair on my hands and the warmth of her breath against my cheeks just feel too damn bittersweet to let go just yet.* "Tanner," *she repeats.*

Even in slumber, I hold tightly to the sound of Beaux's voice saying my name. My mind is playing tricks on me. It has to be mixing the memory of her coming back from that first embed mission and that desperation I felt wanting to see her again with the constant loss I feel now.

"*This is real.* I'm alive. It's me."

That hazy state I'm immersed in between wake and sleep disappears in an instant, and yet I still can't believe that I'm awake because there's no possible way. Once open my eyes, a startled gasp fills the room and shock jump-starts my heart from the depths of loneliness and despair when I look into green eyes that have filled my dreams for so long.

"Beaux?" My voice sounds nothing like my own: It's full of incredulity, hope, disbelief, shock.

She bites her bottom lip, and tears well in her eyes as she nods her head cautiously like I'm going to be mad at her. I'm mad all right but only in the crazy sense because this just isn't possible.

We caress each other's cheeks, faces inches apart as we stare into each other's eyes. It's what I've wished for, what I've told the powers that be that I'd trade anything and everything for to happen . . . but how is this real? I can feel her skin, smell her perfume, see the love in her eyes. Moments that feel like hours pass as I start to believe this could be real.

"Is it really you?" I ask, wanting to look around me, make sure I haven't been transported to another place and time, but am afraid of taking my eyes off her for just one second in case she should vanish.

"I'm so sorry," she says, pressing her lips to mine, and this time I believe it, believe it's real, believe it's *her*. "We had to fake my death, had to erase my cover so I could have a life," she murmurs in between deep kisses, each sentence solidifying the reality that I'm no longer dreaming. "With you."

And on her last word, my heart that had fractured into a million pieces transforms itself into a living, beating, vibrant part of me again. There are so many questions I need to ask, so many things to understand about how and why, but that's for later . . . much later because right now my dream has come true.

"You came back to me," I whisper against her lips as my hands slide down her body and pull her tightly to me, because even air isn't welcome in the space between us.

"I always will," she murmurs as I taste salt in our kiss from the tears of happiness that we're both crying.

And I can't help it, because this is the second chance I never thought I'd get, so I take the kiss deeper, heart pounding with need, and my body reeling with greed.

There is no finesse, no seduction, just two bodies that know each other from memory finding each other in the early-morning light. I'm hard where she's soft. Unwavering needs mix with wants I never thought I'd have the chance to fulfill again. Urgency escalates with each touch. Lips to my neck. Hands to her breasts. I push down her pants, she pulls up her shirt, my fingers dip into the heat of her pussy as a feral growl comes from deep in my throat.

She opens for me without any prompting; I slide into her sweet heat without asking, both of us moaning from the intimacy of that first connection. And this right here, not the endgame, not coming with her name on my lips, has to be the sweetest, most incredible feeling in the whole world. Getting the chance I never thought I'd get again to be a part of her in all ways possible.

I pause in my movements, lean up on my elbows, and look down at my dream, my woman, my hope, all mixed into one incredible package, and I smooth the wisps of hair off her face. Our eyes lock, the intensity of our feelings only becoming stronger now. "You came back to me," I repeat again because I just can't believe it. "Thank you," I whisper as a soft smile spreads across her lips while the moment stretches out between us.

And then I begin to move. Slow strokes and soft murmurs, hushed pleas for more, satisfied sighs of disbelief as we are haloed by the sun's rays as it rises higher in the sky. She comes first, my name on her lips like a feather in the cap of an already perfect moment before I tumble over the edge in what feels like a free fall. And that's perfectly okay because that means I'll land back on top of her, and I don't think there's anywhere else I ever want to be.

I nuzzle my nose under her neck as we just hold on to each other, still connected, hearts beating as one, and life feels absolutely perfect. Chills chase over my skin as I try to fathom that just last night I wished myself to sleep, wished for this all to be a mistake, and somehow it came true.

Time passes, and as much as I want to stay tangled with her forever, I reposition myself half off her body so that I can prop my head up on my elbow and take her in, shock my mind into believing this tangible truth. She looks the same but different somehow. I can't quite put my finger on it, but I don't care because that guarded yet liberated smile on her face owns my soul right now.

"I need to explain," she says.

"I don't care." I lean forward and press my lips against hers. "All that matters is that you're here now."

"I am, but I need to tell you some things," she says with traces of caution in her voice.

"Are you going to leave me again?" My chest constricts even asking the question, but I need to ask, need to prepare myself.

"No!" The way the word rushes from her mouth tells me it's true, and that's all I need to know. "Not unless you want me to go."

"Never." I've never felt more resolute about anything in my life.

"You might not think that after I finish explaining things," she says, and her eyes dart away in an anxious flicker before coming back to mine.

"Never," I say again. "I've already lost you too many times for this lifetime."

"I'm so sorry for doing this to you, for putting you through this, Tanner. You have to believe me when I say that it wasn't an easy choice to make, knowing what it would do to you, but it was the only choice." She reaches out and frames my face with her hands so that she can make sure I don't look away when she speaks. I just stare and nod, wanting an explanation but not really needing one the longer we sit here. She could tell me that she was an alien with three heads and I wouldn't care so long as she's here right now.

"Kids, husband, the white picket fence ... I've never wanted what I called a *real life*. Never. After my parents died—" She stops when my eyes flash up from where my fingers trace a line over her abdomen at the mention of one of the many things we talked about. "I broke cover. It just kind of happened that day. It was so easy with you to be myself after pretending for so long that I was someone else. I don't know. . . . The whole story I told you was true except that my first job after the newspaper was the CIA, not freelance."

"You're fascinating," I murmur, the magnitude of her strength such a turn-on.

"Hardly," she snorts in a self-deprecating fashion. "You need to know that the time I spent with you, the laughs we shared, opening up and telling you I love you was all me, all real. . . . I never faked how I felt for you, even when we were arguing."

Her comment draws a chuckle from me, and I just can't take my eyes or my hands off her because I'm so afraid she will disappear if I do.

"The blast happened. There was chatter of cover being blown and then speculation that the opposition would think that maybe you were in on everything as well. I was out one night, Omid saw me. So stupid on my part really. I was careless, losing my edge. I couldn't be sure he recognized me, but I'm pretty sure he did. I'd been tracking him for a while, thought he was playing both sides of the fence, and if he was the snitch, that meant that you were in danger too since he may have thought we were a team. It killed me to push you away, but I had to do it to keep you safe. I don't think I'll ever be able to say I'm sorry enough for what I put you through."

"Why use Rookie at the hospital, then?" I ask a question I've asked myself a million times but couldn't figure out.

"The agency transferred me there, wanted me to use an alias while they set up the house and the cover there.

Rookie Thomas was the first name that came to mind. A way to keep you close to me. Subconsciously, a part of me hoped that you would come looking for me. I just didn't expect it would be so quickly." She sighs with a little shake of her head. "I shouldn't have expected any less from you, really. I thought by the time you'd figured it out, we'd have moved out. It was stupid on my part for so many reasons. I put you in danger, put Dane and me in danger. . . ."

I purse my lips and try to fathom what it was like on her end, because being left in the dark on my end sucked. "Does Dane know you're alive?"

"No. No one could know except for my CIA handler to keep everyone safe. I'll tell him, but you were first. I had to tell you first."

"Is Beaux your real name?"

"Not anymore," she murmurs with a trace of sadness in her eyes, and I angle my head and stare at her as I wait to find out what it is. "Blair Jane," she says with the cutest scrunch of her nose, like she's unsure of it. "So I can still go by BJ."

"Blair," I murmur, rolling the name around on my tongue. It feels so foreign, and I know it'll take me a long time to get used to it, but it's a lot easier getting used to a new name than to the hole in my heart from thinking she's gone.

"I'll still answer to Rookie, though," she says, a smile spreading on her lips that stirs so many things within me—the strongest of them is peace.

"Good to know." I lean forward and brush a kiss to her lips. "Because I'm bound to call you all of the above. I love you, Beaux Blair Rookie Whatever-your-name-is." I finally get to say it, to tell her, and the only thing that I feel afterward is relief because I know she heard it this time.

I love the sound of her laugh, practically drugged with happiness and tinged with relief. "I love you too," she says, wrapping her arms around me and holding tight.

"So what now, Bea—Blair?"

"I know it takes some getting used to. I might try my hand at real estate or something," she says, causing me to lift my head up and look at her like she's crazy. "You know what they say, location, location—"

"Location," I finish for her with a laugh, appreciating the humor she's trying to inject into this very surreal moment that I still don't think my head or heart have caught up with just yet. "And while I don't quite see that being your calling, at least I'd know you're out of danger . . . but that's not what I meant," I tell her. "I mean, why get out now? Quit? Why do all of this?"

"Because I love you." Her answer is spoken with such conviction, I have no doubt of its truth. "And because I always told myself that if there was ever a day I found myself thinking of the husband and kids and white picket fence, I had to give it up. I loved my job, Tanner. It saved me from so much, and I loved knowing I was making a difference in the grand scheme of things, but the one thing I never thought would happen, happened."

"What?"

"I fell in love with you." Her voice fades off softly, the emotion in it so strong, it flames the feelings within me to epic proportions. "Like head-over-heels, can't-catch-your-breath, can't-live-without-you kind of love. I tried to play cool, tried to act like I didn't feel it, but my God, that first night? It wasn't supposed to be like that. I wasn't supposed to feel like that about you afterward . . . and I did, and it scared the shit out of me, so the only thing I knew to do was to frustrate you, make you want to push me away."

"But you quit," I tell her with a laugh.

"I did, didn't I? Because you were so frustrating, and when you're frustrating, going all alpha male, this is how it's going to be, you are also so damn hot." Her admission makes me smile and builds my ego all at once.

We stare in comfortable silence for a moment, the dust particles dancing around us in the sun's rays as if they're just as excited as I am, when something she said breaks through my scrambled thoughts. "You said I might not still want you here after I know the truth. I know the truth.... Why would you think I'd tell you to leave when I feel exactly the same way?"

The shy smile returns along with tears welling in her eyes that I don't quite understand. I shift again so that I can see her better, one leg hooked over hers, hand resting on her abdomen, and eyes fixed on hers. "Because I want it all, Tanner Thomas. I want late nights laughing and early mornings making love. I want memories and to lay down roots with you. I want you to teach me how to surf and for me to really show you how to shoot a gun," she says with a smirk. "My history has been erased, and so I want to start making a new one with you. I want the white pickets, your last name ... the little boy with skinned knees and sticky kisses. That time away from you after Landstuhl taught me that I want it all, and I know you don't want some of those things, so ..." Her voice fades off as she bites her bottom lip with hesitancy and averts her eyes.

"Hey, hey, hey," I say, immediately needing to correct her way of thinking. "I want that too. All of it. I may not have the white pickets, but that's an easy fix ... and uh, I'm thinking a little girl instead ... one that looks just like her mommy." I rest my forehead to hers and just allow myself to feel this moment, feel her here, real and breathing against me, and I don't think anything else will ever top this moment.

Her chuckle is low and deep and vibrates into my chest and against my lips. "In about eight months we'll find out which one of us is right."

I whip my head back to look at her with surprise, my lips opening to speak, but nothing comes out as I glance down to where my hand rests on her belly, a life I helped create growing somewhere beneath it.

My eyes must ask the question for me because she just nods her head, a tear slipping down her cheek to the upturned corner of her mouth. "Yes."

I was so wrong. Nothing, and I mean nothing, else can top this moment.

My little piece of Heaven after going through so much Hell.

Epilogue

5 months later

"You can't look!" I tell her, pulling her hands away from the blindfold covering her eyes and then directing her through the house with my hands on her shoulders.

"What in the world?" she says, but I can hear the excitement, sense her trying to figure out what I'm doing.

"Stop right here and put your arms over your head." I love the odd expression that appears on her face before it slides into a coy little smile.

"Well, Pulitzer, I know my belly is getting big and all that, but if you wanted to get kinky, all you had to do was ask. These pregnancy hormones have no problem having some fun." Her throaty laugh fills our bedroom as I pull her T-shirt over her head. She does a little wiggle of her hips when I push down her yoga pants, but she keeps her arms up as if I'm cuffing them there with my own hands. "See. I must have expected this, because I'm not wearing any panties."

And she sure as hell isn't. That ache of desire that doesn't ever seem to go away simmers anew at the sight of her in her bra, swollen breasts spilling over, and nothing else. I step back and appreciate the view of her naked body, still beautiful, still petite, but with a little basketball of a belly that makes a pride surge in my chest like I never could have imagined.

I lean forward and press my lips right above her navel. "I've got a surprise for your momma," I murmur against her skin stretched taut and smelling like cocoa butter. And even though I'm in a hurry, I close my eyes momentarily when BJ lowers her hands to the sides of my cheeks and just holds them there in the sweetest of moments because I still can't believe how all of this worked out.

When I step back, I know the questions will start again as her curiosity fires over what I'm up to. "Hands back above your head," I order. She's still thinking I'm going to do something kinky and the idea has never been more appealing while watching her obey my command, but we can do that later. I've got plans first.

First, I pick up the tank top that Rylee had helped me select and after a few fumbling seconds direct her hands through the holes of the sleeves and slide it down over her body, throwing a prayer up that it fits.

"I'm so confused." She giggles as I pull the fabric down over her belly and sigh in relief that it stretches enough to fit around it. Next I pick up the pants with the stretchy waistband, drop to my knees, unable to resist running my fingertips up the line of her legs, and watch the goose bumps that appear in their wake. "Tanner." She sighs from the feeling that causes her head to fall back and lips to fall open.

The sexy sight of her almost makes me want to put off my preparations and keep up this blindfolded game. But not quite. We can do this later. All night if she wants to, but right now I've got plans.

"Put your hands on my shoulders," I tell her when I'm done smoothing my hands back down her legs and direct her hands to my shoulders. I help her into the pants, leg by leg, and pull them up so that they rest just below her bump.

"I could get used to this kind of play," she murmurs, which causes me to chuckle but earns her a swat on the butt in turn.

"Later, Rook. I promise you," I murmur, "I won't forget, but right now I have a bigger surprise for you." The smile comes instantly when I step back and see her in a khaki tank top and camouflage cargos, much like her constant attire when we met.

"Tanner," she pleads as she shifts on her feet, antsy for whatever I have in store for her, and the best part of this whole thing is that I know exactly what's going through BJ's mind because I've left carefully planted clues a few times in the house.

Right now she is thinking that I'm throwing her a surprise baby shower. For the past month, since I've been planning everything for tonight, I've left random Post-it notes on my desk in plain sight about dates and party supplies, I've made cryptic phone calls to Rylee where I hang up suddenly when BJ enters the room, and I've made her register for baby items although she technically knows no one other than my family now. So BJ thinks I'm throwing her a baby shower, and I am in a way, just not the kind she's imagining.

No. Her real baby shower is happening next weekend. Too many surprises in one day might not be good for the baby, and I definitely think this one takes precedence over next weekend's.

Unable to resist her any longer, I lean forward and press a tender kiss against her lips. And even though I pull back when she tries to deepen the kiss, I bring my hands to the side of her face and hold her still while my forehead rests against hers, and I just drink everything about her in—all of the little things I thought I'd never get the chance to experience again—because it's moments like this I'll never take for granted.

"Do you trust me?"

"One hundred percent," she says without hesitation in a way that makes my heart squeeze in my chest but causes me to fall silent while mentally preparing my little family for these next few moments.

"Good. I've got somewhere you need to be," I tell her as I press one more kiss to her lips before sliding my hands down her bare arms and taking her hand in mine. With a gentle squeeze I give it a tug so that she lets me lead her the rest of the way.

Once I clear the sliding glass door of the kitchen out to the backyard, my breath catches because this is so very real now, and I wouldn't have it any other way.

My eyes flicker across the backyard and try to see it how BJ will see it when I remove her blindfold. Glass votives are scattered along the grass, their light adding a soft glow to the sunset's vibrant colors splashed across the evening sky. A mattress sits on the grass, covered in a native fabric that Pauly shipped over to me. I rigged a canopy of sorts over the mattress as well. A woven bag sits atop it, a wine bottle sticking out of the top, while the rest of the wares are hidden. And the finishing touch is a blizzard of bubbles that floats through the air around us, reflecting the colors of the sunset and the light of the candles.

It's as close as I can get to the last night we spent on the rooftop of the hotel when she told me she loved me. I hesitated once to say it back. Right here, right now, I want a do-over of the moment to show her I won't ever hesitate again.

Standing behind BJ with my hands on her shoulders, I lean forward and press a kiss to the bare skin of her nape. "You ready?" I murmur, sounding like I am calm and collected when actually my heartbeat is racing out of control. I can feel her hesitancy mixed with curiosity as the breeze blows, causing her hair to tickle the sides of my face.

I step in front of her and remove the blindfold slowly. She blinks for a few seconds before her eyes find mine and hold my gaze. Even though there is a surprise I've arranged for her that I know she's curious about, when she opens her eyes, she immediately looks straight at me and her gaze does not wander. That little gesture says so much to me about who we are together and the future we have stretched out before us.

And it also solidifies that what I'm about to do is something I've never been more sure of.

Unable to handle my own excitement any longer, I break our hold and step to the side so that I can watch her reaction: the shocked gasp, her hand reaching up to cover her mouth, her widened eyes, and the tears that instantly begin to well in them. She gives herself a few moments to take it all in, to absorb what I've done before she looks over to me with so much love in her eyes, it makes my chest constrict with emotion.

"You gave me the rooftop back," she says with awe in her voice. I just nod, reach out for her hand, and lace my fingers with hers. And then through the surprise she remembers that I changed her clothes and looks down and laughs aloud when she sees her uniform of sorts. "Tanner!"

"Just trying to make it as real as possible." I chuckle as I tug on her hand for her to follow me, but she just stands there, one hand resting on her swollen belly, and her head slowly shaking back and forth as she takes it all in one more time.

I step into her and press my lips to hers, nerves heightened, and yet nothing has ever felt so right to me. "I have more to give you."

"Oh I believe you've already given me enough." She laughs, her hand moving in a circle over our baby she's carrying. "But I want to see it all!" Her eyes light up as she releases my hand and walks down the steps toward the replica rooftop setting.

My feet are rooted in place as I watch her move down the path. She waves her hands to try to catch some of the bubbles and turns around like a child, enjoying the simplicity, arms out, face towards the sky. Déjà vu transports me to that last morning we had together when I snapped her picture with my camera phone and wondered how she'd look on my back porch and if we could withstand everyday life in the real world.

We've proven that and then some, our relationship flourishing with this second chance at love. Life has changed so much in the five months since she has come back to me: moving in together, learning the ins and outs of each other's personalities that we'd missed in hotel living, adjusting to the sudden changes but loving every single minute of it, even the growing pains, understanding that the simple blessing of each other's company is the biggest extravagance and greatest part about finding your other half. Then add to that quitting my job in spite of her protests. Explaining to her that I got the second chance with her I'd prayed for; I wasn't going to travel overseas on assignment and miss a single second with her or the baby.

My transition to a new job as an investigator for a local news station hasn't gone without some bumps along the way, but it allowed me the freedom to finish and publish my novel. I can't believe how successful it's been. But then again, with a heroine based on Beaux, how can it not?

It's been crazy. All of it. I never thought hanging up

my credentials would be so easy for me. But the best part is that every single change has brought us to this moment, right now.

She walks into the blizzard of bubbles with her face to the sun and a laugh on her lips. And there is something about watching her like this that makes me step back and enjoy the feeling of my heart beating faster. She looks better than I imagined she would right here when I envisioned it all of those months ago.

She stops, arms out to her sides, bubbles clinging to her hair, and smiles at me. "You gonna come dance with me?" she asks as I move toward her.

"In a minute. I even have music this time . . . but first I have other surprises for you," I say as I take her hand and bring her to the mattress, holding her hands to help as she lowers herself to sit down.

"The bag!" she exclaims. "You kept it?" Wonderment and nostalgia fill her eyes when I nod.

"It's the only thing I had left from that night, so when I packed to come home, I brought it with me." I shrug away the thought of how desperately lonely I was without her.

"That's so sweet." She traces a finger along it. "Wine?"

"One glass won't harm the baby. I asked the doctor."

She throws her head back and laughs as she thrusts the bottle at me to open since she's done without it for this long. "I figured you'd ask the doctor about sex in the third trimester, not wine."

"Well, I did ask that too." I wink at her with my smile a permanent fixture on my lips.

"Of course you did! Now what else is in here?" she asks. "Can I open it?"

"Mmm-hmm," I murmur, trying to focus on pouring the wine and not spilling it while I keep watching her pull things from the bag.

"Wow, you really made sure this was authentic," she says as she takes out cheese and chocolate, and then a soft sigh of pleasure falls from her mouth as she pulls out the last item in the bag. "Bubbles," she murmurs, her fingers toying with the lid and her eyes finding mine.

"Bubbles."

"Don't you think there are enough of them floating around us?" she teases as she leans forward and brushes her mouth against mine. I close my eyes and flick my tongue between her lips, drinking her in before I pull back and look in her eyes.

"I think we should add to them. Don't you? Match the moment and then we can add a different ending to it, don't you think?"

"I like that idea," she murmurs against my lips before leaning back, granting me a coy little smile as she twists open the top of the bottle.

My heart lodges in my throat and it takes everything I have to not fidget or tell her to hurry up or anything else of the sort because this is all I've thought about since the blast that rocked our world took her from me and then brought her back. This moment. How I'd do it if I got a second chance. I got one, so I'm not looking back.

When she twists the cap off, I watch her brow furrow when she notices there isn't any bubble liquid inside the container. She ever so slowly pulls the wand out, her breath hitching when she notices the platinum and diamond engagement ring attached to the end of it. Her eyes flash up to mine as she looks back at the ring and then at me again.

"Tanner . . . ," she says cautiously although her eyes light up with happiness.

"How'd that get there?" I tease as I reach out and take the wand from her.

"No. Mine!" she says as she pulls her hand back so that I can't take it from her before throwing her head back and laughing. And that laugh . . . It's one I'll carry with me to my death because it embodies the personality of the woman I love, how carefree and happy she is now. How I've helped her to achieve that. How we've found it together.

I press my lips to hers, my nerves skittering out of control but my heart never steadier. "Yes, it is yours, but I'm kind of old-fashioned and want to do this the right way if you'll let me."

Her smile softens as she brings a hand up to my face and mouths, "I love you," before reaching out the bubble wand to me, tears welling in her eyes.

"I wanted to make tonight perfect for you. So many things I need to say, want to say, but I thought this"—I gesture to the setting around us—"would say a lot of it for me." I take a moment and breathe in before I continue. "I loved you before I even knew the real you. I loved you that night when you told me you loved me up on the rooftop and I hesitated to say it back to you . . . because one, I wanted it to mean something, and two, because I couldn't. When you told me, you knocked me on my ass, jump-started my heart, proved to me how real love was supposed to feel. So I hesitated, didn't say it back, and then I cursed myself for so many days and weeks afterward because then I was too late and couldn't say it to you."

I take her hands in mine before looking back up to the green of her eyes. "So tonight I want to tell you there is no hesitation on my part. I learned my lesson. I love you, Beaux BJ Blair Rookie." Her laugh rings out, and I love that even though her hands are steady, a tinge of nerves edges the sound because that shows this means something to her too. "And I don't want to waste another moment hesitating on starting our life together. You're it for me. You and this baby are all I've ever wanted when I never thought I wanted this life. You give me the hum, the buzz, the adrenaline rush I've spent my life chasing every time I think of you, each time I kiss you, and just knowing you came back to me. You're all I need, all I want, and I can't wait to spend the rest of my life with you. Will you marry me?" My question hangs in the air, hope weighing it down and bubbles lifting it back up as she just stares at me and a ghost of a smile curls up the corners of her mouth.

"I guess that means I'd better withdraw the restraining order, then, huh?"

Relief surges through me with the nervous laughter that falls from my lips, because even though I was sure of the answer, that's a pretty steep cliff for a man to be teetering on. "So, that's a yes?"

"On one condition."

"Anything," I say without hesitation.

"That you put that blindfold back on me later." She raises her eyebrows and laughs.

"I'll do whatever you want with it as long as I know you're tied to me for life."

She leans in and brushes her lips to mine and murmurs against them, "Then the answer is yes."

"Yes?"

"Yes," she says.

That buzz? It roars in like a goddamn tornado, wreaking havoc and devastating every single part of my body, but I'm okay with it. Because who knew the hum that I've lived by on the hard beat would end up giving me the love I was missing to make my heart beat?

Turn the page for an exclusive bonus scene!
See what Beaux was thinking when
she first laid eyes on Tanner....

Tanner Thomas is a household name on the foreign beat. I've heard he's a strict professional who is returning to the field after a tough blow with the loss of his partner. The unfortunate turn of events is admittedly horrible, but it makes him a perfect match for me. Someone who probably doesn't want to team up with anyone new and by the laws of human nature won't want to get close to anyone right now.

Laughter erupts on the other side of the room, causing me to glance over to where I last caught a glimpse of Tanner's back. As always on a mission, disinterest is my best friend. It allows me to slip below the radar, slide seamlessly into the flow of things, and always remain on the periphery.

But as I observe the various reporters, producers, and photographers working their way toward him, it strikes me there is something different in the atmosphere tonight. The general mood in the room is lighter, energetic, and in some inexplicable way has a sense of hope.

I don't want to attribute it to the presence of Tanner

Thomas. It's ludicrous to believe that a single person can breathe life into a community as has happened tonight.

But there's no denying it either.

And it's not just the alcohol flowing more freely than normal. There's a current in the room that's indescribable. It's like they know he's finally returned, so things are going to start happening here again instead of the day-after-day monotony that has been the norm since I arrived more than two weeks ago.

"C'mon, T-squared!" someone yells with a slap of his hand on the bar, and I start craning my head back and forth to see between the crowd of bodies from my spot on the other side of the bar.

"I'm game if you're game!" A voice booms before I can catch a glimpse of what's going on. I don't need to see whose lips are moving to know it was Tanner speaking, because chills raced over my skin at the sound of the familiar baritone I know from watching his broadcasts. It's likely just the knowledge that I'm so close to pulling my boots up and wading straight into the thick of my cover that causes the goose bumps to come. That undeniable thrill of anticipation.

That has to be the cause of the sudden fluttery feeling in my stomach.

Another reporter I've spoken to on a few occasions, Gus, I believe is his name, hands me a shot with a whoop of a laugh, and before I can even ask why, a hush falls over the room.

"Shh. Shh. Shh." Pauly, a fellow reporter, climbs atop a chair, a shot glass filled with amber liquid in one hand and his other motioning for the lot of us to quiet down. He looks down to his right, and for the first time I catch a fleeting glimpse of Tanner's face before the crowd shifts and I lose sight of him again. "Tanner Thomas . . . we are so glad to see your ugly ass back in this shithole. I'm sure once you hand our asses to us time and again by getting the story first, we'll want you to leave, but for now we're glad you're here. Slainte!"

"Slainte!" I say back in unison with the rest of the crowd; then the sound of swearing fills my ears as the burn of the alcohol hits everyone's throats.

Needing to appear to be a part of the group, I take a sip, but I know well enough that a drunk woman in a city like this is just asking for trouble. And I get in enough trouble on my own, thank you.

When I glance back through the crowd again, I'm startled when I lock eyes with Tanner. It's only a split second of time, just long enough for me to tip my shot glass to him before someone moves and blocks our connection, but it's enough to have me holding my breath and for that fluttering to return in my belly.

I sit there in complete indecision for a second, since that momentary connection disarmed me for some reason when I'm hard to rattle. *Jesus, Beaux, it's not like you've never met a mark before.* Exhaling slowly, I tell myself that I need to keep my wits. It was stupid for me to search him out since I don't plan on introducing myself to him face-to-face until our assigned meeting at ten tomorrow morning. Besides, my new boss, Rafe, might not have even told him about me yet. He warned me Tanner was going to resist the idea of a new partner, that he might be tough on me. Little did Rafe know that in my line of work, tough is an everyday norm.

So if I don't plan on meeting Tanner until tomorrow, why do I keep looking back to where he's sitting? What am I going to gain with one more glimpse of him?

Absolutely nothing.

And yet I look again. This time there is a complete break in the crowd, and I catch Pauly's eyes. By the way he smirks at me, then looks over to Tanner and throws his head back with a laugh, I know they are talking about me. Call it woman's intuition or just plain curiosity, but I know. And now I definitely can't look away.

The problem, though, is that not looking away means that my gaze moves from Pauly to Tanner, and this time I'm afforded more than just a glimpse of him. I'm granted the whole entire package.

Dark hair frames his tanned face, and there's something intriguing about his eyes that I can't quite put my finger on across the distance. I don't have a chance to consider it for very long because when he shifts his gaze and his eyes lock on mine, I freeze in place—lips shocked open, heart skipping a beat—and a flash of something I want to deny as being attraction flickers through me.

But this time I recover quickly and turn my lips up into a slow, knowing smile as we hold each other's gaze. In contrast to the flash of hunger I catch in his eyes, he nods his head nonchalantly with an arrogant curl to his mouth before looking away.

But I keep staring.

And there's something about the whole exchange that infuriates me.

I need to remember he's just my cover, the man I need to partner up with to protect my ass. So there's no reason to be irritated that he just reeled me in with those eyes and then disregarded me without so much as a second look. Ironically it's the exact same thing I had planned on doing to him—use my looks right off the bat if I sensed any attraction in order to catch him off guard enough to use my brain and intuition to do my job.

I may be an agent, but first and foremost I'm a woman, and no woman likes to be made to feel inconsequential. For the first time in forever I am pissed about someone not noticing me.

Agitated and irritated, I'm suddenly tossing back the

shot I had no intention of drinking. The burn comes fast, and I hope my sense follows suit, because no man has ever thrown me off my game when it comes to work, romantically or otherwise—and yet with a single glance, Tanner Thomas has done just that.

I turn the glass around in circles on the scarred table-top as I try to figure out what exactly it was about the exchange that instantly had him getting beneath my skin. It was ten seconds tops, and yet those ten seconds packed a punch I never expected.

It had to be the look he gave me. While I've seen him a hundred times filing live reports—and I've both appreciated his looks and admired his skills—nothing prepared me for the absolute intensity in his eyes. Not to mention the flash fire of heat that surged in my lower belly when our gazes met.

And with that last thought, I'm immediately shoving my chair back. All my best laid plans have gone out the window: play it cool, meet face-to-face for the first time tomorrow, fly under the radar. I've made a living on being able to read people, and in that brief meeting of our eyes, he was able to get a visceral reaction out of me. That in itself is rare. Even more unheard of is for me to take the bait and say fuck it to my rules, which is exactly what I'm doing by walking across the bar to face this head-on.

There's something about the contradiction between the look in his eyes and his rigid posture that tells me he doesn't like to be handled. Wants all of the control. And God yes, in a lover that's sexy as hell, but in a man I have to work with under difficult circumstances, it's not so appealing. I need to get the upper hand here so I can control the situation before it even starts.

Fate has to be on my side because the barstool next to Tanner is vacant when I approach. So I slide into the seat, face him, and wait for him to look my way. I know he senses my presence. I can see the stiffening of his posture, the fleeting tension in his fingers, but he doesn't lift his eyes from where he's tracing lines over the grooves on the scarred wood bar top.

He's attractive in an odd combination of rugged mixed with preppy pretty boy. Camera-worthy looks but with a hint of edge to the lines giving character to his face.

The seconds pass as I wait him out, questioning my decision to come over here, but I won't back down now. I'm not wishy-washy. Hate women that are. I didn't get where I am professionally by being a damn doormat. But standing here waiting for him to glance my way suddenly unnerves me.

"Whoever you're looking for, I'm not him," he says without looking up.

The part of me that felt uncertainty sags in relief and welcomes his hostility. I can definitely work with his lack of warmth, hold on to it, and use it to my advantage to find my footing. He has no clue that we're about to enter into a partnership.

"I don't believe I'm looking for anything." I feign nonchalance, don't want to give him any more than he is giving me and yet at the same time hope it brings a reaction out of him. Something. Anything.

"Good."

Well, that wasn't exactly what I was looking for, but at least he hasn't gotten up and left. I glance up to the bartender and then back toward Tanner. "Whiskey sour," I order from the bartender, and notice a slight startle of Tanner's head in my periphery. I smirk, his reaction giving me the perfect in to get his full attention. "And put it on his tab."

Bingo. Tanner snaps his head up and immediately

meets my gaze. If I thought the intensity in his eyes was powerful before, it's tenfold now. The problem is that it's not just the intensity that pins me immobile, but also the unique amethyst color of his eyes mixed with his undeniable good looks. Proximity to him might not have been a good idea because I find myself captivated by him.

A completely foreign and unwelcome feeling hits me so fast that I shove away from the bar top. I maintain my smirking expression and the challenging look I'm giving him even as my insides somersault into nothingness and that quick ache of lust hits me head-on. The flash of intrigue commingled with amusement in his eyes tells me that he'd love nothing more than for me to be the typical female I'm sure he's used to dealing with: compliant, starstruck, fumbling over her words.

He's got another think coming if that's what he's expecting.

"I don't believe I offered to buy you one." He leans back and angles his head, eyes assessing and daring me all at once.

"Well, I don't believe I asked you to be an asshole either, so the drink's on you." The comment is off my tongue before I can think it through. We stare at each other like two caged animals circling, each trying to figure the other one out, and knowing regardless of our indifference, there is definitely a game of some sort being played between us. Good thing I know what that game is.

"Then I guess you should steer clear of me and neither of us will have to worry about me being an asshole." He grunts the words out, and I don't know whether I should be glad or upset about his response.

On one hand, his lack of interest could make this whole mission easier. He'll leave me alone, let me do my thing, so long as I get my work done when he needs it. On the other hand, he's damn attractive, and it could be extremely beneficial to use sex appeal to my advantage. Reel him in, keep him under my wing, and get my job done quicker by playing the innocent-female card.

The problem with using sex appeal, though, is that I've watched other female agents play theirs up, draw lines, erase them, redraw them, and in the end get hurt by becoming too emotionally invested.

All my training has warned me that there will be one person who will make me cross that line. *No way. Not me.* The job, the mission, the objective, all three mean way too much to cross any lines, regardless of the sexual chemistry I feel licking at my heels as I stand here and hold his stare.

I wait for the comment I can see forming on his lips to come, but just as unexpected as this conversation has been, he breaks our eye contact without saying another word and refocuses on the glass in his hand.

"So you're the one, huh?" My thoughts turn to words before I realize what I'm saying, and disbelief robs me from saying anything else as Tanner turns to look at me again, glass stopped midway to his lips, and that way he has of staring straight into you and seeing every single thing you want to hide.

"The one?"

And without any pertinent words being exchanged or even so much as an introduction being made, I know without a doubt that Tanner Thomas is the one person who's going to make me question crossing that damn line. Call it a gut reaction or a psychotic episode, but I have a feeling that this mission is going to be anything but the easy get in, get out, get done type that I had planned on it being.

And it will have nothing to do with the mission but rather everything to do with the attractive man before me and his inquisitive eyes.

Once I process the thought, try to laugh it off, and ferret it away to worry about and obsess over later, I scramble to answer his question hanging heavy in the air between us. Make the comment relevant somehow, some way.

"Yep, the one that every reporter in this room hates and wants to be all at the same time," I explain, speaking nothing but the truth I've come to learn while waiting for him to arrive.

Skepticism causes him to narrow his eyes, and amusement has him pursing his lips as he tries to figure out if he believes me. I'm not sure if he does because he breaks our stare and motions to the bartender for a bottle of whiskey. The exchange of money for the bottle happens quickly. Tanner scoots his chair back, grabs the neck of the fifth of alcohol, and gives me a half-cocked, arrogant smirk.

"Yep, I'm the one." He turns his back to me and strides away.

Cocky son of a bitch. And he most definitely is, yet I still watch him leave the bar, lifting the bottle up to the protests of the other journalists gathered to welcome him back.

And even when he's cleared the doorway and I can no longer see him, I'm still watching. There's just something about him when I most definitely don't want there to be.

He's the one all right.

Hopefully he's the one I can avoid.

QUINLAN

The Southern California heat mixed with the second week of school has really done a number on me. I'm ready to melt into the cool air-conditioning of the Fine Arts offices as I pull open the door, tired from a late night hanging out with Layla—my fault but still aggravating nonetheless—and having had to deal with some dipshit undergrads in the teaching assistant session I just came from didn't help matters.

Generally I don't mind if a student doesn't get a concept. I have no problem helping them so that they understand. But when the students are too busy chasing skirts and worrying about who the Trojans take on this weekend to listen, it's not my problem they received bad marks on their first pop quiz.

And it's not helping my mood that I need to get laid something fierce. And not by my own hand. There's nothing worse than a woman in need of a good orgasm.

Or two.

Or three.

I drop my backpack on the counter with a sudden resolve to rectify the situation with the first willing candidate who meets my discriminating standards. Then again I'm on the verge of being desperate enough that I might throw them out of the window for the right mistake.

I start rifling through the bazillion pieces of paper stuffed in my mailbox—such is the life of a graduate student in the Cinematic Arts. Shit, save a tree people, use e-mail. I automatically toss the ones about elective seminars into the recycle bin without even reading them because at the beginning of a semester the last thing I have time for is something that does nothing to further help me write my dissertation.

"Quinlan! Just the person I wanted to see!"

As I turn around to face my graduate adviser, the smile comes naturally to my face since I'm one of the select few fortunate enough to be under her tutelage. "Hi, Dr. Stevens." She gives me a stern look that causes me to laugh at the formality of my greeting, so I cave to her oft-repeated request and correct myself. "Hi, Carla."

"Better." She laughs the word out. "Now, I'm not looking for my husband when you say that," she says, referring to her spouse, who is a cardiologist.

I nod my head in agreement. "Why do I have the feeling that I'm not going to like the fact that you wanted to see me?"

Please God don't let her ask me to add something else to my already overflowing plate full of obligations, deadlines, and drafts I need to write.

"I'm kind of in a jam and I need your help." She scrunches up her nose like she knows I'm not going to be too happy with what she's going to say next. "Like I'll give you a three-week extension on your first draft due date kind of help."

I worry my bottom lip between my teeth and know that no matter what she asks, I'll say yes. She's my mentor for God's sake. Anything not to disappoint her. "Okay?" I draw the word out into a question, fearful and curious all at the same time.

"Well, Dr. Elliot has brought in someone for a seminar that is starting" — she looks down at her watch and winces — "well, it started about five minutes ago actually. Anyway he's asked if I can help him. His TA, Callie, was supposed to do it, but she had a last-minute schedule change to accommodate one of her professors . . . and all of his other teaching assistants have classes right now. . . ."

I bite back the urge to make a smart-ass comment about how Callie's conflict is the need to flirt ridiculously with the professor she has the hots for, university protocol be damned. Instead I look at Carla and blow out an audible breath, certain that my expression reflects my displeasure.

I'm usually on top of all of the department's goings-on but my last-minute trip to the Sonoma race to watch Colton mixed with playing bestie to nurse Layla through her unexpected breakup and the usual first month of school discord has left me in the dark about course specifics. It had better be a damn good class if I'm going to have to be stuck sitting through it.

"You know I'm agreeing to this because I'm already behind on my draft and need those weeks, right?"

"Exactly!" She smirks. "I don't have that PhD behind my name for nothing."

"That's low." I just shake my head as I reach over to grab my bag. "So give me the details."

"You're a lifesaver!" She reaches out and pats my shoulder. "So the seminar is on sex, drugs, and rock and roll in a manner of speaking." She quirks her eyebrow up, asking if I'm okay with that.

Like I have a choice. I can just imagine some stiff professor giving a seminar about something so completely foreign to him. Now I'm going to have to waste my time mollycoddling someone when I have so many other things that would be a better use of my time. Sounds like a real *barn burner*.

"Who's teaching it?" I ask, my tone reflecting the cynicism I feel over the contradiction between teacher and subject.

"A guest lecturer. I forget his name but he's a member of some popular band." She rolls her eyes. Her musical taste includes only classical music and jazz. "Oh and he's cute," she says with a smile and then cuts me off before I can ask her any more details. "Now shoo—he's probably mangling the sound system as we speak. Microphone on upside down or something. Class is in the GFA building, room sixty-nine."

Mentally I roll my eyes at the room number, thinking how something else that number represents would be a much better way to occupy my time than listening to a monotone oration. And I wonder how big of a name he can really be if Carla's worried that he has his mic on upside down.

I shake my head one more time and sling my bag over my shoulder. "Thank you, Quinlan," she says in a saccharine sweet tone that makes me laugh.

"Just so you know, I'm cursing you right now," I say over my shoulder as I open the door and begin the journey across campus.

I'm winded, hotter than hell, and cussing out Carla even more by the time I reach the closed door of the lecture hall. When I pull it open and step into the lobby, I can hear laughter from the students beyond the open theater doors.

Two coeds exit the bathroom across the foyer from me, both way overdressed for students attending a lecture, and one is applying lipstick while the other giggles uncontrollably. They walk past me and I hear hushed comments about how they "just had to see for themselves" if he's as hot in person and "damn security for kicking them out" before they push through the doors I've just entered

My curiosity is now definitely piqued. Who the hell is the guest lecturer if there is security here?

Maybe it's one of Dad's friends. Stranger things have happened.

"So you see, it was the Grammys—it's not like you can say no to him when he just won album of the year and asks you to hang out. Little did I know," the male voice says in a low tenor that's almost a contradiction: smooth like velvet but with a rasp that pulls at my libido and makes me think of bedroom murmurs and hot sex, "that I'd go with him and walk into a private club where everything is laid out like candy—drugs, women, record producers. He turned to me and said, 'Welcome to Hollywood, son.' Shit, I looked at Vince here and thought, is this what I have to do to make it here? Play this game? Or can I do this the old-fashioned way? And I don't mean sleep my way to the top either."

The room erupts into laughter with a few whistles as I clear the doorway. I recognize him immediately. He may be on the stage at a distance but his face, his presence, is unmistakable. I've seen it gracing tabloids. *TMZ*, *Rolling Stone*—you name it, he's been on their cover.

He's Hawkin Play, front man and lead singer of the highly popular rock band Bent.

And according to his most recent press coverage, a man on the path to a drug-fueled destruction. So that exaggeration most likely means he was caught in possession of some drugs.

Why in the hell is he here?

I walk farther into the auditorium and falter at the top of the steps because just as my ears are attuned to his voice, my body reacts immediately to the overpowering sight of him.

And I sure as hell don't want it to.

I tell myself it's just because I need some action. That my battery-operated boyfriend is getting old and the visceral reaction of my racing pulse or the catch in my breath is just from my dry spell. Well, not really a complete dry spell per se, but rather a lack of toe-curling, mind-numbing, knock-you-on-your-ass sex that I haven't been able to find lately. It's the good lays that are hard to come by.

Don't even think about it. He may be hot, but shit, I grew up with Colton, the ultimate player, so this girl knows what a player sounds and acts like. And from everything I've seen splashed across headlines and social media, Hawkin plays the part to perfection.

But the notion that just like the drug rumors blasted across the magazines, his reputation as a player could be manufactured just as easily lingers in my subconscious. I stare at him again as the class laughs, his ease in front of a large crowd more than apparent, and I immediately wonder if I had a chance with him if I'd take it.

What is wrong with me? My head says to stop thinking thoughts like that, things that are never going to happen, while my body is telling my legs to *open wide*.

I force myself away from thinking such ludicrous thoughts and focus instead on finding a seat in the room packed full of coeds. I begin walking slowly down the aisles, glancing back and forth to try to find an open spot but there's not a single one available.

I glance forward to see a beefy guy walking toward me with an irritated expression on his face. It immediately hits me that I have nothing to prove I should be in this class, no paper, nothing to show to the security that appears to be bearing down on me that I'm not a fangirl and have a legitimate reason for attending the lecture. Well, maybe they'll kick me out and then he won't have a TA for the day.

Just one less class I'll have to sit through. And one less asshole I'll have to deal with.

He approaches me and reaches out a very muscular arm toward me. "Course paperwork?" He asks in a hushed whisper, trying to not disrupt whatever Mr. Rock Star at the front of the class is babbling on and on about.

I take in a deep breath, trying to figure how I'm going to play this. What I really want to do and what I know is right are two different things so I suck it up and take the higher road.

Reluctantly.

"I don't have anything," I whisper back. "But I'm the TA for the course."

"Sure you are." He chuckles with a roll of his eyes. "TA doesn't stand for tits and ass, honey."

I clench my jaw, reining in my frustration as we begin to draw the attention of those around us. "I just came from the department offices; I don't have—"

"Is there a problem, Axe?" His liquid sex of a voice booms across the room, causing all of the heads in the room to whip over toward us on the stairway.

Axe, I presume, turns his body to look back at Hawkin, which opens up his line of sight to see me.

"No problem," Axe says and before he can say anything else, Hawke speaks again.

"So nice of you to show up on time." Sarcasm drips from his voice, and my eyes snap up to meet his despite the distance between us.

And I swear I hate everything about myself right now because I feel a jolt to my system and quick bang of lust between my thighs as our eyes connect and that slow, I'm-a-god-you-can-bow-before-me smile curls up one side of his mouth.

And damn it to hell if that doesn't make him look even sexier.

But good looks sure as hell don't make him any less of an asshole.

My own lips pull into a tight, scowling grimace, thoughts firing but the damn words don't come because I'm still momentarily frozen by whatever just ricocheted between us.

"Well, at least you're quiet, huh? Not one to disrupt unless you count arguing with Axe on the stairs."

How did I know he was going to be a prick? "I wasn't arguing. I'm not a—"

"Look," he says, cutting me off. "There's one seat left and it's right here." He points to a space right in front of the lectern when a man hurriedly stands and vacates it. I watch the occupant stroll to the side of the room and turn to lean his back against the wall, arms crossed, grin wide, as all the while he shakes his head at Hawkin like they have a private joke between them.

He seems vaguely familiar but I don't get a chance to figure it out because Hawkin speaks to me again. "C'mon now. I don't bite—right, guys?" He says to the rest of the lecture hall and the audience erupts in a cacophony of hoots and hollers egging me on to go take the seat.

I also hear a few offers from the females that they'll take the seat if I don't.

I'm sure they would. Particularly a seat that's astride his hips if my hunch is right.

"Please, take your time. We like waiting." His voice floats through the room but grates on my nerves.

I grit my teeth as I move reluctantly, my anger escalating with each step I descend toward the front of the room. As much as I don't want to be here, dealing with the likes of a cocky asshole like him, my graduate career does have requirements, and I really don't think pissing off who I have a feeling will be one of the most popular lecturers of the year is the brightest idea.

But hell if I don't want to tell him to kiss my ass with that smart mouth of his while I stride up the steps toward the exit and flip him the bird instead.

But my degree is more important so I swallow my pride along with my anger, even though I'd much rather verbalize it as I reach the front row. Keeping my eyes fastened to his, I refuse to let him think he's gotten the upper hand despite me following his directive and taking the seat he so *graciously* offered.

I reach the seat and stop before I sit down and stand my ground, my eyebrows arched and eyes telling him everything my lips can't. He meets them challenge for challenge while all the while those lips of his smirk and taunt me.

I force my eyes to remain forward, not to wander and take in the whole of him because I don't want to see how sexy-hot he is face-to-face, don't want to notice his cologne that makes me think of fresh air with a subtle hint of musk, don't want to feel my cheeks flush because I know my nipples just hardened and I'm quite sure they're more than obvious through the thin layer of my bra's lace and my cotton T-shirt.

After a moment, when I know I have no point I can really make in front of several hundred students, I lower my eyes and take my seat. But instead of continuing on right away, he stands in front of me a few seconds more, making sure I know who won this ridiculous little show of control between us.

And of course as he stands in front of me with his hips right at my eye level, I can't help the two thoughts colliding: the one of him being in control with the one of just how well his worn denim jeans are filled out behind that button fly of his.

I immediately chastise myself. Tell myself that it's my sex-deprived brain—well, more like other deprived body parts—that is directing my thoughts like a nympho. And that alone fuels my dislike of Hawkin even more because I should be focused on being pissed off at him rather than wondering about how he performs in *other* ways . . . off the stage.